JEREMY

THE STRANGE ONES

GALLERY 13

New York   London   Toronto   Sydney   New Delhi

Gallery 13
An Imprint of Simon & Schuster, Inc.
1230 Avenue of the Americas
New York, NY 10020

"Catching Squirrels" by Velocity Girl. Used with permission.

Copyright © 2020 by Jeremy Jusay
Portions of this work were previously self-published by the author in the publication *Karass*.

First Gallery 13 trade paperback edition January 2020

GALLERY 13 and colophon are trademarks of Simon & Schuster, Inc.

For information about special discounts for bulk purchases, please contact Simon & Schuster Special Sales at 1-866-506-1949 or business@simonandschuster.com.

The Simon & Schuster Speakers Bureau can bring authors to your live event. For more information or to book an event, contact the Simon & Schuster Speakers Bureau at 1-866-248-3049 or visit our website at www.simonspeakers.com.

Manufactured in the United States of America

1   3   5   7   9   10   8   6   4   2

Library of Congress Cataloging-in-Publication Data
Names: Jusay, Jeremy, author, artist.
Title: The strange ones / Jeremy Jusay.
Description: First Gallery 13 trade paperback edition. | New York : Gallery 13, 2020.
Identifiers: LCCN 2019035437 (print) | LCCN 2019035438 (ebook) | ISBN 9781982101121 (trade paperback) | ISBN 9781982101169 (ebook)
Subjects: LCSH: Friendship—Comic books, strips, etc. | Graphic novels.
Classification: LCC PN6727.J87 S77 2020 (print) | LCC PN6727.J87 (ebook) | DDC 741.5/973—dc23
LC record available at https://lccn.loc.gov/2019035437
LC ebook record available at https://lccn.loc.gov/2019035438

ISBN 978-1-9821-0112-1
ISBN 978-1-9821-0116-9 (ebook)

For my friend Sam

Introduction

Walking through a crowded Woodbridge shopping mall in New Jersey alongside my dad when I was about ten or eleven, I made zigzag motions for no reason at all. My path looked like a sine wave if seen from above. "Stop doing that, Jerry," my dad said. "People will think you're crazy."

Years later, I was bored and lonely at my summer job as an engineering aide with the US Army Corps of Engineers at 26 Federal Plaza in downtown Manhattan, in between my first and second years at Polytechnic University in Brooklyn (long before NYU bought them out), when I thought up the idea for *The Strange Ones*. It would be about a boy and a girl from Staten Island going to school in the city. The boy would look somewhat like me, of course, and the girl would look like a mix between Winona Ryder and about every other girl I'd ever fallen in love with. I didn't know too much about their story at that point, only that they were weirdos.

Fast-forward about two years and I'm falling behind in my classes after becoming obsessed with zines, combat boots, and alternative music. Franck and Anjeline were more developed as characters in my mind by then. At the same time, I wrote an autobiographical prose novella called *Porcupine* about my bouts with bad skin and self-hatred. I published this serially in my zine *Karass*, along with other contributors' submissions of prose and poetry. I found working on the zine, getting it printed up at the local copy shop, dropping flyers all over town, selling a few copies to Tower Records on Broadway—hell, even having my own post office box—so much more rewarding than studying something like the aerodynamics of an Airbus A320 that I decided to quit Poly in the middle of the spring semester of my junior year. It was not an easy decision, but for me in those days it was a choice between art and death. A scene in *Joe Versus the Volcano* also played a pivotal role.

Output slowed after I transferred to the School of Visual Arts that same year. I remember thinking every day how lucky I was to be there, how cool it was to be surrounded by people as peculiar as me (although I was an old man by comparison, with my choirboy haircut, button-down shirts, and '50s-era trench coat), and how grateful I was that I was finally learning to do something that I have loved doing since I was little: drawing cartoons. Looking back, I am amazed at the roster of teachers I had then: Joe Orlando (EC Comics) was a drawing teacher, Klaus Janson (DC's *The Dark Knight Returns*) instructed me on comics storytelling, and Brian Walker (*Beetle Bailey*) taught me cartooning history. I rubbed elbows with artists like Abby Denson, Gerard Way, Tomer Hanuka, Dean Haspiel, and Aaron Augenblick. While I was a freshman, *The Strange Ones* made its debut in *Karass* #6 on November 30, 1994. People seemed to like the comic, calling it sweet, well-drawn, and genuine. Any kind of feedback was intoxicating to me and motivated me to work even harder on the next issue. At one point Kurt Vonnegut even wrote me a letter (after I sent him a copy of *Karass*, of course), praising the zine as a "humane and lively publication." Subsequent chapters were published throughout my time at SVA, until 1996, when the fourth chapter appeared in *Karass #9*. The zine, as well as the comic, would not surface again until a decade later.

In that time, I graduated, found love, found dot-com work, got laid off, broke up with said love, then found animation work as a background designer at Augenblick Studios in Dumbo, Brooklyn (where I happily remain to this day). It wasn't until I met Kseniya Yarosh around 2006 through a missed connections ad on Craigslist and realized that zines were a thing again (she put out a personal rag about her dating experiences and would later create the acclaimed zine *I Love Bad Movies* with her now-husband Matt Carman) that I decided to resurrect *Karass*, and thus *The Strange Ones*. After *Karass #10* debuted with the fifth chapter of the comic, the story was put on hold yet again.

The remaining story of Franck and Anjeline lived on solely in my imagination, and whenever I would be walking down subway platforms, standing in elevators, or sitting in doctors' office waiting rooms, I would go over snippets of dialogue or construct panel layouts in my mind, thinking someday I would finally have enough time to sit down and finish the damn thing.

The following years would see *Karass #10* and a collected volume of the first five chapters of *The Strange Ones* being sold at random zine and comic book shows. Then in 2017 I received a message from Margaret O'Connor, an old friend and former *Karass* contributor who was now a literary agent, asking if she could pitch *The Strange Ones* to some comic book companies that were looking to publish illustrated memoirs. I said sure, why not.

And that's why you're holding this book from Gallery 13, more than twenty-five years after the story was conceived in a government engineering office.

I hope you enjoy it.

Jeremy Jusay
October 2019
New York City

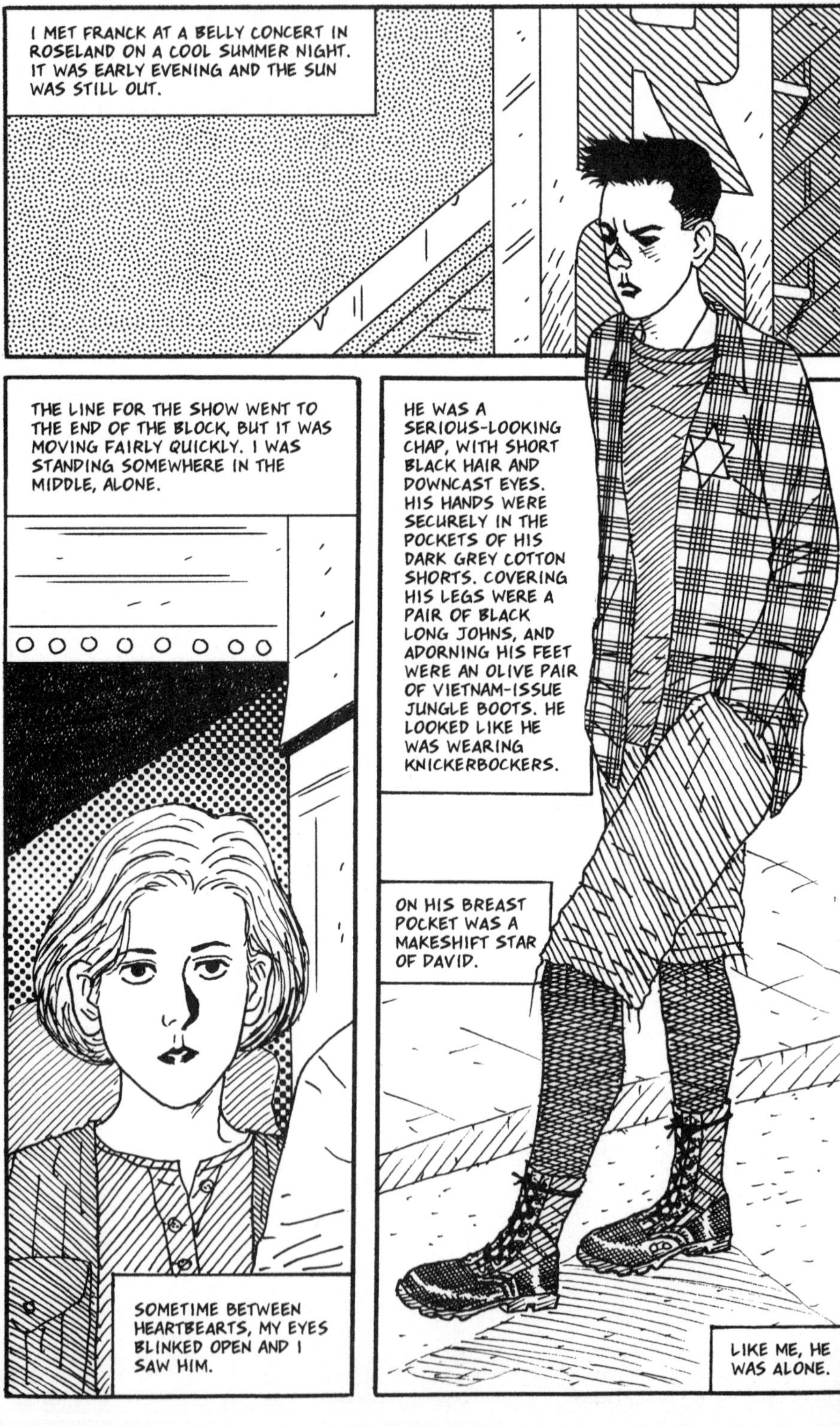
I MET FRANCK AT A BELLY CONCERT IN ROSELAND ON A COOL SUMMER NIGHT. IT WAS EARLY EVENING AND THE SUN WAS STILL OUT.
THE LINE FOR THE SHOW WENT TO THE END OF THE BLOCK, BUT IT WAS MOVING FAIRLY QUICKLY. I WAS STANDING SOMEWHERE IN THE MIDDLE, ALONE.
SOMETIME BETWEEN HEARTBEARTS, MY EYES BLINKED OPEN AND I SAW HIM.
HE WAS A SERIOUS-LOOKING CHAP, WITH SHORT BLACK HAIR AND DOWNCAST EYES. HIS HANDS WERE SECURELY IN THE POCKETS OF HIS DARK GREY COTTON SHORTS. COVERING HIS LEGS WERE A PAIR OF BLACK LONG JOHNS, AND ADORNING HIS FEET WERE AN OLIVE PAIR OF VIETNAM-ISSUE JUNGLE BOOTS. HE LOOKED LIKE HE WAS WEARING KNICKERBOCKERS.
ON HIS BREAST POCKET WAS A MAKESHIFT STAR OF DAVID.
LIKE ME, HE WAS ALONE.

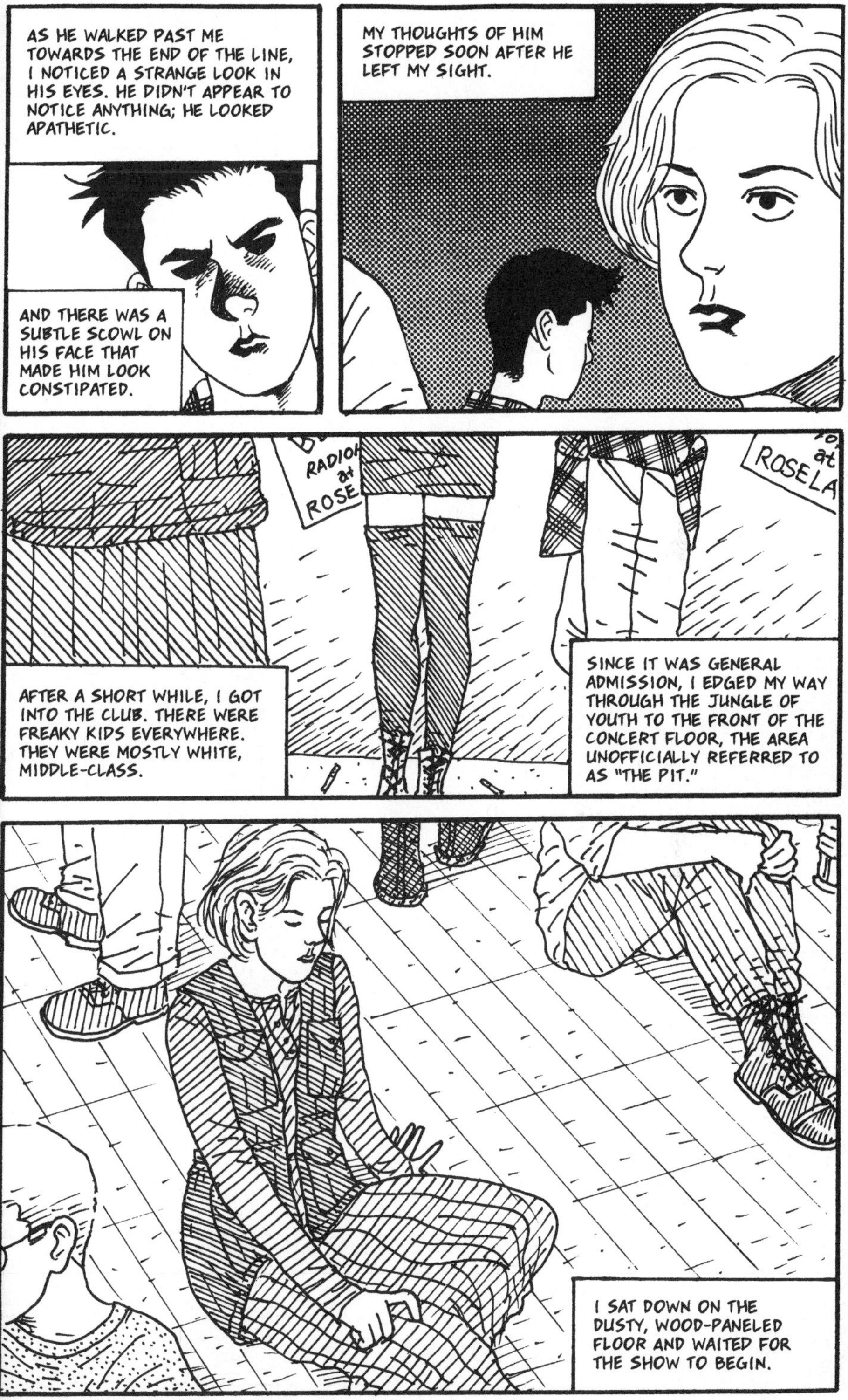
AS HE WALKED PAST ME TOWARDS THE END OF THE LINE, I NOTICED A STRANGE LOOK IN HIS EYES. HE DIDN'T APPEAR TO NOTICE ANYTHING; HE LOOKED APATHETIC.
AND THERE WAS A SUBTLE SCOWL ON HIS FACE THAT MADE HIM LOOK CONSTIPATED.
MY THOUGHTS OF HIM STOPPED SOON AFTER HE LEFT MY SIGHT.
RADIOH at ROSE
at ROSELA
AFTER A SHORT WHILE, I GOT INTO THE CLUB. THERE WERE FREAKY KIDS EVERYWHERE. THEY WERE MOSTLY WHITE, MIDDLE-CLASS.
SINCE IT WAS GENERAL ADMISSION, I EDGED MY WAY THROUGH THE JUNGLE OF YOUTH TO THE FRONT OF THE CONCERT FLOOR, THE AREA UNOFFICIALLY REFERRED TO AS "THE PIT."
I SAT DOWN ON THE DUSTY, WOOD-PANELED FLOOR AND WAITED FOR THE SHOW TO BEGIN.

RO1009   G.A.   GEN ADM   M-TYPE
17.00   GEN ADM   SEC   SEAT   17.00

G.A.
CA   1
GEN ADM
TMC602 M
14AUG93

BELLY

ROSELAND
239 W 52ND ST. .NYC
SAT AUG 14, 1993 7:3

Belly

GOOD FOR ONE FARE

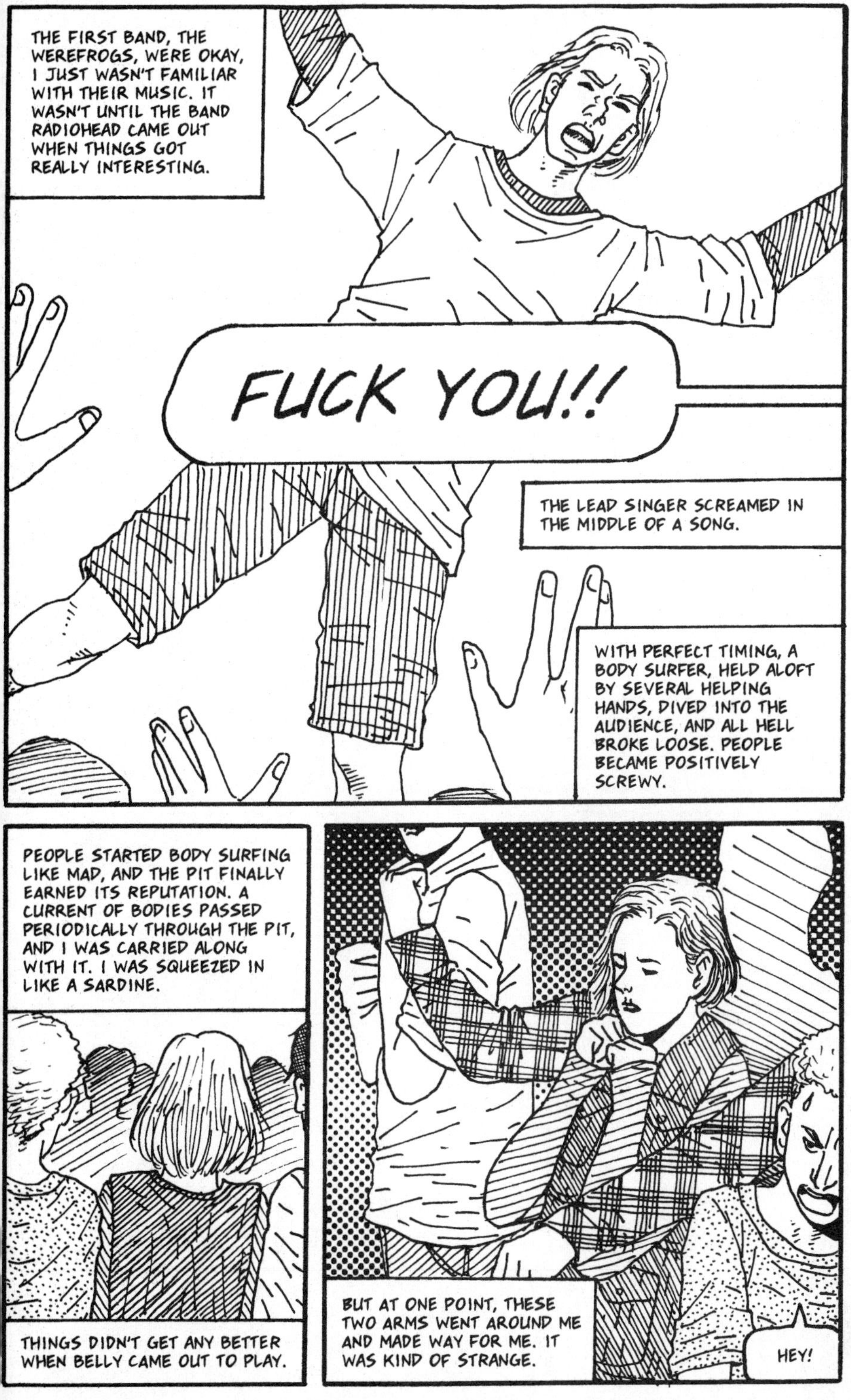
THE FIRST BAND, THE WEREFROGS, WERE OKAY, I JUST WASN'T FAMILIAR WITH THEIR MUSIC. IT WASN'T UNTIL THE BAND RADIOHEAD CAME OUT WHEN THINGS GOT REALLY INTERESTING.
FUCK YOU!!
THE LEAD SINGER SCREAMED IN THE MIDDLE OF A SONG.
WITH PERFECT TIMING, A BODY SURFER, HELD ALOFT BY SEVERAL HELPING HANDS, DIVED INTO THE AUDIENCE, AND ALL HELL BROKE LOOSE. PEOPLE BECAME POSITIVELY SCREWY.
PEOPLE STARTED BODY SURFING LIKE MAD, AND THE PIT FINALLY EARNED ITS REPUTATION. A CURRENT OF BODIES PASSED PERIODICALLY THROUGH THE PIT, AND I WAS CARRIED ALONG WITH IT. I WAS SQUEEZED IN LIKE A SARDINE.
THINGS DIDN'T GET ANY BETTER WHEN BELLY CAME OUT TO PLAY.
BUT AT ONE POINT, THESE TWO ARMS WENT AROUND ME AND MADE WAY FOR ME. IT WAS KIND OF STRANGE.
HEY!

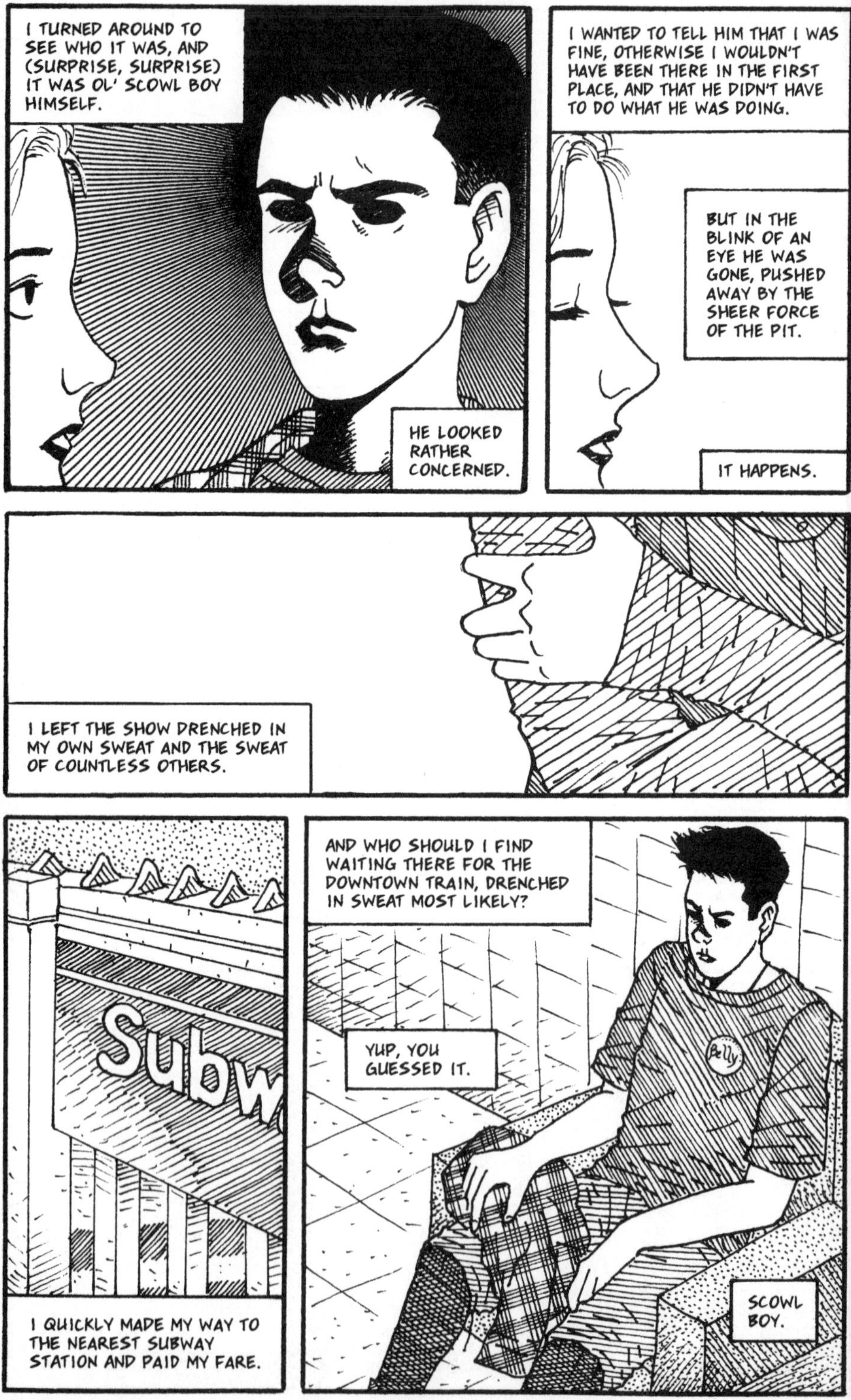
I TURNED AROUND TO SEE WHO IT WAS, AND (SURPRISE, SURPRISE) IT WAS OL' SCOWL BOY HIMSELF.
HE LOOKED RATHER CONCERNED.
I WANTED TO TELL HIM THAT I WAS FINE, OTHERWISE I WOULDN'T HAVE BEEN THERE IN THE FIRST PLACE, AND THAT HE DIDN'T HAVE TO DO WHAT HE WAS DOING.
BUT IN THE BLINK OF AN EYE HE WAS GONE, PUSHED AWAY BY THE SHEER FORCE OF THE PIT.
IT HAPPENS.
I LEFT THE SHOW DRENCHED IN MY OWN SWEAT AND THE SWEAT OF COUNTLESS OTHERS.
Subw
I QUICKLY MADE MY WAY TO THE NEAREST SUBWAY STATION AND PAID MY FARE.
AND WHO SHOULD I FIND WAITING THERE FOR THE DOWNTOWN TRAIN, DRENCHED IN SWEAT MOST LIKELY?
YUP, YOU GUESSED IT.
Belly
SCOWL BOY.

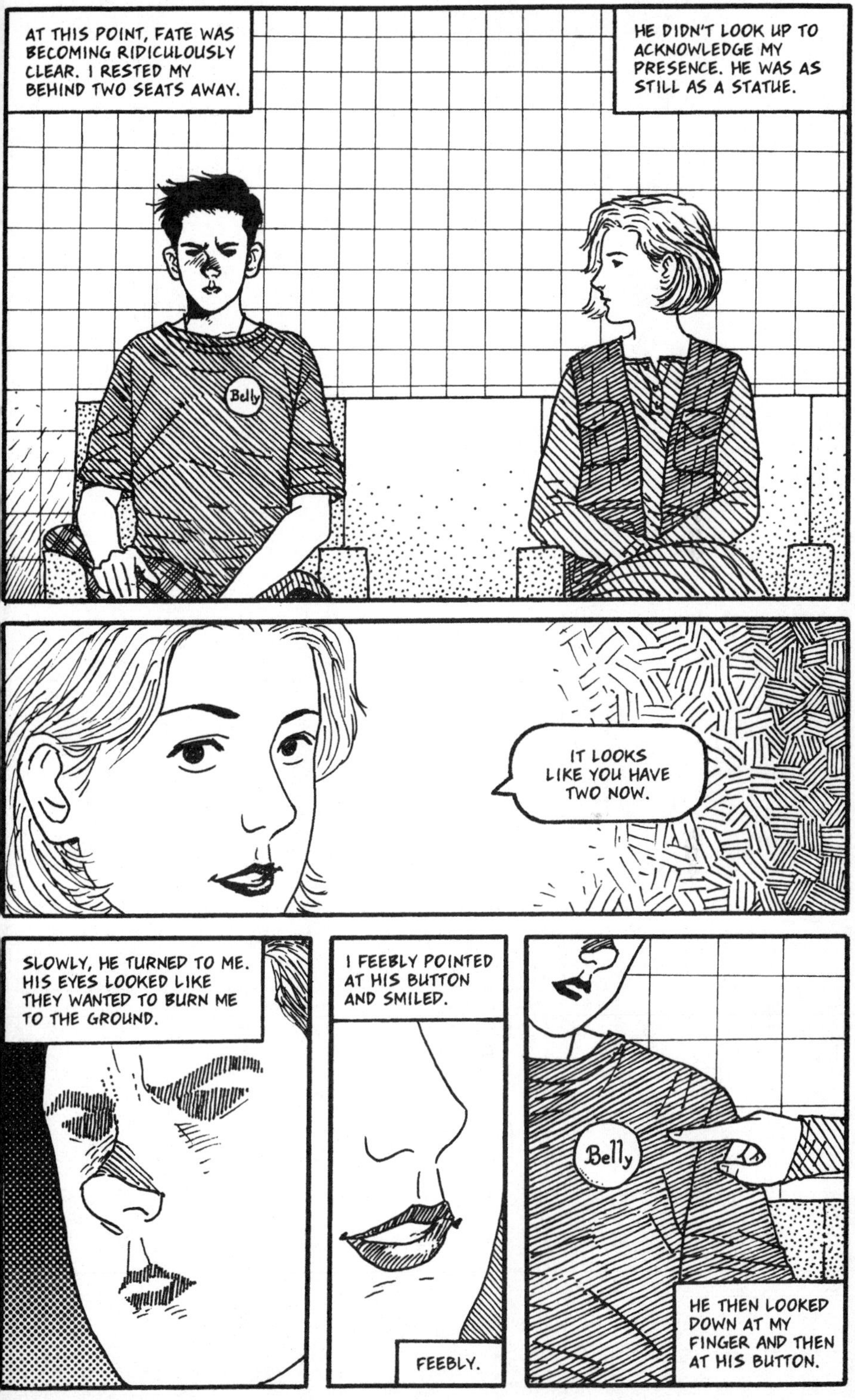

AT THIS POINT, FATE WAS BECOMING RIDICULOUSLY CLEAR. I RESTED MY BEHIND TWO SEATS AWAY.
HE DIDN'T LOOK UP TO ACKNOWLEDGE MY PRESENCE. HE WAS AS STILL AS A STATUE.
Belly
IT LOOKS LIKE YOU HAVE TWO NOW.
SLOWLY, HE TURNED TO ME. HIS EYES LOOKED LIKE THEY WANTED TO BURN ME TO THE GROUND.
I FEEBLY POINTED AT HIS BUTTON AND SMILED.
FEEBLY.
Belly
HE THEN LOOKED DOWN AT MY FINGER AND THEN AT HIS BUTTON.

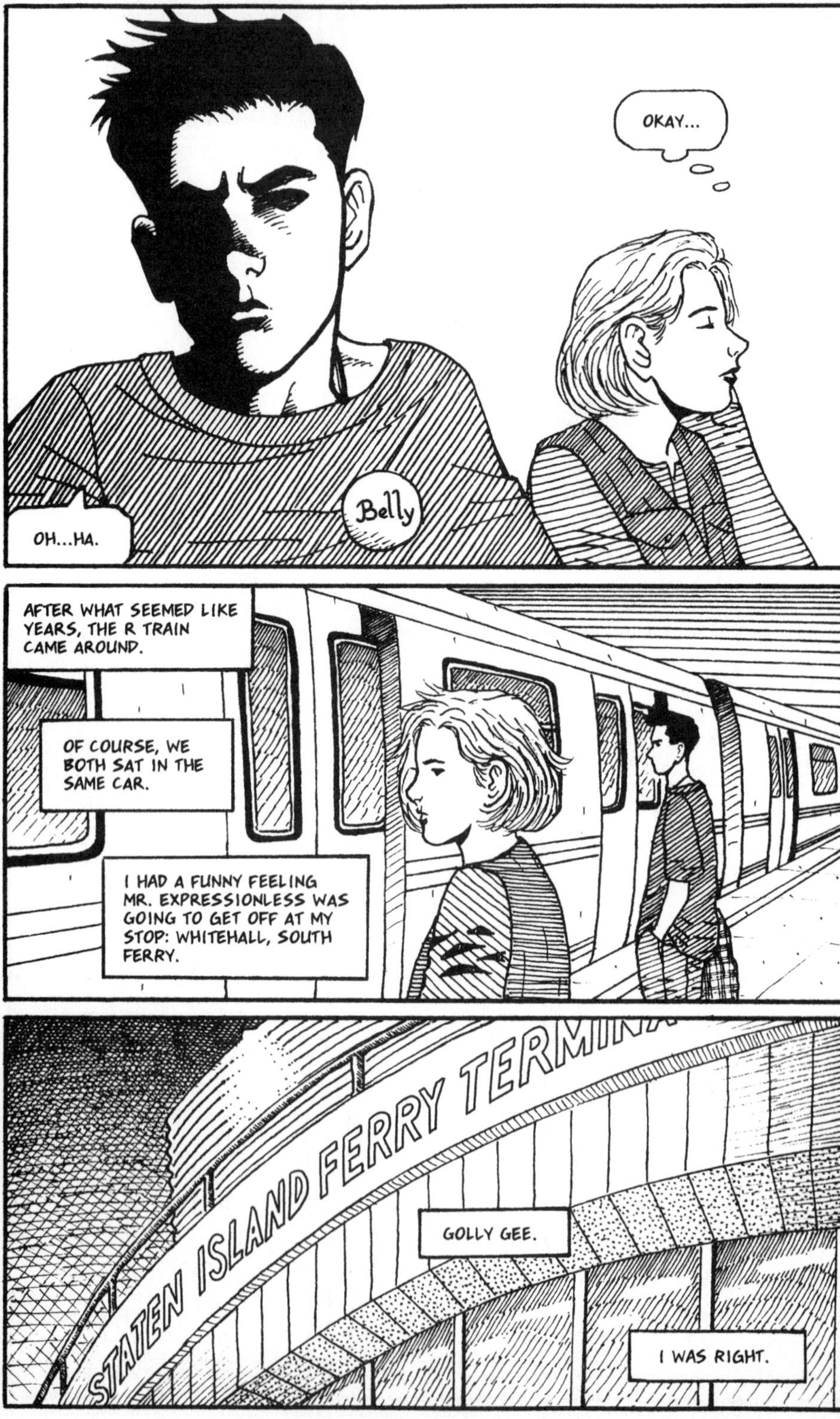
OKAY...
OH...HA.
Belly
AFTER WHAT SEEMED LIKE YEARS, THE R TRAIN CAME AROUND.
OF COURSE, WE BOTH SAT IN THE SAME CAR.
I HAD A FUNNY FEELING MR. EXPRESSIONLESS WAS GOING TO GET OFF AT MY STOP: WHITEHALL, SOUTH FERRY.
STATEN ISLAND FERRY TERMINA
GOLLY GEE.
I WAS RIGHT.

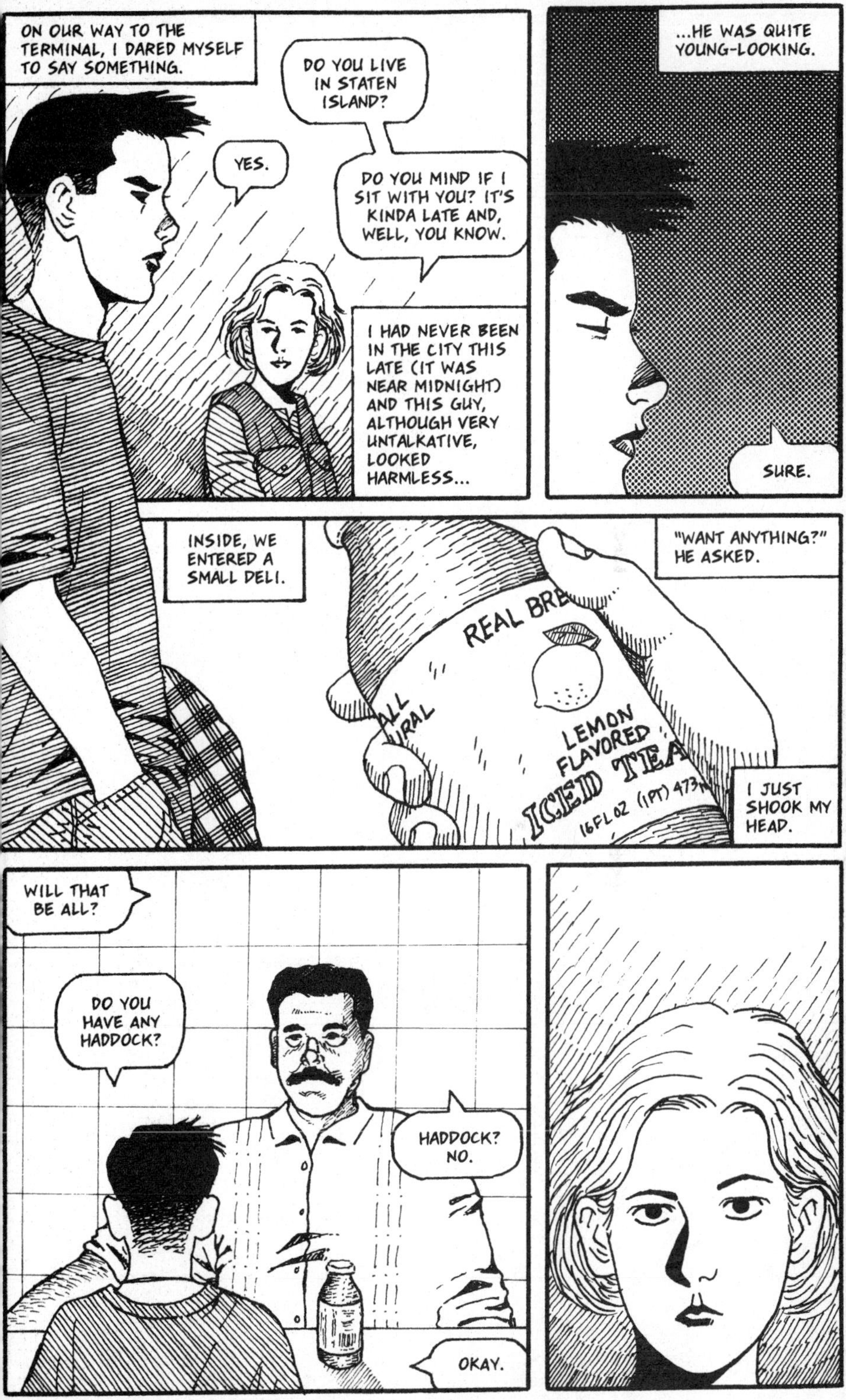
ON OUR WAY TO THE TERMINAL, I DARED MYSELF TO SAY SOMETHING.
DO YOU LIVE IN STATEN ISLAND?
YES.
DO YOU MIND IF I SIT WITH YOU? IT'S KINDA LATE AND, WELL, YOU KNOW.
I HAD NEVER BEEN IN THE CITY THIS LATE (IT WAS NEAR MIDNIGHT) AND THIS GUY, ALTHOUGH VERY UNTALKATIVE, LOOKED HARMLESS...
...HE WAS QUITE YOUNG-LOOKING.
SURE.
INSIDE, WE ENTERED A SMALL DELI.
REAL BRE
LEMON FLAVORED ICED TEA
16FL OZ (1PT) 473
"WANT ANYTHING?" HE ASKED.
I JUST SHOOK MY HEAD.
WILL THAT BE ALL?
DO YOU HAVE ANY HADDOCK?
HADDOCK? NO.
OKAY.

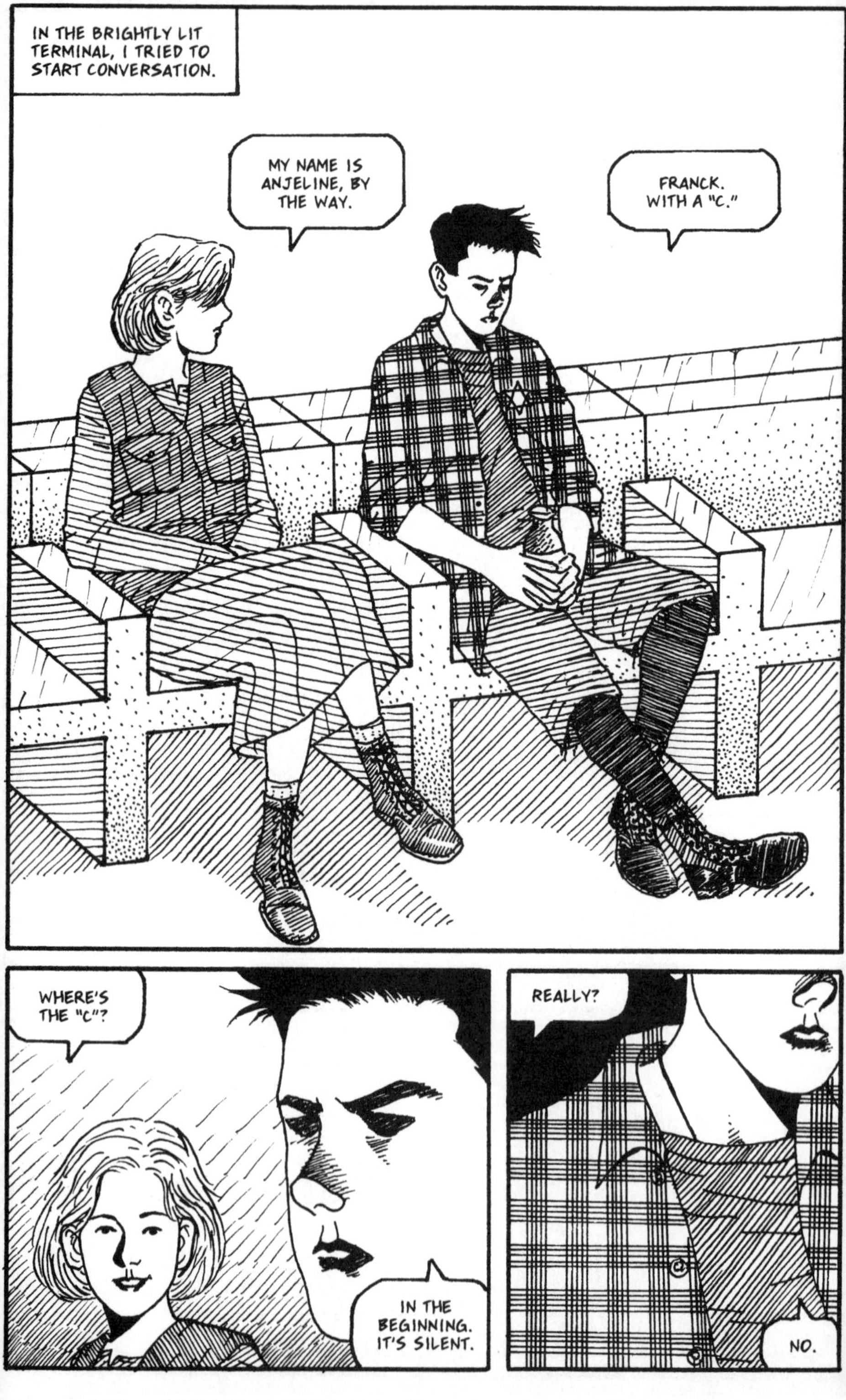
IN THE BRIGHTLY LIT TERMINAL, I TRIED TO START CONVERSATION.
MY NAME IS ANJELINE, BY THE WAY.
FRANCK. WITH A "C."
WHERE'S THE "C"?
IN THE BEGINNING. IT'S SILENT.
REALLY?
NO.

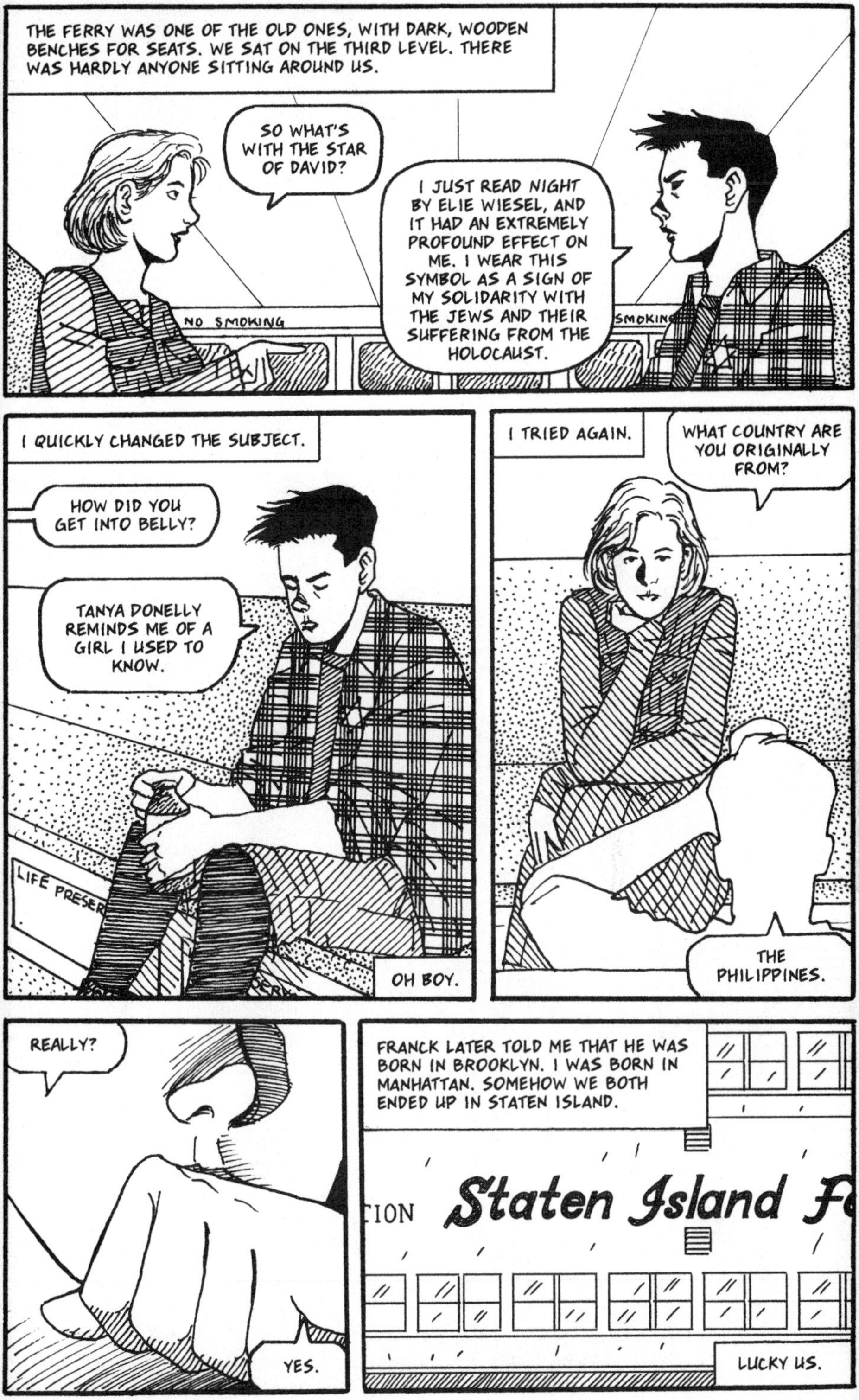
THE FERRY WAS ONE OF THE OLD ONES, WITH DARK, WOODEN BENCHES FOR SEATS. WE SAT ON THE THIRD LEVEL. THERE WAS HARDLY ANYONE SITTING AROUND US.
SO WHAT'S WITH THE STAR OF DAVID?
I JUST READ NIGHT BY ELIE WIESEL, AND IT HAD AN EXTREMELY PROFOUND EFFECT ON ME. I WEAR THIS SYMBOL AS A SIGN OF MY SOLIDARITY WITH THE JEWS AND THEIR SUFFERING FROM THE HOLOCAUST.
NO SMOKING
I QUICKLY CHANGED THE SUBJECT.
HOW DID YOU GET INTO BELLY?
TANYA DONELLY REMINDS ME OF A GIRL I USED TO KNOW.
OH BOY.
I TRIED AGAIN.
WHAT COUNTRY ARE YOU ORIGINALLY FROM?
THE PHILIPPINES.
REALLY?
YES.
FRANCK LATER TOLD ME THAT HE WAS BORN IN BROOKLYN. I WAS BORN IN MANHATTAN. SOMEHOW WE BOTH ENDED UP IN STATEN ISLAND.
Staten Island
LUCKY US.

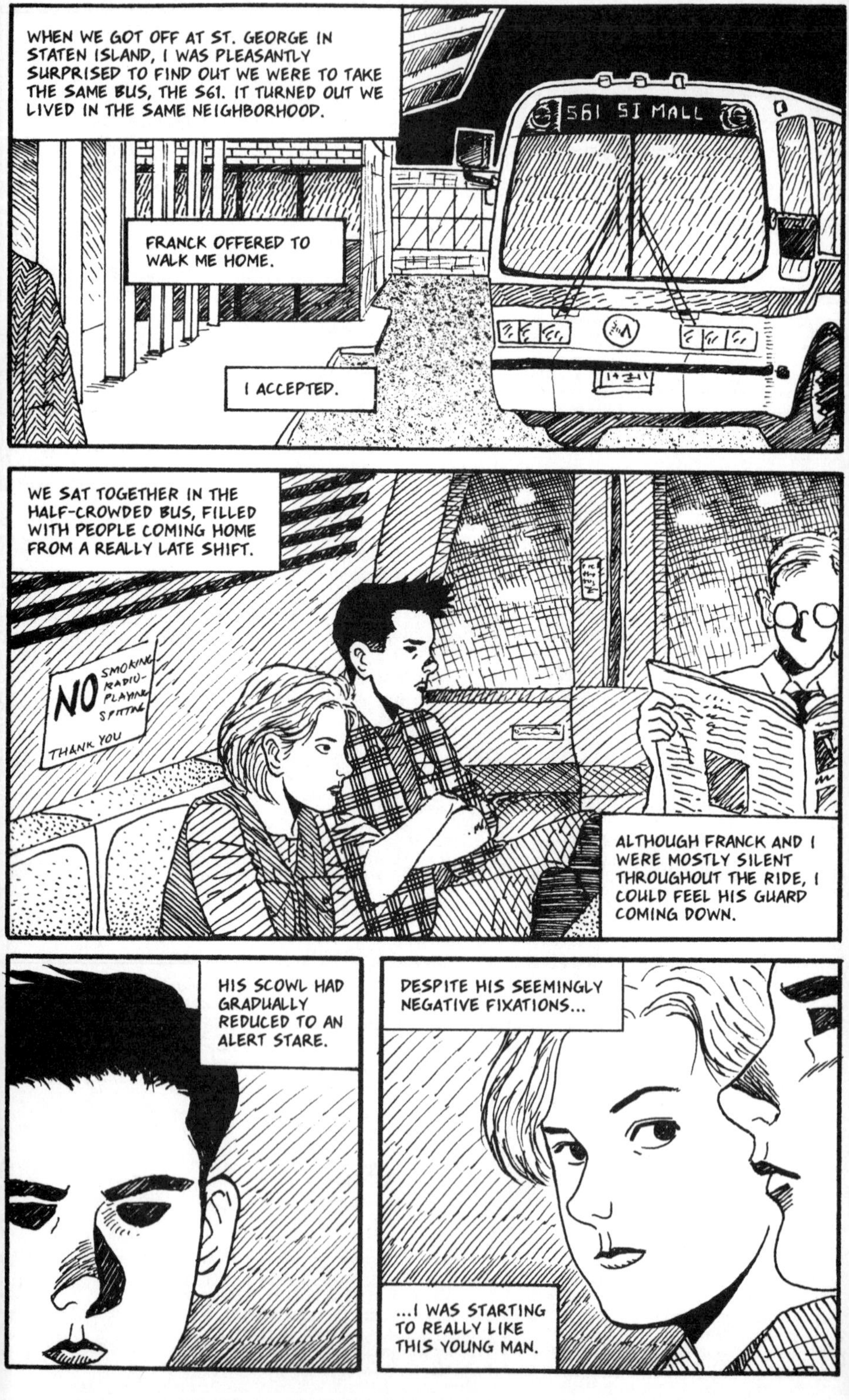
WHEN WE GOT OFF AT ST. GEORGE IN STATEN ISLAND, I WAS PLEASANTLY SURPRISED TO FIND OUT WE WERE TO TAKE THE SAME BUS, THE S61. IT TURNED OUT WE LIVED IN THE SAME NEIGHBORHOOD.
S61 SI MALL
FRANCK OFFERED TO WALK ME HOME.
I ACCEPTED.
WE SAT TOGETHER IN THE HALF-CROWDED BUS, FILLED WITH PEOPLE COMING HOME FROM A REALLY LATE SHIFT.
NO SMOKING RADIO-PLAYING SPITTING
THANK YOU
ALTHOUGH FRANCK AND I WERE MOSTLY SILENT THROUGHOUT THE RIDE, I COULD FEEL HIS GUARD COMING DOWN.
HIS SCOWL HAD GRADUALLY REDUCED TO AN ALERT STARE.
DESPITE HIS SEEMINGLY NEGATIVE FIXATIONS...
...I WAS STARTING TO REALLY LIKE THIS YOUNG MAN.

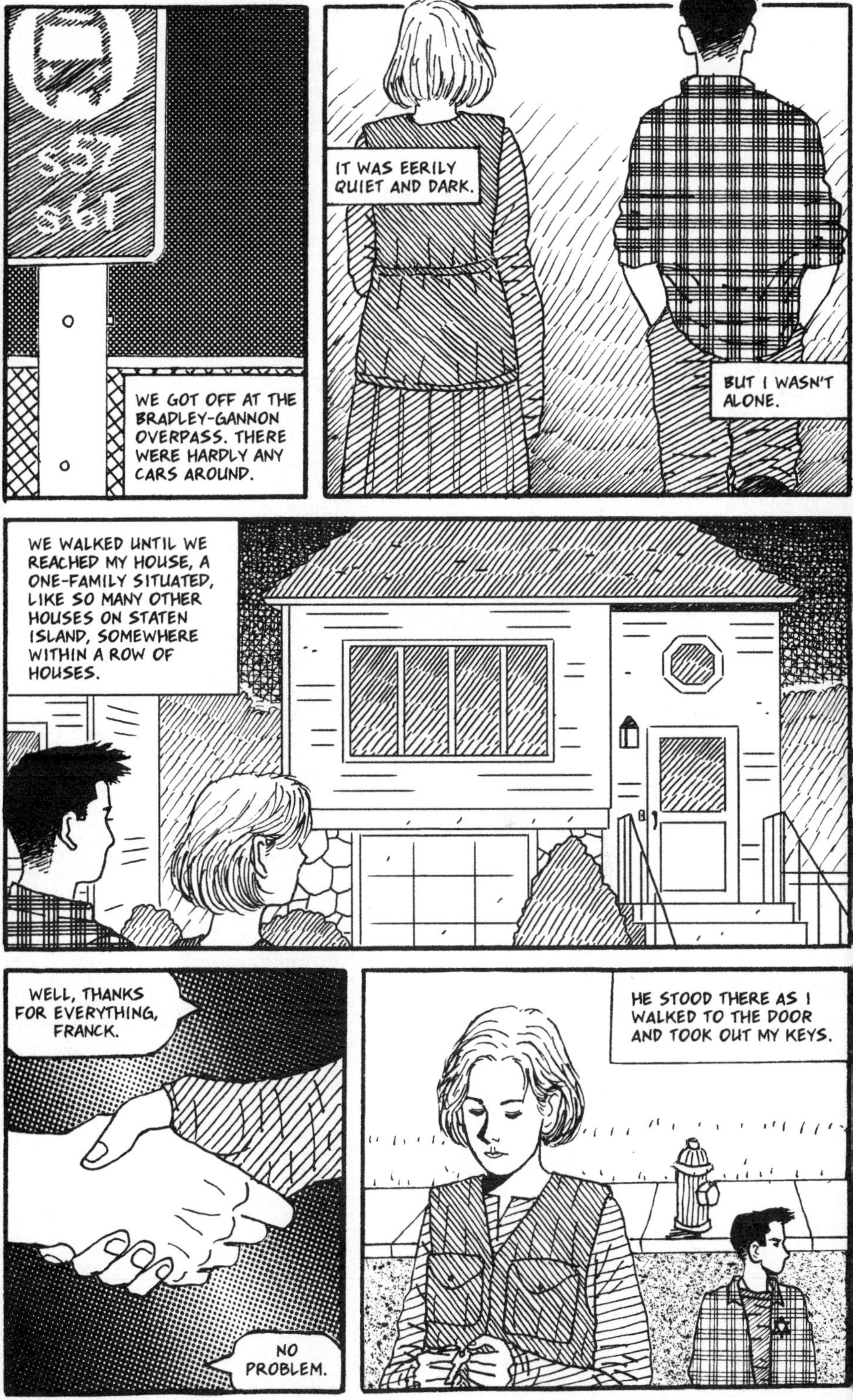
S57
S61
WE GOT OFF AT THE BRADLEY-GANNON OVERPASS. THERE WERE HARDLY ANY CARS AROUND.
IT WAS EERILY QUIET AND DARK.
BUT I WASN'T ALONE.
WE WALKED UNTIL WE REACHED MY HOUSE, A ONE-FAMILY SITUATED, LIKE SO MANY OTHER HOUSES ON STATEN ISLAND, SOMEWHERE WITHIN A ROW OF HOUSES.
WELL, THANKS FOR EVERYTHING, FRANCK.
NO PROBLEM.
HE STOOD THERE AS I WALKED TO THE DOOR AND TOOK OUT MY KEYS.

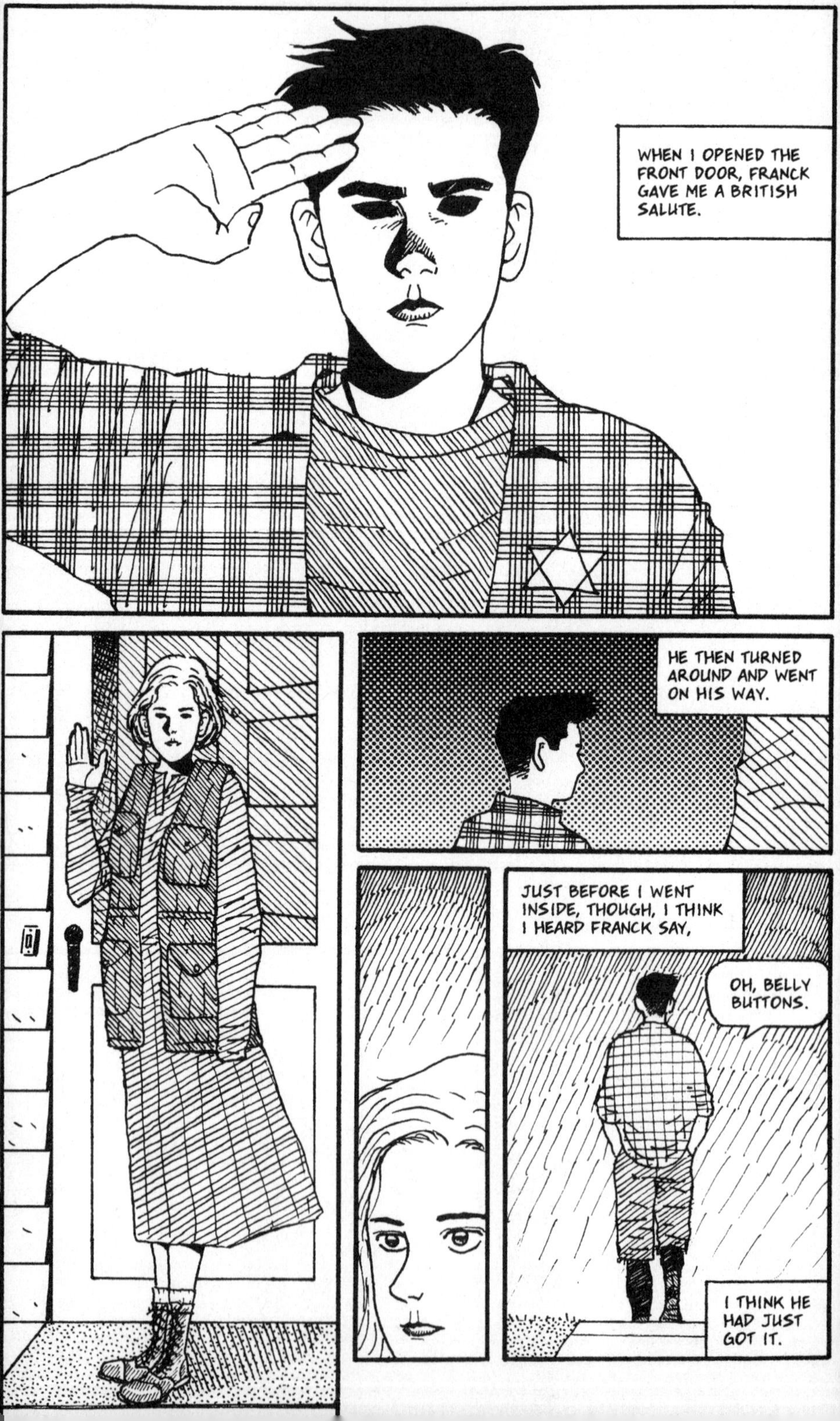
WHEN I OPENED THE FRONT DOOR, FRANCK GAVE ME A BRITISH SALUTE.
HE THEN TURNED AROUND AND WENT ON HIS WAY.
JUST BEFORE I WENT INSIDE, THOUGH, I THINK I HEARD FRANCK SAY,
OH, BELLY BUTTONS.
I THINK HE HAD JUST GOT IT.

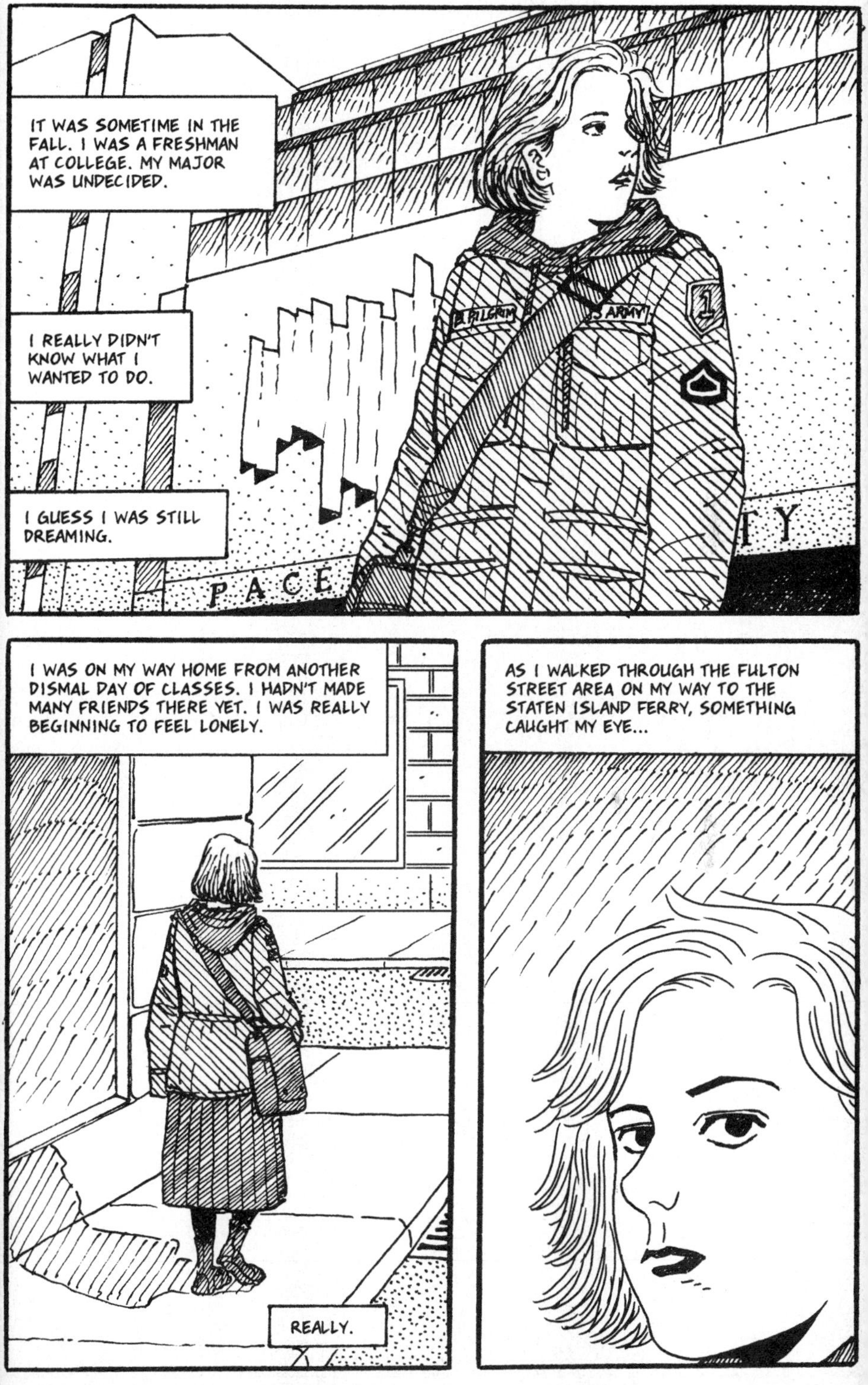
IT WAS SOMETIME IN THE FALL. I WAS A FRESHMAN AT COLLEGE. MY MAJOR WAS UNDECIDED.
I REALLY DIDN'T KNOW WHAT I WANTED TO DO.
I GUESS I WAS STILL DREAMING.
ARMY
PACE
I WAS ON MY WAY HOME FROM ANOTHER DISMAL DAY OF CLASSES. I HADN'T MADE MANY FRIENDS THERE YET. I WAS REALLY BEGINNING TO FEEL LONELY.
REALLY.
AS I WALKED THROUGH THE FULTON STREET AREA ON MY WAY TO THE STATEN ISLAND FERRY, SOMETHING CAUGHT MY EYE...

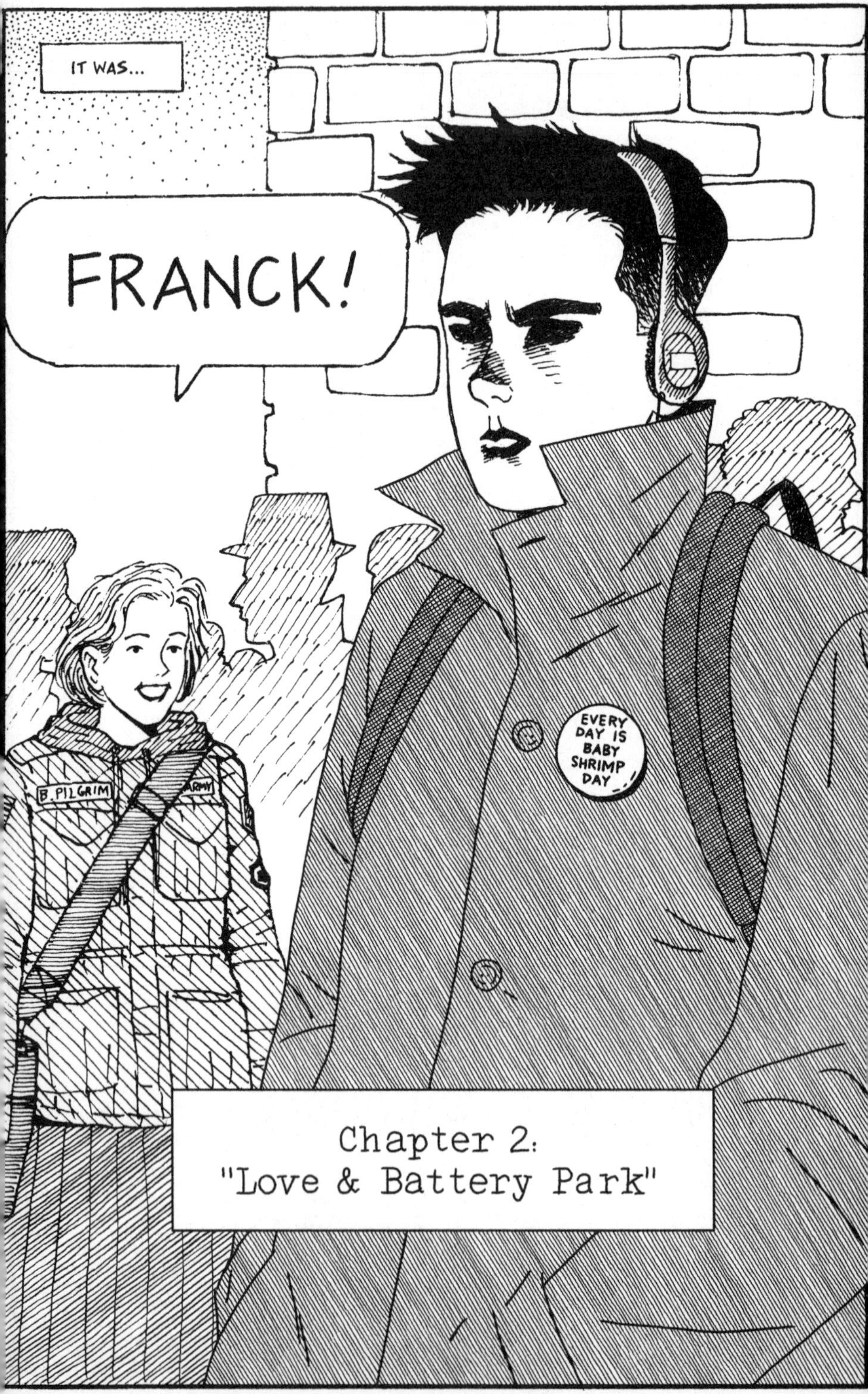
IT WAS...
FRANCK!
B. PILGRIM
ARMY
EVERY DAY IS BABY SHRIMP DAY
Chapter 2:
"Love & Battery Park"

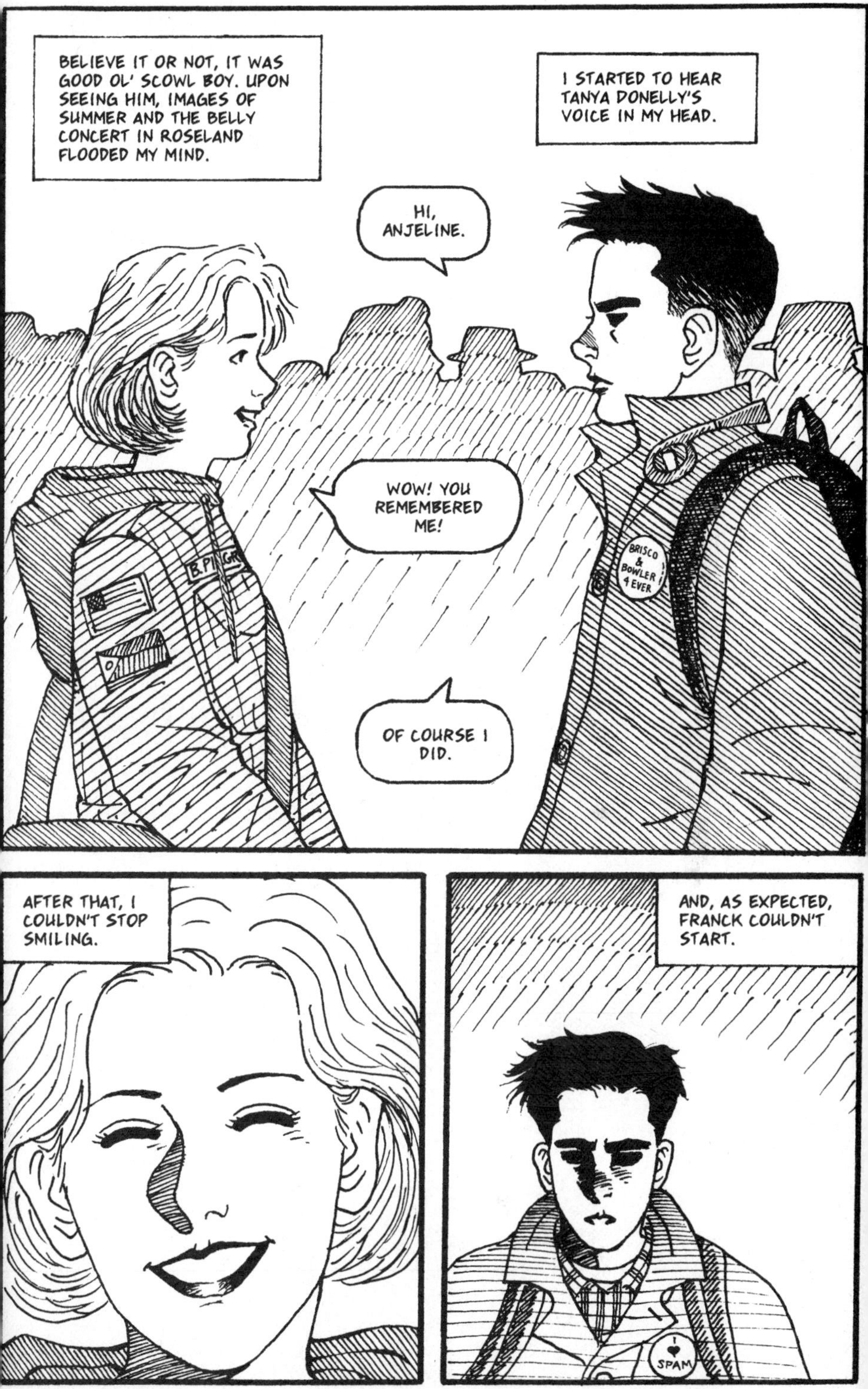
BELIEVE IT OR NOT, IT WAS GOOD OL' SCOWL BOY. UPON SEEING HIM, IMAGES OF SUMMER AND THE BELLY CONCERT IN ROSELAND FLOODED MY MIND.
I STARTED TO HEAR TANYA DONELLY'S VOICE IN MY HEAD.
HI, ANJELINE.
WOW! YOU REMEMBERED ME!
BRISCO & BOWLER 4 EVER
OF COURSE I DID.
AFTER THAT, I COULDN'T STOP SMILING.
AND, AS EXPECTED, FRANCK COULDN'T START.
I ♥ SPAM

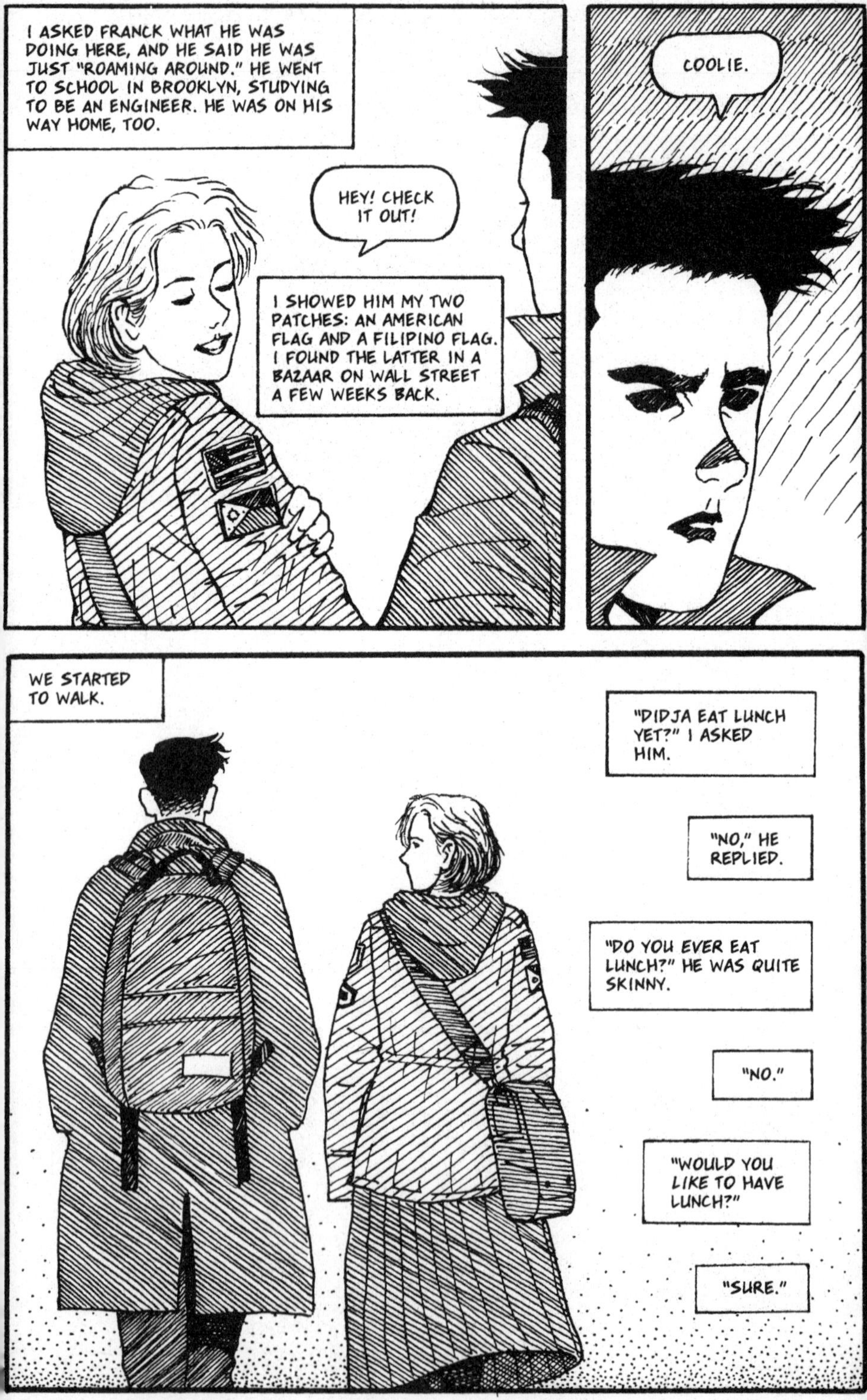
I ASKED FRANCK WHAT HE WAS DOING HERE, AND HE SAID HE WAS JUST "ROAMING AROUND." HE WENT TO SCHOOL IN BROOKLYN, STUDYING TO BE AN ENGINEER. HE WAS ON HIS WAY HOME, TOO.
HEY! CHECK IT OUT!
I SHOWED HIM MY TWO PATCHES: AN AMERICAN FLAG AND A FILIPINO FLAG. I FOUND THE LATTER IN A BAZAAR ON WALL STREET A FEW WEEKS BACK.
COOLIE.
WE STARTED TO WALK.
"DIDJA EAT LUNCH YET?" I ASKED HIM.
"NO," HE REPLIED.
"DO YOU EVER EAT LUNCH?" HE WAS QUITE SKINNY.
"NO."
"WOULD YOU LIKE TO HAVE LUNCH?"
"SURE."

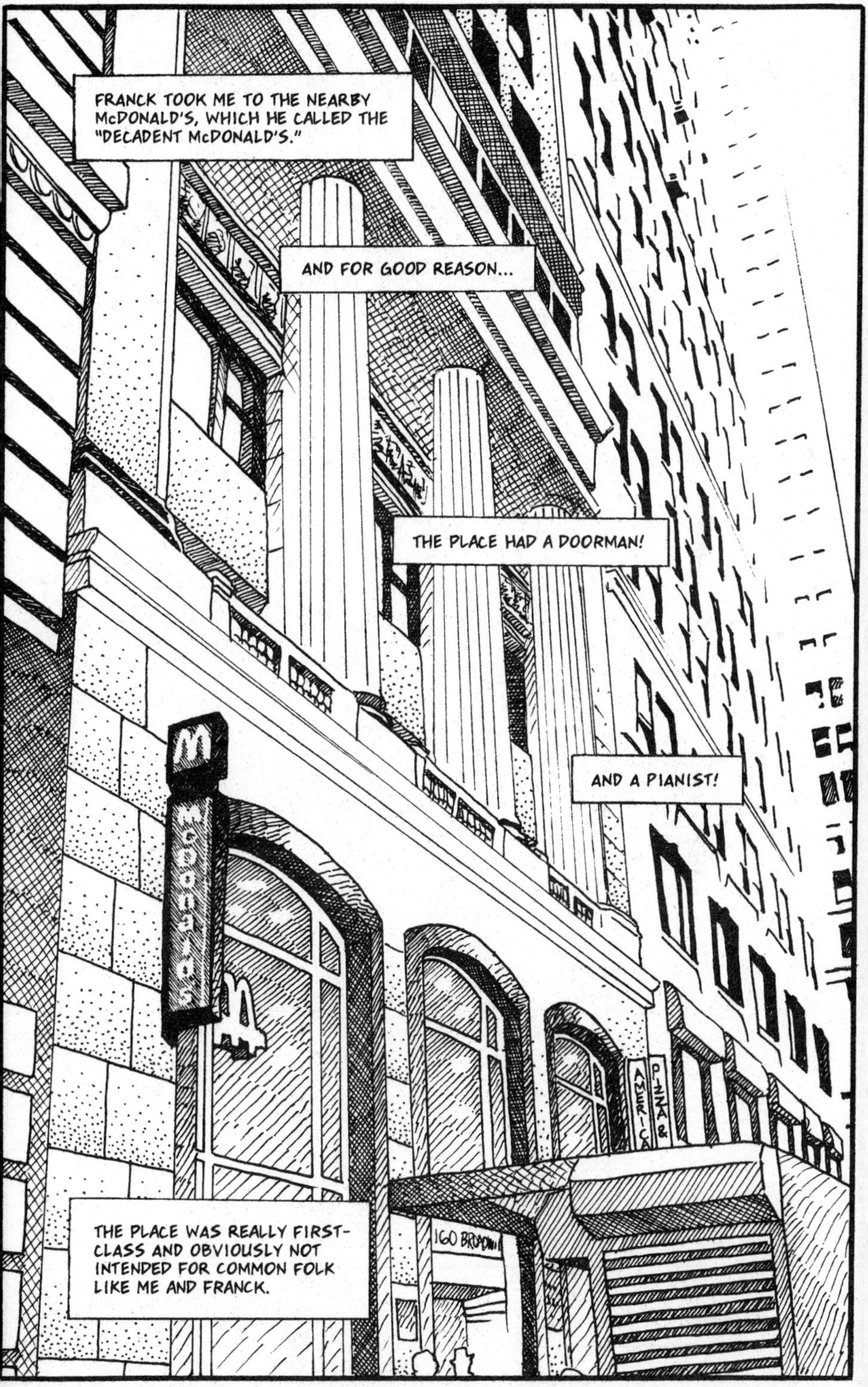
FRANCK TOOK ME TO THE NEARBY McDONALD'S, WHICH HE CALLED THE "DECADENT McDONALD'S."
AND FOR GOOD REASON...
THE PLACE HAD A DOORMAN!
AND A PIANIST!
THE PLACE WAS REALLY FIRST-CLASS AND OBVIOUSLY NOT INTENDED FOR COMMON FOLK LIKE ME AND FRANCK.
McDonald's
PIZZA & AMERICA
160 BROADW

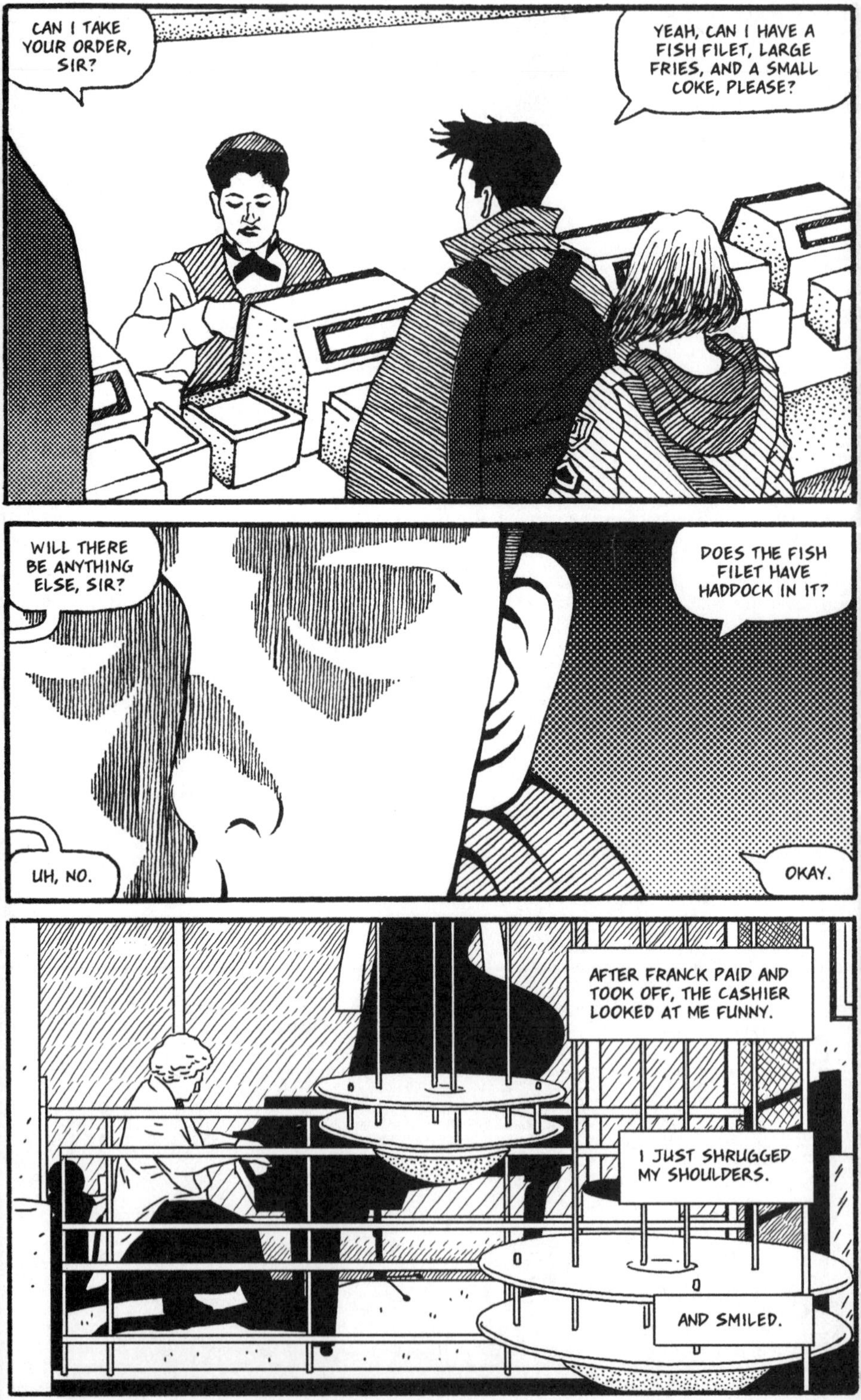
CAN I TAKE YOUR ORDER, SIR?
YEAH, CAN I HAVE A FISH FILET, LARGE FRIES, AND A SMALL COKE, PLEASE?
WILL THERE BE ANYTHING ELSE, SIR?
DOES THE FISH FILET HAVE HADDOCK IN IT?
UH, NO.
OKAY.
AFTER FRANCK PAID AND TOOK OFF, THE CASHIER LOOKED AT ME FUNNY.
I JUST SHRUGGED MY SHOULDERS.
AND SMILED.

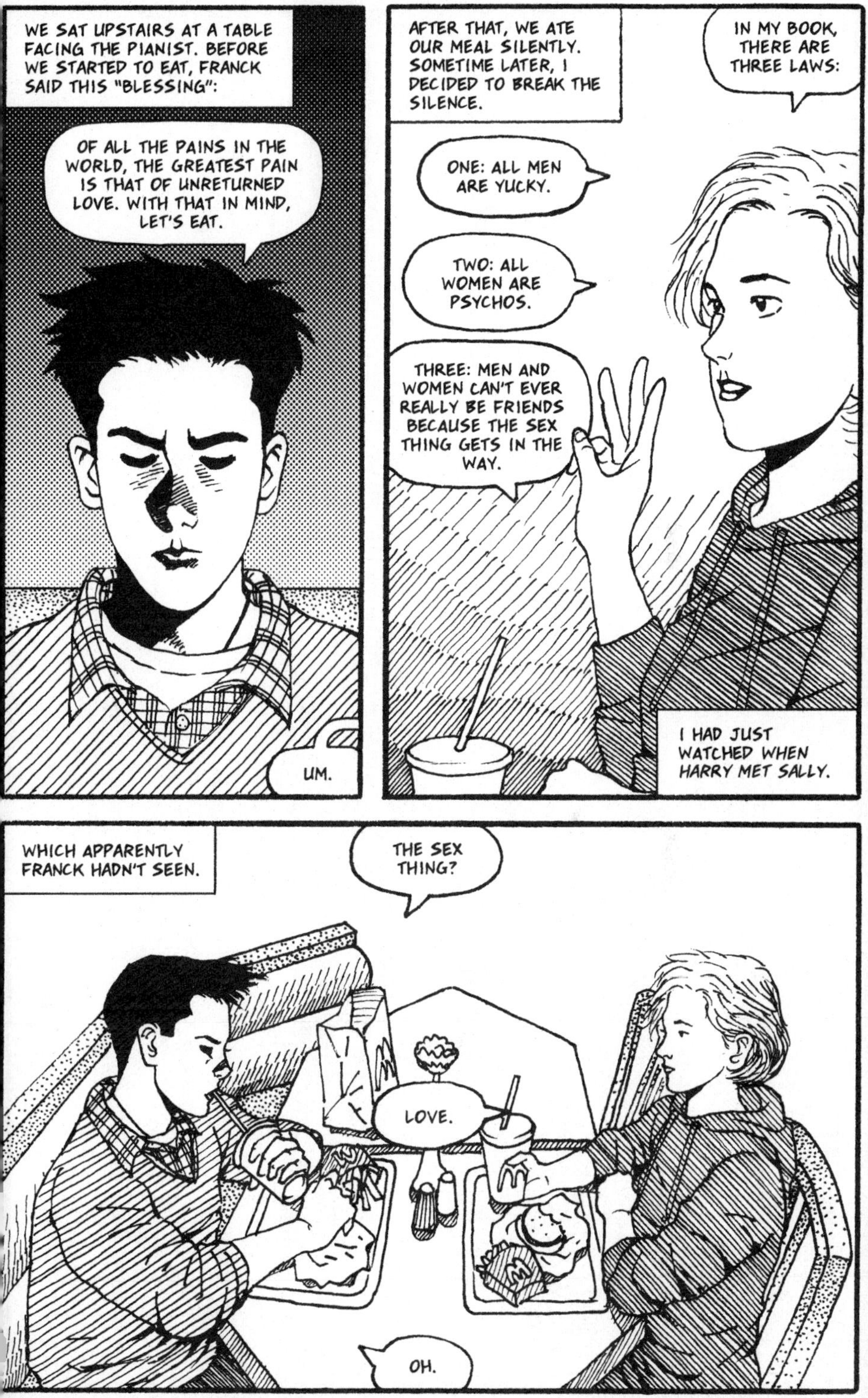
WE SAT UPSTAIRS AT A TABLE FACING THE PIANIST. BEFORE WE STARTED TO EAT, FRANCK SAID THIS "BLESSING":
OF ALL THE PAINS IN THE WORLD, THE GREATEST PAIN IS THAT OF UNRETURNED LOVE. WITH THAT IN MIND, LET'S EAT.
UM.
AFTER THAT, WE ATE OUR MEAL SILENTLY. SOMETIME LATER, I DECIDED TO BREAK THE SILENCE.
IN MY BOOK, THERE ARE THREE LAWS:
ONE: ALL MEN ARE YUCKY.
TWO: ALL WOMEN ARE PSYCHOS.
THREE: MEN AND WOMEN CAN'T EVER REALLY BE FRIENDS BECAUSE THE SEX THING GETS IN THE WAY.
I HAD JUST WATCHED WHEN HARRY MET SALLY.
WHICH APPARENTLY FRANCK HADN'T SEEN.
THE SEX THING?
LOVE.
OH.

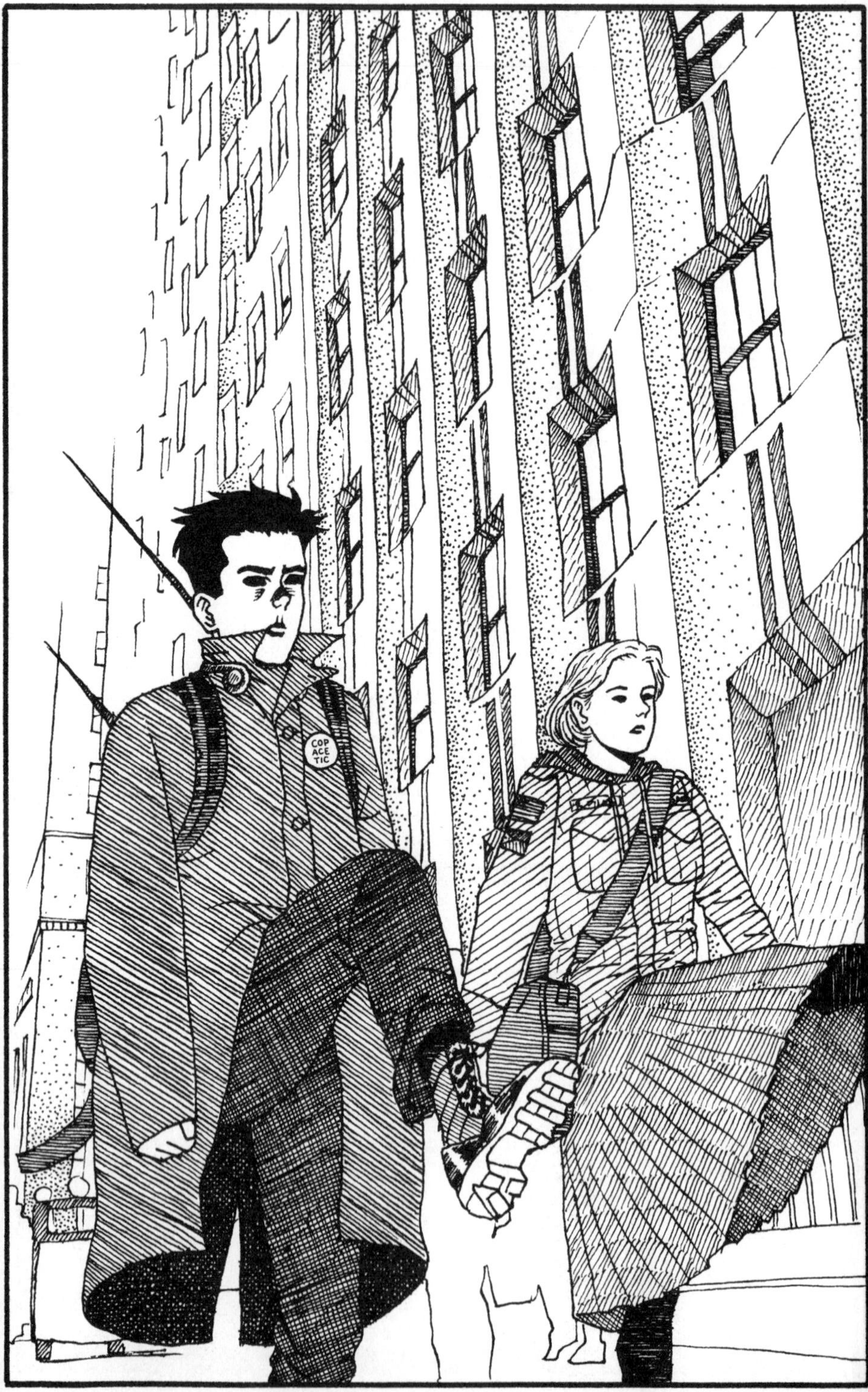
COP
ACE
TIC

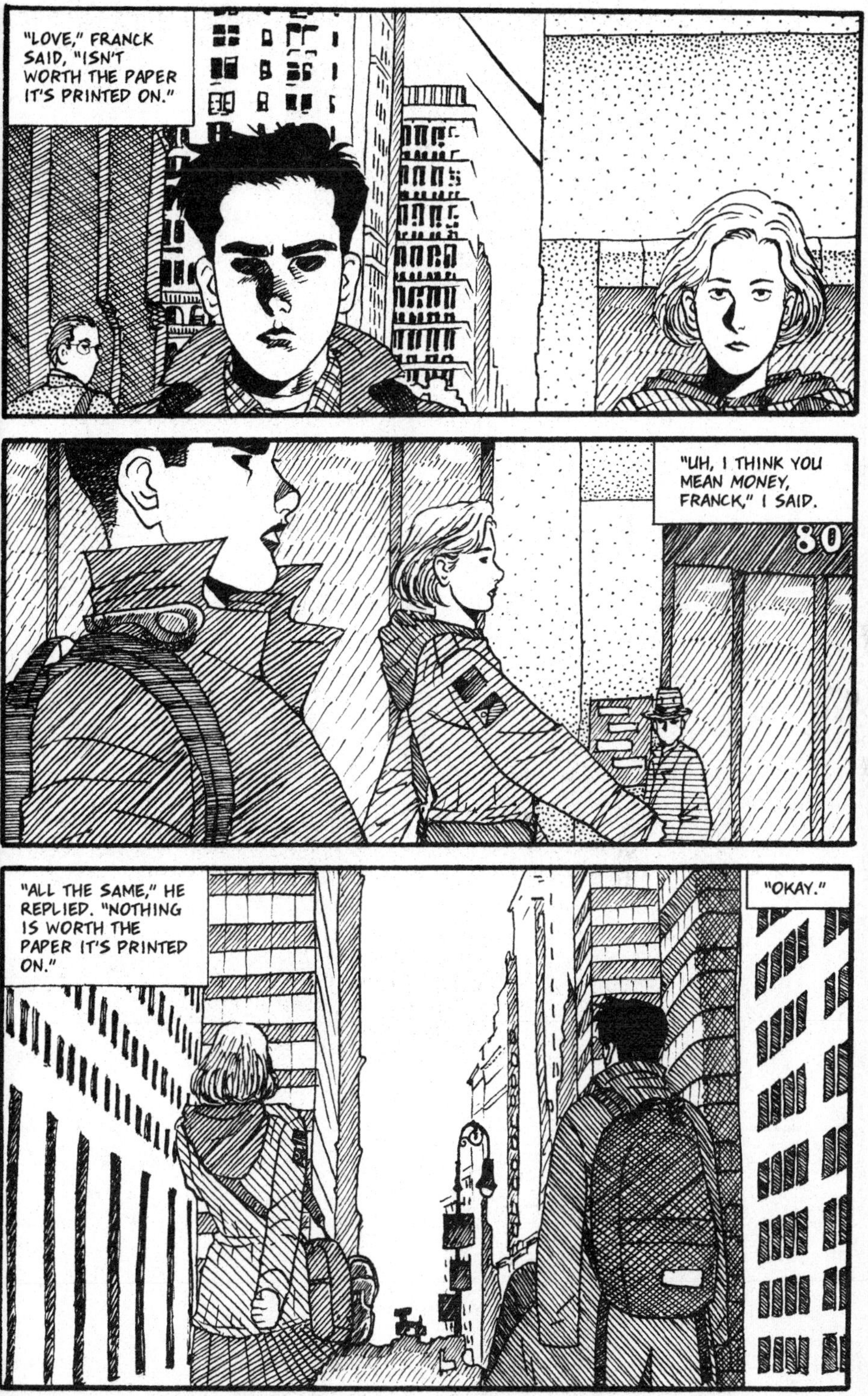
"LOVE," FRANCK SAID, "ISN'T WORTH THE PAPER IT'S PRINTED ON."
"UH, I THINK YOU MEAN MONEY, FRANCK," I SAID.
80
"ALL THE SAME," HE REPLIED. "NOTHING IS WORTH THE PAPER IT'S PRINTED ON."
"OKAY."

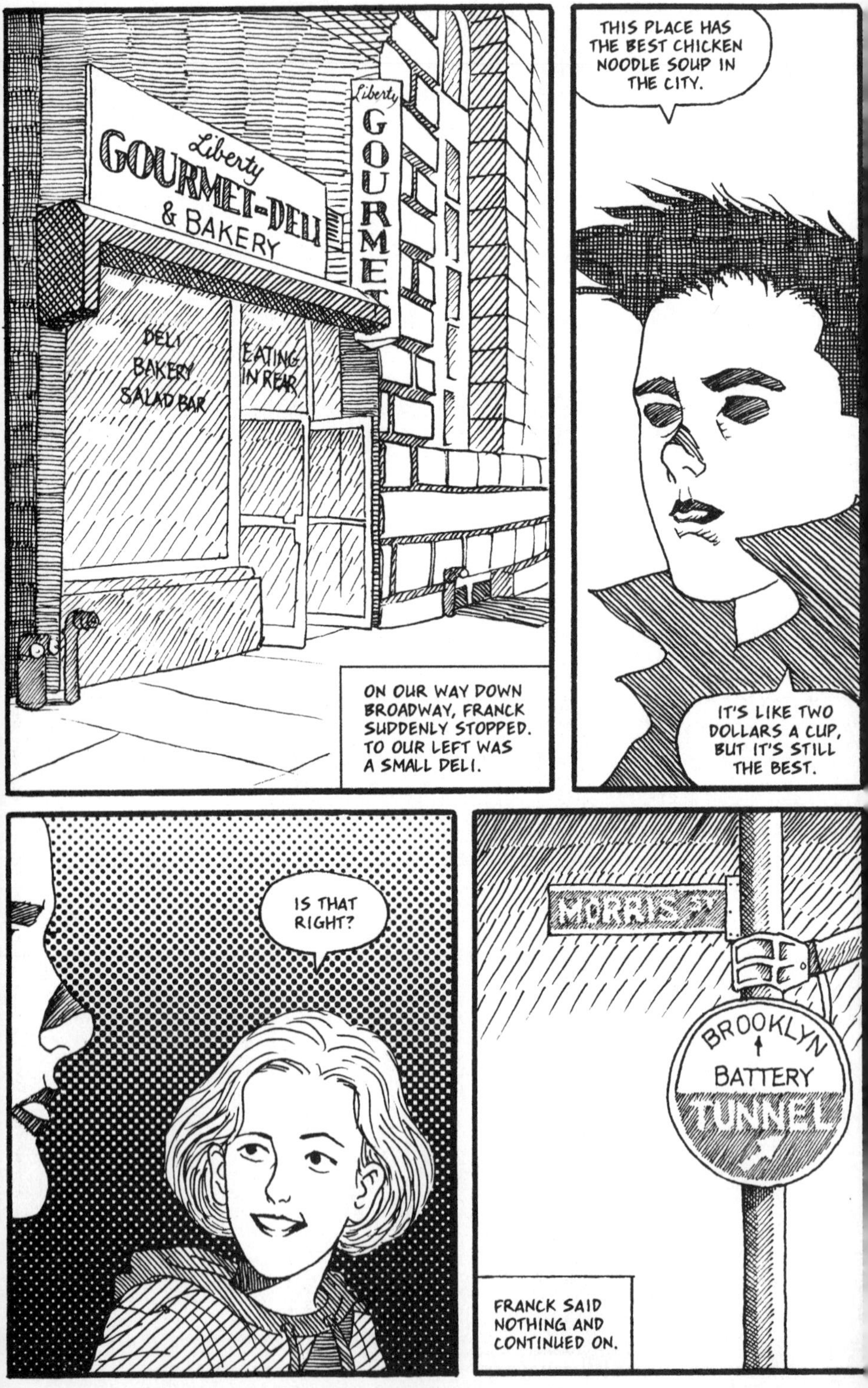
Liberty
GOURMET-DELI
& BAKERY
Liberty
GOURMET
DELI
BAKERY
SALAD BAR
EATING
IN REAR
ON OUR WAY DOWN BROADWAY, FRANCK SUDDENLY STOPPED. TO OUR LEFT WAS A SMALL DELI.
THIS PLACE HAS THE BEST CHICKEN NOODLE SOUP IN THE CITY.
IT'S LIKE TWO DOLLARS A CUP, BUT IT'S STILL THE BEST.
IS THAT RIGHT?
MORRIS ST
BROOKLYN
BATTERY
TUNNEL
FRANCK SAID NOTHING AND CONTINUED ON.

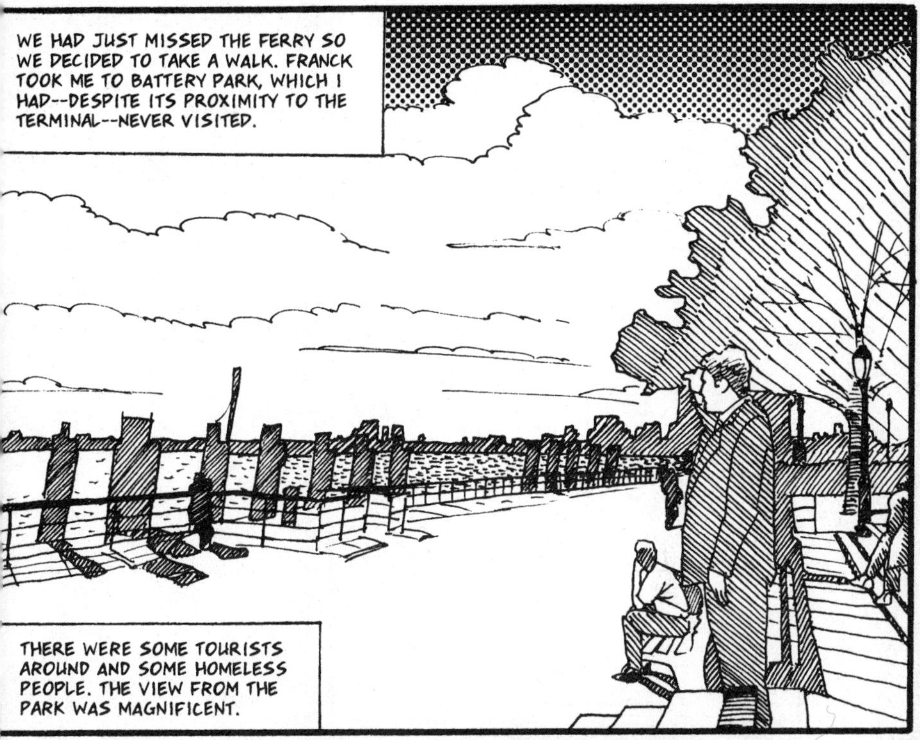
WE HAD JUST MISSED THE FERRY SO WE DECIDED TO TAKE A WALK. FRANCK TOOK ME TO BATTERY PARK, WHICH I HAD--DESPITE ITS PROXIMITY TO THE TERMINAL--NEVER VISITED.
THERE WERE SOME TOURISTS AROUND AND SOME HOMELESS PEOPLE. THE VIEW FROM THE PARK WAS MAGNIFICENT.

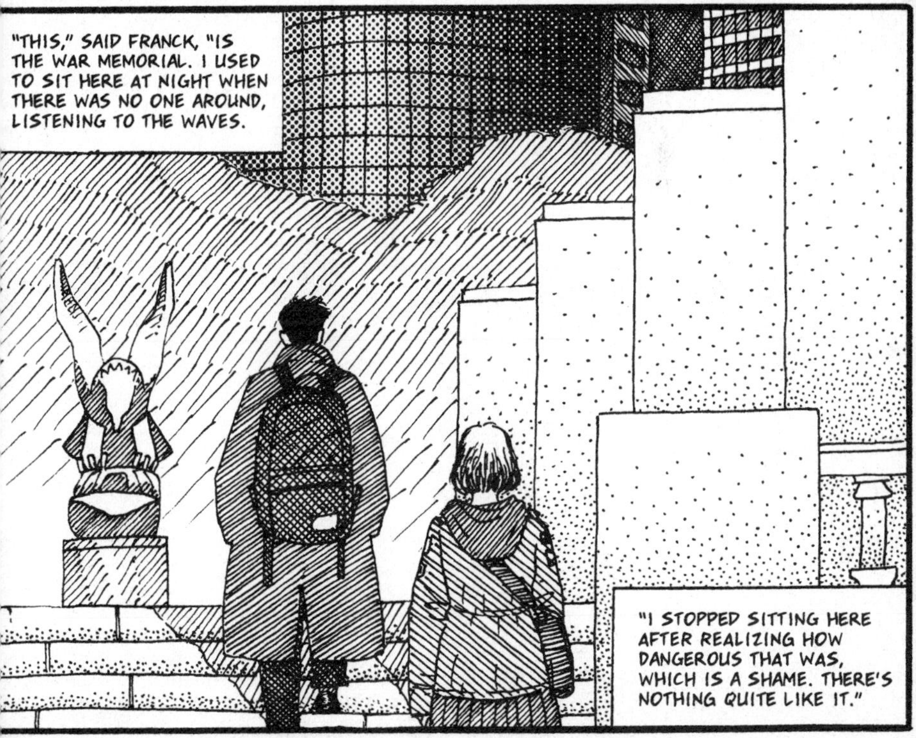
"THIS," SAID FRANCK, "IS THE WAR MEMORIAL. I USED TO SIT HERE AT NIGHT WHEN THERE WAS NO ONE AROUND, LISTENING TO THE WAVES.
"I STOPPED SITTING HERE AFTER REALIZING HOW DANGEROUS THAT WAS, WHICH IS A SHAME. THERE'S NOTHING QUITE LIKE IT."

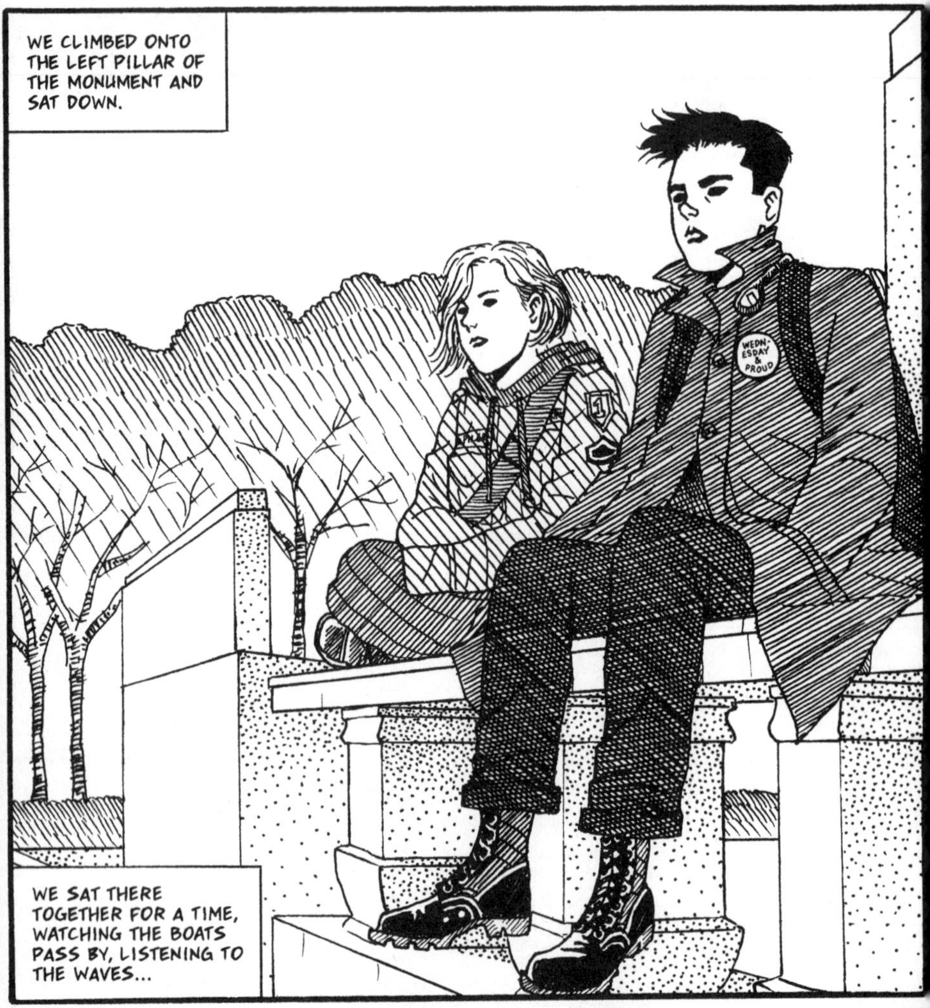
WE CLIMBED ONTO THE LEFT PILLAR OF THE MONUMENT AND SAT DOWN.
WEDNESDAY & PROUD
WE SAT THERE TOGETHER FOR A TIME, WATCHING THE BOATS PASS BY, LISTENING TO THE WAVES...

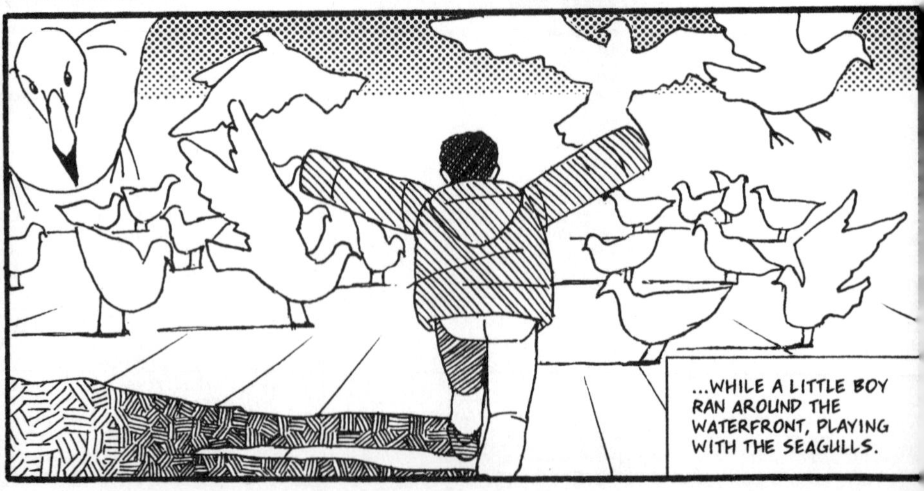
...WHILE A LITTLE BOY RAN AROUND THE WATERFRONT, PLAYING WITH THE SEAGULLS.

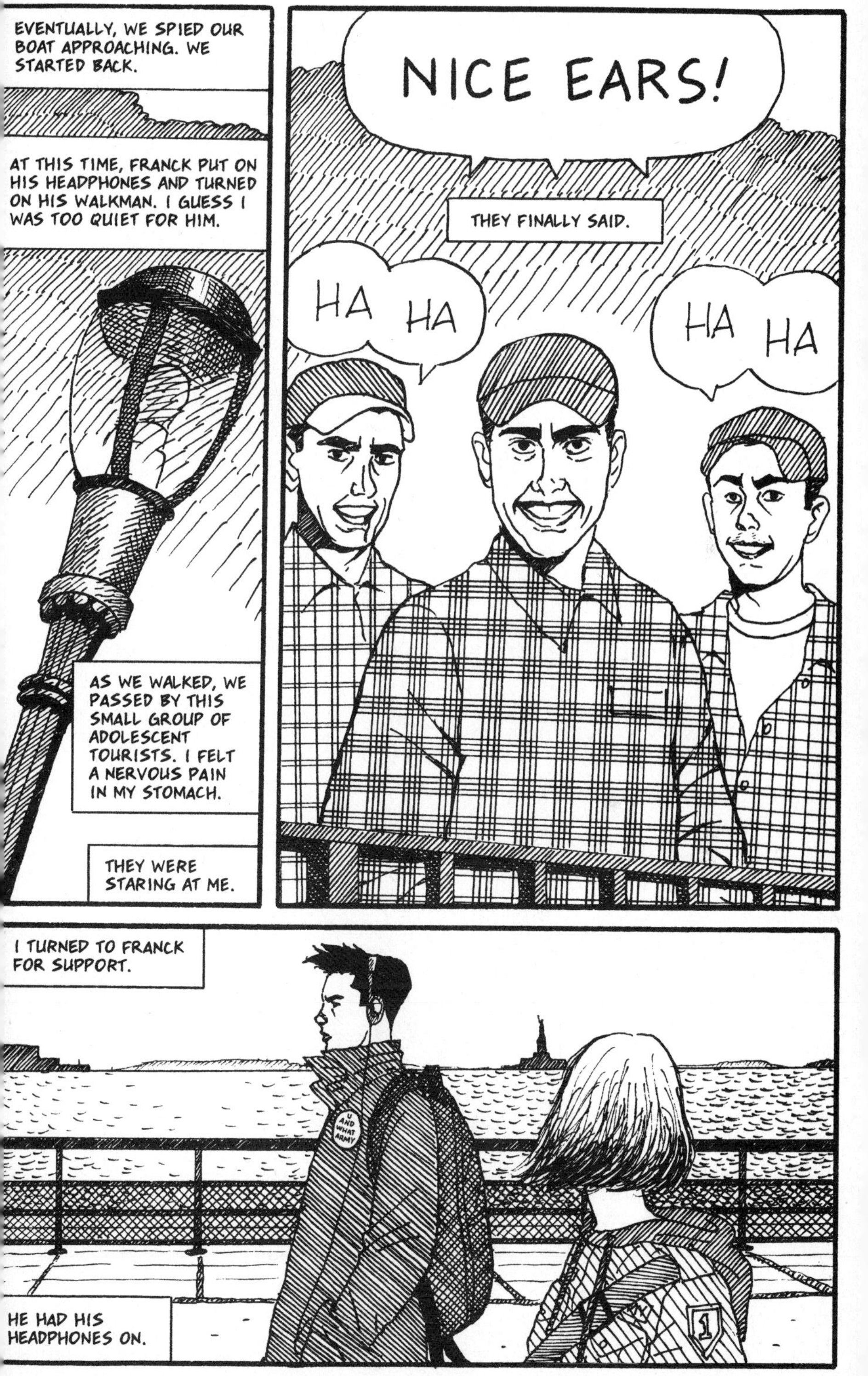
EVENTUALLY, WE SPIED OUR BOAT APPROACHING. WE STARTED BACK.
AT THIS TIME, FRANCK PUT ON HIS HEADPHONES AND TURNED ON HIS WALKMAN. I GUESS I WAS TOO QUIET FOR HIM.
AS WE WALKED, WE PASSED BY THIS SMALL GROUP OF ADOLESCENT TOURISTS. I FELT A NERVOUS PAIN IN MY STOMACH.
THEY WERE STARING AT ME.
NICE EARS!
THEY FINALLY SAID.
HA HA
HA HA
I TURNED TO FRANCK FOR SUPPORT.
U AND WHAT ARMY
HE HAD HIS HEADPHONES ON.

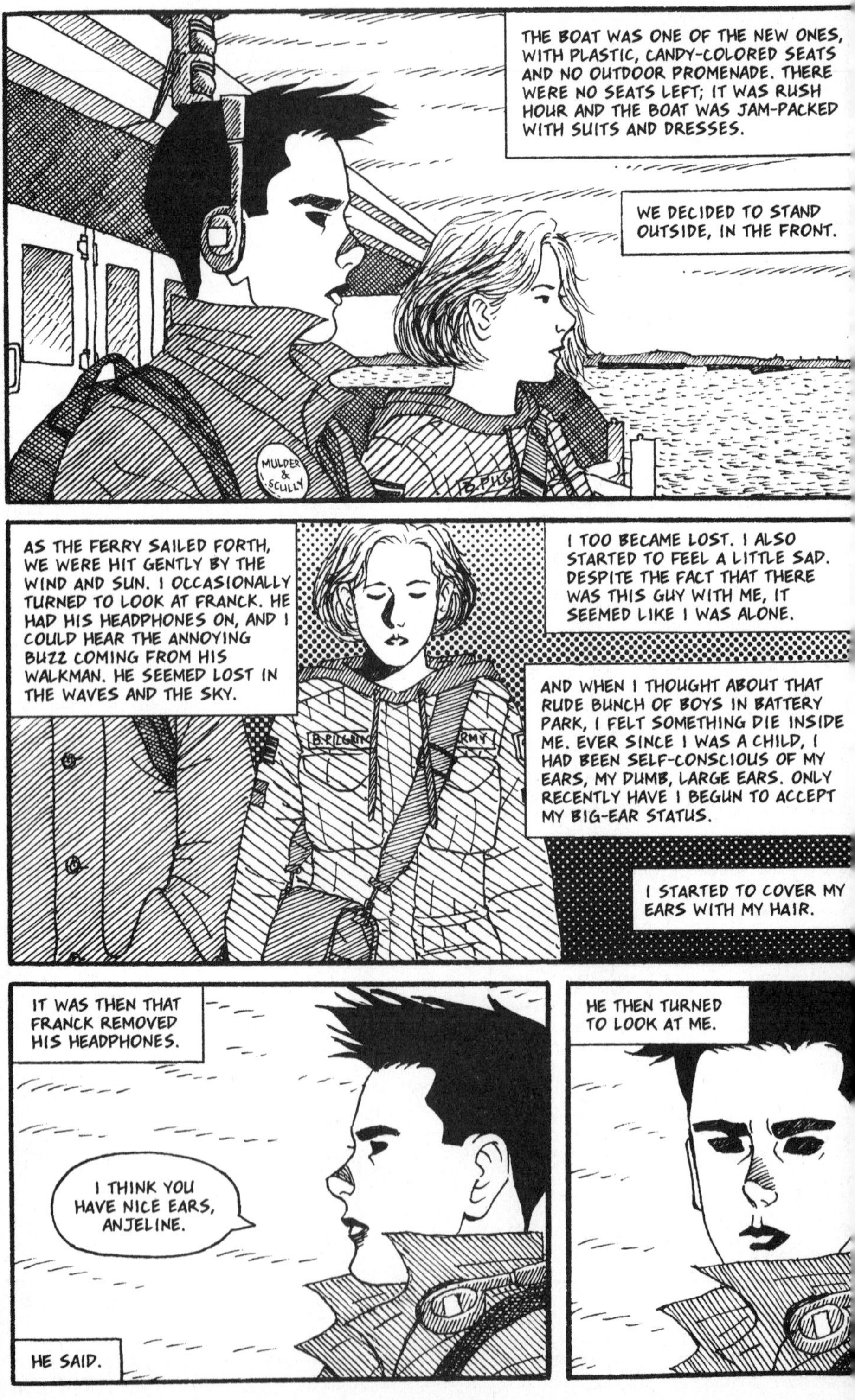
THE BOAT WAS ONE OF THE NEW ONES, WITH PLASTIC, CANDY-COLORED SEATS AND NO OUTDOOR PROMENADE. THERE WERE NO SEATS LEFT; IT WAS RUSH HOUR AND THE BOAT WAS JAM-PACKED WITH SUITS AND DRESSES.
WE DECIDED TO STAND OUTSIDE, IN THE FRONT.
MULDER & SCULLY
AS THE FERRY SAILED FORTH, WE WERE HIT GENTLY BY THE WIND AND SUN. I OCCASIONALLY TURNED TO LOOK AT FRANCK. HE HAD HIS HEADPHONES ON, AND I COULD HEAR THE ANNOYING BUZZ COMING FROM HIS WALKMAN. HE SEEMED LOST IN THE WAVES AND THE SKY.
I TOO BECAME LOST. I ALSO STARTED TO FEEL A LITTLE SAD. DESPITE THE FACT THAT THERE WAS THIS GUY WITH ME, IT SEEMED LIKE I WAS ALONE.
AND WHEN I THOUGHT ABOUT THAT RUDE BUNCH OF BOYS IN BATTERY PARK, I FELT SOMETHING DIE INSIDE ME. EVER SINCE I WAS A CHILD, I HAD BEEN SELF-CONSCIOUS OF MY EARS, MY DUMB, LARGE EARS. ONLY RECENTLY HAVE I BEGUN TO ACCEPT MY BIG-EAR STATUS.
I STARTED TO COVER MY EARS WITH MY HAIR.
IT WAS THEN THAT FRANCK REMOVED HIS HEADPHONES.
I THINK YOU HAVE NICE EARS, ANJELINE.
HE SAID.
HE THEN TURNED TO LOOK AT ME.

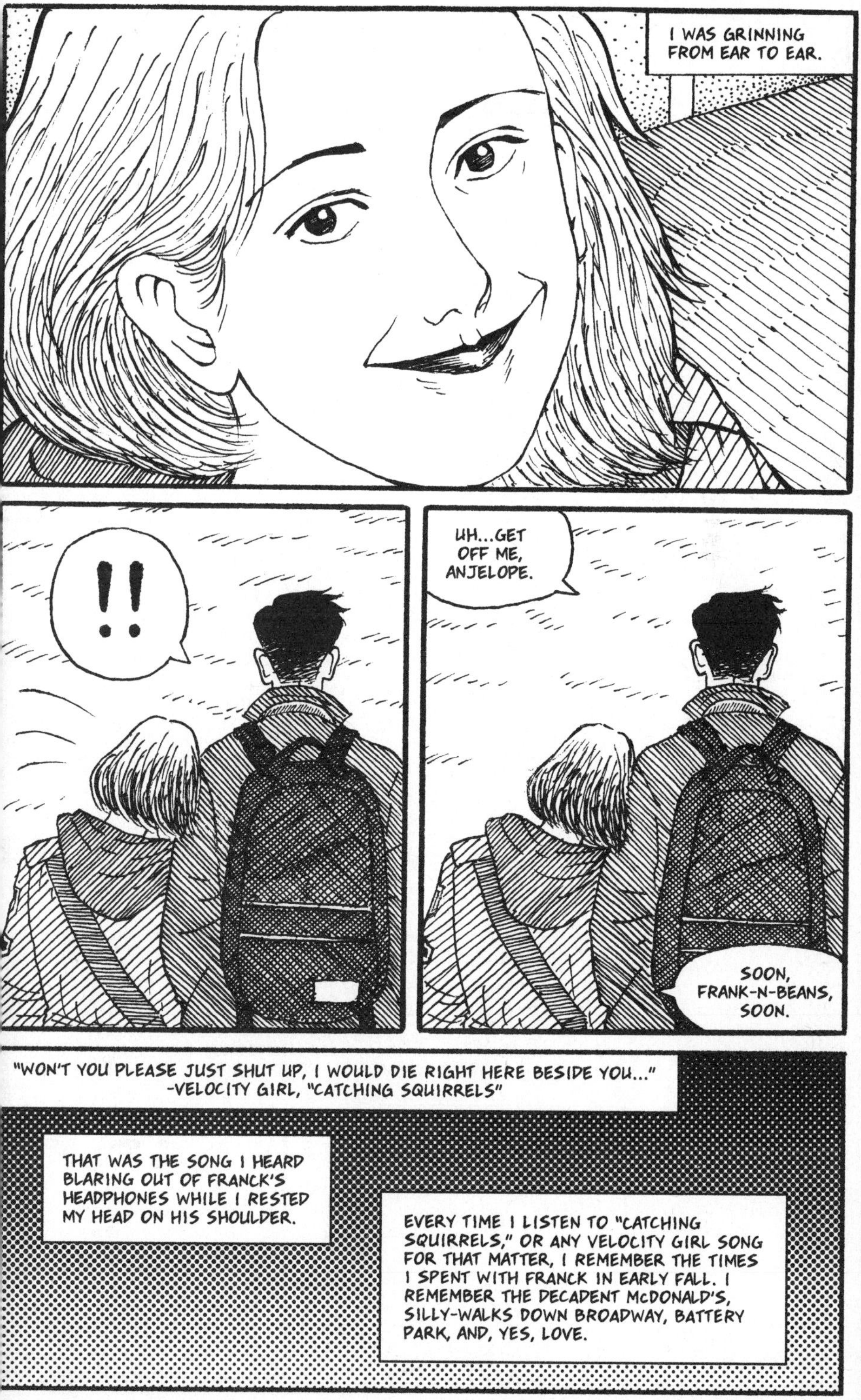
I WAS GRINNING FROM EAR TO EAR.
!!
UH...GET OFF ME, ANJELOPE.
SOON, FRANK-N-BEANS, SOON.
"WON'T YOU PLEASE JUST SHUT UP, I WOULD DIE RIGHT HERE BESIDE YOU..."
-VELOCITY GIRL, "CATCHING SQUIRRELS"
THAT WAS THE SONG I HEARD BLARING OUT OF FRANCK'S HEADPHONES WHILE I RESTED MY HEAD ON HIS SHOULDER.
EVERY TIME I LISTEN TO "CATCHING SQUIRRELS," OR ANY VELOCITY GIRL SONG FOR THAT MATTER, I REMEMBER THE TIMES I SPENT WITH FRANCK IN EARLY FALL. I REMEMBER THE DECADENT McDONALD'S, SILLY-WALKS DOWN BROADWAY, BATTERY PARK, AND, YES, LOVE.

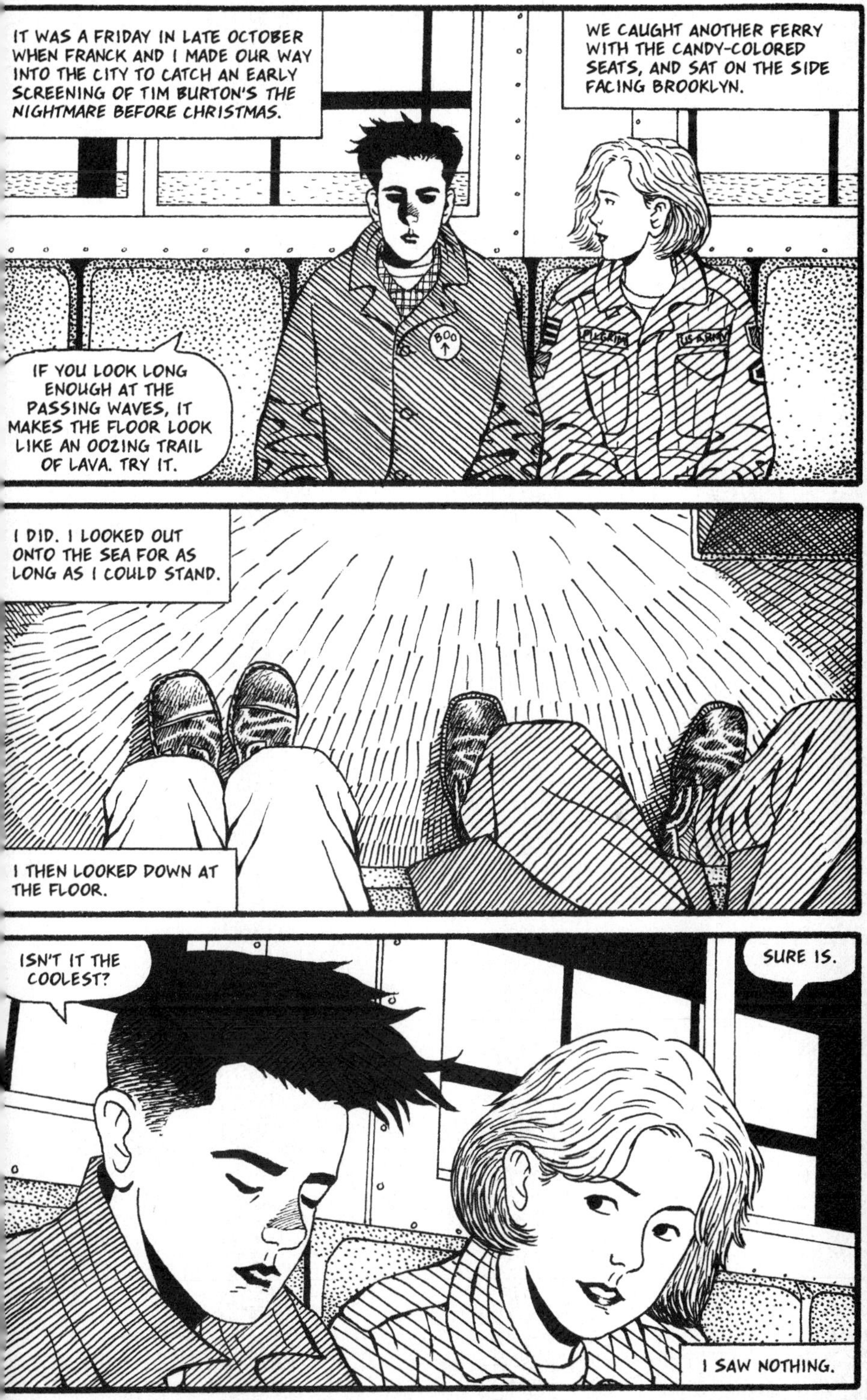
IT WAS A FRIDAY IN LATE OCTOBER WHEN FRANCK AND I MADE OUR WAY INTO THE CITY TO CATCH AN EARLY SCREENING OF TIM BURTON'S THE NIGHTMARE BEFORE CHRISTMAS.
WE CAUGHT ANOTHER FERRY WITH THE CANDY-COLORED SEATS, AND SAT ON THE SIDE FACING BROOKLYN.
BOO
PILGRIM
US ARMY
IF YOU LOOK LONG ENOUGH AT THE PASSING WAVES, IT MAKES THE FLOOR LOOK LIKE AN OOZING TRAIL OF LAVA. TRY IT.
I DID. I LOOKED OUT ONTO THE SEA FOR AS LONG AS I COULD STAND.
I THEN LOOKED DOWN AT THE FLOOR.
ISN'T IT THE COOLEST?
SURE IS.
I SAW NOTHING.

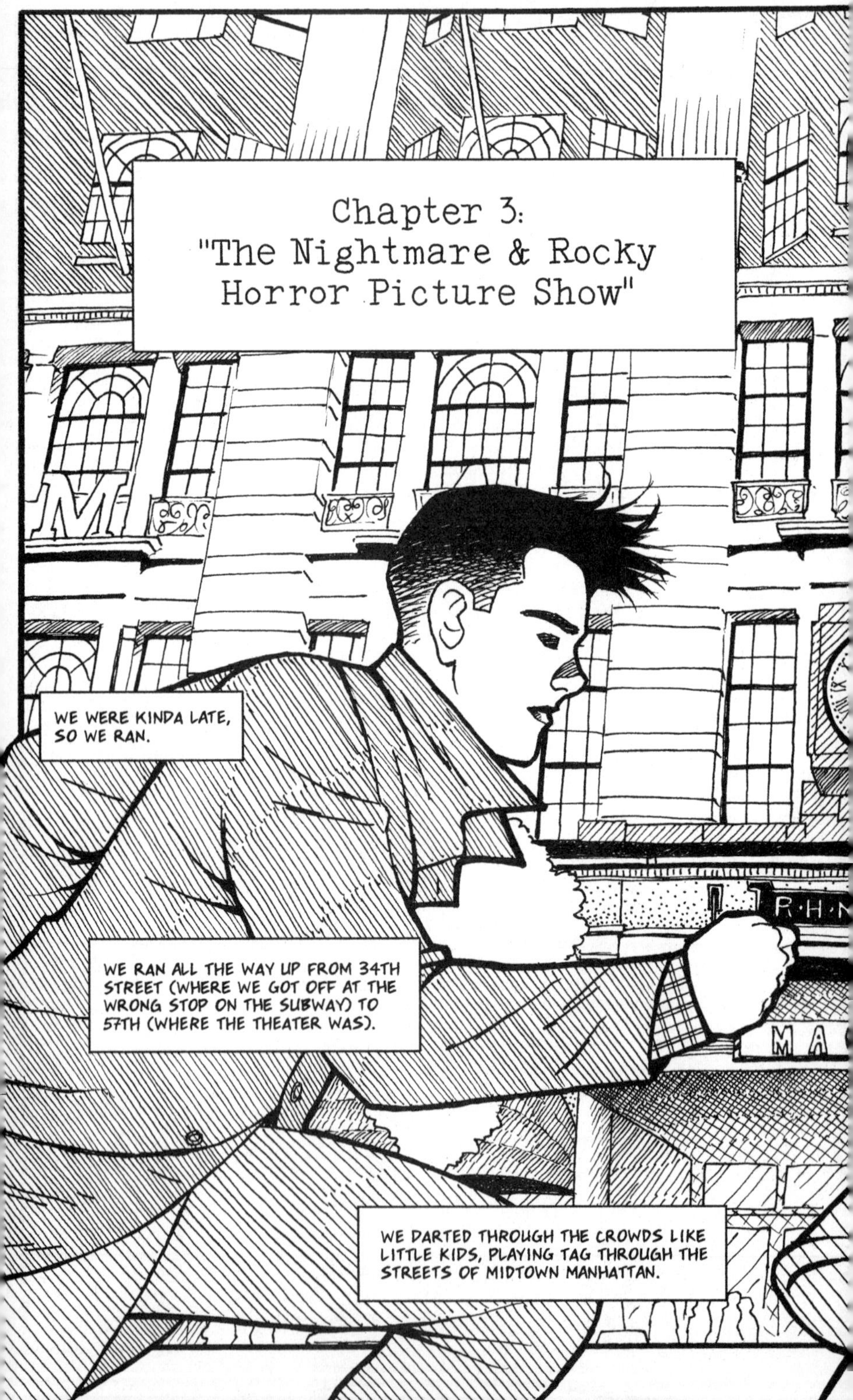
Chapter 3:
"The Nightmare & Rocky Horror Picture Show"
WE WERE KINDA LATE, SO WE RAN.
WE RAN ALL THE WAY UP FROM 34TH STREET (WHERE WE GOT OFF AT THE WRONG STOP ON THE SUBWAY) TO 57TH (WHERE THE THEATER WAS).
WE DARTED THROUGH THE CROWDS LIKE LITTLE KIDS, PLAYING TAG THROUGH THE STREETS OF MIDTOWN MANHATTAN.

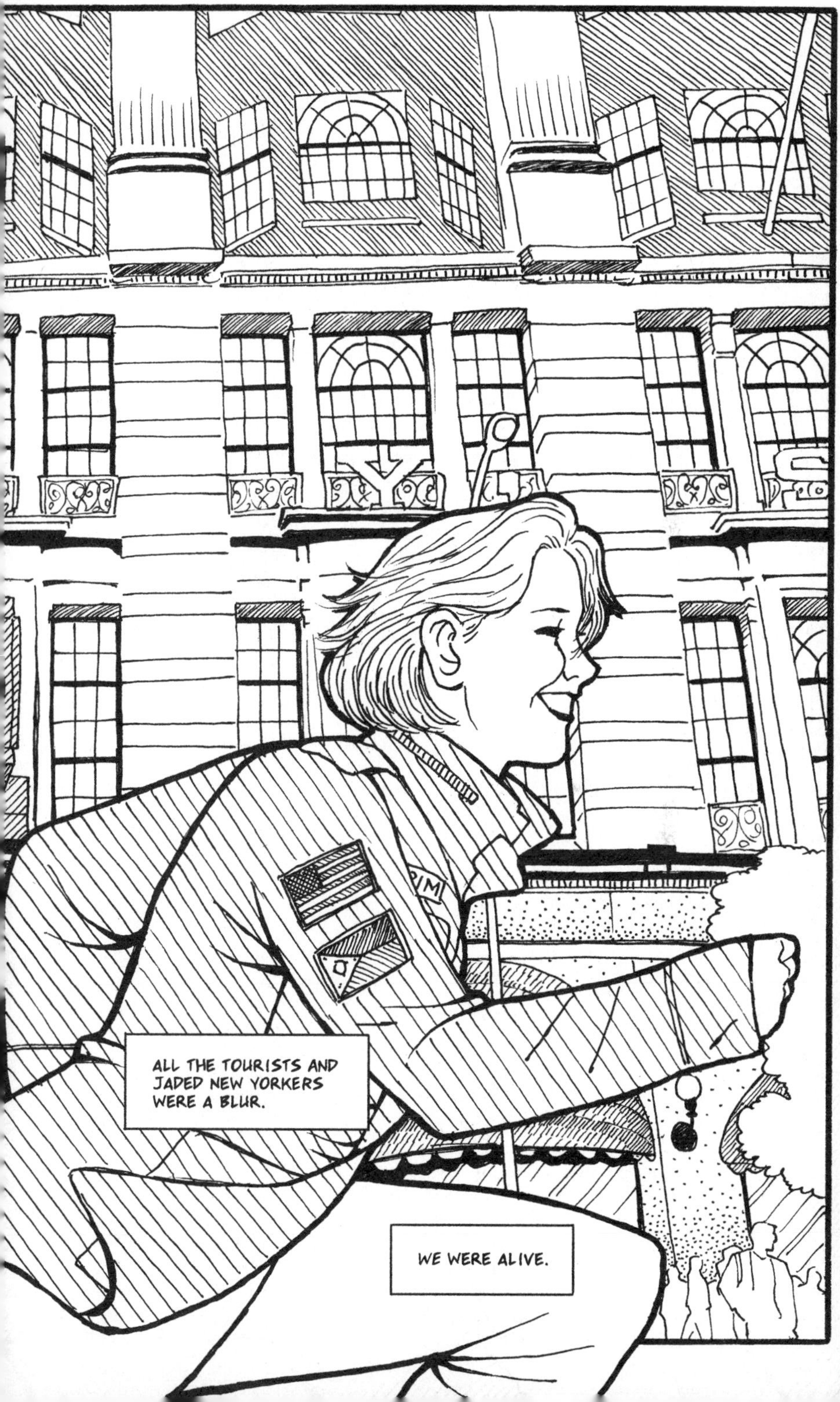
ALL THE TOURISTS AND JADED NEW YORKERS WERE A BLUR.
WE WERE ALIVE.

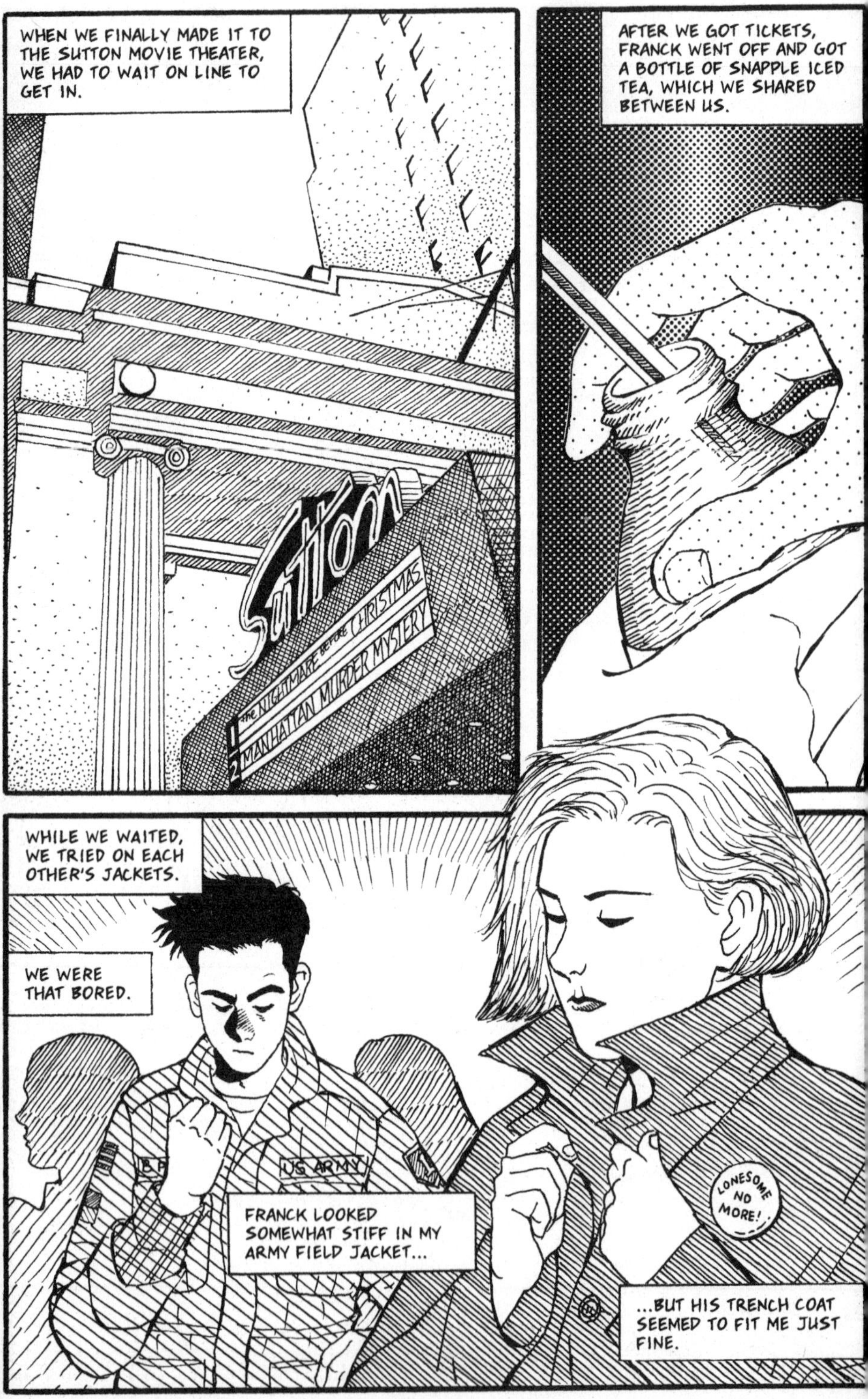
WHEN WE FINALLY MADE IT TO THE SUTTON MOVIE THEATER, WE HAD TO WAIT ON LINE TO GET IN.
Sutton
1 THE NIGHTMARE BEFORE CHRISTMAS
2 MANHATTAN MURDER MYSTERY
AFTER WE GOT TICKETS, FRANCK WENT OFF AND GOT A BOTTLE OF SNAPPLE ICED TEA, WHICH WE SHARED BETWEEN US.
WHILE WE WAITED, WE TRIED ON EACH OTHER'S JACKETS.
WE WERE THAT BORED.
US ARMY
FRANCK LOOKED SOMEWHAT STIFF IN MY ARMY FIELD JACKET...
LONESOME NO MORE!
...BUT HIS TRENCH COAT SEEMED TO FIT ME JUST FINE.

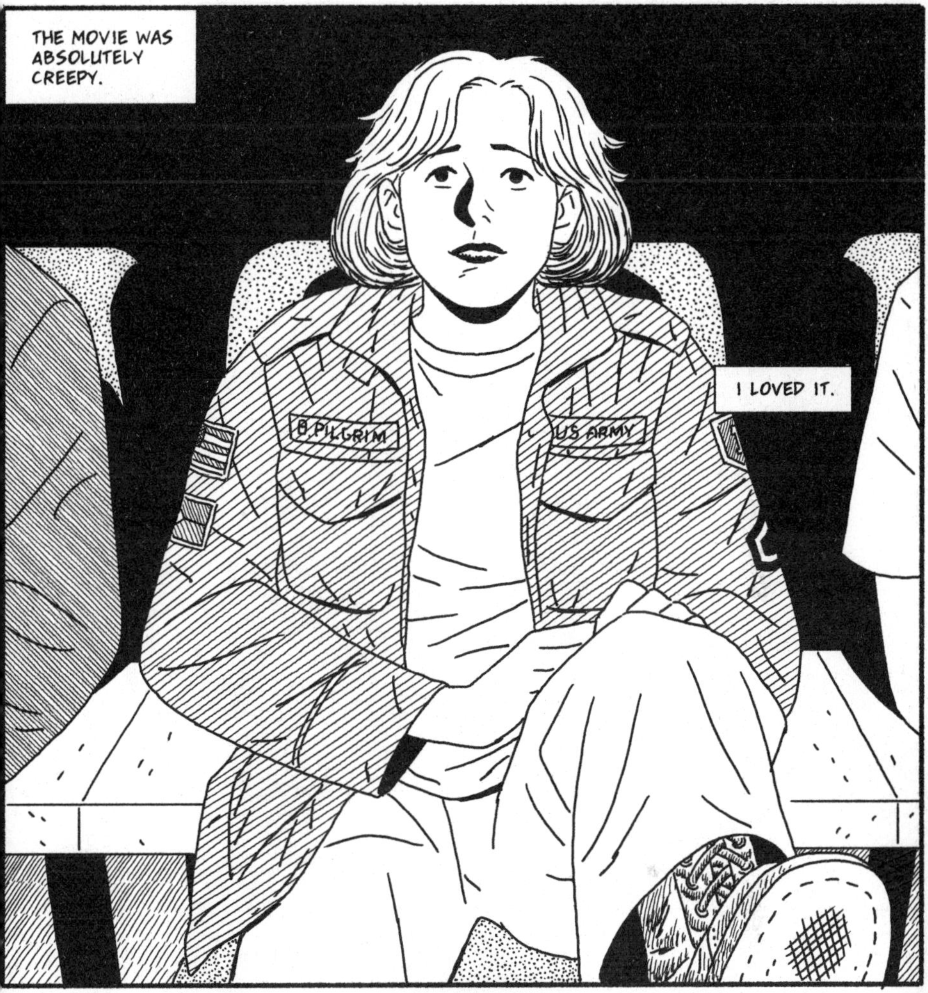
THE MOVIE WAS ABSOLUTELY CREEPY.
B PILGRIM
US ARMY
I LOVED IT.

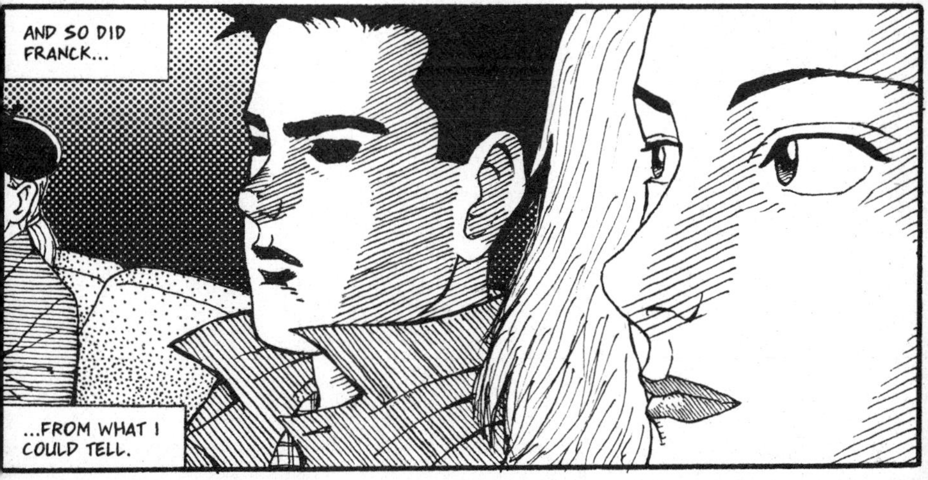
AND SO DID FRANCK...
...FROM WHAT I COULD TELL.

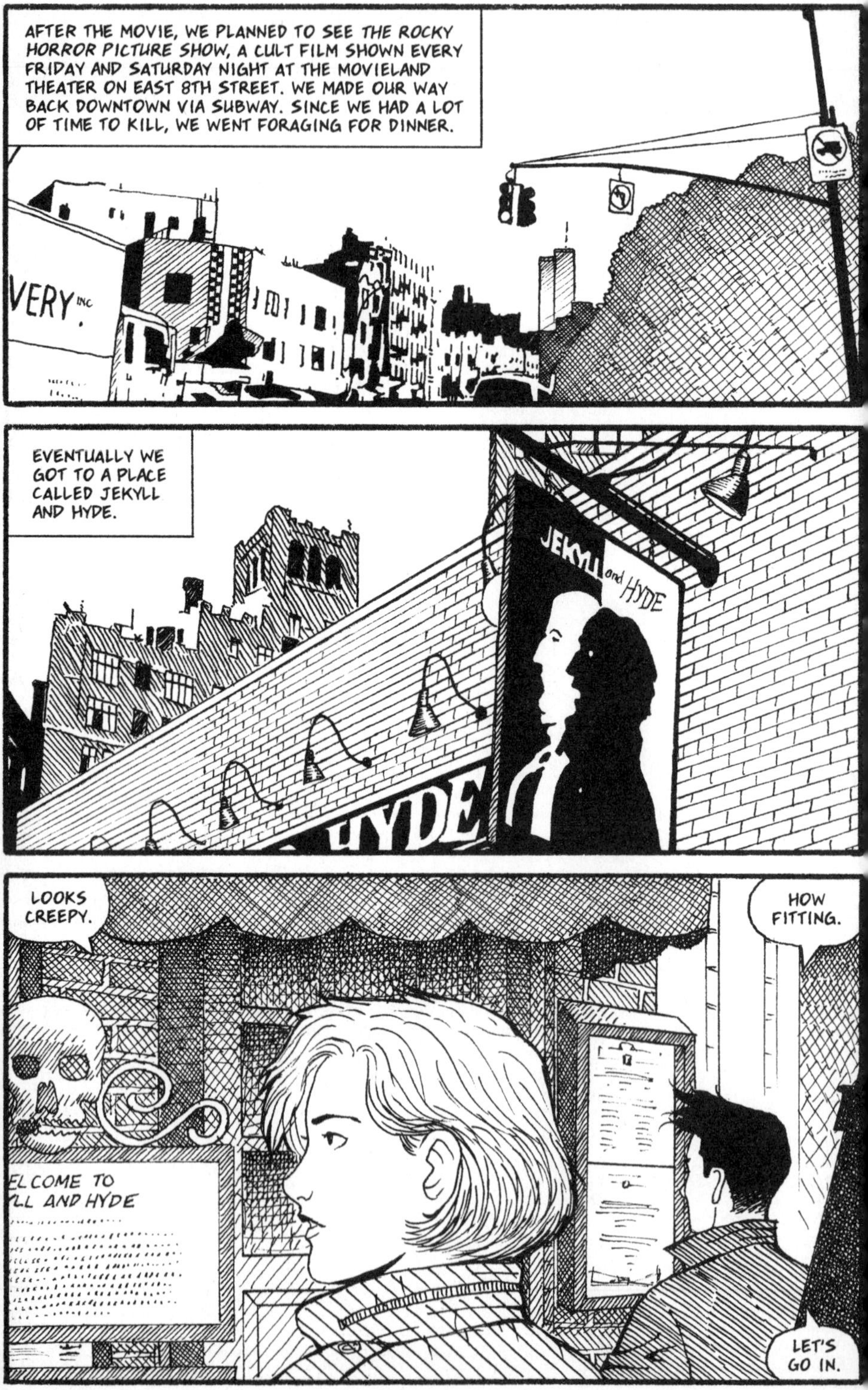
AFTER THE MOVIE, WE PLANNED TO SEE THE ROCKY HORROR PICTURE SHOW, A CULT FILM SHOWN EVERY FRIDAY AND SATURDAY NIGHT AT THE MOVIELAND THEATER ON EAST 8TH STREET. WE MADE OUR WAY BACK DOWNTOWN VIA SUBWAY. SINCE WE HAD A LOT OF TIME TO KILL, WE WENT FORAGING FOR DINNER.
VERY INC.
EVENTUALLY WE GOT TO A PLACE CALLED JEKYLL AND HYDE.
JEKYLL and HYDE
HYDE
LOOKS CREEPY.
HOW FITTING.
ELCOME TO
YLL AND HYDE
LET'S GO IN.

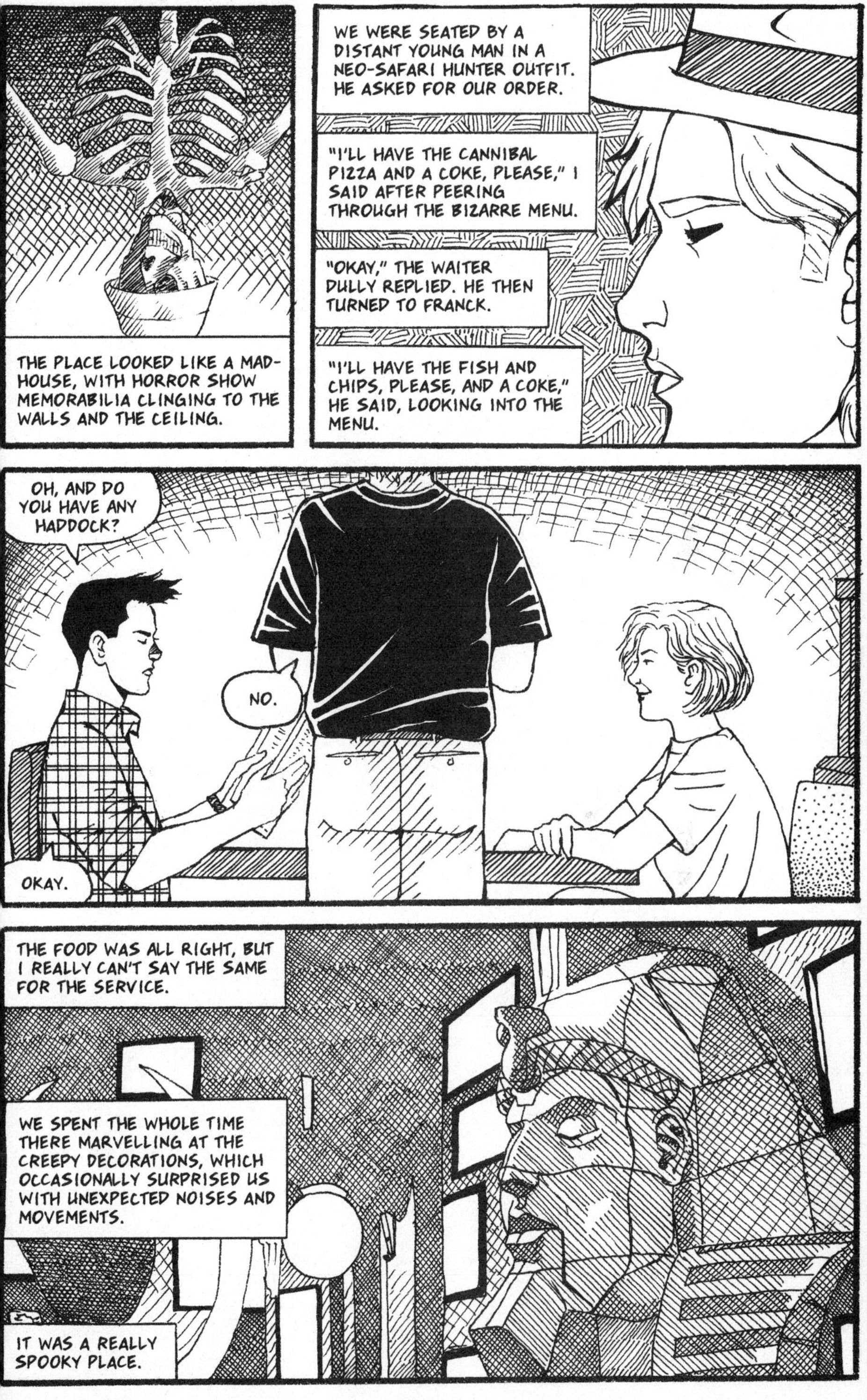
THE PLACE LOOKED LIKE A MAD-HOUSE, WITH HORROR SHOW MEMORABILIA CLINGING TO THE WALLS AND THE CEILING.
WE WERE SEATED BY A DISTANT YOUNG MAN IN A NEO-SAFARI HUNTER OUTFIT. HE ASKED FOR OUR ORDER.
"I'LL HAVE THE CANNIBAL PIZZA AND A COKE, PLEASE," I SAID AFTER PEERING THROUGH THE BIZARRE MENU.
"OKAY," THE WAITER DULLY REPLIED. HE THEN TURNED TO FRANCK.
"I'LL HAVE THE FISH AND CHIPS, PLEASE, AND A COKE," HE SAID, LOOKING INTO THE MENU.
OH, AND DO YOU HAVE ANY HADDOCK?
NO.
OKAY.
THE FOOD WAS ALL RIGHT, BUT I REALLY CAN'T SAY THE SAME FOR THE SERVICE.
WE SPENT THE WHOLE TIME THERE MARVELLING AT THE CREEPY DECORATIONS, WHICH OCCASIONALLY SURPRISED US WITH UNEXPECTED NOISES AND MOVEMENTS.
IT WAS A REALLY SPOOKY PLACE.

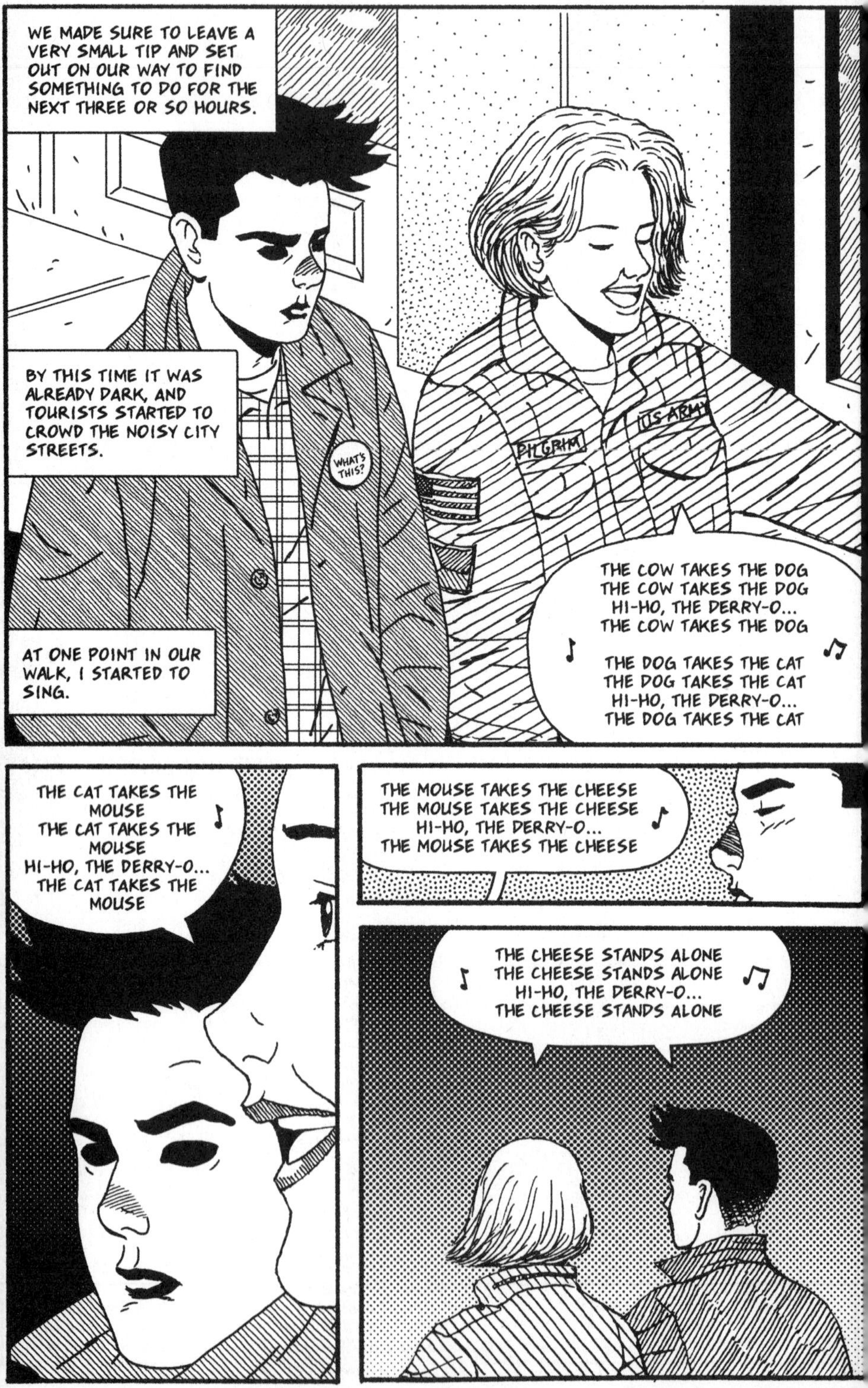
WE MADE SURE TO LEAVE A VERY SMALL TIP AND SET OUT ON OUR WAY TO FIND SOMETHING TO DO FOR THE NEXT THREE OR SO HOURS.
BY THIS TIME IT WAS ALREADY DARK, AND TOURISTS STARTED TO CROWD THE NOISY CITY STREETS.
WHAT'S THIS?
PILGRIM
US ARMY
AT ONE POINT IN OUR WALK, I STARTED TO SING.
THE COW TAKES THE DOG THE COW TAKES THE DOG HI-HO, THE DERRY-O... THE COW TAKES THE DOG
THE DOG TAKES THE CAT THE DOG TAKES THE CAT HI-HO, THE DERRY-O... THE DOG TAKES THE CAT
THE CAT TAKES THE MOUSE THE CAT TAKES THE MOUSE HI-HO, THE DERRY-O... THE CAT TAKES THE MOUSE
THE MOUSE TAKES THE CHEESE THE MOUSE TAKES THE CHEESE HI-HO, THE DERRY-O... THE MOUSE TAKES THE CHEESE
THE CHEESE STANDS ALONE THE CHEESE STANDS ALONE HI-HO, THE DERRY-O... THE CHEESE STANDS ALONE

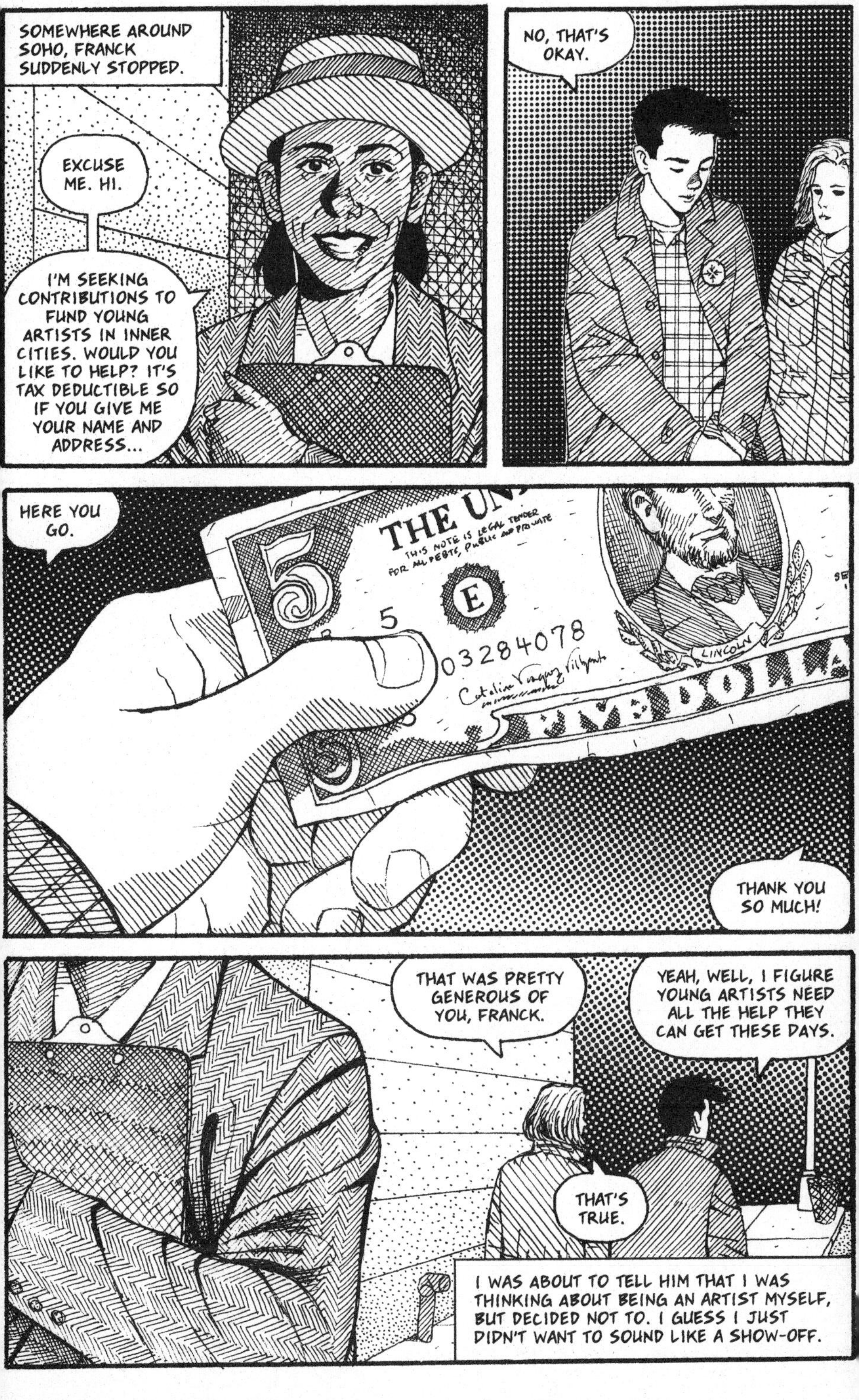
SOMEWHERE AROUND SOHO, FRANCK SUDDENLY STOPPED.
EXCUSE ME. HI.
I'M SEEKING CONTRIBUTIONS TO FUND YOUNG ARTISTS IN INNER CITIES. WOULD YOU LIKE TO HELP? IT'S TAX DEDUCTIBLE SO IF YOU GIVE ME YOUR NAME AND ADDRESS...
NO, THAT'S OKAY.
HERE YOU GO.
THE UN
THIS NOTE IS LEGAL TENDER FOR ALL DEBTS, PUBLIC AND PRIVATE
E
5
03284078
LINCOLN
THANK YOU SO MUCH!
THAT WAS PRETTY GENEROUS OF YOU, FRANCK.
YEAH, WELL, I FIGURE YOUNG ARTISTS NEED ALL THE HELP THEY CAN GET THESE DAYS.
THAT'S TRUE.
I WAS ABOUT TO TELL HIM THAT I WAS THINKING ABOUT BEING AN ARTIST MYSELF, BUT DECIDED NOT TO. I GUESS I JUST DIDN'T WANT TO SOUND LIKE A SHOW-OFF.

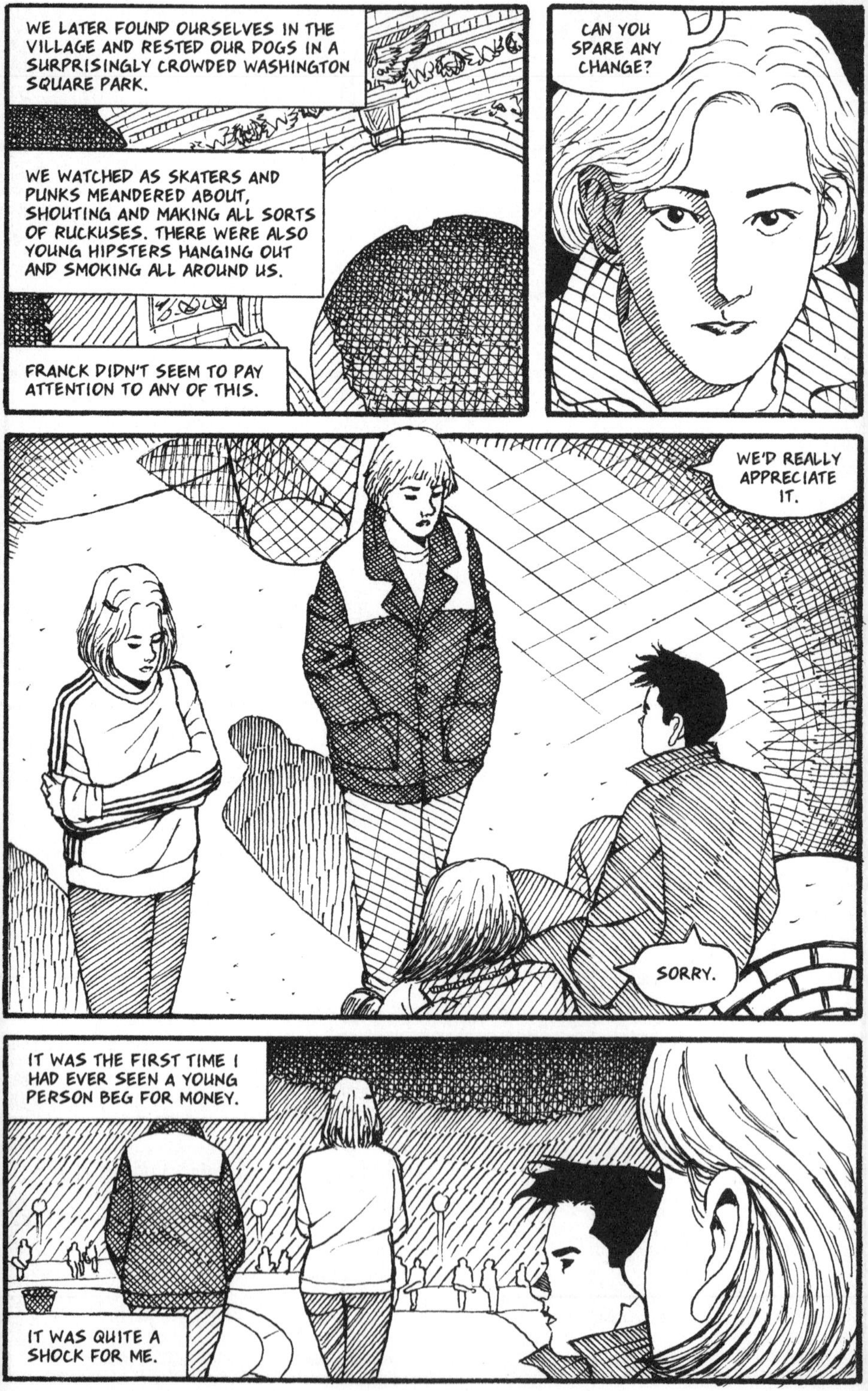
WE LATER FOUND OURSELVES IN THE VILLAGE AND RESTED OUR DOGS IN A SURPRISINGLY CROWDED WASHINGTON SQUARE PARK.
WE WATCHED AS SKATERS AND PUNKS MEANDERED ABOUT, SHOUTING AND MAKING ALL SORTS OF RUCKUSES. THERE WERE ALSO YOUNG HIPSTERS HANGING OUT AND SMOKING ALL AROUND US.
FRANCK DIDN'T SEEM TO PAY ATTENTION TO ANY OF THIS.
CAN YOU SPARE ANY CHANGE?
WE'D REALLY APPRECIATE IT.
SORRY.
IT WAS THE FIRST TIME I HAD EVER SEEN A YOUNG PERSON BEG FOR MONEY.
IT WAS QUITE A SHOCK FOR ME.

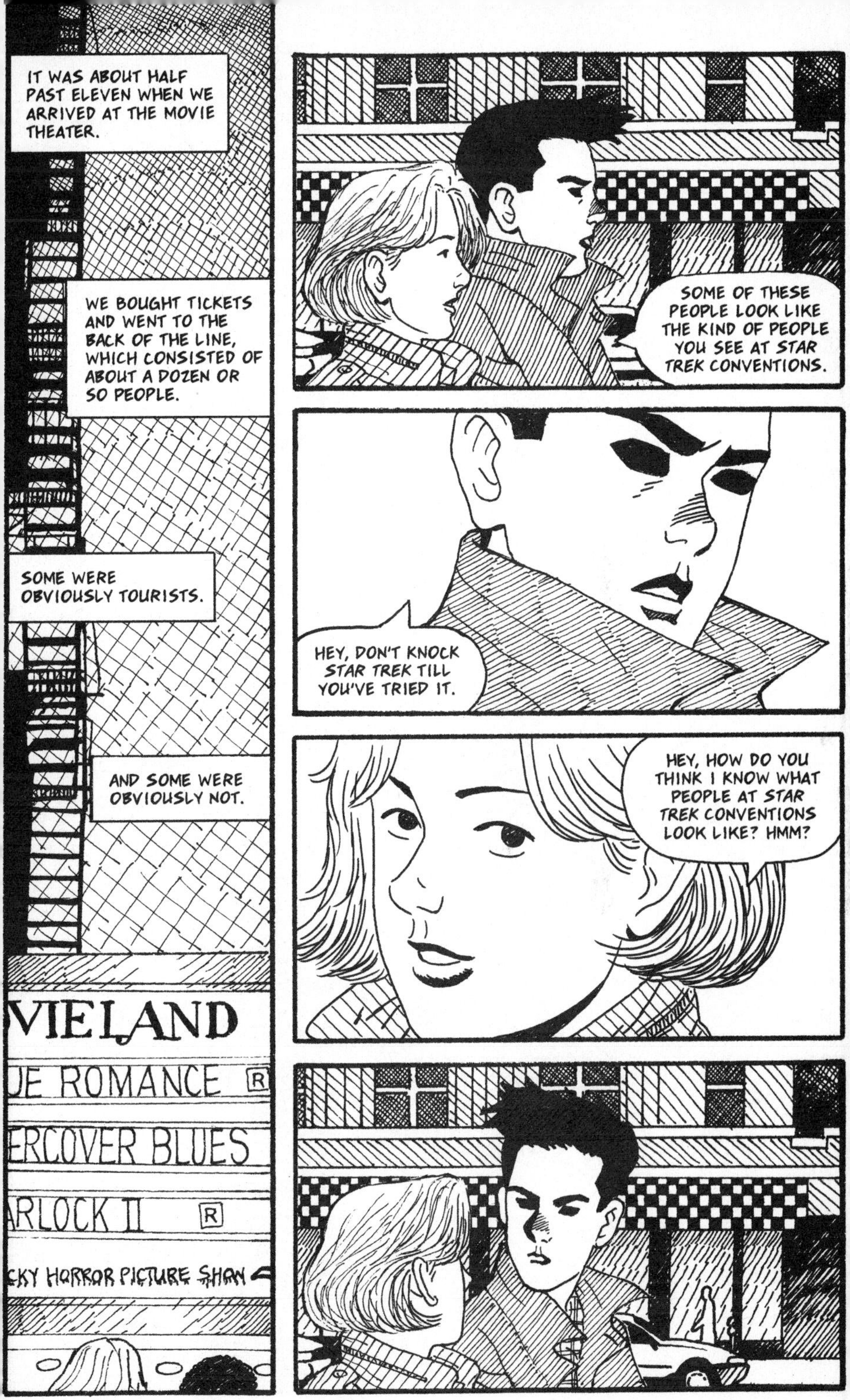
IT WAS ABOUT HALF PAST ELEVEN WHEN WE ARRIVED AT THE MOVIE THEATER.
WE BOUGHT TICKETS AND WENT TO THE BACK OF THE LINE, WHICH CONSISTED OF ABOUT A DOZEN OR SO PEOPLE.
SOME WERE OBVIOUSLY TOURISTS.
AND SOME WERE OBVIOUSLY NOT.
VIELAND
UE ROMANCE R
ERCOVER BLUES
ARLOCK II R
CKY HORROR PICTURE SHOW
SOME OF THESE PEOPLE LOOK LIKE THE KIND OF PEOPLE YOU SEE AT STAR TREK CONVENTIONS.
HEY, DON'T KNOCK STAR TREK TILL YOU'VE TRIED IT.
HEY, HOW DO YOU THINK I KNOW WHAT PEOPLE AT STAR TREK CONVENTIONS LOOK LIKE? HMM?

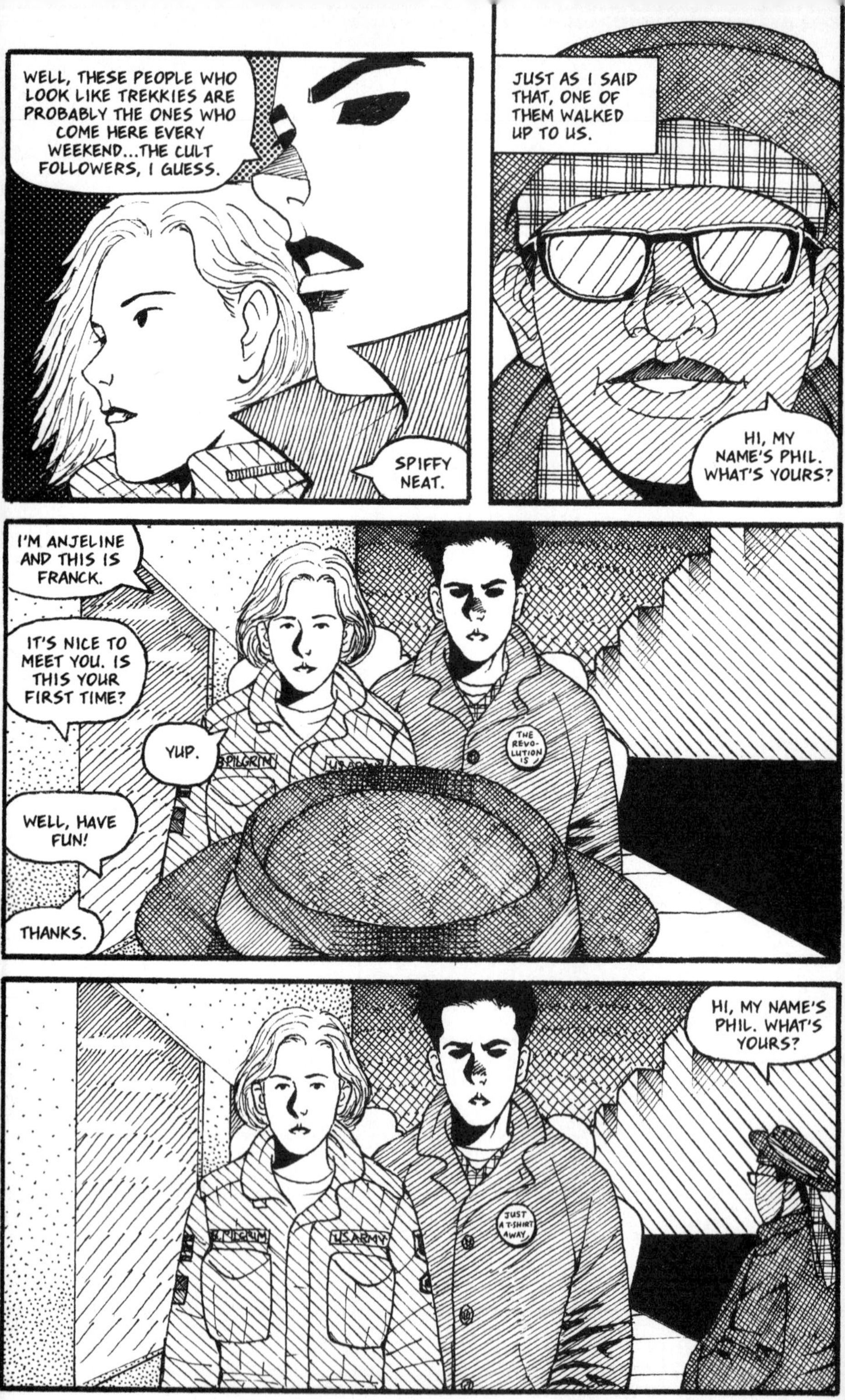
WELL, THESE PEOPLE WHO LOOK LIKE TREKKIES ARE PROBABLY THE ONES WHO COME HERE EVERY WEEKEND...THE CULT FOLLOWERS, I GUESS.
SPIFFY NEAT.
JUST AS I SAID THAT, ONE OF THEM WALKED UP TO US.
HI, MY NAME'S PHIL. WHAT'S YOURS?
I'M ANJELINE AND THIS IS FRANCK.
IT'S NICE TO MEET YOU. IS THIS YOUR FIRST TIME?
YUP.
WELL, HAVE FUN!
THANKS.
THE REVO-LUTION IS
HI, MY NAME'S PHIL. WHAT'S YOURS?
JUST A T-SHIRT AWAY.

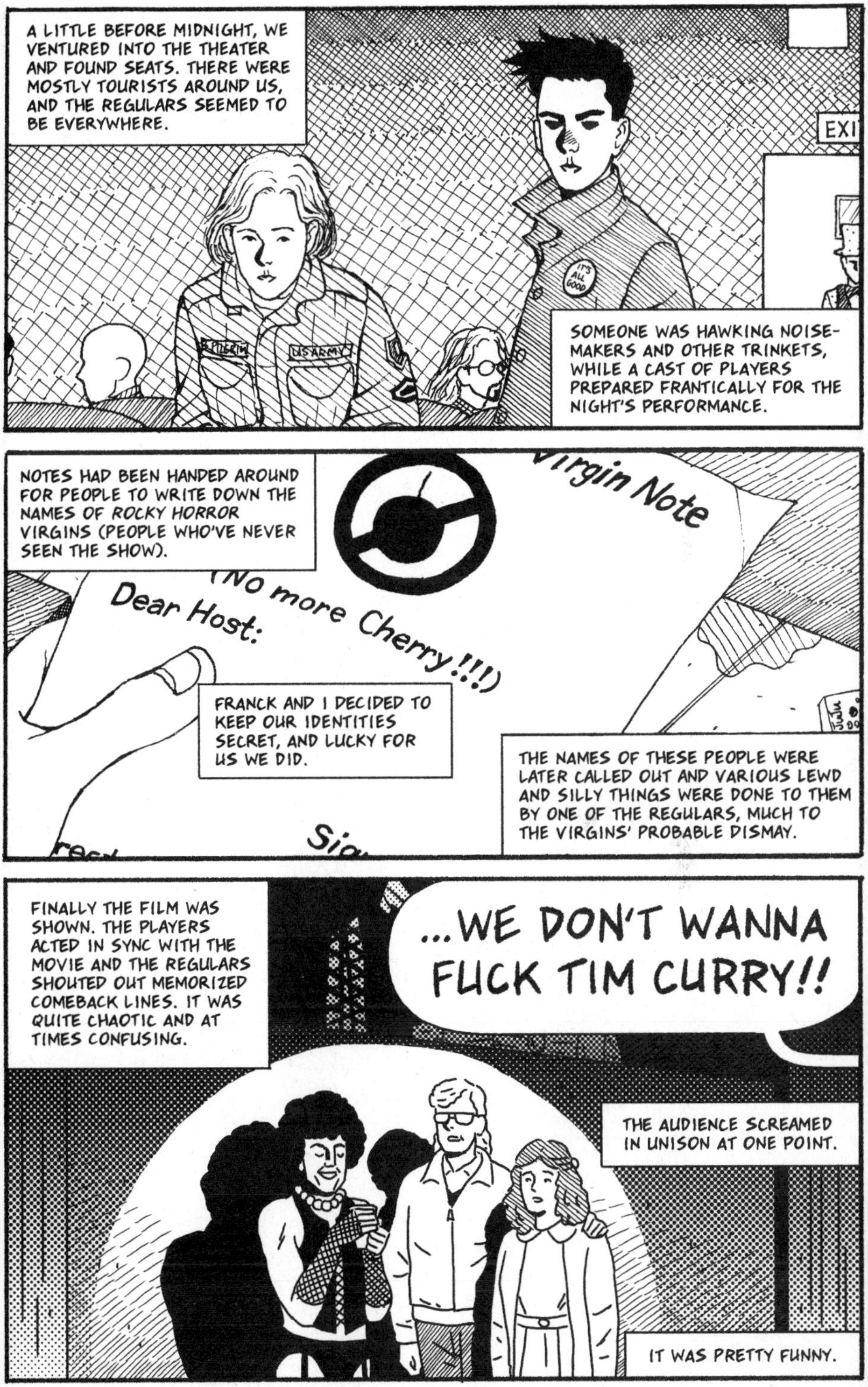
A LITTLE BEFORE MIDNIGHT, WE VENTURED INTO THE THEATER AND FOUND SEATS. THERE WERE MOSTLY TOURISTS AROUND US, AND THE REGULARS SEEMED TO BE EVERYWHERE.
IT'S ALL GOOD
US ARMY
SOMEONE WAS HAWKING NOISEMAKERS AND OTHER TRINKETS, WHILE A CAST OF PLAYERS PREPARED FRANTICALLY FOR THE NIGHT'S PERFORMANCE.
NOTES HAD BEEN HANDED AROUND FOR PEOPLE TO WRITE DOWN THE NAMES OF *ROCKY HORROR* VIRGINS (PEOPLE WHO'VE NEVER SEEN THE SHOW).
Virgin Note
(No more Cherry!!!)
Dear Host:
FRANCK AND I DECIDED TO KEEP OUR IDENTITIES SECRET, AND LUCKY FOR US WE DID.
THE NAMES OF THESE PEOPLE WERE LATER CALLED OUT AND VARIOUS LEWD AND SILLY THINGS WERE DONE TO THEM BY ONE OF THE REGULARS, MUCH TO THE VIRGINS' PROBABLE DISMAY.
FINALLY THE FILM WAS SHOWN. THE PLAYERS ACTED IN SYNC WITH THE MOVIE AND THE REGULARS SHOUTED OUT MEMORIZED COMEBACK LINES. IT WAS QUITE CHAOTIC AND AT TIMES CONFUSING.
...WE DON'T WANNA FUCK TIM CURRY!!
THE AUDIENCE SCREAMED IN UNISON AT ONE POINT.
IT WAS PRETTY FUNNY.

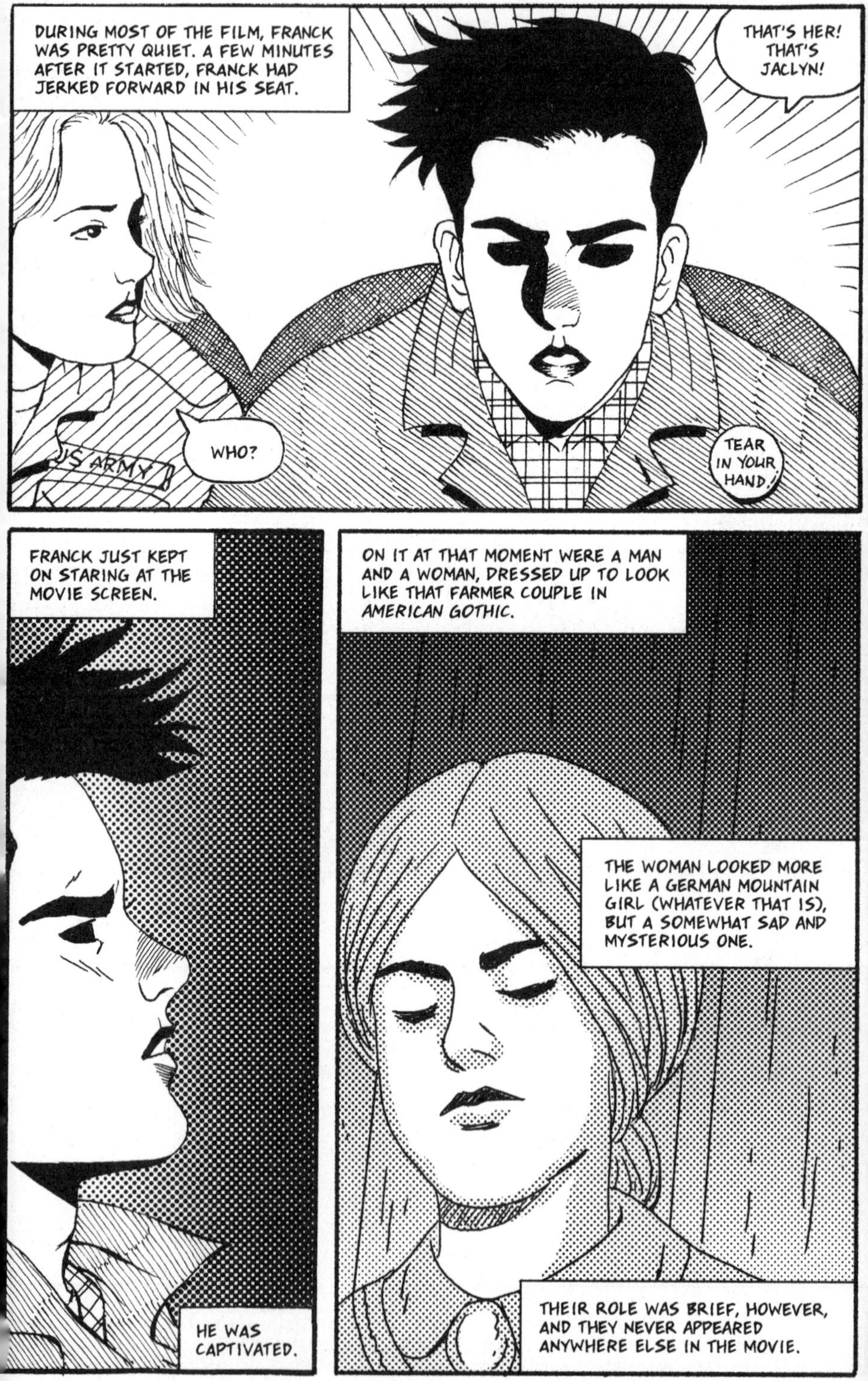
DURING MOST OF THE FILM, FRANCK WAS PRETTY QUIET. A FEW MINUTES AFTER IT STARTED, FRANCK HAD JERKED FORWARD IN HIS SEAT.
THAT'S HER! THAT'S JACLYN!
WHO?
TEAR IN YOUR HAND!
US ARMY
FRANCK JUST KEPT ON STARING AT THE MOVIE SCREEN.
HE WAS CAPTIVATED.
ON IT AT THAT MOMENT WERE A MAN AND A WOMAN, DRESSED UP TO LOOK LIKE THAT FARMER COUPLE IN AMERICAN GOTHIC.
THE WOMAN LOOKED MORE LIKE A GERMAN MOUNTAIN GIRL (WHATEVER THAT IS), BUT A SOMEWHAT SAD AND MYSTERIOUS ONE.
THEIR ROLE WAS BRIEF, HOWEVER, AND THEY NEVER APPEARED ANYWHERE ELSE IN THE MOVIE.

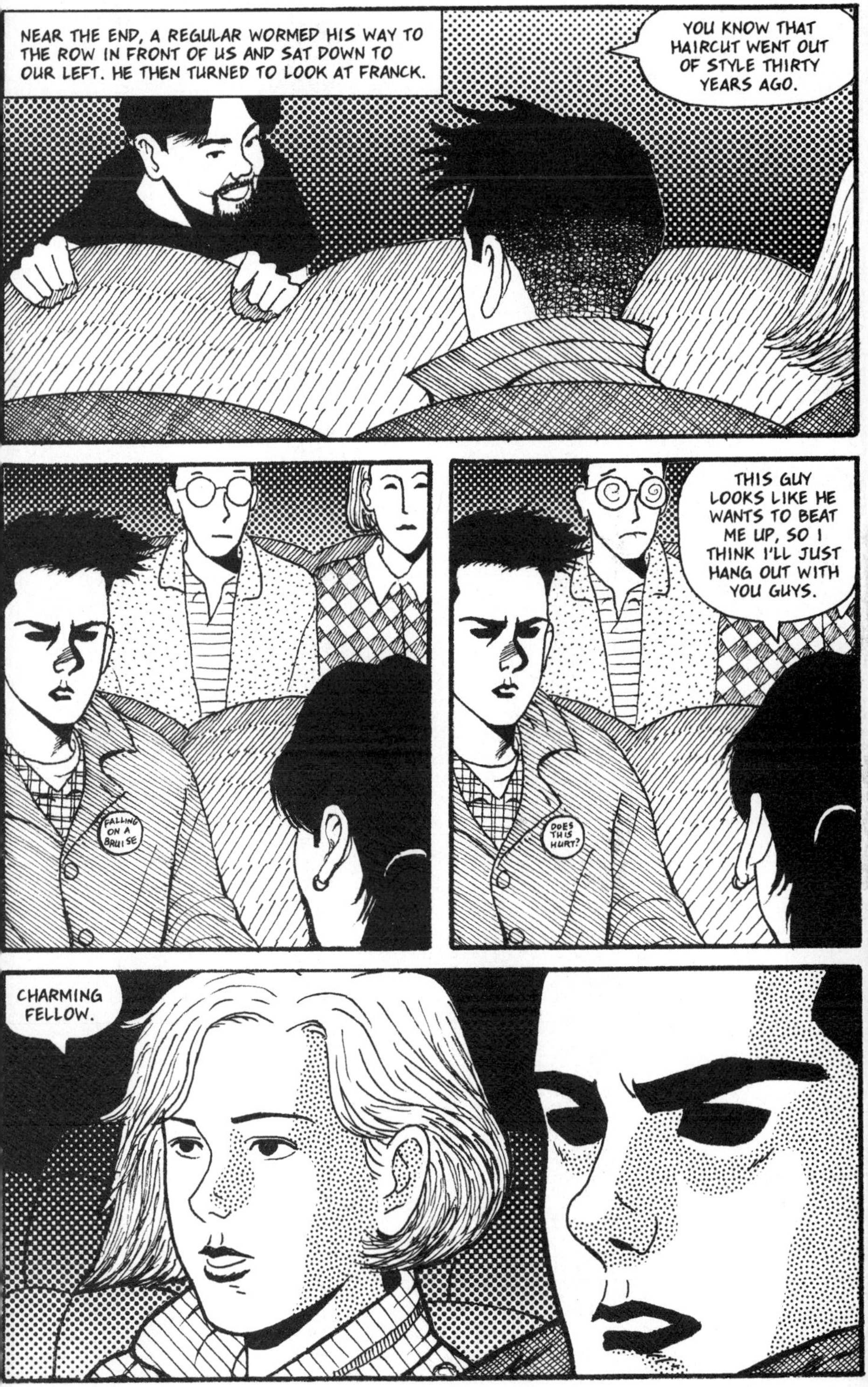
NEAR THE END, A REGULAR WORMED HIS WAY TO THE ROW IN FRONT OF US AND SAT DOWN TO OUR LEFT. HE THEN TURNED TO LOOK AT FRANCK.
YOU KNOW THAT HAIRCUT WENT OUT OF STYLE THIRTY YEARS AGO.
FALLING ON A BRUISE
DOES THIS HURT?
THIS GUY LOOKS LIKE HE WANTS TO BEAT ME UP, SO I THINK I'LL JUST HANG OUT WITH YOU GUYS.
CHARMING FELLOW.

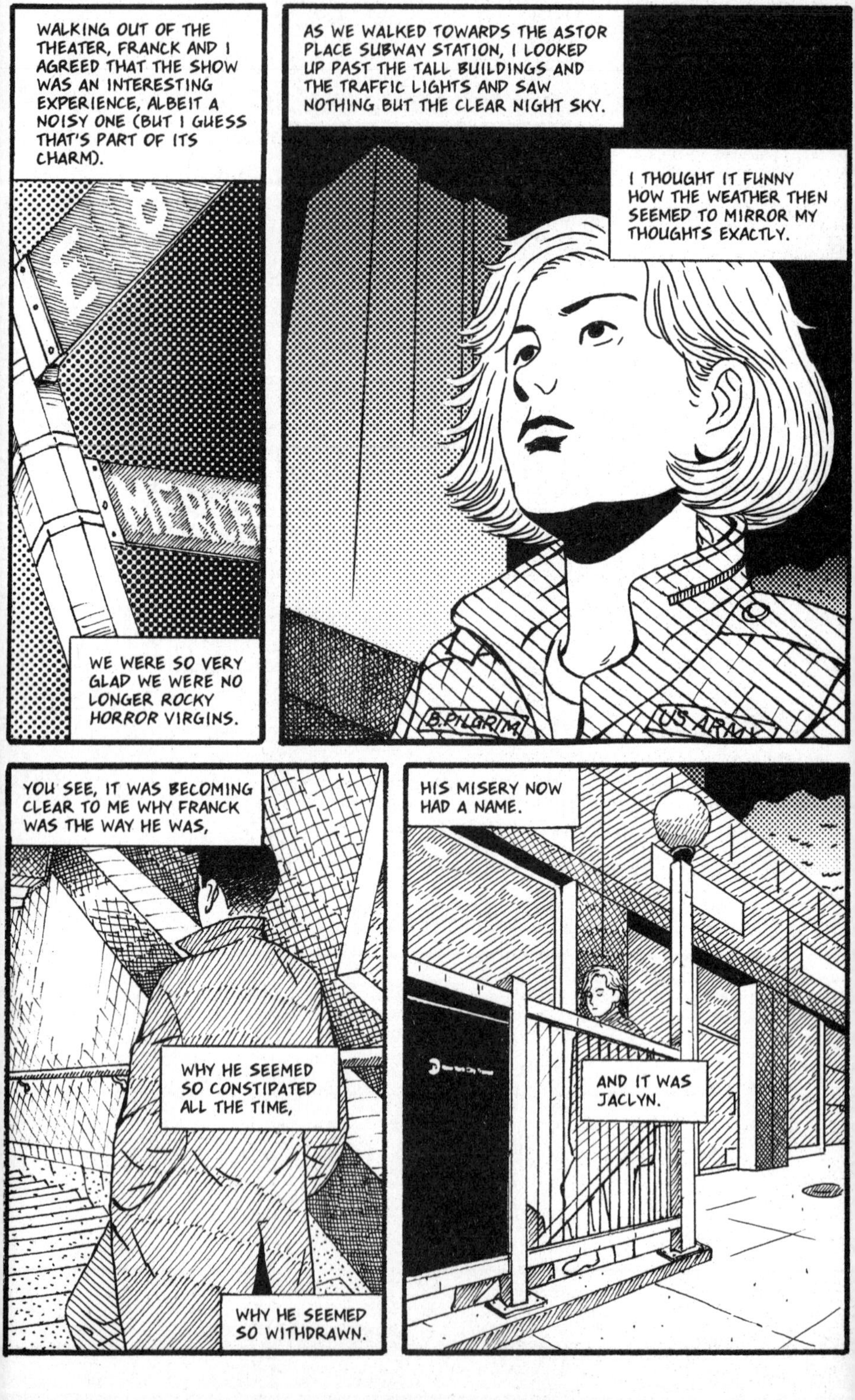
WALKING OUT OF THE THEATER, FRANCK AND I AGREED THAT THE SHOW WAS AN INTERESTING EXPERIENCE, ALBEIT A NOISY ONE (BUT I GUESS THAT'S PART OF ITS CHARM).
WE WERE SO VERY GLAD WE WERE NO LONGER ROCKY HORROR VIRGINS.
AS WE WALKED TOWARDS THE ASTOR PLACE SUBWAY STATION, I LOOKED UP PAST THE TALL BUILDINGS AND THE TRAFFIC LIGHTS AND SAW NOTHING BUT THE CLEAR NIGHT SKY.
I THOUGHT IT FUNNY HOW THE WEATHER THEN SEEMED TO MIRROR MY THOUGHTS EXACTLY.
B.PILGRIM
YOU SEE, IT WAS BECOMING CLEAR TO ME WHY FRANCK WAS THE WAY HE WAS,
WHY HE SEEMED SO CONSTIPATED ALL THE TIME,
WHY HE SEEMED SO WITHDRAWN.
HIS MISERY NOW HAD A NAME.
AND IT WAS JACLYN.

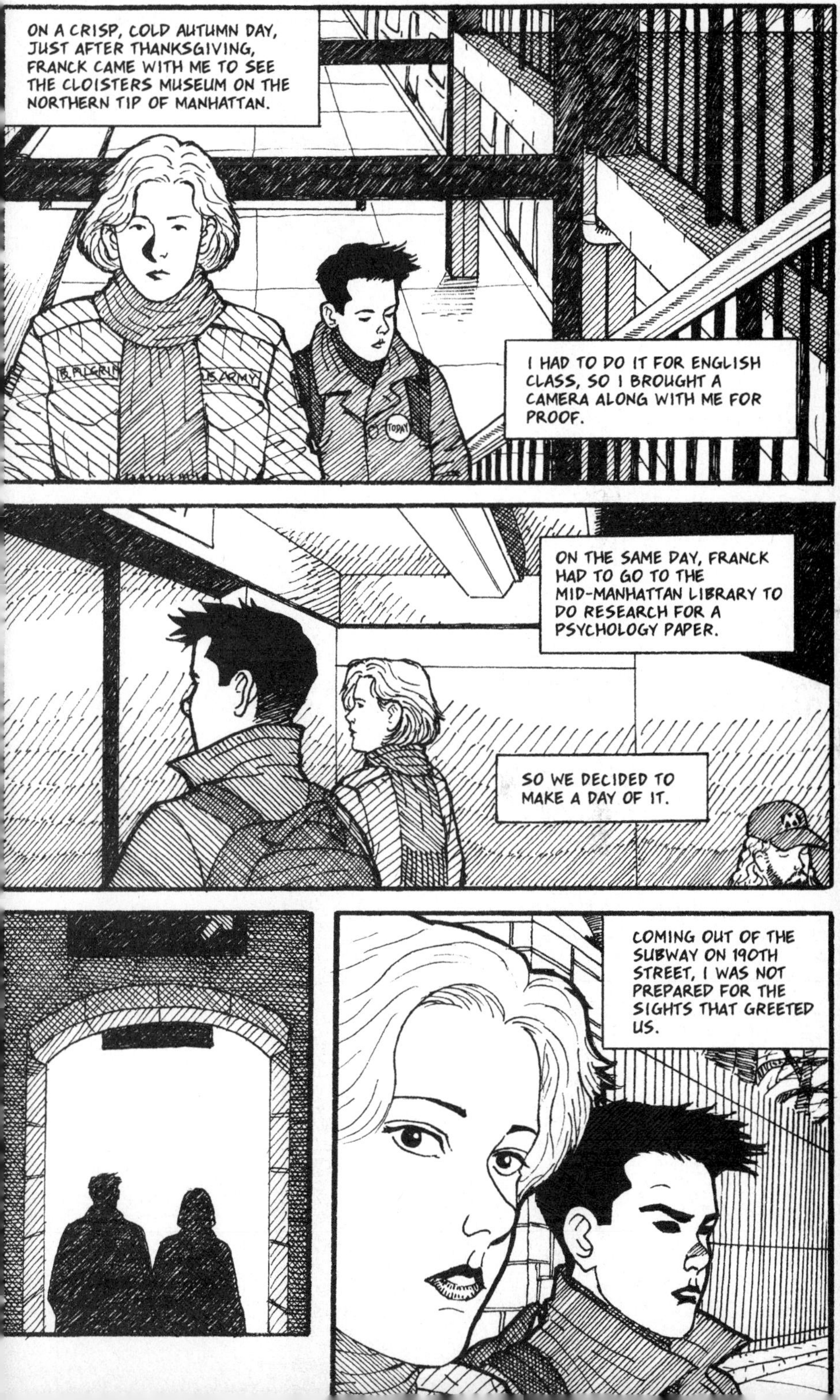
ON A CRISP, COLD AUTUMN DAY, JUST AFTER THANKSGIVING, FRANCK CAME WITH ME TO SEE THE CLOISTERS MUSEUM ON THE NORTHERN TIP OF MANHATTAN.
US ARMY
TODAY
I HAD TO DO IT FOR ENGLISH CLASS, SO I BROUGHT A CAMERA ALONG WITH ME FOR PROOF.
ON THE SAME DAY, FRANCK HAD TO GO TO THE MID-MANHATTAN LIBRARY TO DO RESEARCH FOR A PSYCHOLOGY PAPER.
SO WE DECIDED TO MAKE A DAY OF IT.
COMING OUT OF THE SUBWAY ON 190TH STREET, I WAS NOT PREPARED FOR THE SIGHTS THAT GREETED US.

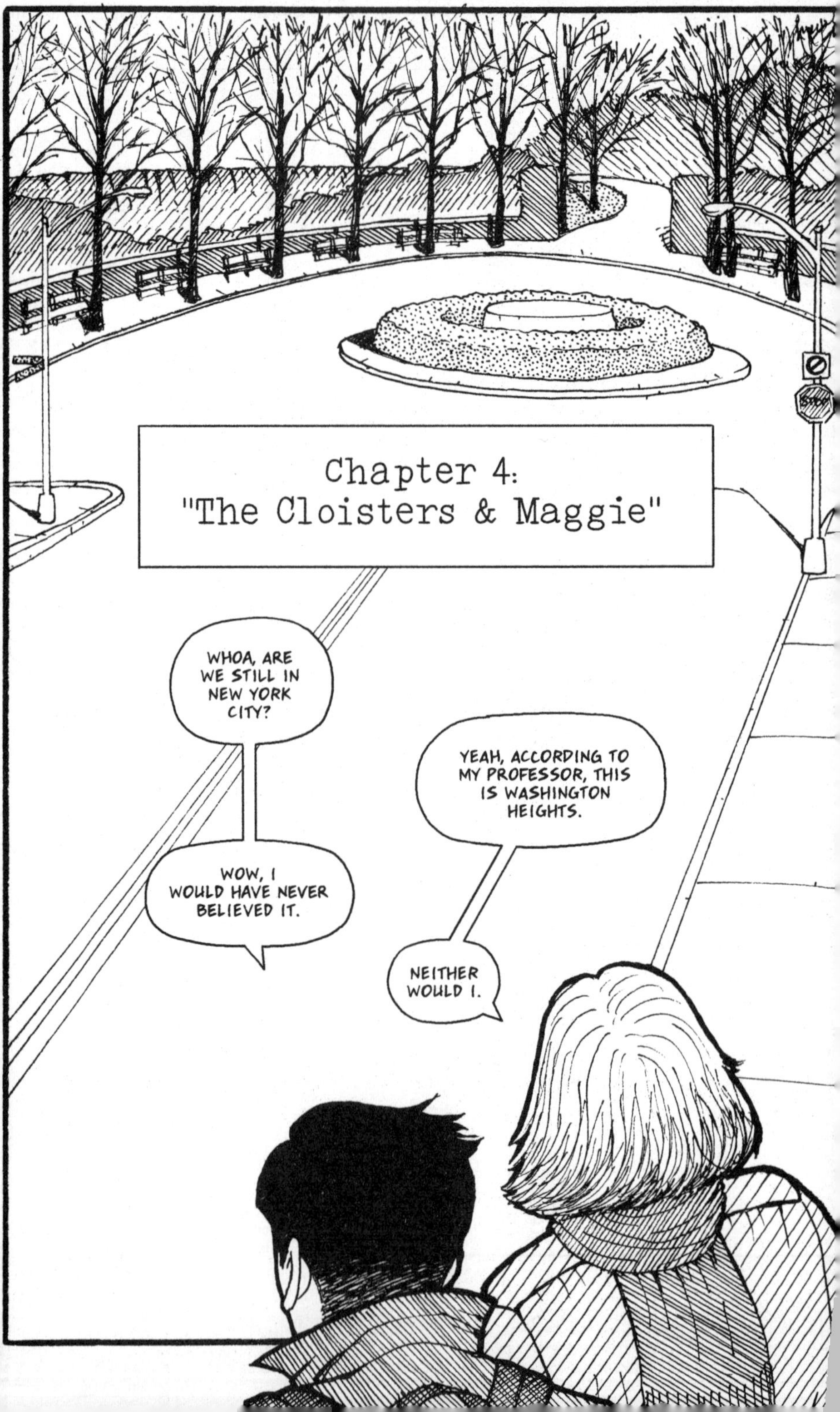
Chapter 4:
"The Cloisters & Maggie"
WHOA, ARE WE STILL IN NEW YORK CITY?
WOW, I WOULD HAVE NEVER BELIEVED IT.
YEAH, ACCORDING TO MY PROFESSOR, THIS IS WASHINGTON HEIGHTS.
NEITHER WOULD I.

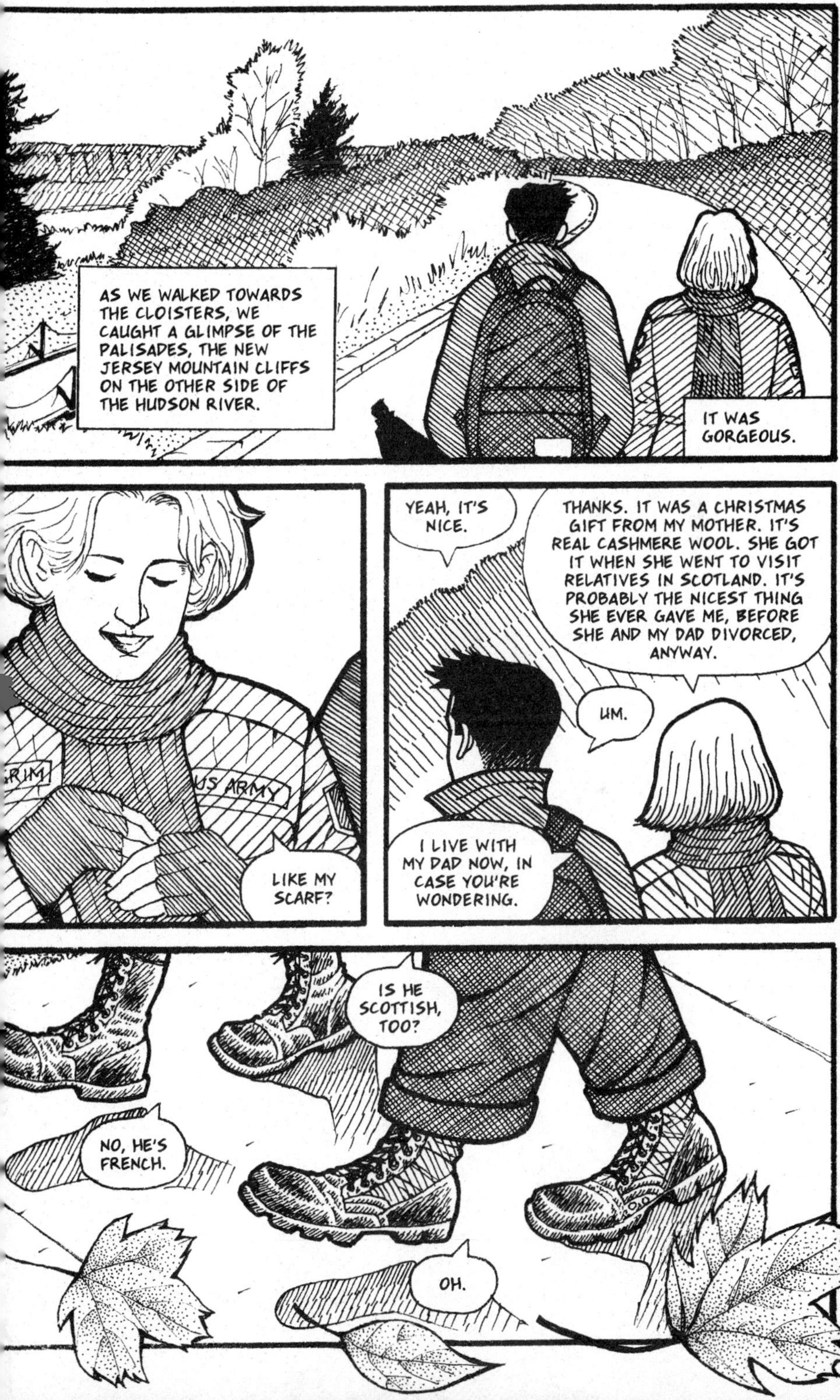
AS WE WALKED TOWARDS THE CLOISTERS, WE CAUGHT A GLIMPSE OF THE PALISADES, THE NEW JERSEY MOUNTAIN CLIFFS ON THE OTHER SIDE OF THE HUDSON RIVER.
IT WAS GORGEOUS.
RIM
US ARMY
LIKE MY SCARF?
YEAH, IT'S NICE.
THANKS. IT WAS A CHRISTMAS GIFT FROM MY MOTHER. IT'S REAL CASHMERE WOOL. SHE GOT IT WHEN SHE WENT TO VISIT RELATIVES IN SCOTLAND. IT'S PROBABLY THE NICEST THING SHE EVER GAVE ME, BEFORE SHE AND MY DAD DIVORCED, ANYWAY.
UM.
I LIVE WITH MY DAD NOW, IN CASE YOU'RE WONDERING.
IS HE SCOTTISH, TOO?
NO, HE'S FRENCH.
OH.

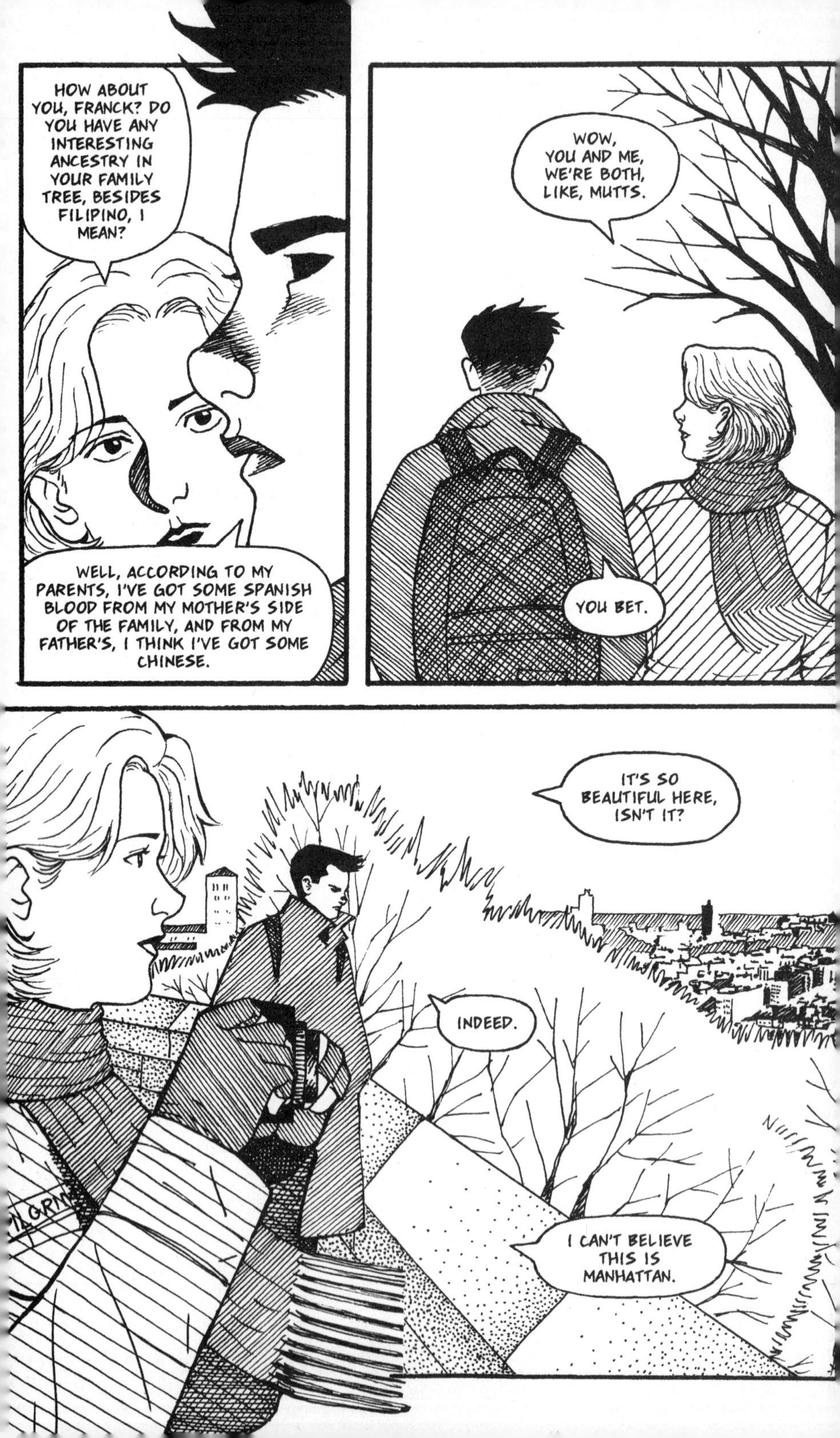
HOW ABOUT YOU, FRANCK? DO YOU HAVE ANY INTERESTING ANCESTRY IN YOUR FAMILY TREE, BESIDES FILIPINO, I MEAN?
WELL, ACCORDING TO MY PARENTS, I'VE GOT SOME SPANISH BLOOD FROM MY MOTHER'S SIDE OF THE FAMILY, AND FROM MY FATHER'S, I THINK I'VE GOT SOME CHINESE.
WOW, YOU AND ME, WE'RE BOTH, LIKE, MUTTS.
YOU BET.
IT'S SO BEAUTIFUL HERE, ISN'T IT?
INDEED.
I CAN'T BELIEVE THIS IS MANHATTAN.

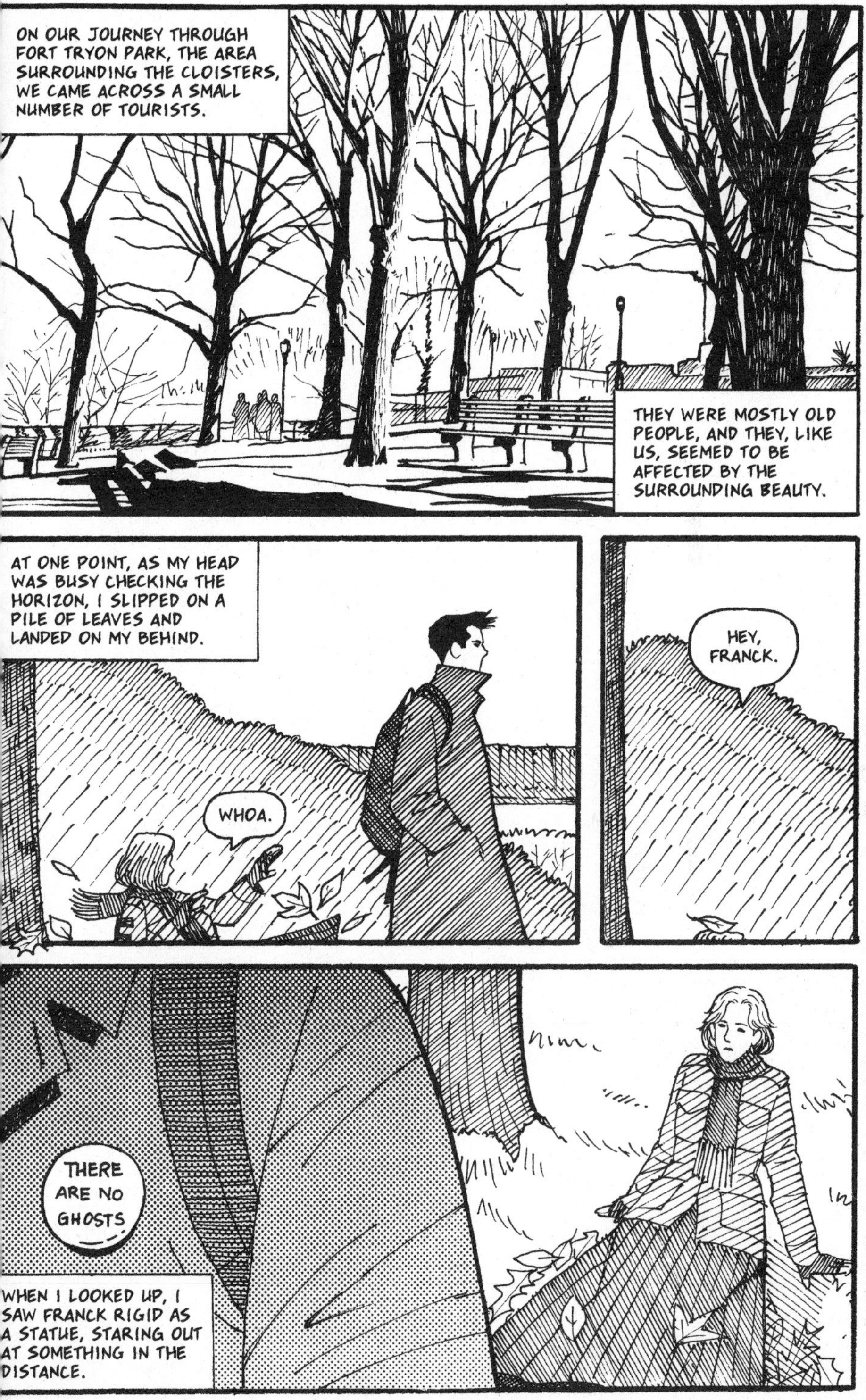
ON OUR JOURNEY THROUGH FORT TRYON PARK, THE AREA SURROUNDING THE CLOISTERS, WE CAME ACROSS A SMALL NUMBER OF TOURISTS.
THEY WERE MOSTLY OLD PEOPLE, AND THEY, LIKE US, SEEMED TO BE AFFECTED BY THE SURROUNDING BEAUTY.
AT ONE POINT, AS MY HEAD WAS BUSY CHECKING THE HORIZON, I SLIPPED ON A PILE OF LEAVES AND LANDED ON MY BEHIND.
WHOA.
HEY, FRANCK.
THERE ARE NO GHOSTS
WHEN I LOOKED UP, I SAW FRANCK RIGID AS A STATUE, STARING OUT AT SOMETHING IN THE DISTANCE.

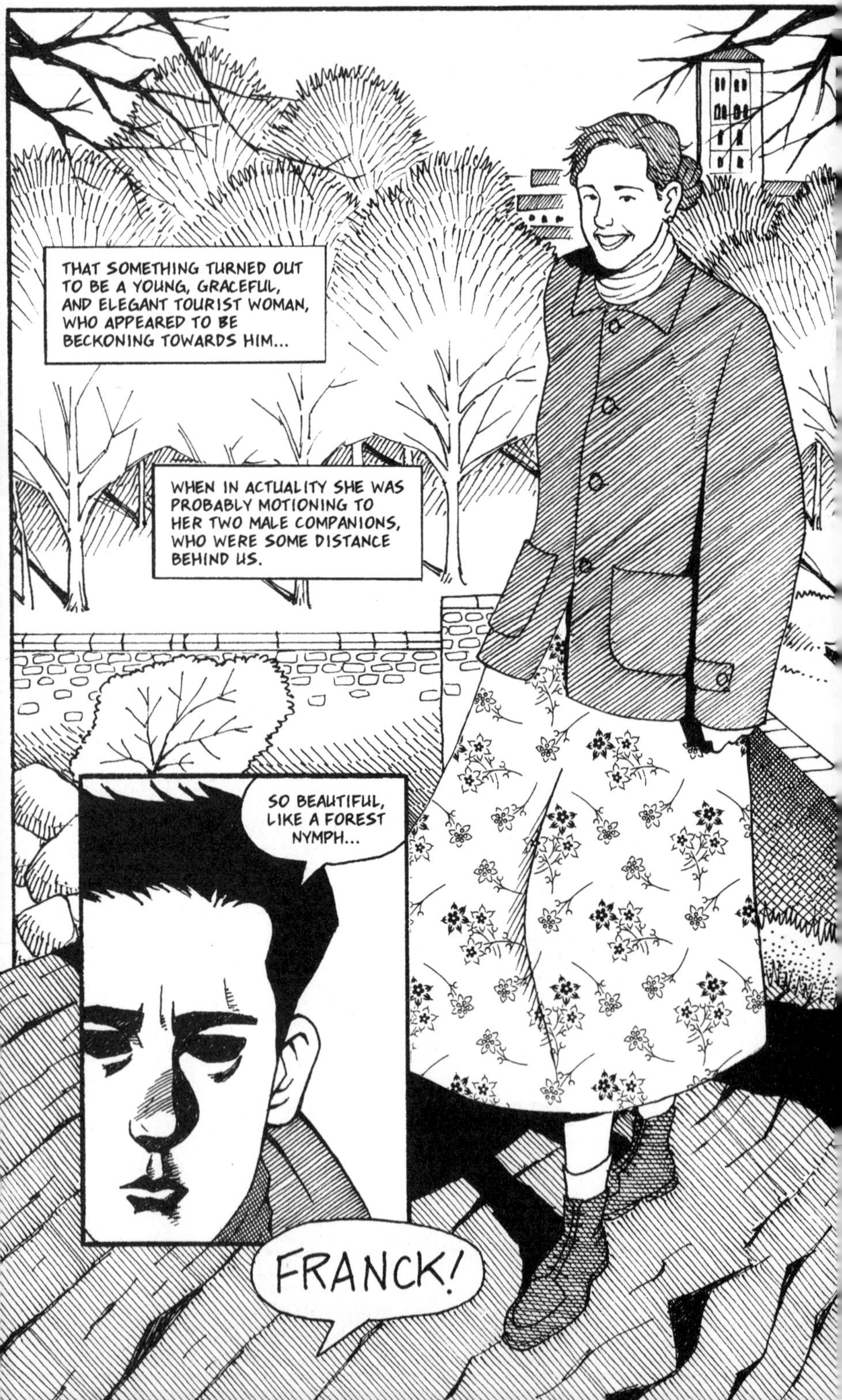
THAT SOMETHING TURNED OUT TO BE A YOUNG, GRACEFUL, AND ELEGANT TOURIST WOMAN, WHO APPEARED TO BE BECKONING TOWARDS HIM...
WHEN IN ACTUALITY SHE WAS PROBABLY MOTIONING TO HER TWO MALE COMPANIONS, WHO WERE SOME DISTANCE BEHIND US.
SO BEAUTIFUL, LIKE A FOREST NYMPH...
FRANCK!

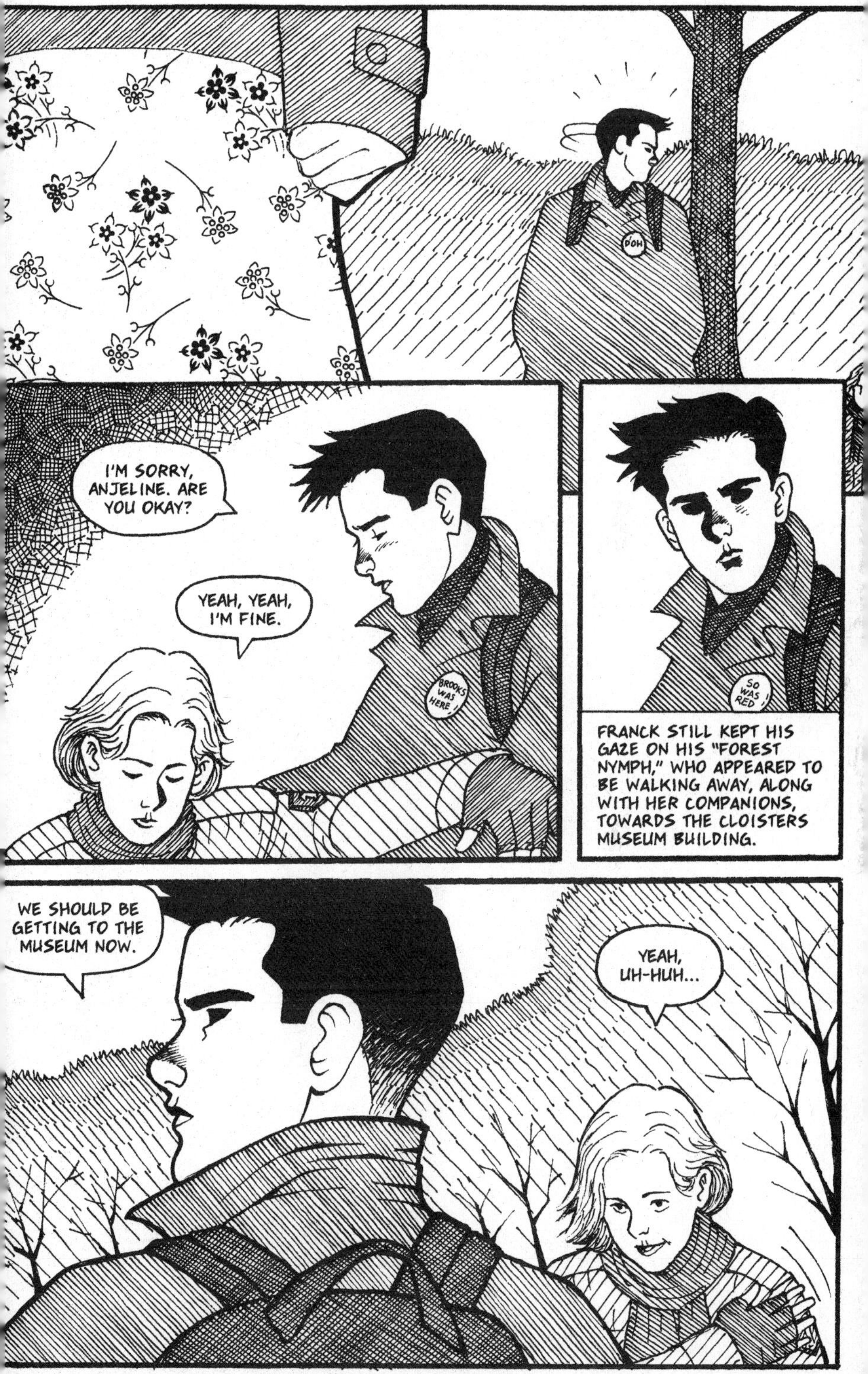
DOH
I'M SORRY, ANJELINE. ARE YOU OKAY?
YEAH, YEAH, I'M FINE.
BROOKS WAS HERE!
SO WAS RED!
FRANCK STILL KEPT HIS GAZE ON HIS "FOREST NYMPH," WHO APPEARED TO BE WALKING AWAY, ALONG WITH HER COMPANIONS, TOWARDS THE CLOISTERS MUSEUM BUILDING.
WE SHOULD BE GETTING TO THE MUSEUM NOW.
YEAH, UH-HUH...

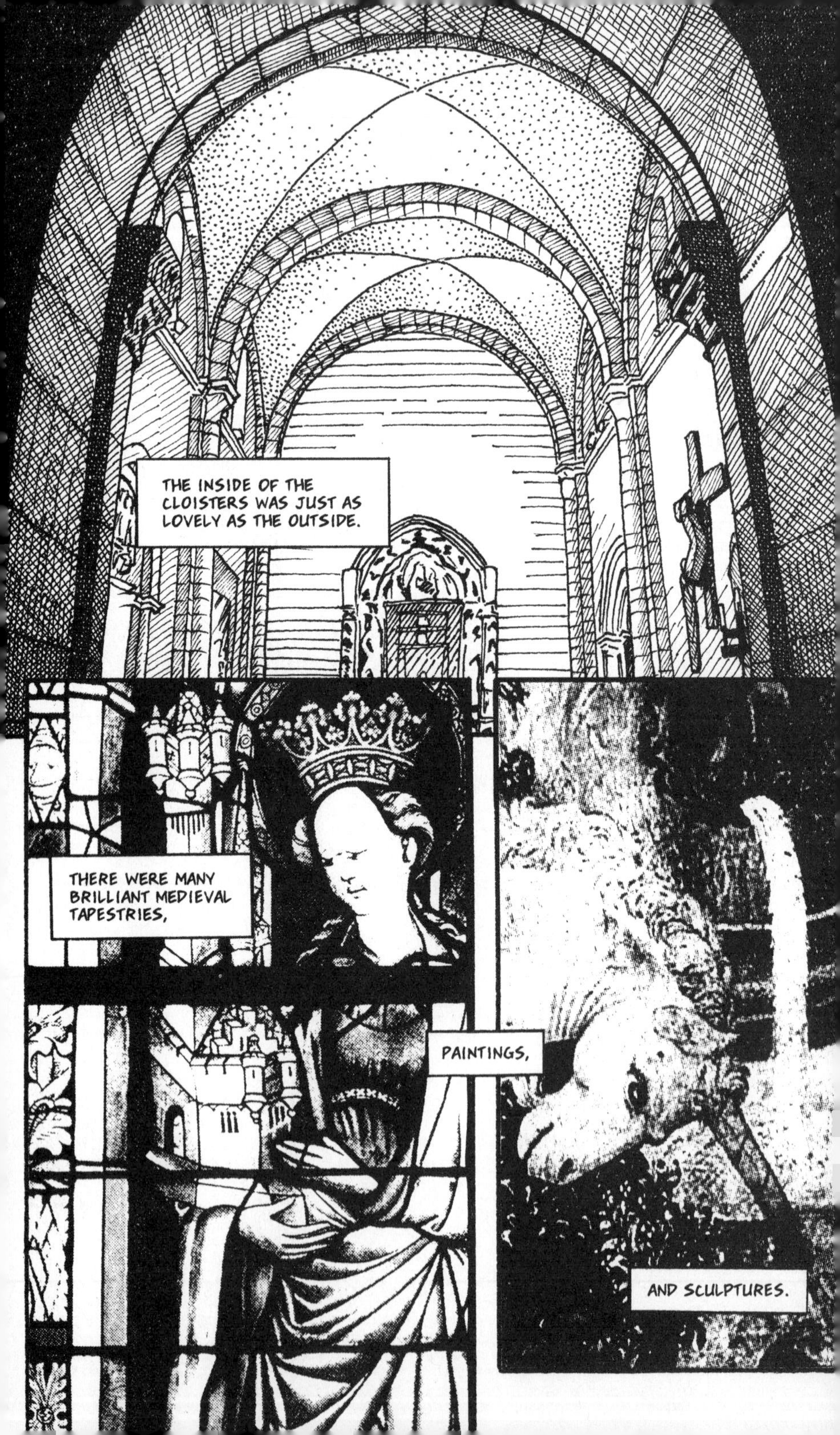
THE INSIDE OF THE CLOISTERS WAS JUST AS LOVELY AS THE OUTSIDE.
THERE WERE MANY BRILLIANT MEDIEVAL TAPESTRIES,
PAINTINGS,
AND SCULPTURES.

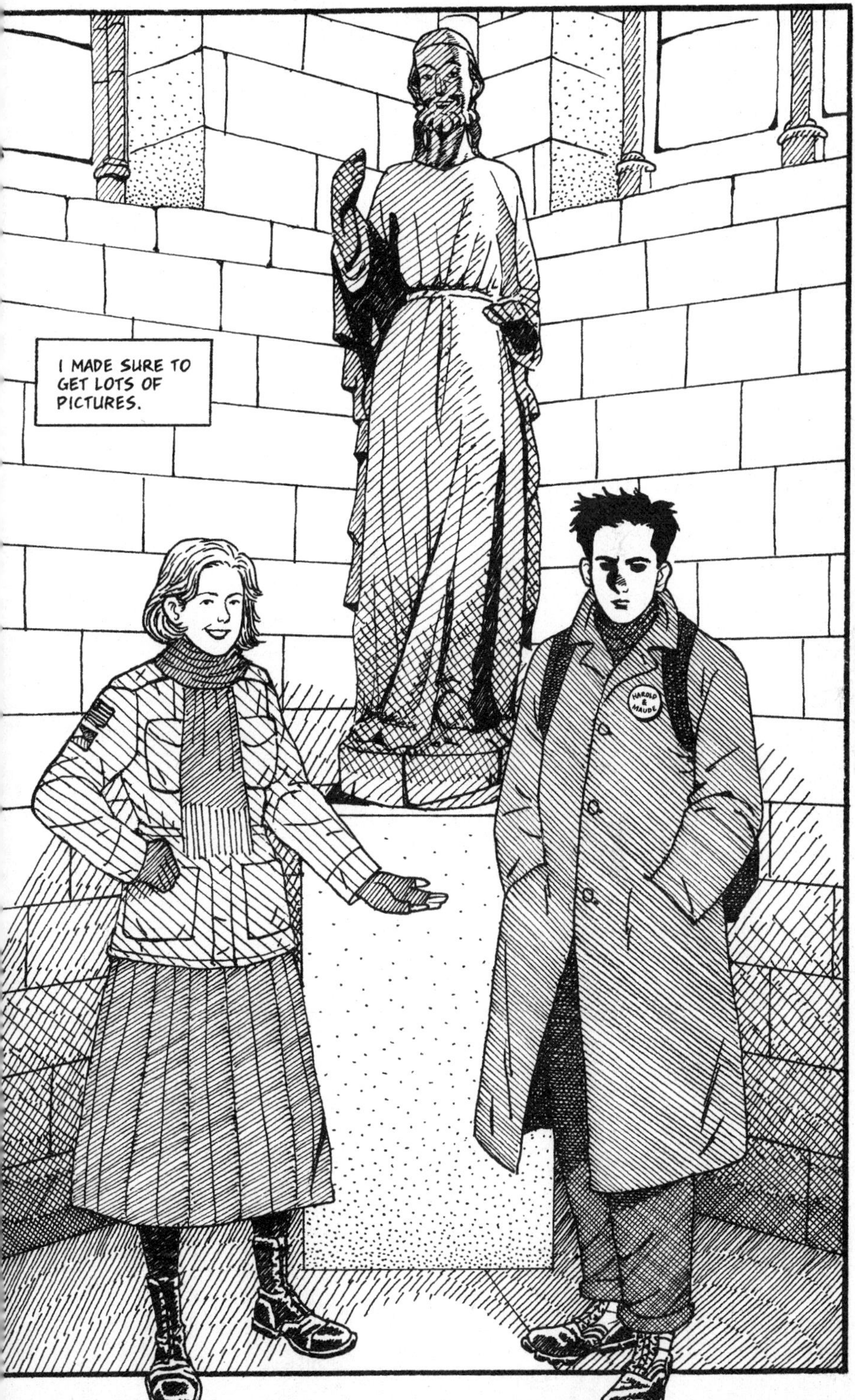
I MADE SURE TO GET LOTS OF PICTURES.
HAROLD & MAUDE

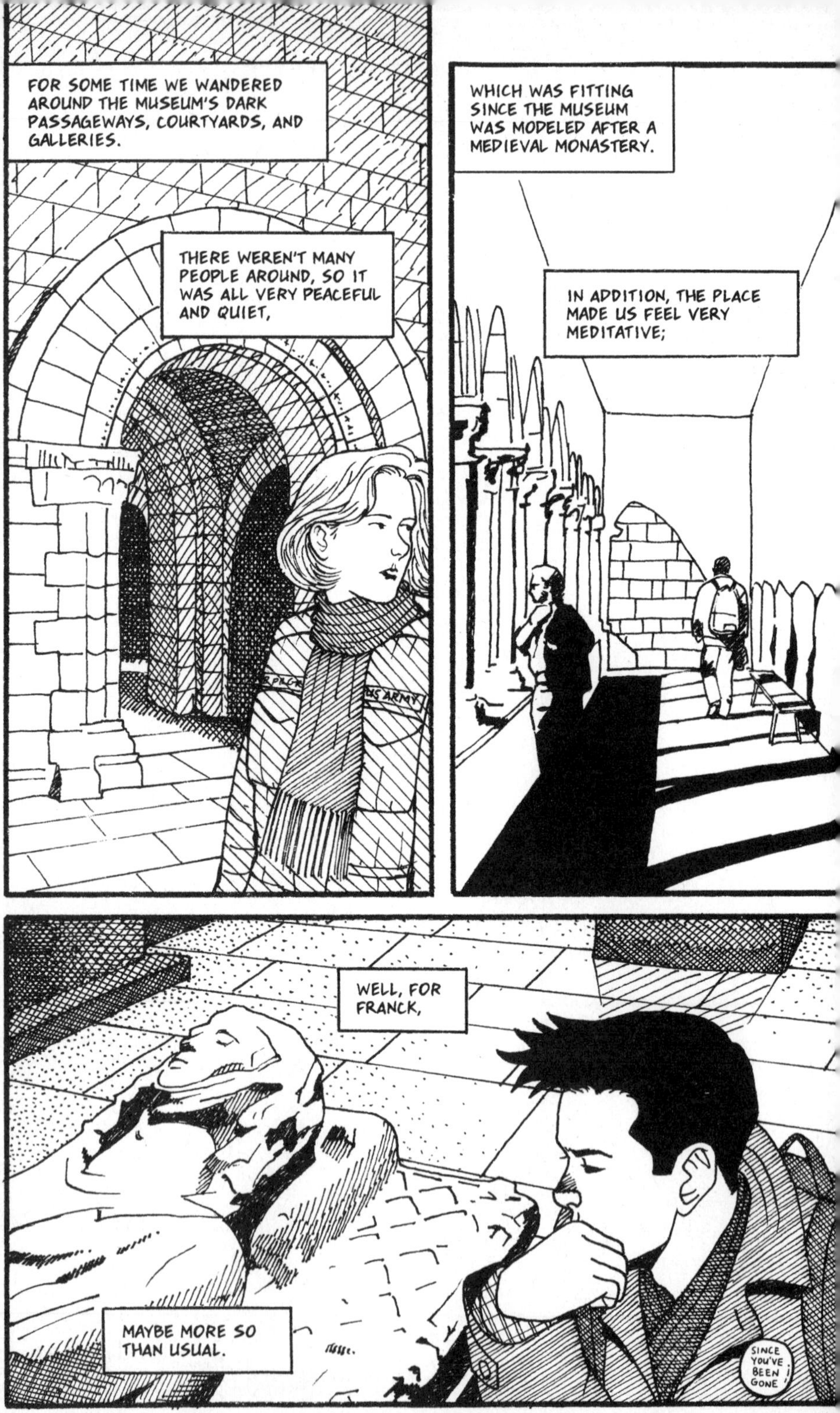
FOR SOME TIME WE WANDERED AROUND THE MUSEUM'S DARK PASSAGEWAYS, COURTYARDS, AND GALLERIES.
THERE WEREN'T MANY PEOPLE AROUND, SO IT WAS ALL VERY PEACEFUL AND QUIET,
US ARMY
WHICH WAS FITTING SINCE THE MUSEUM WAS MODELED AFTER A MEDIEVAL MONASTERY.
IN ADDITION, THE PLACE MADE US FEEL VERY MEDITATIVE;
WELL, FOR FRANCK,
MAYBE MORE SO THAN USUAL.
SINCE YOU'VE BEEN GONE

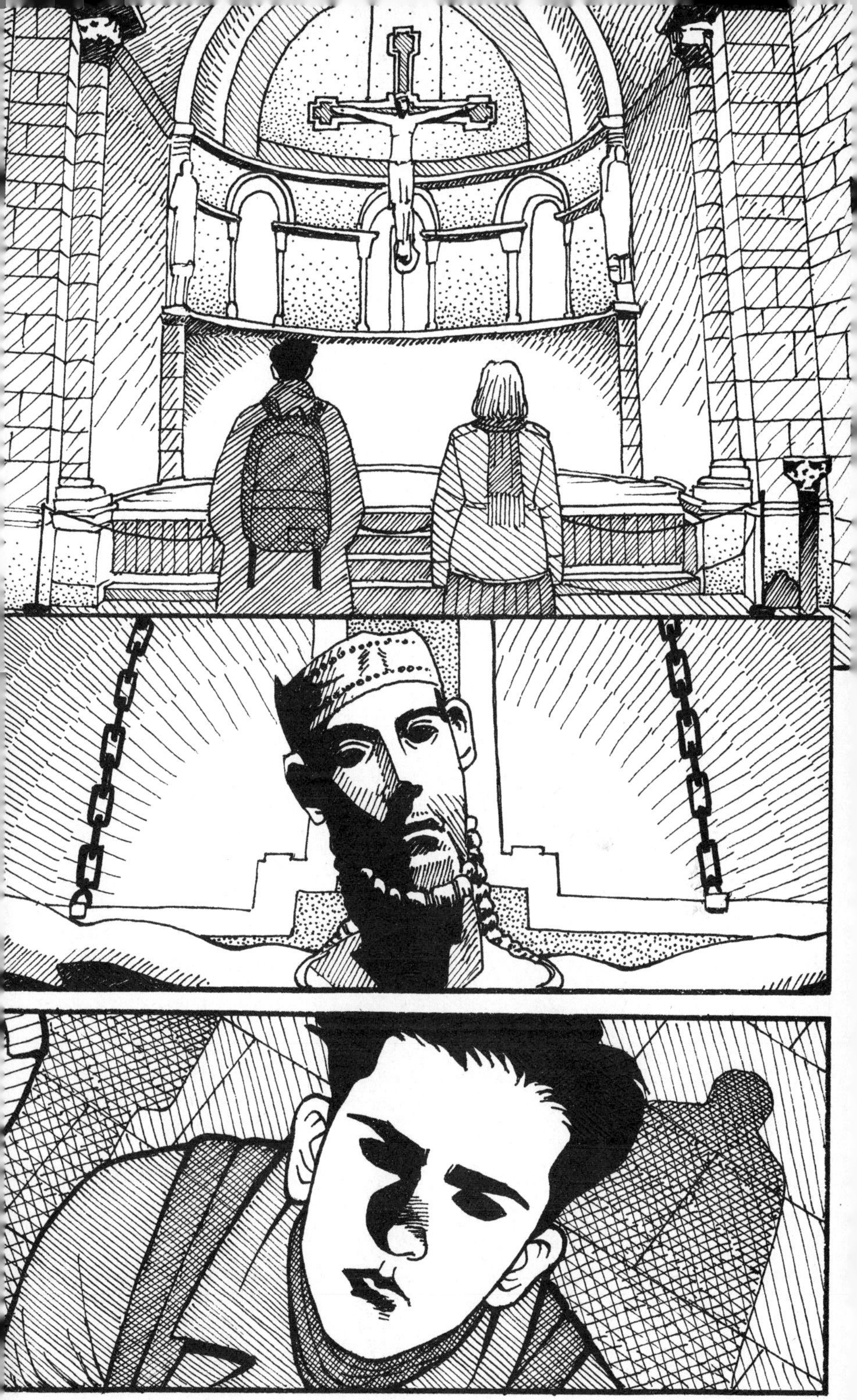

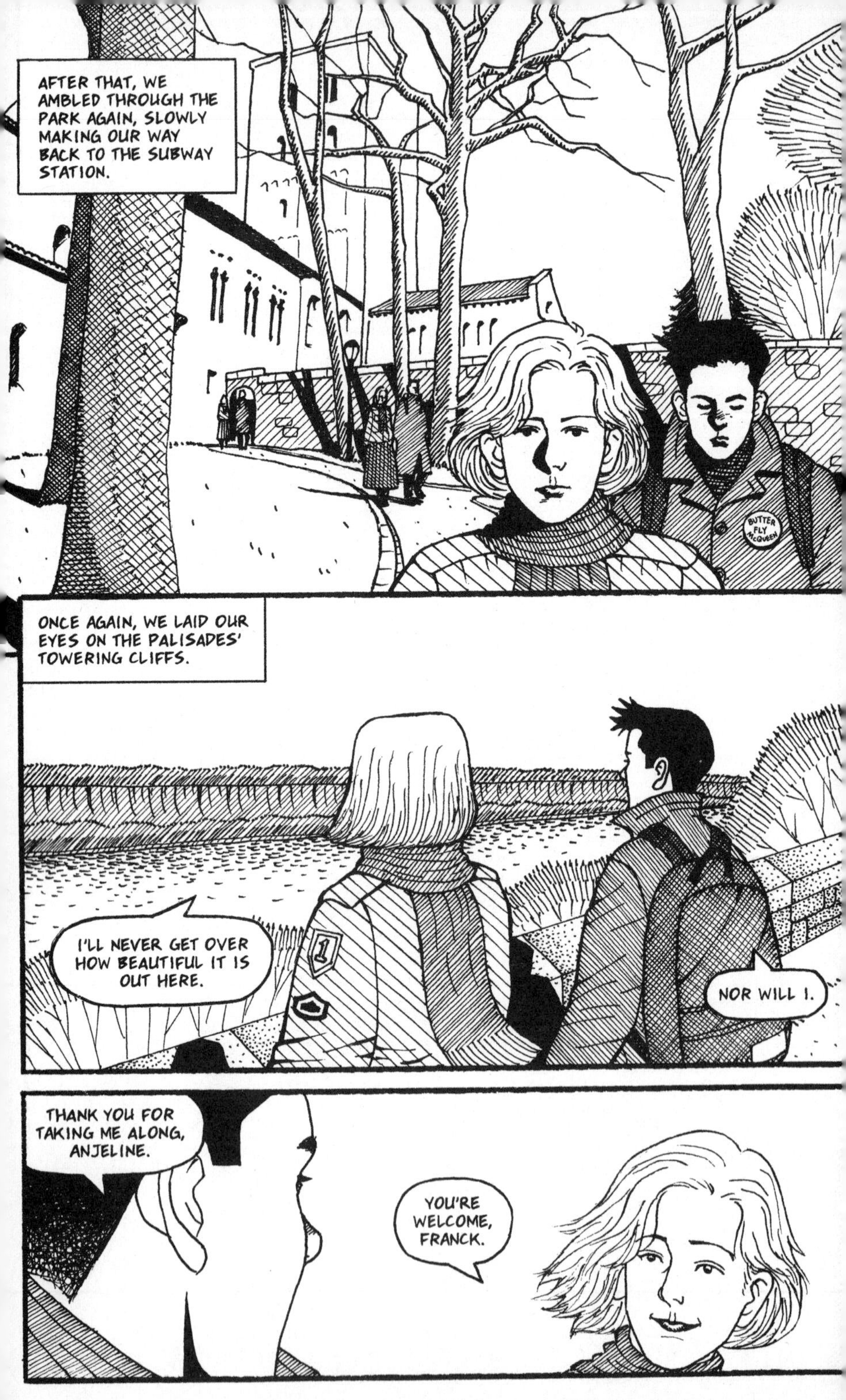
AFTER THAT, WE AMBLED THROUGH THE PARK AGAIN, SLOWLY MAKING OUR WAY BACK TO THE SUBWAY STATION.
BUTTER FLY McQUEEN
ONCE AGAIN, WE LAID OUR EYES ON THE PALISADES' TOWERING CLIFFS.
I'LL NEVER GET OVER HOW BEAUTIFUL IT IS OUT HERE.
NOR WILL I.
THANK YOU FOR TAKING ME ALONG, ANJELINE.
YOU'RE WELCOME, FRANCK.

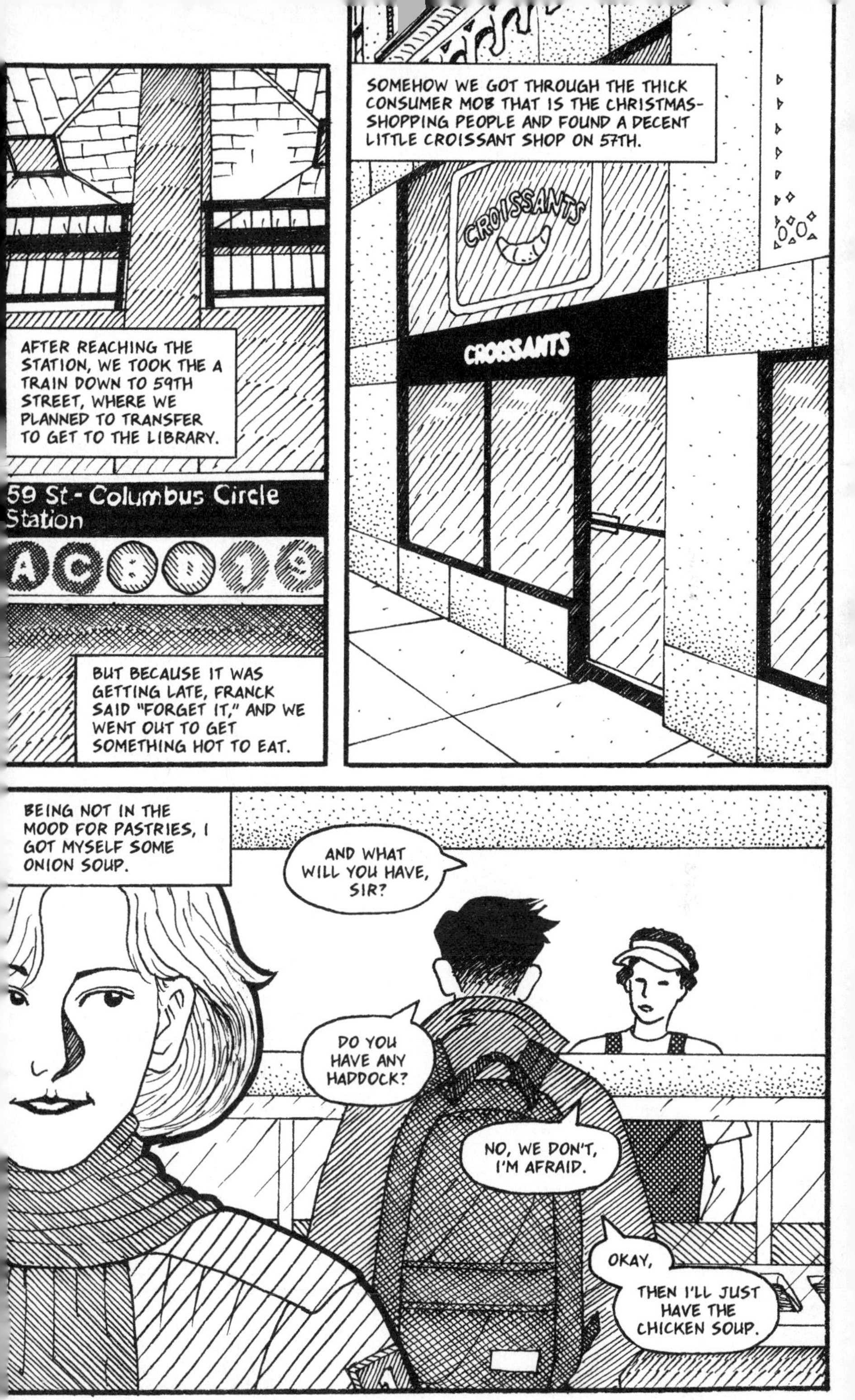
AFTER REACHING THE STATION, WE TOOK THE A TRAIN DOWN TO 59TH STREET, WHERE WE PLANNED TO TRANSFER TO GET TO THE LIBRARY.
59 St - Columbus Circle Station
BUT BECAUSE IT WAS GETTING LATE, FRANCK SAID "FORGET IT," AND WE WENT OUT TO GET SOMETHING HOT TO EAT.
SOMEHOW WE GOT THROUGH THE THICK CONSUMER MOB THAT IS THE CHRISTMAS-SHOPPING PEOPLE AND FOUND A DECENT LITTLE CROISSANT SHOP ON 57TH.
CROISSANTS
CROISSANTS
BEING NOT IN THE MOOD FOR PASTRIES, I GOT MYSELF SOME ONION SOUP.
AND WHAT WILL YOU HAVE, SIR?
DO YOU HAVE ANY HADDOCK?
NO, WE DON'T, I'M AFRAID.
OKAY,
THEN I'LL JUST HAVE THE CHICKEN SOUP.

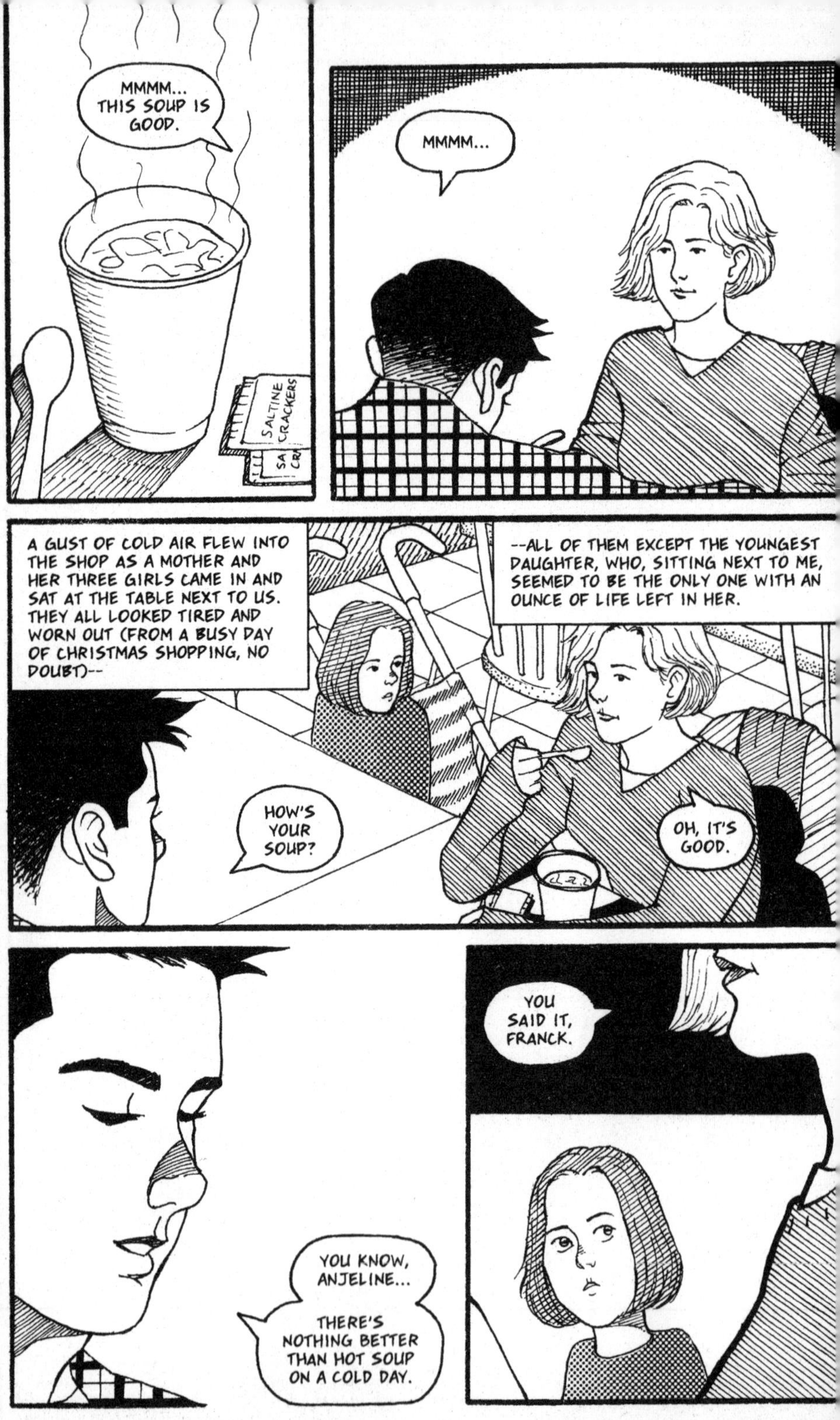
MMMM... THIS SOUP IS GOOD.
SALTINE CRACKERS
MMMM...
A GUST OF COLD AIR FLEW INTO THE SHOP AS A MOTHER AND HER THREE GIRLS CAME IN AND SAT AT THE TABLE NEXT TO US. THEY ALL LOOKED TIRED AND WORN OUT (FROM A BUSY DAY OF CHRISTMAS SHOPPING, NO DOUBT)--
--ALL OF THEM EXCEPT THE YOUNGEST DAUGHTER, WHO, SITTING NEXT TO ME, SEEMED TO BE THE ONLY ONE WITH AN OUNCE OF LIFE LEFT IN HER.
HOW'S YOUR SOUP?
OH, IT'S GOOD.
YOU KNOW, ANJELINE...
THERE'S NOTHING BETTER THAN HOT SOUP ON A COLD DAY.
YOU SAID IT, FRANCK.

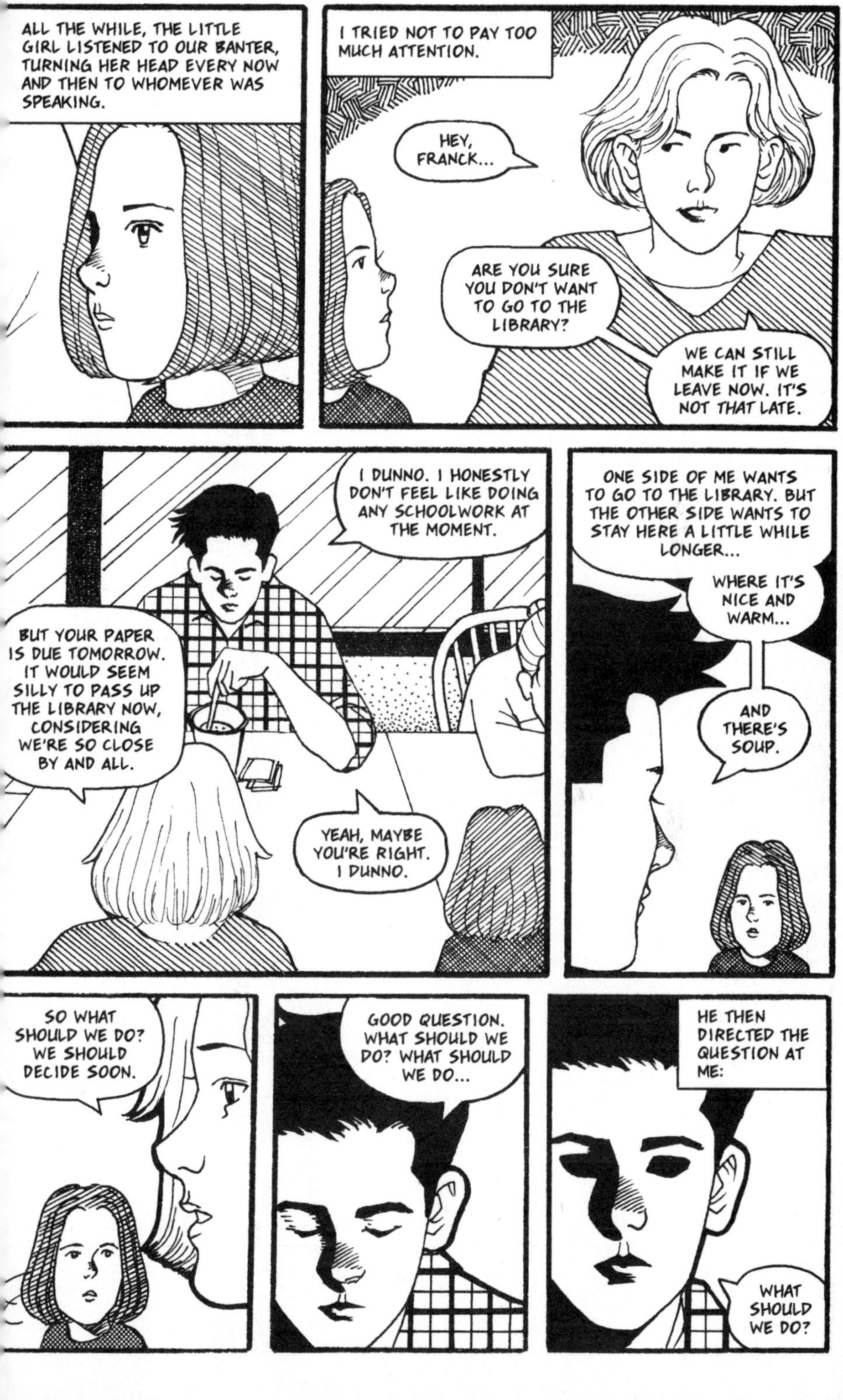
ALL THE WHILE, THE LITTLE GIRL LISTENED TO OUR BANTER, TURNING HER HEAD EVERY NOW AND THEN TO WHOMEVER WAS SPEAKING.
I TRIED NOT TO PAY TOO MUCH ATTENTION.
HEY, FRANCK...
ARE YOU SURE YOU DON'T WANT TO GO TO THE LIBRARY?
WE CAN STILL MAKE IT IF WE LEAVE NOW. IT'S NOT THAT LATE.
I DUNNO. I HONESTLY DON'T FEEL LIKE DOING ANY SCHOOLWORK AT THE MOMENT.
BUT YOUR PAPER IS DUE TOMORROW. IT WOULD SEEM SILLY TO PASS UP THE LIBRARY NOW, CONSIDERING WE'RE SO CLOSE BY AND ALL.
YEAH, MAYBE YOU'RE RIGHT. I DUNNO.
ONE SIDE OF ME WANTS TO GO TO THE LIBRARY. BUT THE OTHER SIDE WANTS TO STAY HERE A LITTLE WHILE LONGER...
WHERE IT'S NICE AND WARM...
AND THERE'S SOUP.
SO WHAT SHOULD WE DO? WE SHOULD DECIDE SOON.
GOOD QUESTION. WHAT SHOULD WE DO? WHAT SHOULD WE DO...
HE THEN DIRECTED THE QUESTION AT ME:
WHAT SHOULD WE DO?

WHAT SHOULD WE DO?

I ANSWERED BACK.

FRANCK'S EYES THEN WENT TO THE EAVESDROPPING LITTLE GIRL.

WHAT SHOULD WE DO?

THE LOOK SHE GAVE ME AFTER THAT WAS SUCH THAT I JUST HAD TO SMILE.

I THEN LOOKED AT FRANCK.

HE HAD TO SMILE, TOO.

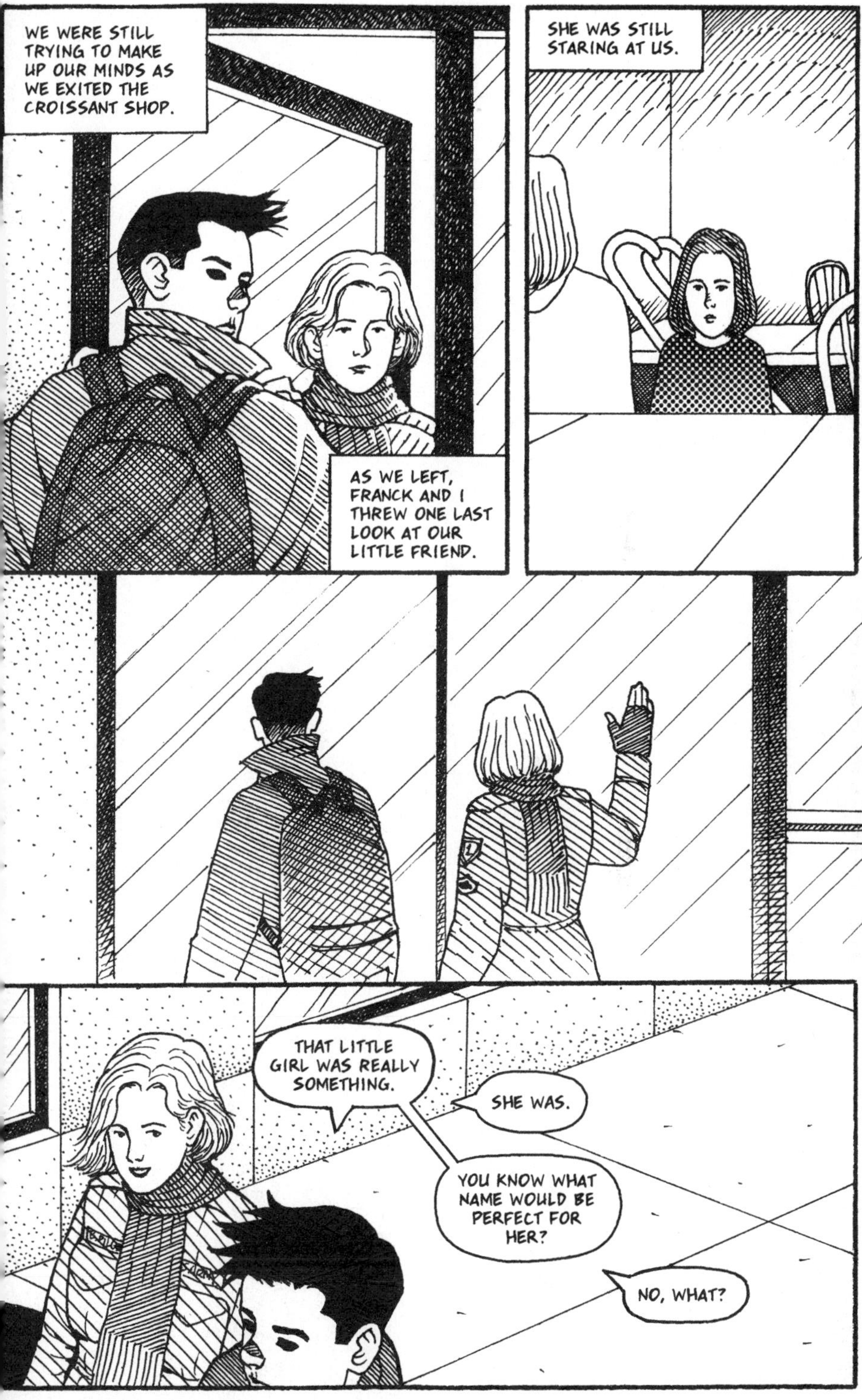
WE WERE STILL TRYING TO MAKE UP OUR MINDS AS WE EXITED THE CROISSANT SHOP.
AS WE LEFT, FRANCK AND I THREW ONE LAST LOOK AT OUR LITTLE FRIEND.
SHE WAS STILL STARING AT US.
THAT LITTLE GIRL WAS REALLY SOMETHING.
SHE WAS.
YOU KNOW WHAT NAME WOULD BE PERFECT FOR HER?
NO, WHAT?

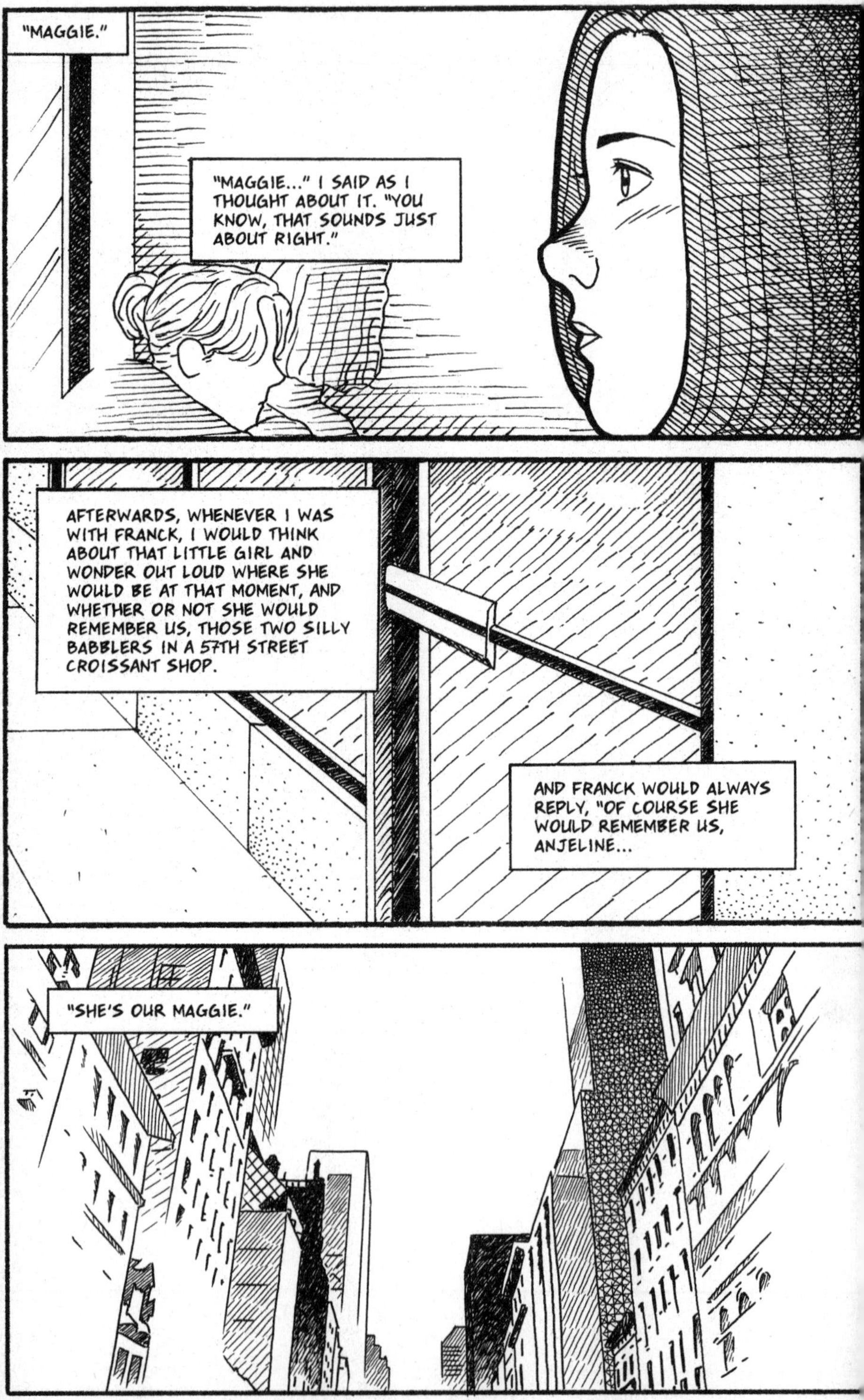
"MAGGIE."
"MAGGIE..." I SAID AS I THOUGHT ABOUT IT. "YOU KNOW, THAT SOUNDS JUST ABOUT RIGHT."
AFTERWARDS, WHENEVER I WAS WITH FRANCK, I WOULD THINK ABOUT THAT LITTLE GIRL AND WONDER OUT LOUD WHERE SHE WOULD BE AT THAT MOMENT, AND WHETHER OR NOT SHE WOULD REMEMBER US, THOSE TWO SILLY BABBLERS IN A 57TH STREET CROISSANT SHOP.
AND FRANCK WOULD ALWAYS REPLY, "OF COURSE SHE WOULD REMEMBER US, ANJELINE...
"SHE'S OUR MAGGIE."

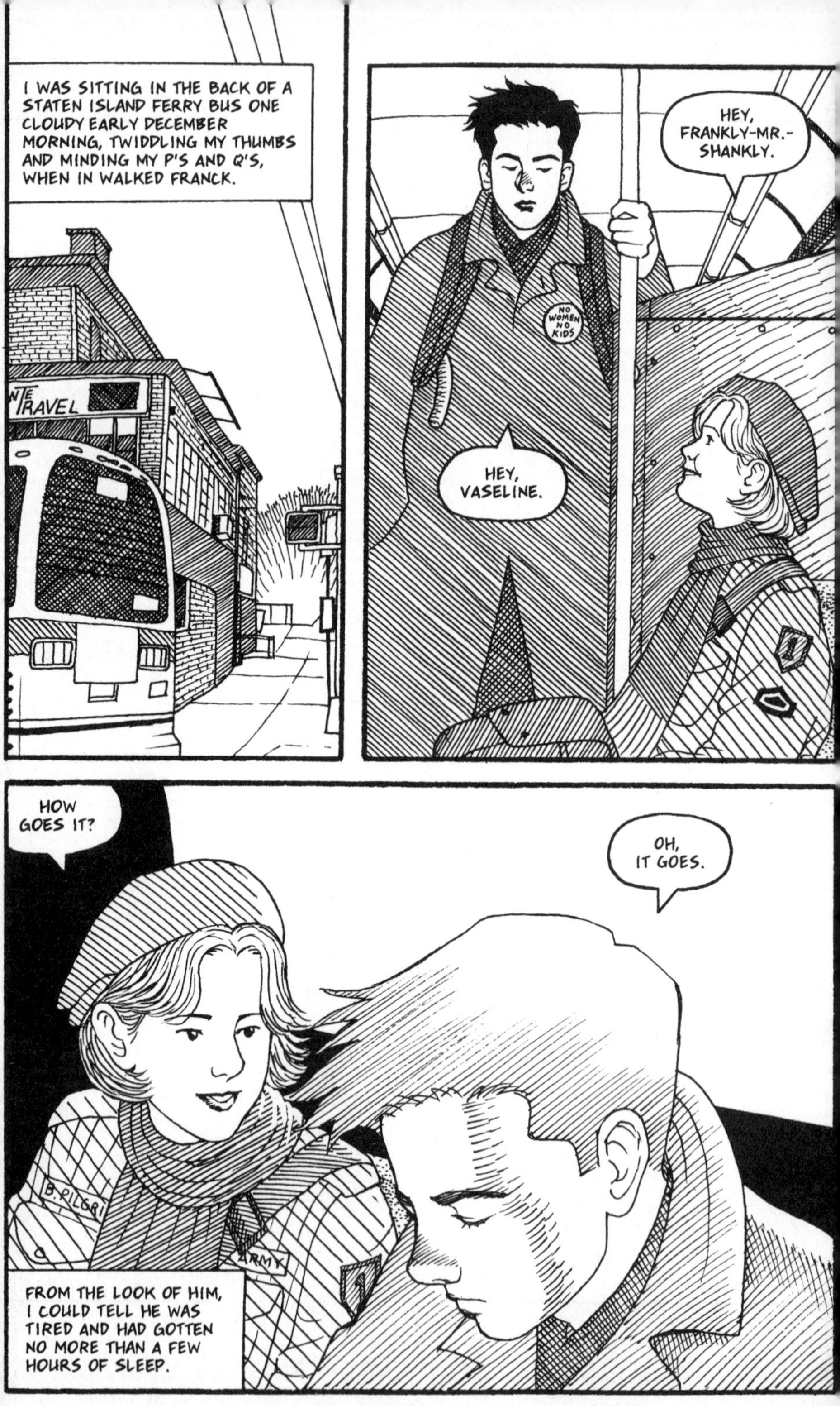
I WAS SITTING IN THE BACK OF A STATEN ISLAND FERRY BUS ONE CLOUDY EARLY DECEMBER MORNING, TWIDDLING MY THUMBS AND MINDING MY P'S AND Q'S, WHEN IN WALKED FRANCK.
TRAVEL
HEY, FRANKLY-MR.-SHANKLY.
NO WOMEN NO KIDS
HEY, VASELINE.
HOW GOES IT?
OH, IT GOES.
B. PILGRI
ARMY
FROM THE LOOK OF HIM, I COULD TELL HE WAS TIRED AND HAD GOTTEN NO MORE THAN A FEW HOURS OF SLEEP.

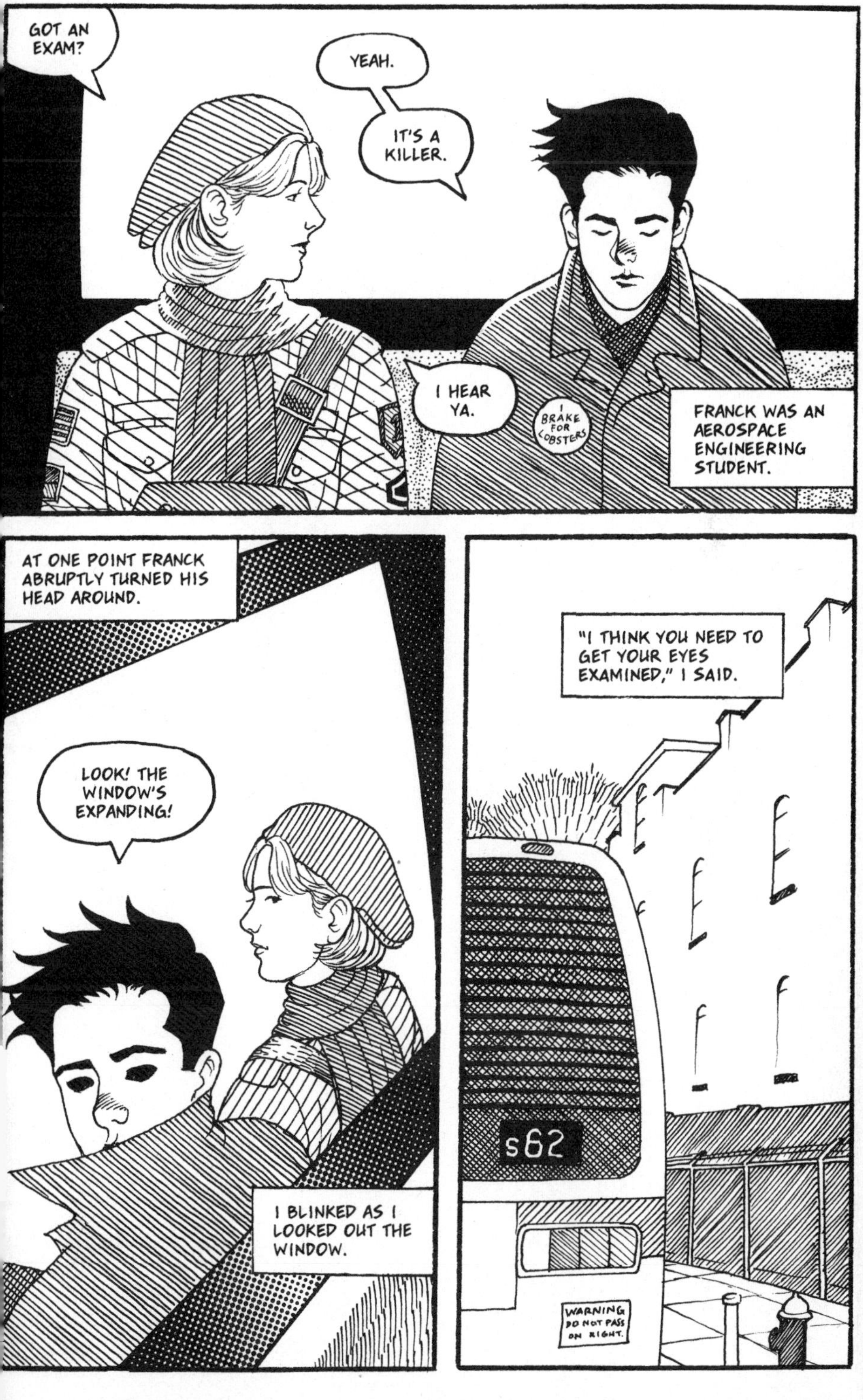
GOT AN EXAM?
YEAH.
IT'S A KILLER.
I HEAR YA.
I BRAKE FOR LOBSTERS
FRANCK WAS AN AEROSPACE ENGINEERING STUDENT.
AT ONE POINT FRANCK ABRUPTLY TURNED HIS HEAD AROUND.
LOOK! THE WINDOW'S EXPANDING!
I BLINKED AS I LOOKED OUT THE WINDOW.
"I THINK YOU NEED TO GET YOUR EYES EXAMINED," I SAID.
S62
WARNING DO NOT PASS ON RIGHT.

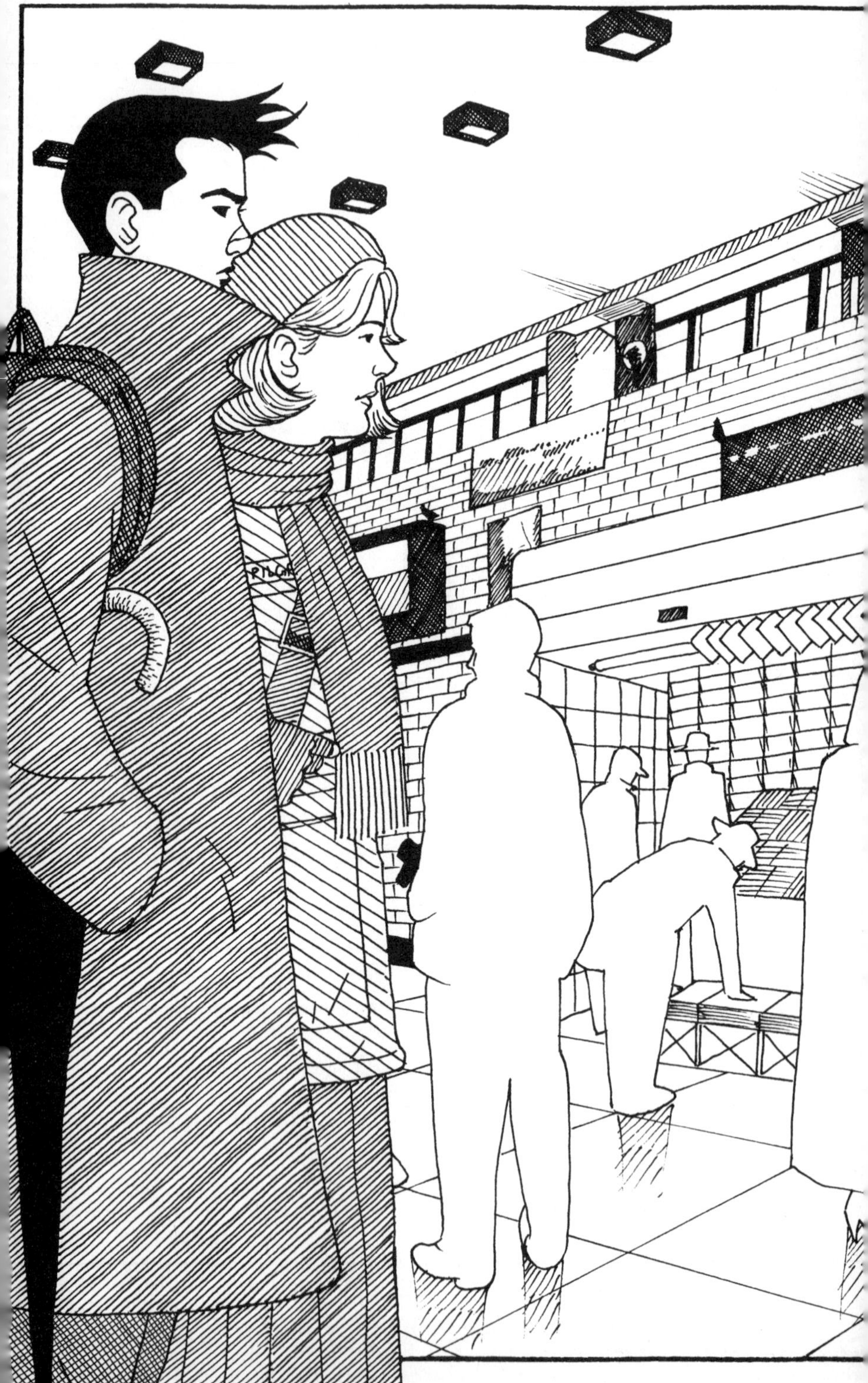

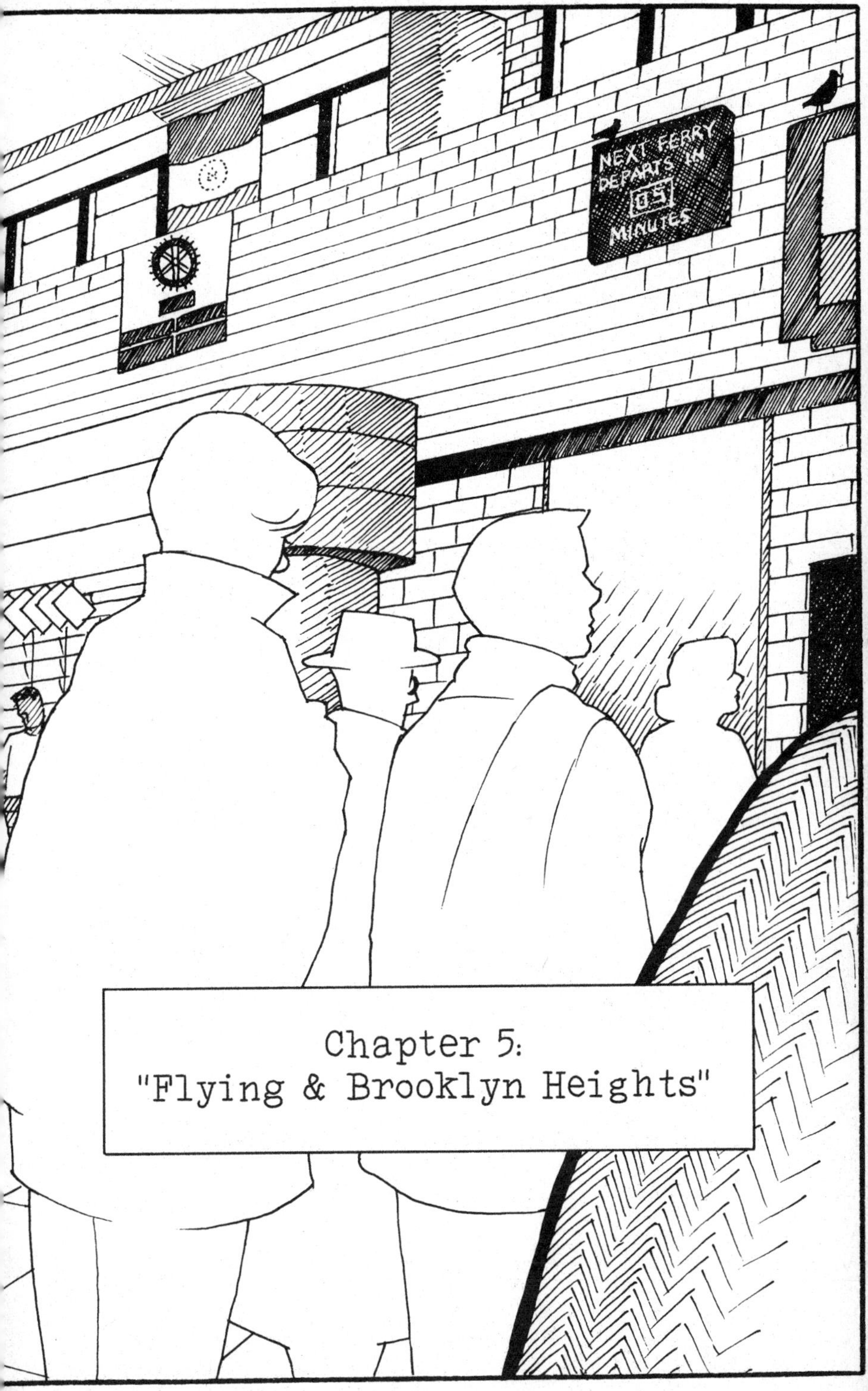
NEXT FERRY DEPARTS IN 05 MINUTES

Chapter 5: "Flying & Brooklyn Heights"

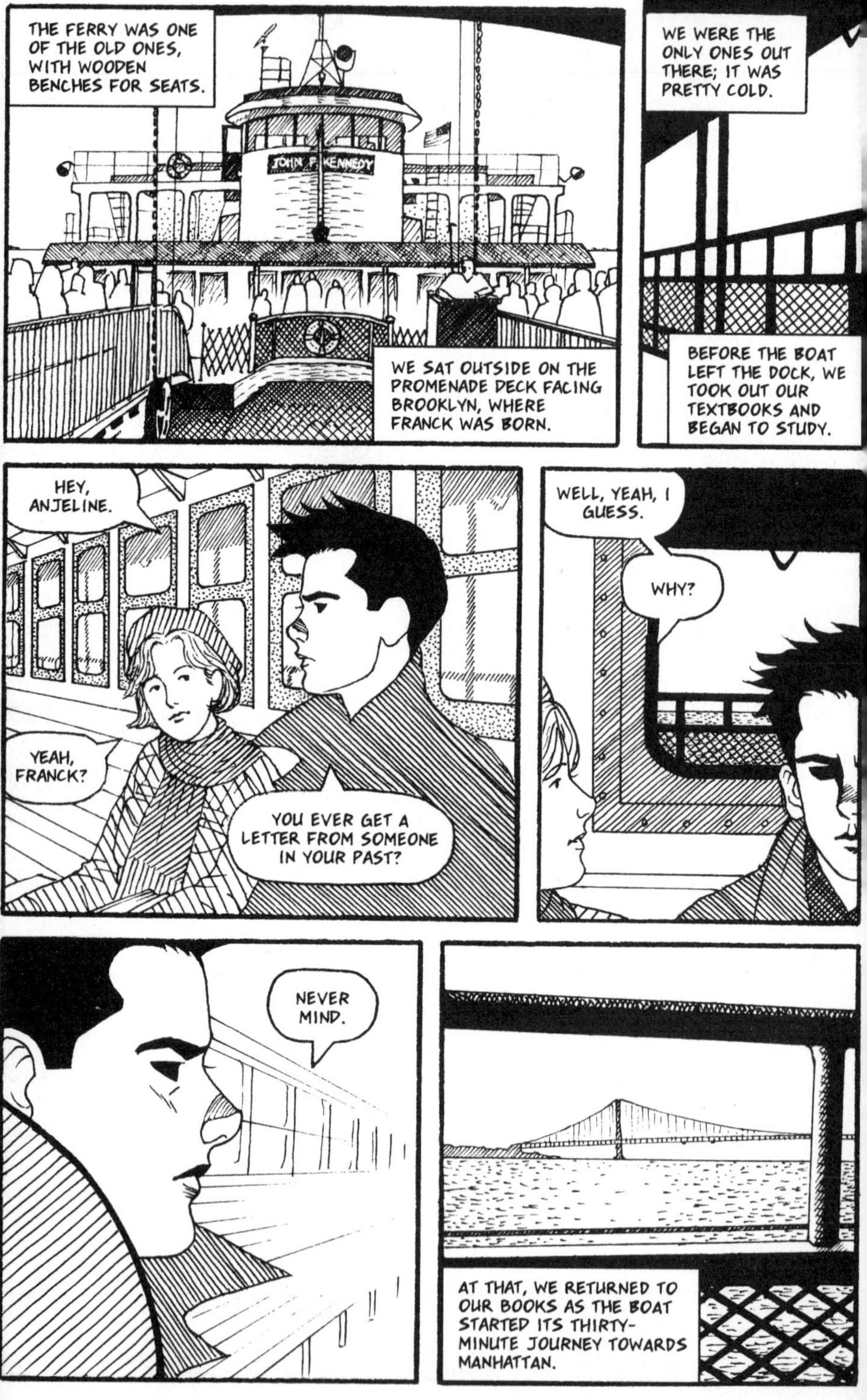

THE FERRY WAS ONE OF THE OLD ONES, WITH WOODEN BENCHES FOR SEATS.
JOHN F. KENNEDY
WE SAT OUTSIDE ON THE PROMENADE DECK FACING BROOKLYN, WHERE FRANCK WAS BORN.
WE WERE THE ONLY ONES OUT THERE; IT WAS PRETTY COLD.
BEFORE THE BOAT LEFT THE DOCK, WE TOOK OUT OUR TEXTBOOKS AND BEGAN TO STUDY.
HEY, ANJELINE.
YEAH, FRANCK?
YOU EVER GET A LETTER FROM SOMEONE IN YOUR PAST?
WELL, YEAH, I GUESS.
WHY?
NEVER MIND.
AT THAT, WE RETURNED TO OUR BOOKS AS THE BOAT STARTED ITS THIRTY-MINUTE JOURNEY TOWARDS MANHATTAN.

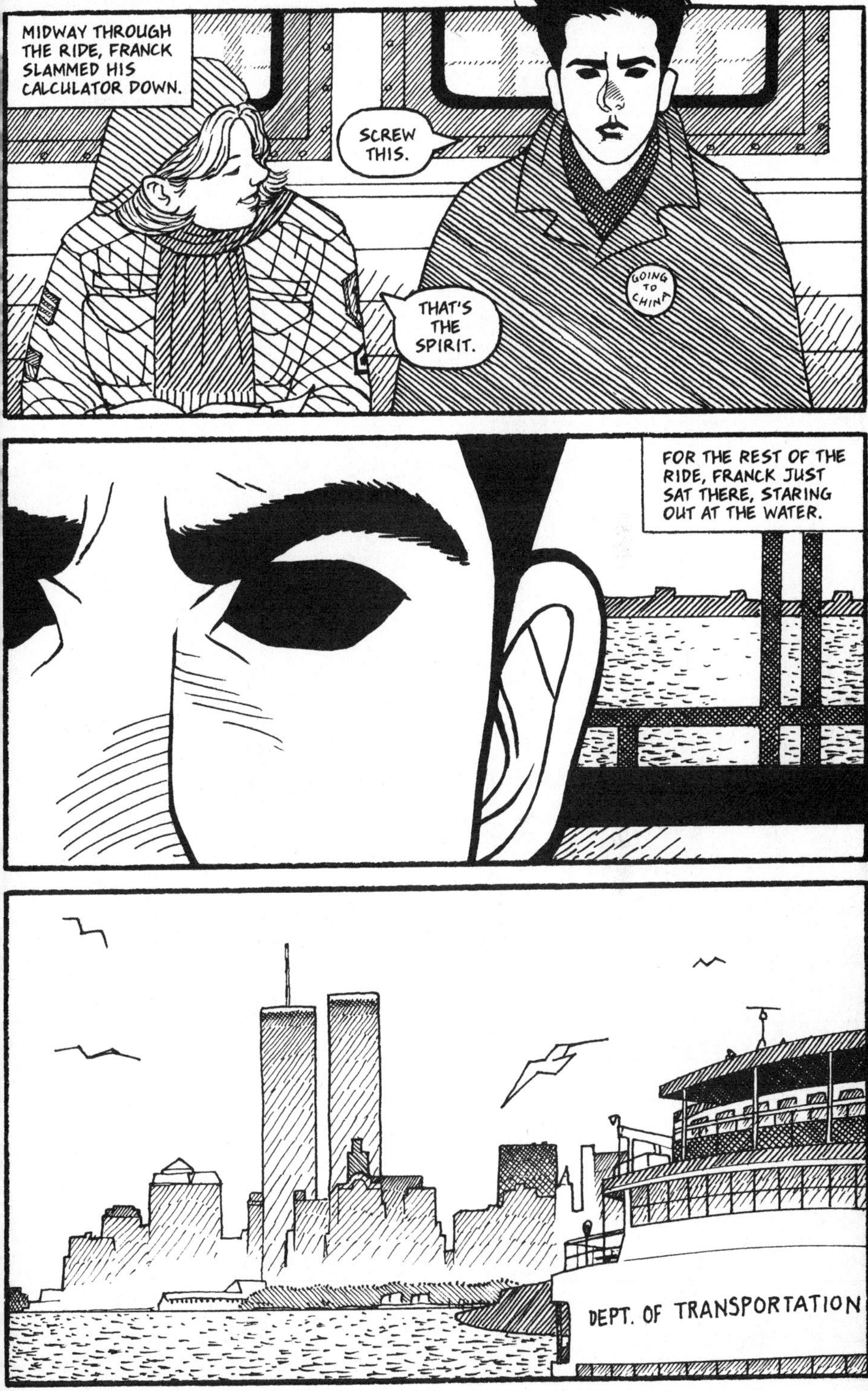
MIDWAY THROUGH THE RIDE, FRANCK SLAMMED HIS CALCULATOR DOWN.
SCREW THIS.
GOING TO CHINA
THAT'S THE SPIRIT.
FOR THE REST OF THE RIDE, FRANCK JUST SAT THERE, STARING OUT AT THE WATER.
DEPT. OF TRANSPORTATION

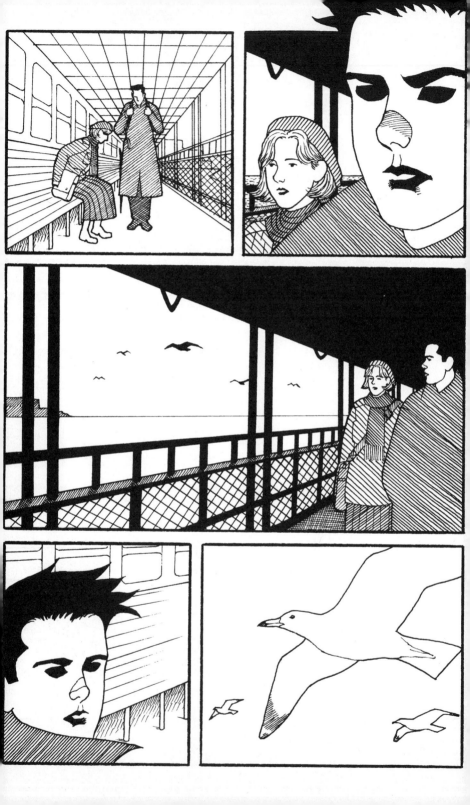

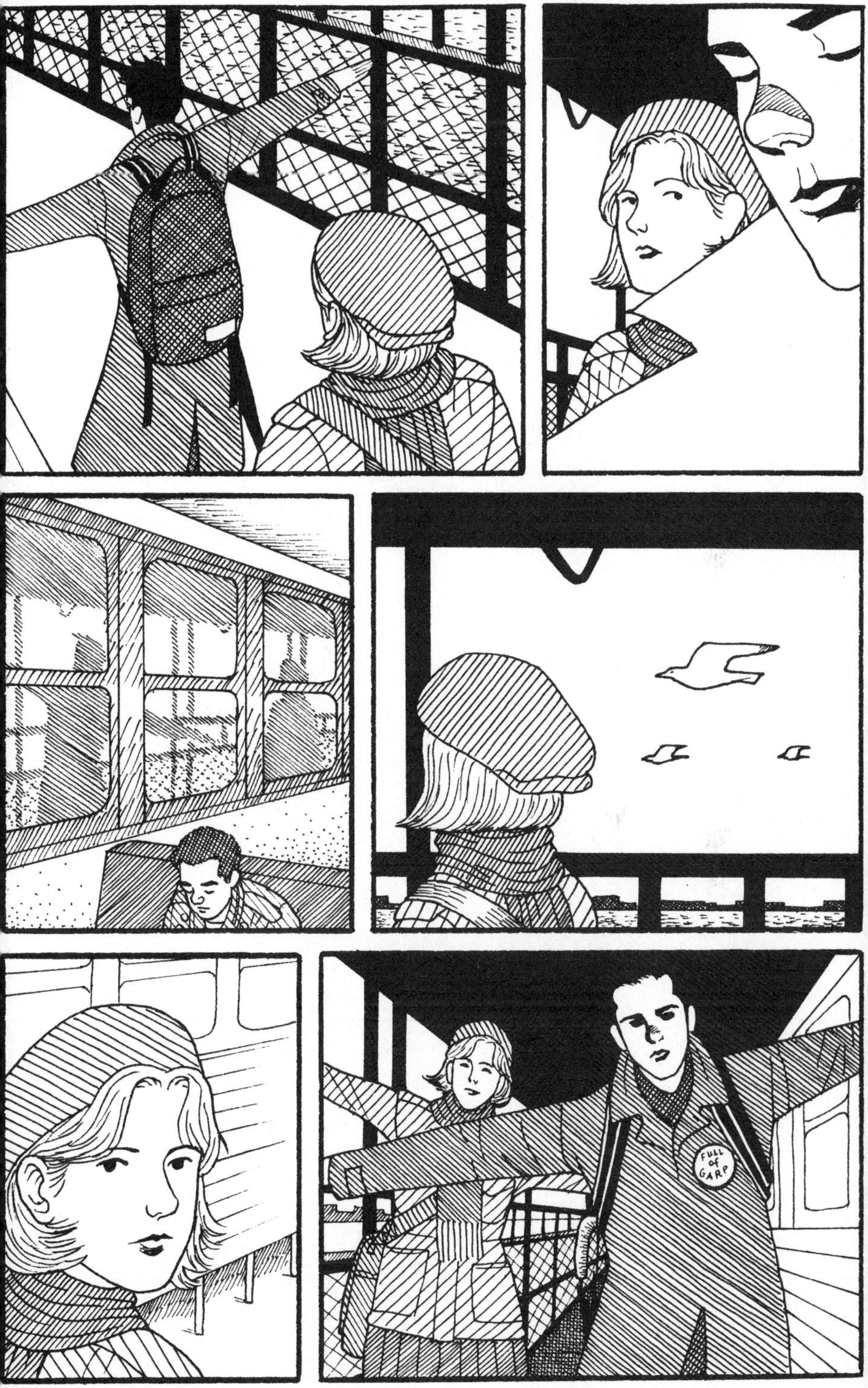
FULL of GARP

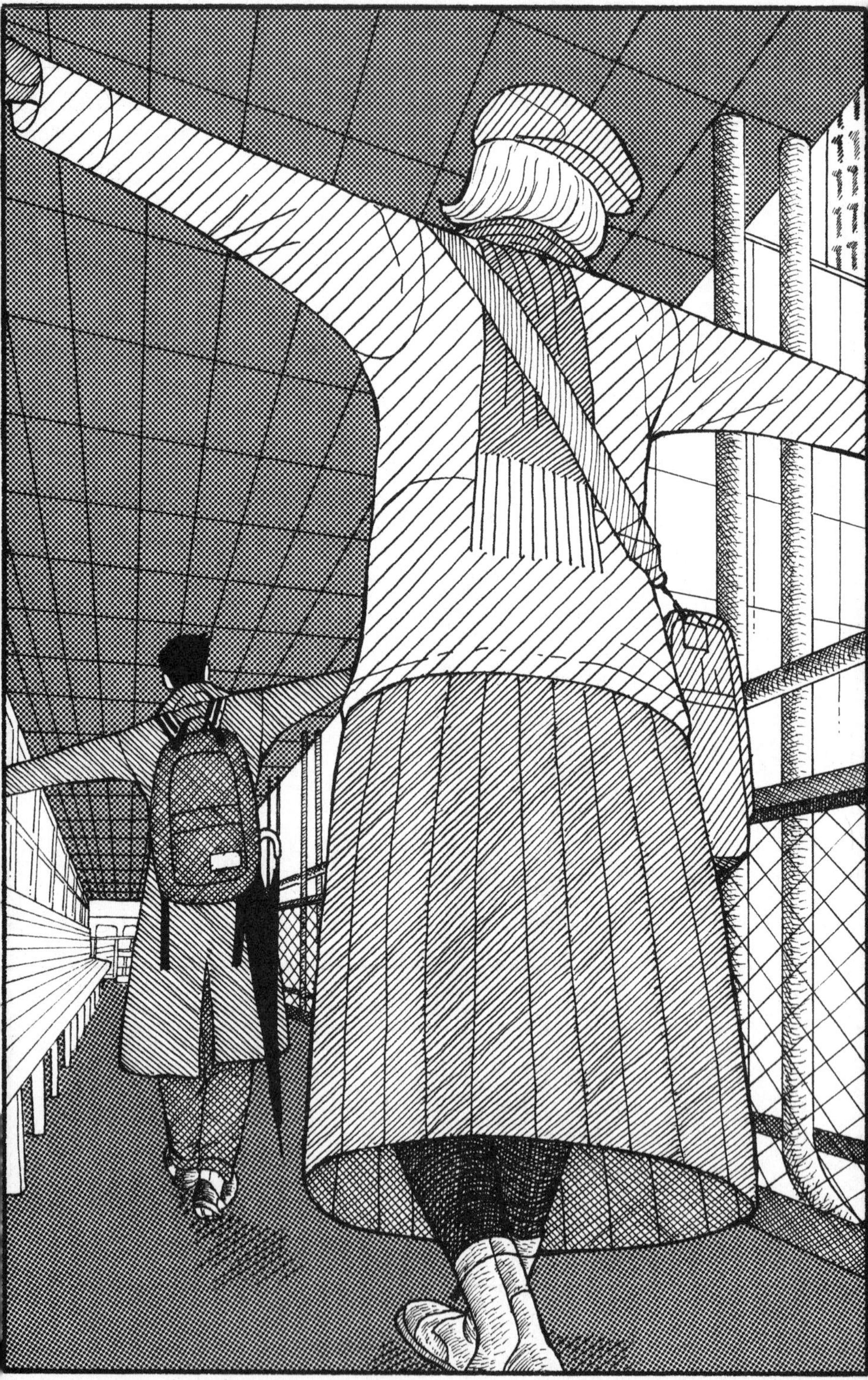

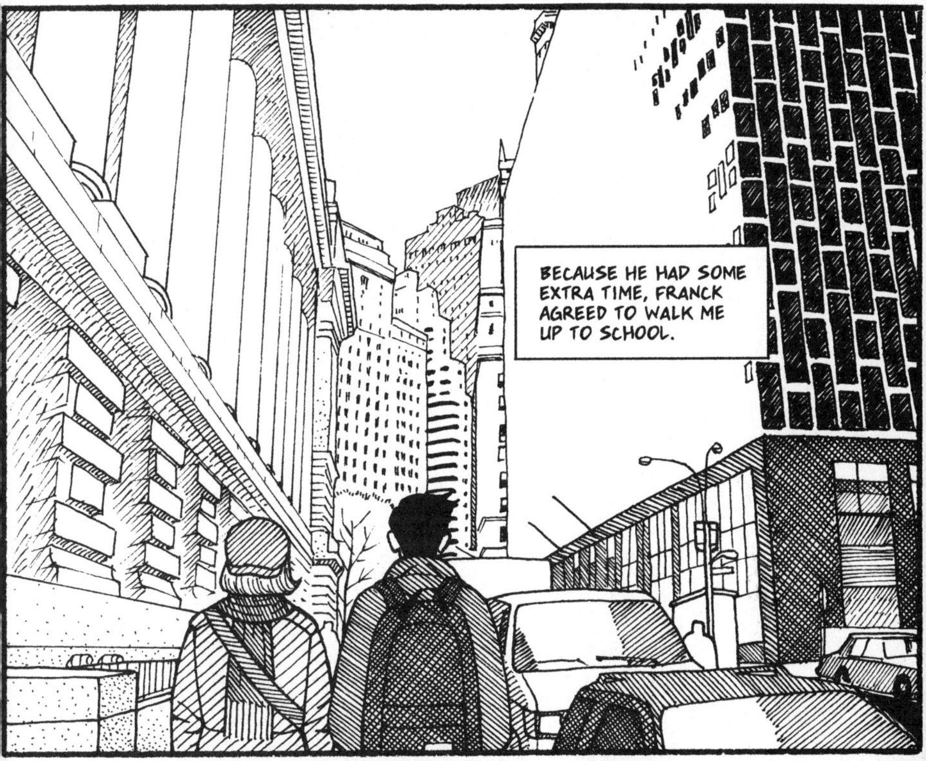
BECAUSE HE HAD SOME EXTRA TIME, FRANCK AGREED TO WALK ME UP TO SCHOOL.

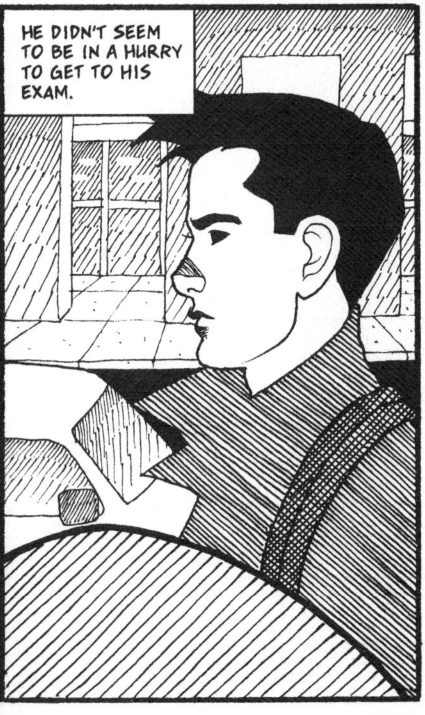
HE DIDN'T SEEM TO BE IN A HURRY TO GET TO HIS EXAM.

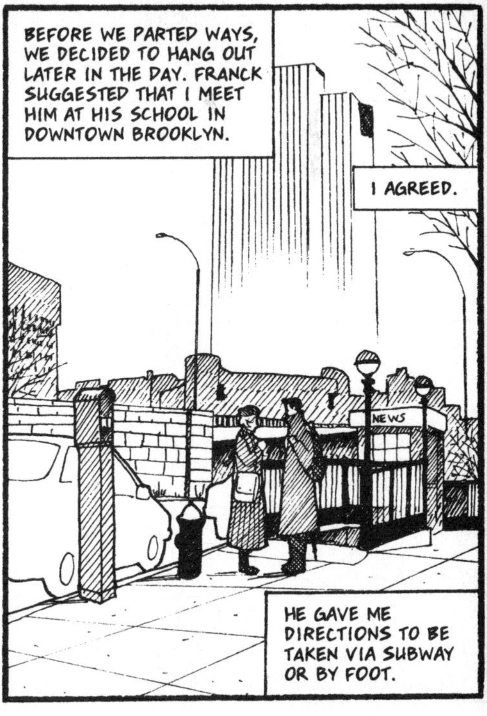
BEFORE WE PARTED WAYS, WE DECIDED TO HANG OUT LATER IN THE DAY. FRANCK SUGGESTED THAT I MEET HIM AT HIS SCHOOL IN DOWNTOWN BROOKLYN.
I AGREED.
NEWS
HE GAVE ME DIRECTIONS TO BE TAKEN VIA SUBWAY OR BY FOOT.

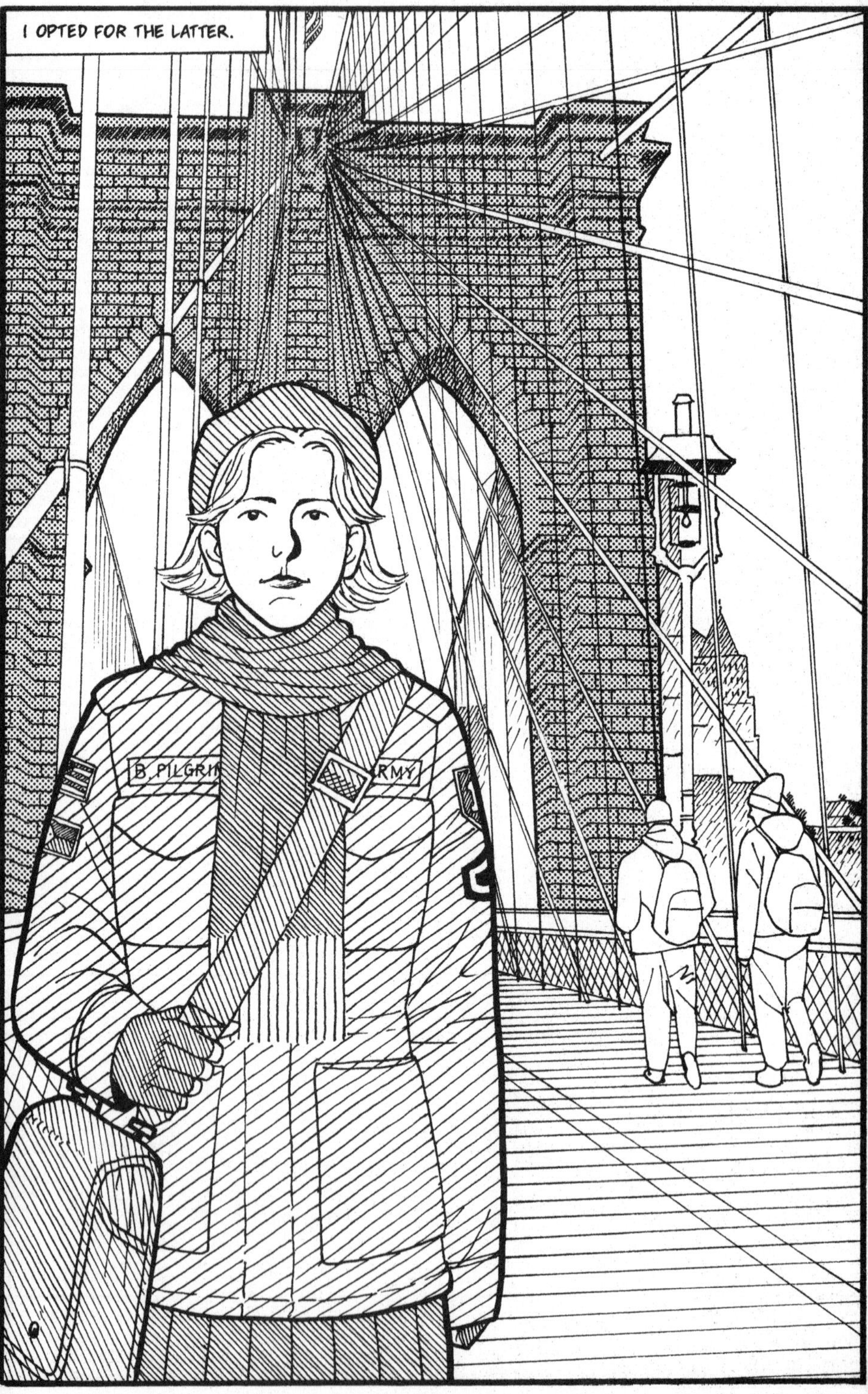
I OPTED FOR THE LATTER.
B. PILGRIM
ARMY

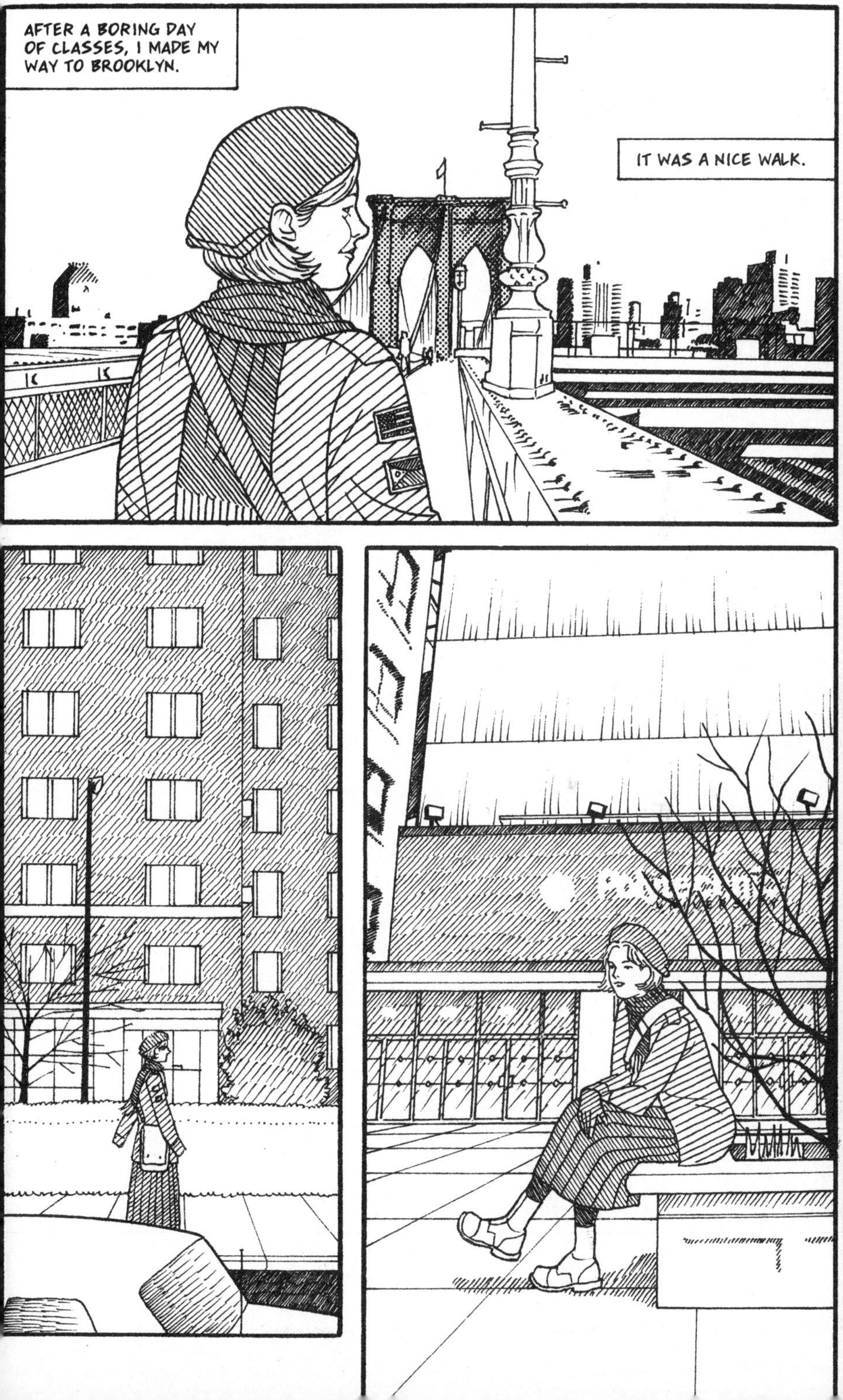
AFTER A BORING DAY OF CLASSES, I MADE MY WAY TO BROOKLYN.
IT WAS A NICE WALK.

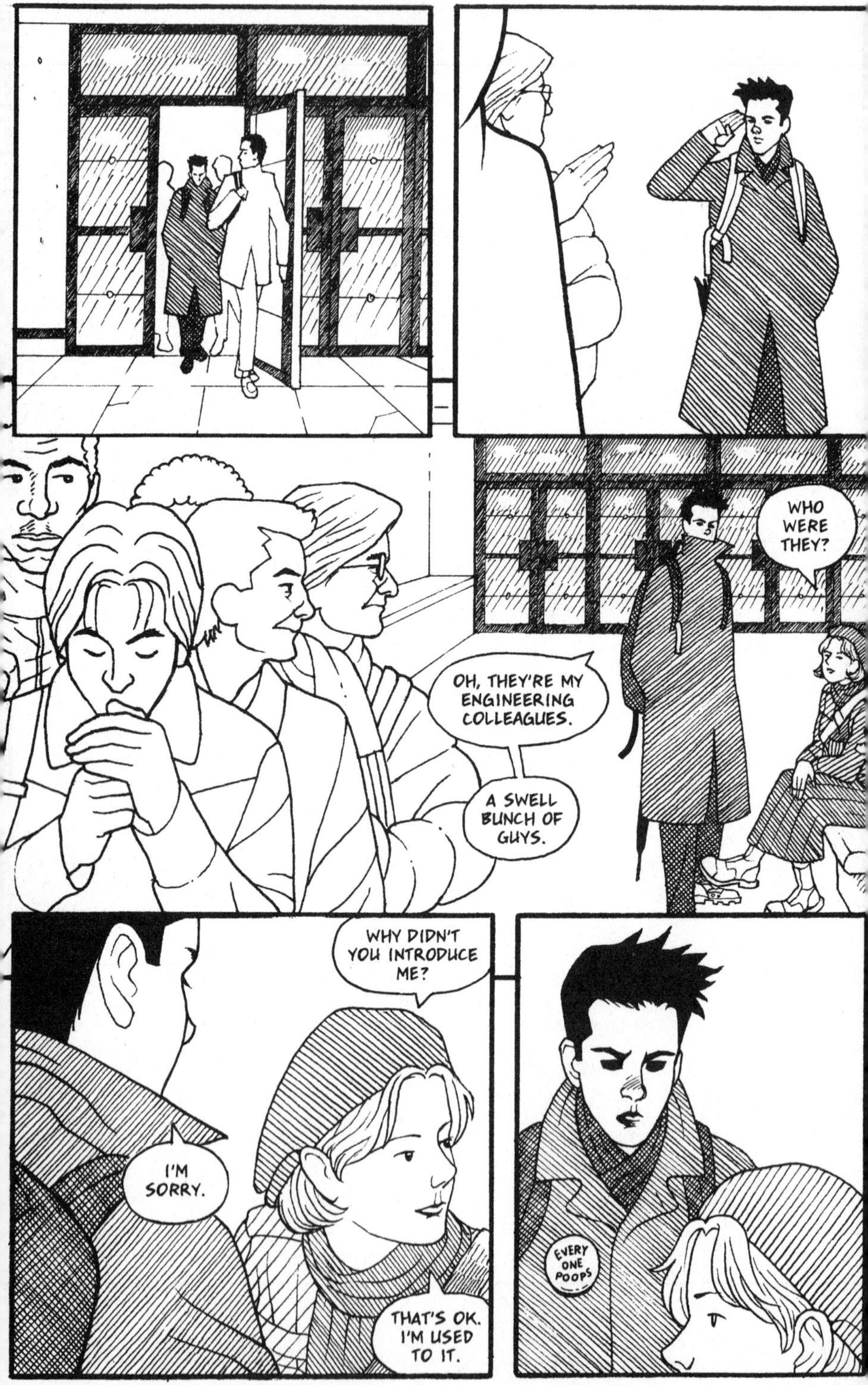
WHO WERE THEY?
OH, THEY'RE MY ENGINEERING COLLEAGUES.
A SWELL BUNCH OF GUYS.
WHY DIDN'T YOU INTRODUCE ME?
I'M SORRY.
THAT'S OK. I'M USED TO IT.
EVERY ONE POOPS

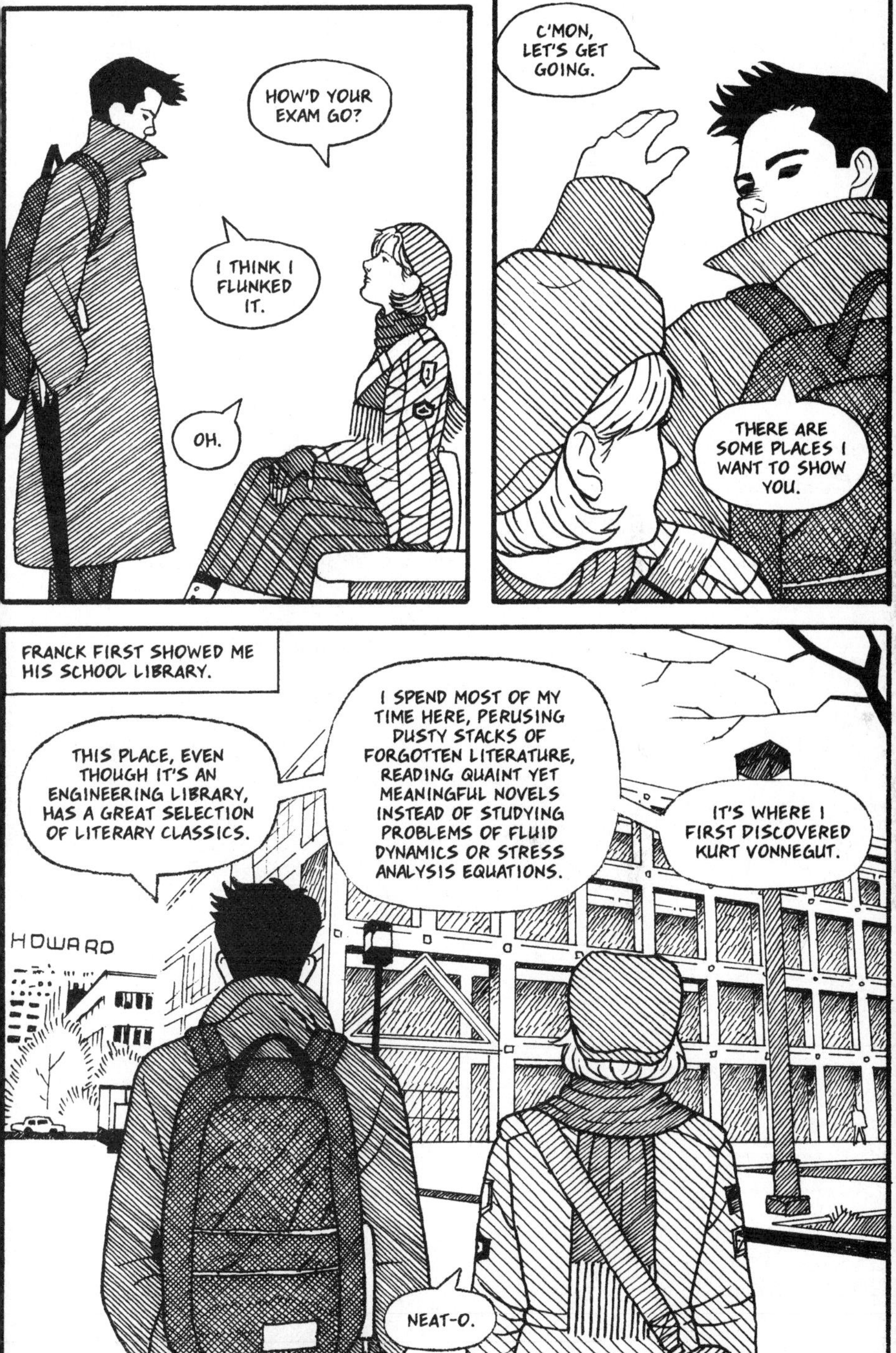
HOW'D YOUR EXAM GO?
I THINK I FLUNKED IT.
OH.
C'MON, LET'S GET GOING.
THERE ARE SOME PLACES I WANT TO SHOW YOU.
FRANCK FIRST SHOWED ME HIS SCHOOL LIBRARY.
THIS PLACE, EVEN THOUGH IT'S AN ENGINEERING LIBRARY, HAS A GREAT SELECTION OF LITERARY CLASSICS.
I SPEND MOST OF MY TIME HERE, PERUSING DUSTY STACKS OF FORGOTTEN LITERATURE, READING QUAINT YET MEANINGFUL NOVELS INSTEAD OF STUDYING PROBLEMS OF FLUID DYNAMICS OR STRESS ANALYSIS EQUATIONS.
IT'S WHERE I FIRST DISCOVERED KURT VONNEGUT.
HOWARD
NEAT-O.

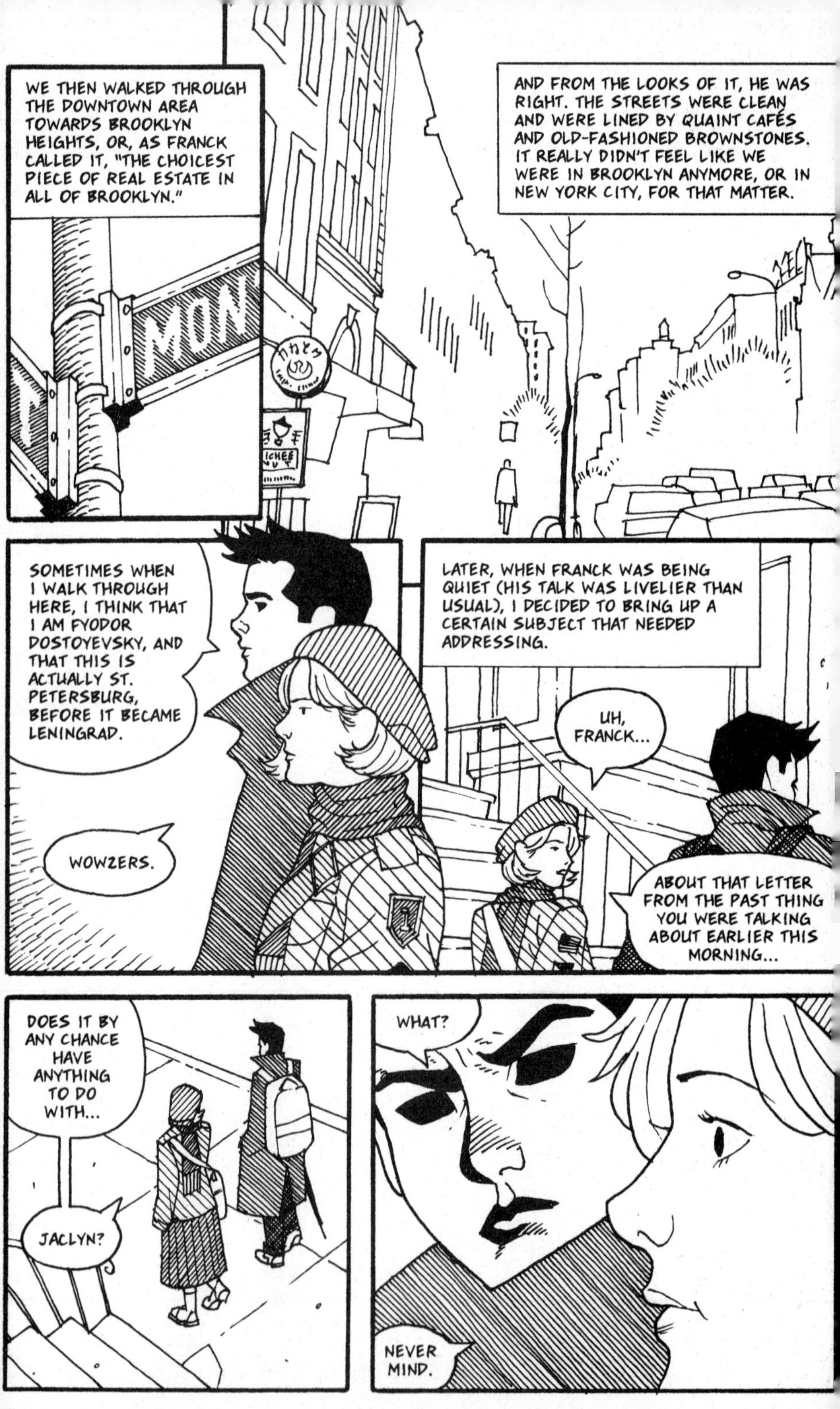
WE THEN WALKED THROUGH THE DOWNTOWN AREA TOWARDS BROOKLYN HEIGHTS, OR, AS FRANCK CALLED IT, "THE CHOICEST PIECE OF REAL ESTATE IN ALL OF BROOKLYN."
MON
AND FROM THE LOOKS OF IT, HE WAS RIGHT. THE STREETS WERE CLEAN AND WERE LINED BY QUAINT CAFÉS AND OLD-FASHIONED BROWNSTONES. IT REALLY DIDN'T FEEL LIKE WE WERE IN BROOKLYN ANYMORE, OR IN NEW YORK CITY, FOR THAT MATTER.
SOMETIMES WHEN I WALK THROUGH HERE, I THINK THAT I AM FYODOR DOSTOYEVSKY, AND THAT THIS IS ACTUALLY ST. PETERSBURG, BEFORE IT BECAME LENINGRAD.
WOWZERS.
LATER, WHEN FRANCK WAS BEING QUIET (HIS TALK WAS LIVELIER THAN USUAL), I DECIDED TO BRING UP A CERTAIN SUBJECT THAT NEEDED ADDRESSING.
UH, FRANCK...
ABOUT THAT LETTER FROM THE PAST THING YOU WERE TALKING ABOUT EARLIER THIS MORNING...
DOES IT BY ANY CHANCE HAVE ANYTHING TO DO WITH...
JACLYN?
WHAT?
NEVER MIND.

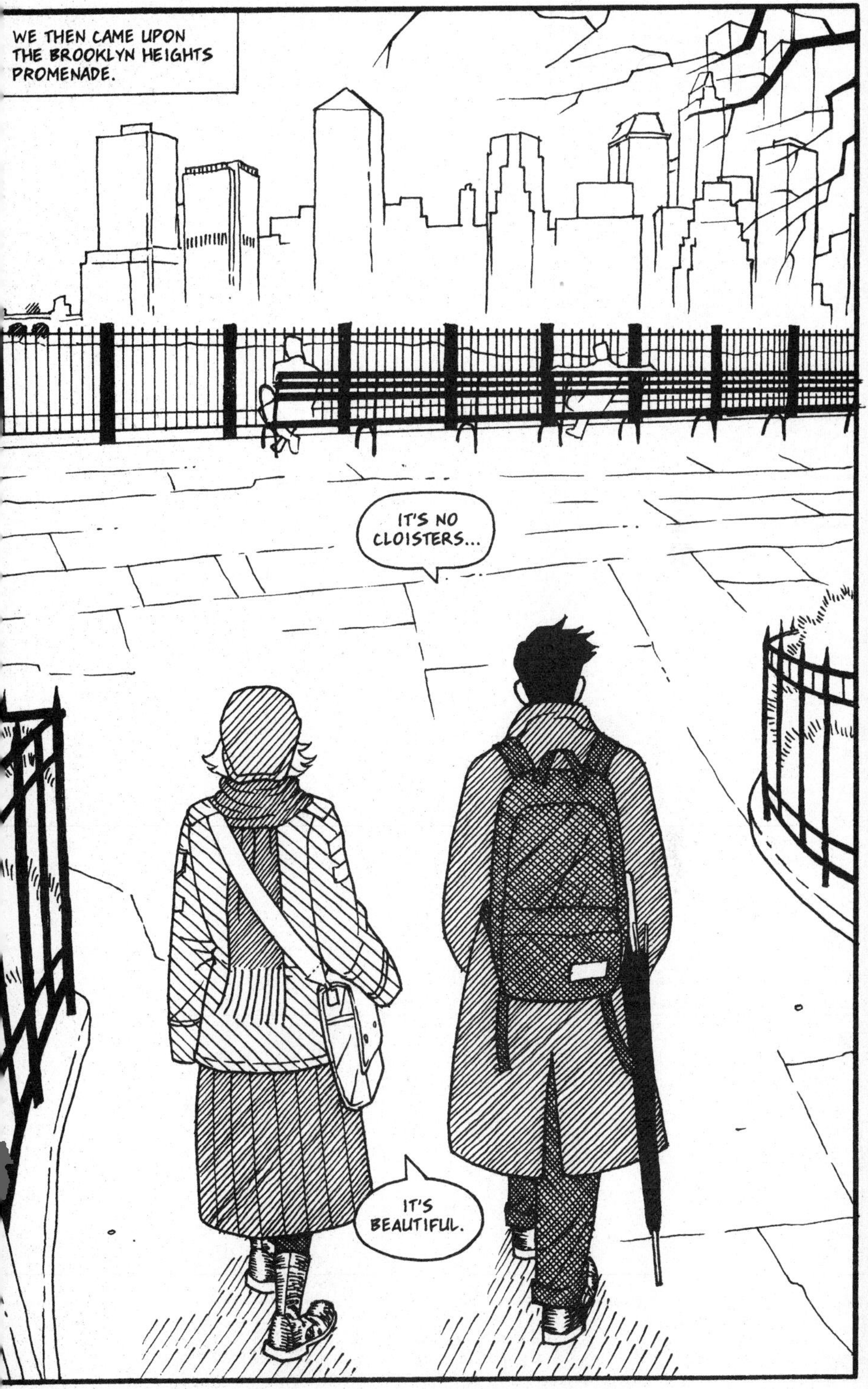
WE THEN CAME UPON THE BROOKLYN HEIGHTS PROMENADE.
IT'S NO CLOISTERS...
IT'S BEAUTIFUL.

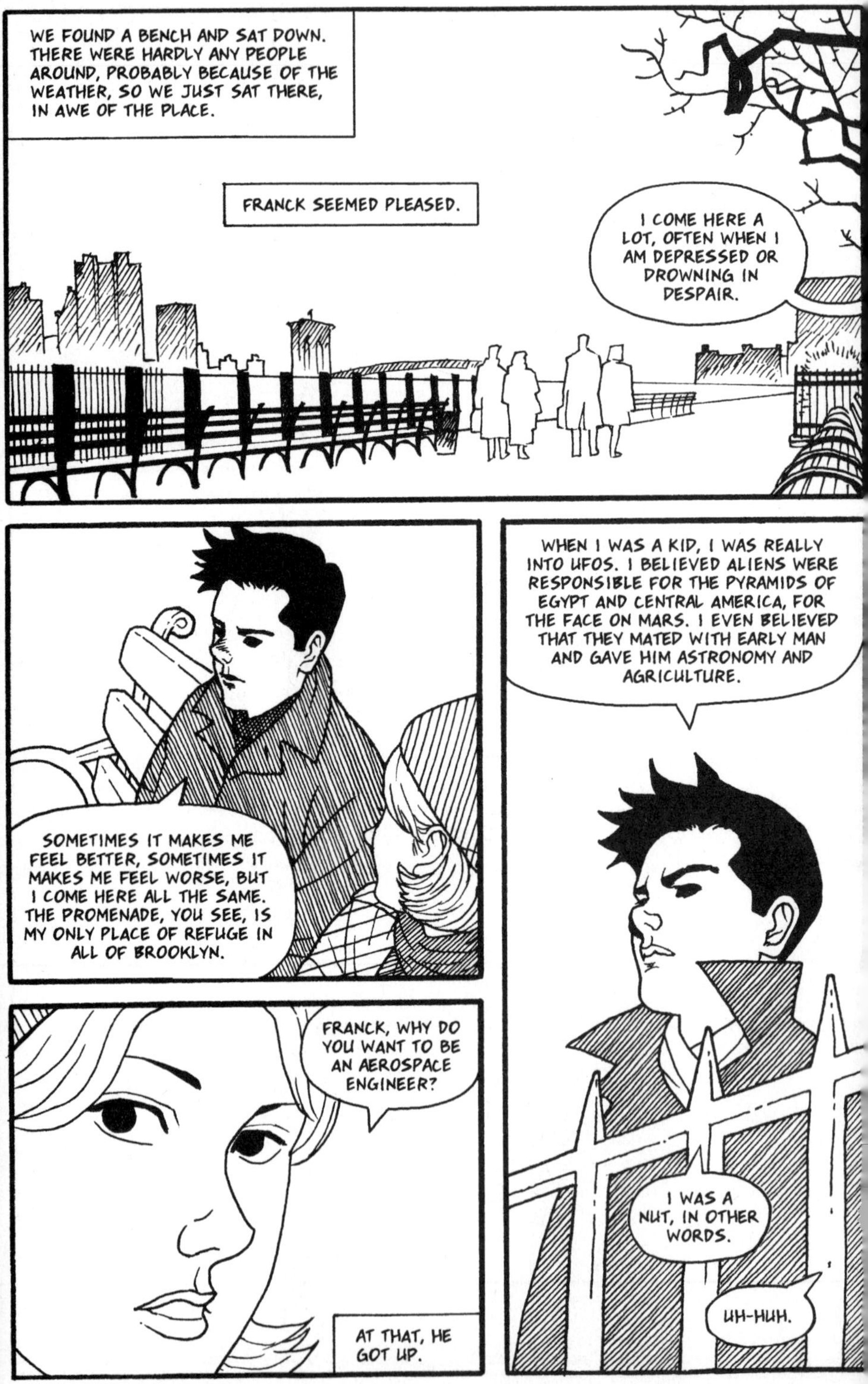
WE FOUND A BENCH AND SAT DOWN. THERE WERE HARDLY ANY PEOPLE AROUND, PROBABLY BECAUSE OF THE WEATHER, SO WE JUST SAT THERE, IN AWE OF THE PLACE.
FRANCK SEEMED PLEASED.
I COME HERE A LOT, OFTEN WHEN I AM DEPRESSED OR DROWNING IN DESPAIR.
SOMETIMES IT MAKES ME FEEL BETTER, SOMETIMES IT MAKES ME FEEL WORSE, BUT I COME HERE ALL THE SAME. THE PROMENADE, YOU SEE, IS MY ONLY PLACE OF REFUGE IN ALL OF BROOKLYN.
FRANCK, WHY DO YOU WANT TO BE AN AEROSPACE ENGINEER?
AT THAT, HE GOT UP.
WHEN I WAS A KID, I WAS REALLY INTO UFOS. I BELIEVED ALIENS WERE RESPONSIBLE FOR THE PYRAMIDS OF EGYPT AND CENTRAL AMERICA, FOR THE FACE ON MARS. I EVEN BELIEVED THAT THEY MATED WITH EARLY MAN AND GAVE HIM ASTRONOMY AND AGRICULTURE.
I WAS A NUT, IN OTHER WORDS.
UH-HUH.

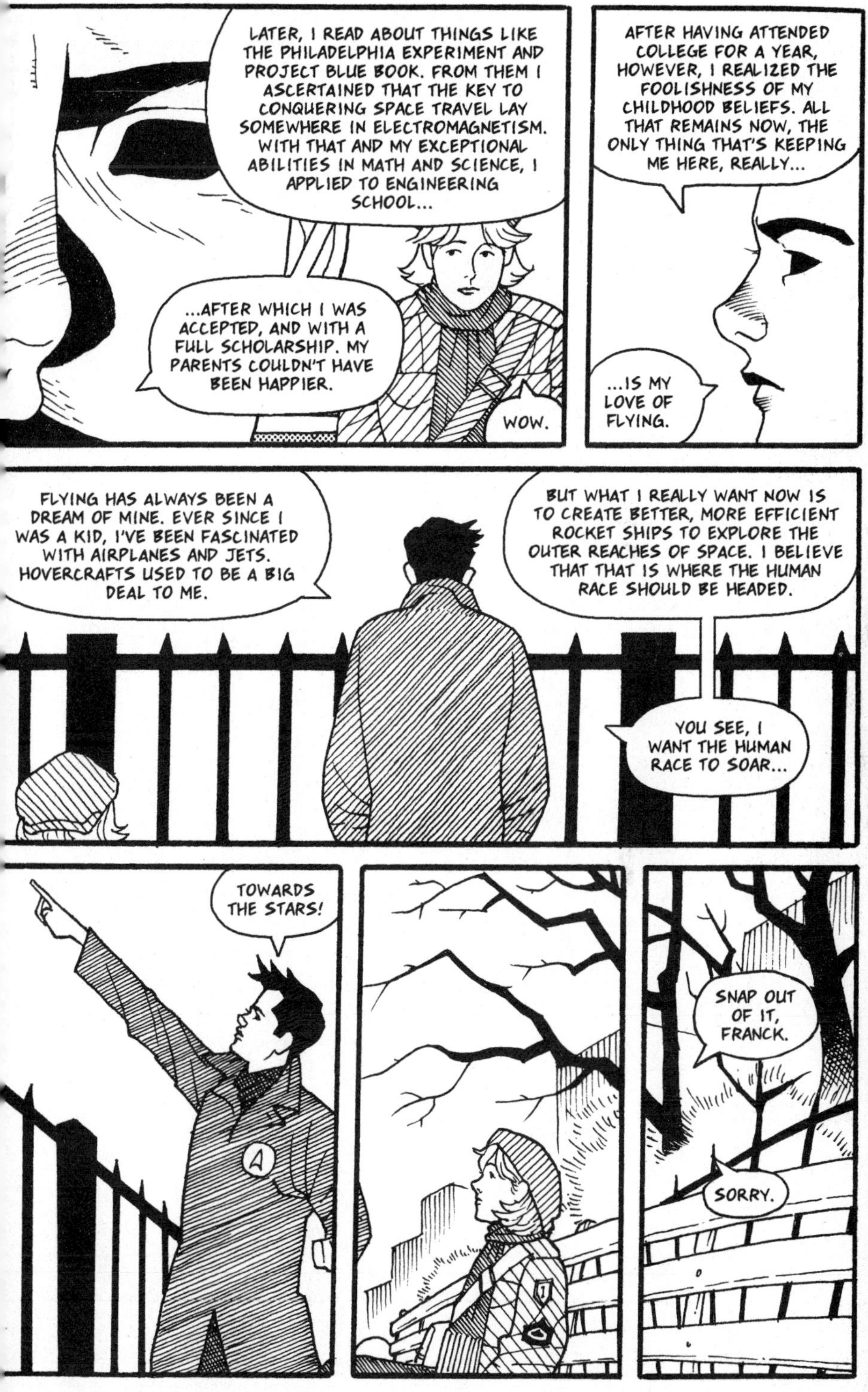
LATER, I READ ABOUT THINGS LIKE THE PHILADELPHIA EXPERIMENT AND PROJECT BLUE BOOK. FROM THEM I ASCERTAINED THAT THE KEY TO CONQUERING SPACE TRAVEL LAY SOMEWHERE IN ELECTROMAGNETISM. WITH THAT AND MY EXCEPTIONAL ABILITIES IN MATH AND SCIENCE, I APPLIED TO ENGINEERING SCHOOL...
...AFTER WHICH I WAS ACCEPTED, AND WITH A FULL SCHOLARSHIP. MY PARENTS COULDN'T HAVE BEEN HAPPIER.
WOW.
AFTER HAVING ATTENDED COLLEGE FOR A YEAR, HOWEVER, I REALIZED THE FOOLISHNESS OF MY CHILDHOOD BELIEFS. ALL THAT REMAINS NOW, THE ONLY THING THAT'S KEEPING ME HERE, REALLY...
...IS MY LOVE OF FLYING.
FLYING HAS ALWAYS BEEN A DREAM OF MINE. EVER SINCE I WAS A KID, I'VE BEEN FASCINATED WITH AIRPLANES AND JETS. HOVERCRAFTS USED TO BE A BIG DEAL TO ME.
BUT WHAT I REALLY WANT NOW IS TO CREATE BETTER, MORE EFFICIENT ROCKET SHIPS TO EXPLORE THE OUTER REACHES OF SPACE. I BELIEVE THAT THAT IS WHERE THE HUMAN RACE SHOULD BE HEADED.
YOU SEE, I WANT THE HUMAN RACE TO SOAR...
TOWARDS THE STARS!
SNAP OUT OF IT, FRANCK.
SORRY.

I THINK IT'S COOL THAT YOU KNOW WHAT YOU WANT TO DO. I WISH I DID.

DON'T YOU WORRY ABOUT THAT. IT'S QUITE COMMON FOR FIRST YEAR STUDENTS NOT TO KNOW WHAT KIND OF CAREER THEY WANT TO PURSUE. JUST HANG IN THERE. IT'LL COME TO YOU EVENTUALLY.

I HOPE SO.

I KNOW IT WILL.

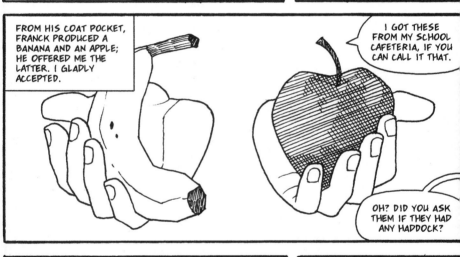

FROM HIS COAT POCKET, FRANCK PRODUCED A BANANA AND AN APPLE; HE OFFERED ME THE LATTER. I GLADLY ACCEPTED.

I GOT THESE FROM MY SCHOOL CAFETERIA, IF YOU CAN CALL IT THAT.

OH? DID YOU ASK THEM IF THEY HAD ANY HADDOCK?

HUH?

NOTHING.

IT STARTED TO RAIN, SO WE PUT OUR FRUIT AWAY FOR LATER.

FRANCK OPENED HIS UMBRELLA AND WE GOT UP TO LEAVE.

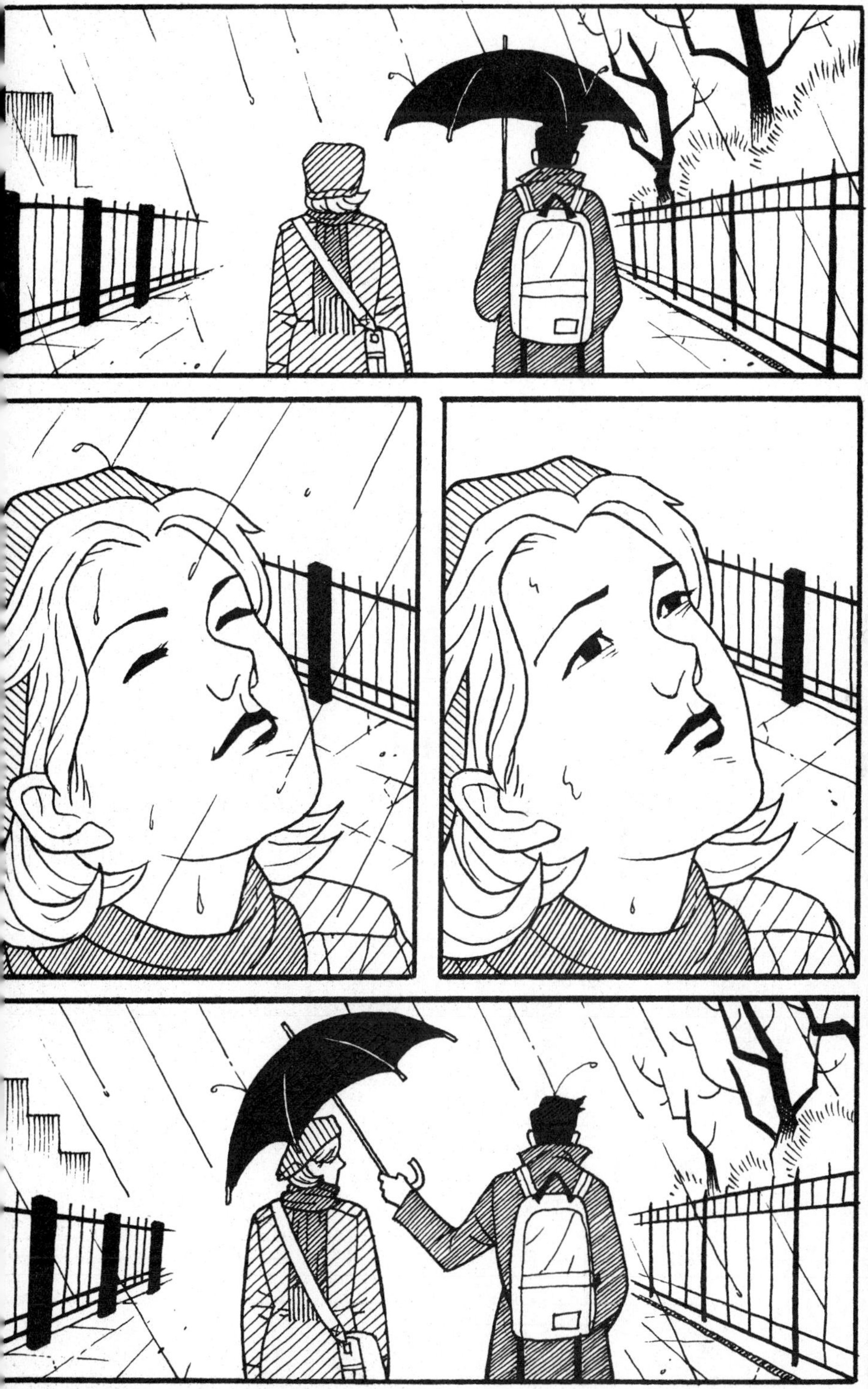

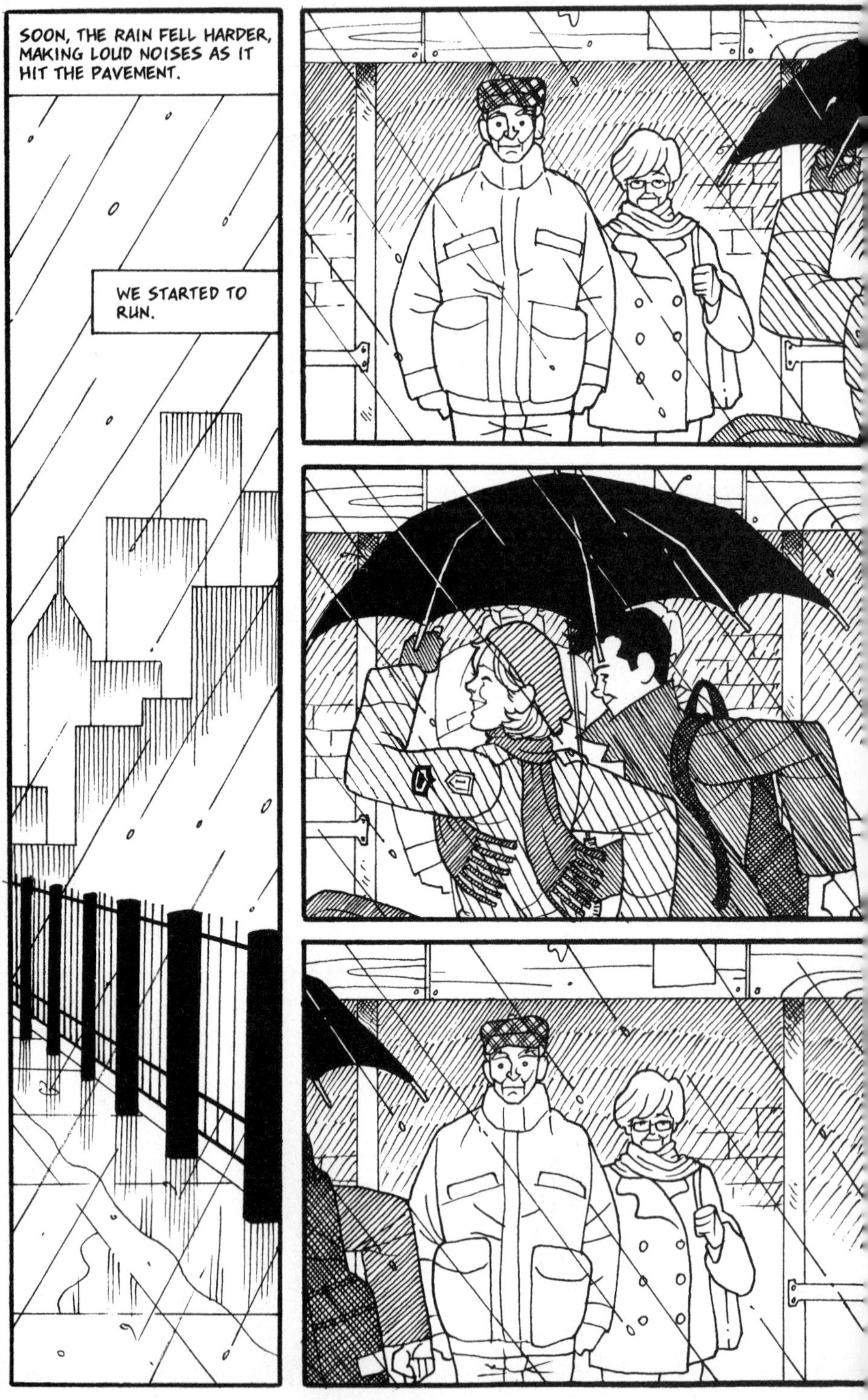
SOON, THE RAIN FELL HARDER, MAKING LOUD NOISES AS IT HIT THE PAVEMENT.
WE STARTED TO RUN.

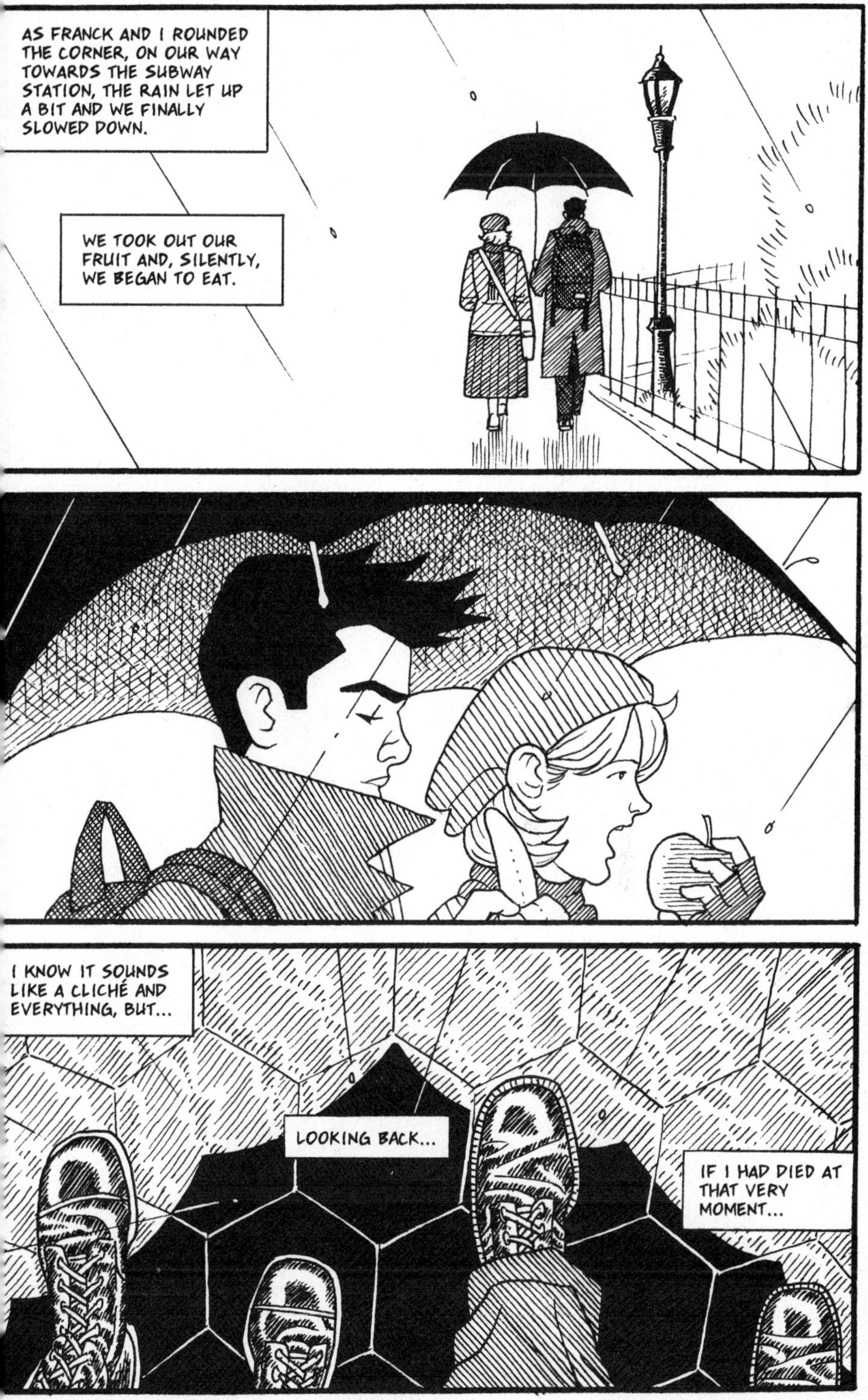
AS FRANCK AND I ROUNDED THE CORNER, ON OUR WAY TOWARDS THE SUBWAY STATION, THE RAIN LET UP A BIT AND WE FINALLY SLOWED DOWN.
WE TOOK OUT OUR FRUIT AND, SILENTLY, WE BEGAN TO EAT.
I KNOW IT SOUNDS LIKE A CLICHÉ AND EVERYTHING, BUT...
LOOKING BACK...
IF I HAD DIED AT THAT VERY MOMENT...

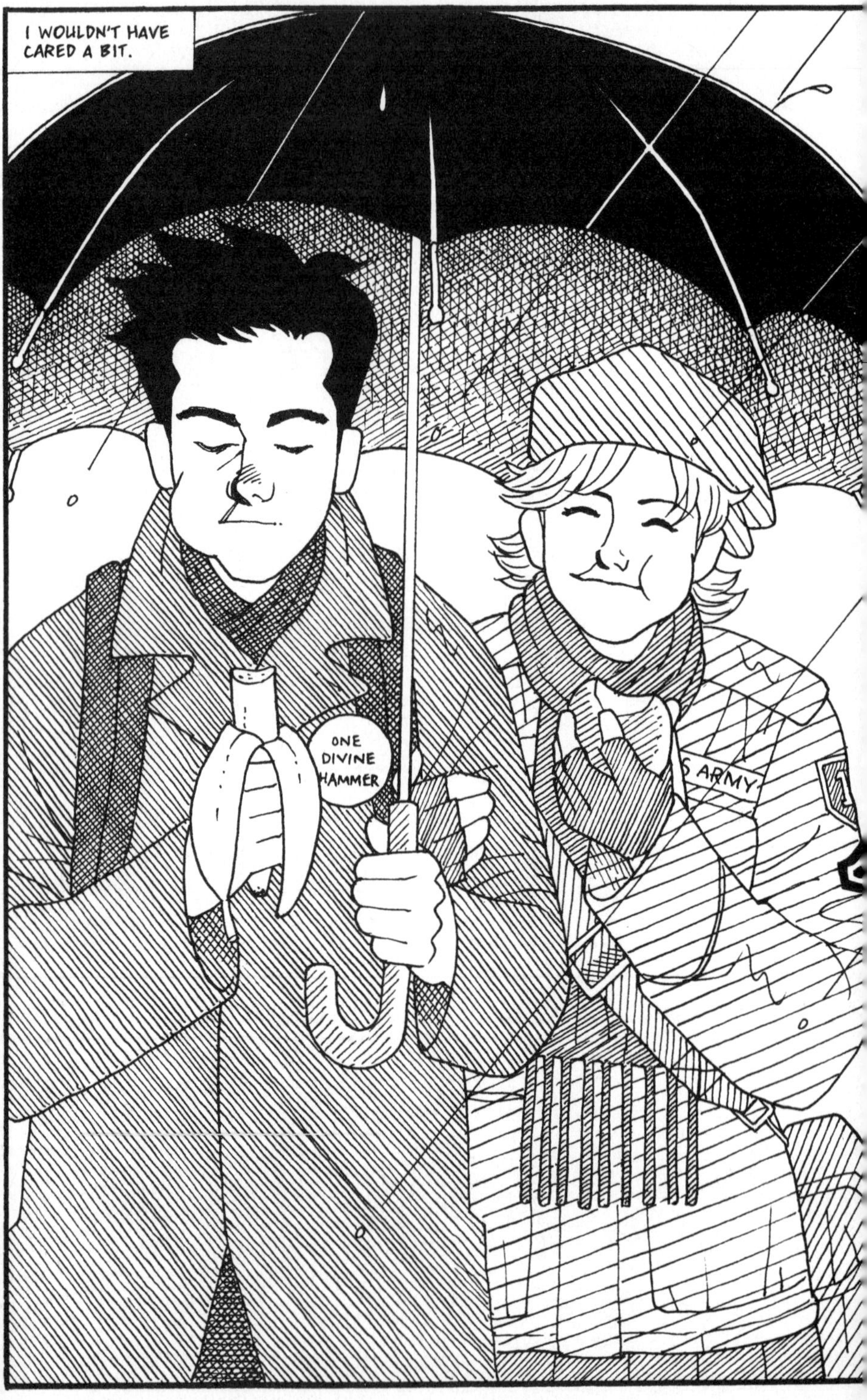
I WOULDN'T HAVE CARED A BIT.
ONE DIVINE HAMMER
S ARMY

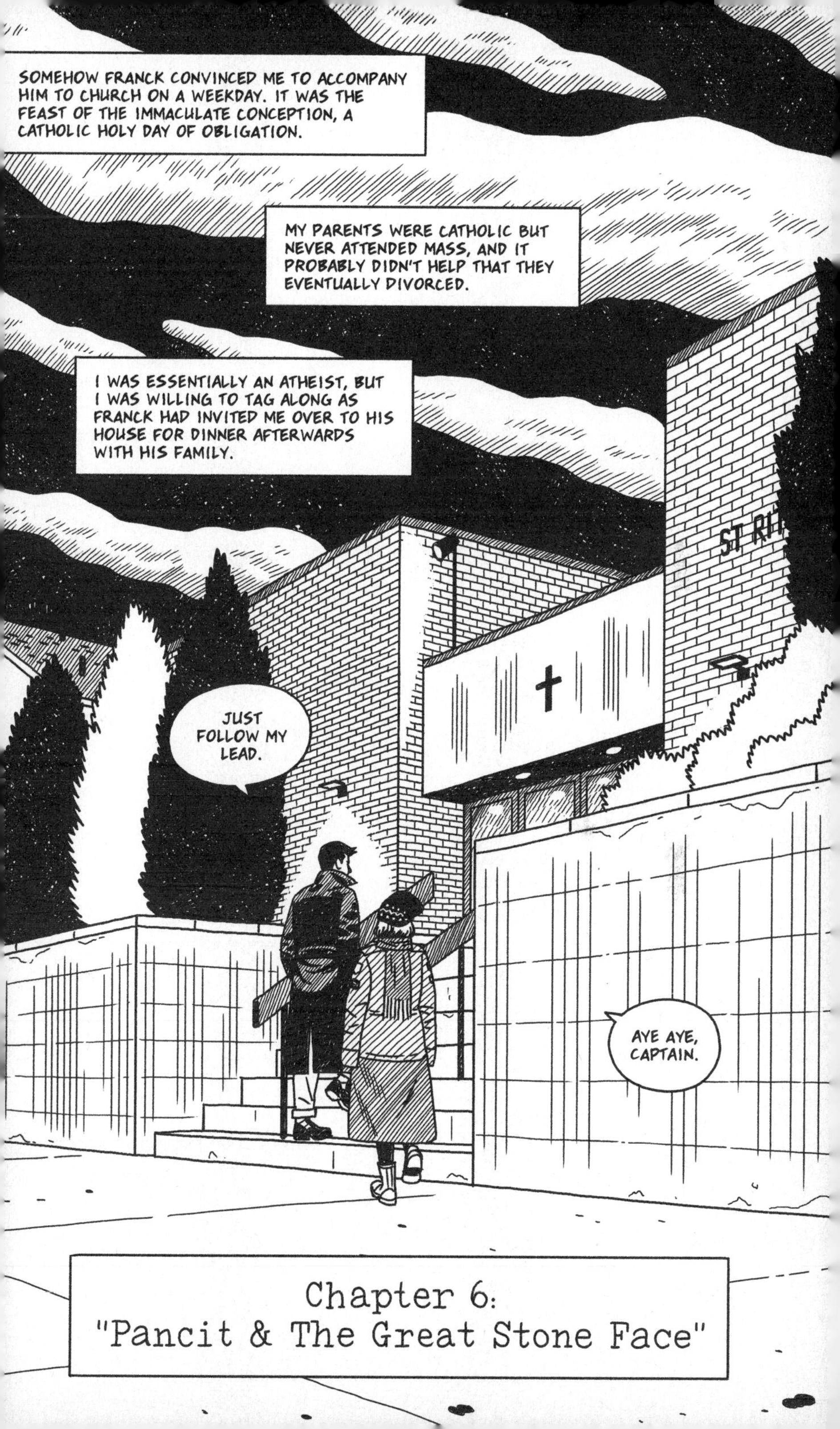
SOMEHOW FRANCK CONVINCED ME TO ACCOMPANY HIM TO CHURCH ON A WEEKDAY. IT WAS THE FEAST OF THE IMMACULATE CONCEPTION, A CATHOLIC HOLY DAY OF OBLIGATION.
MY PARENTS WERE CATHOLIC BUT NEVER ATTENDED MASS, AND IT PROBABLY DIDN'T HELP THAT THEY EVENTUALLY DIVORCED.
I WAS ESSENTIALLY AN ATHEIST, BUT I WAS WILLING TO TAG ALONG AS FRANCK HAD INVITED ME OVER TO HIS HOUSE FOR DINNER AFTERWARDS WITH HIS FAMILY.
JUST FOLLOW MY LEAD.
AYE AYE, CAPTAIN.

Chapter 6:
"Pancit & The Great Stone Face"

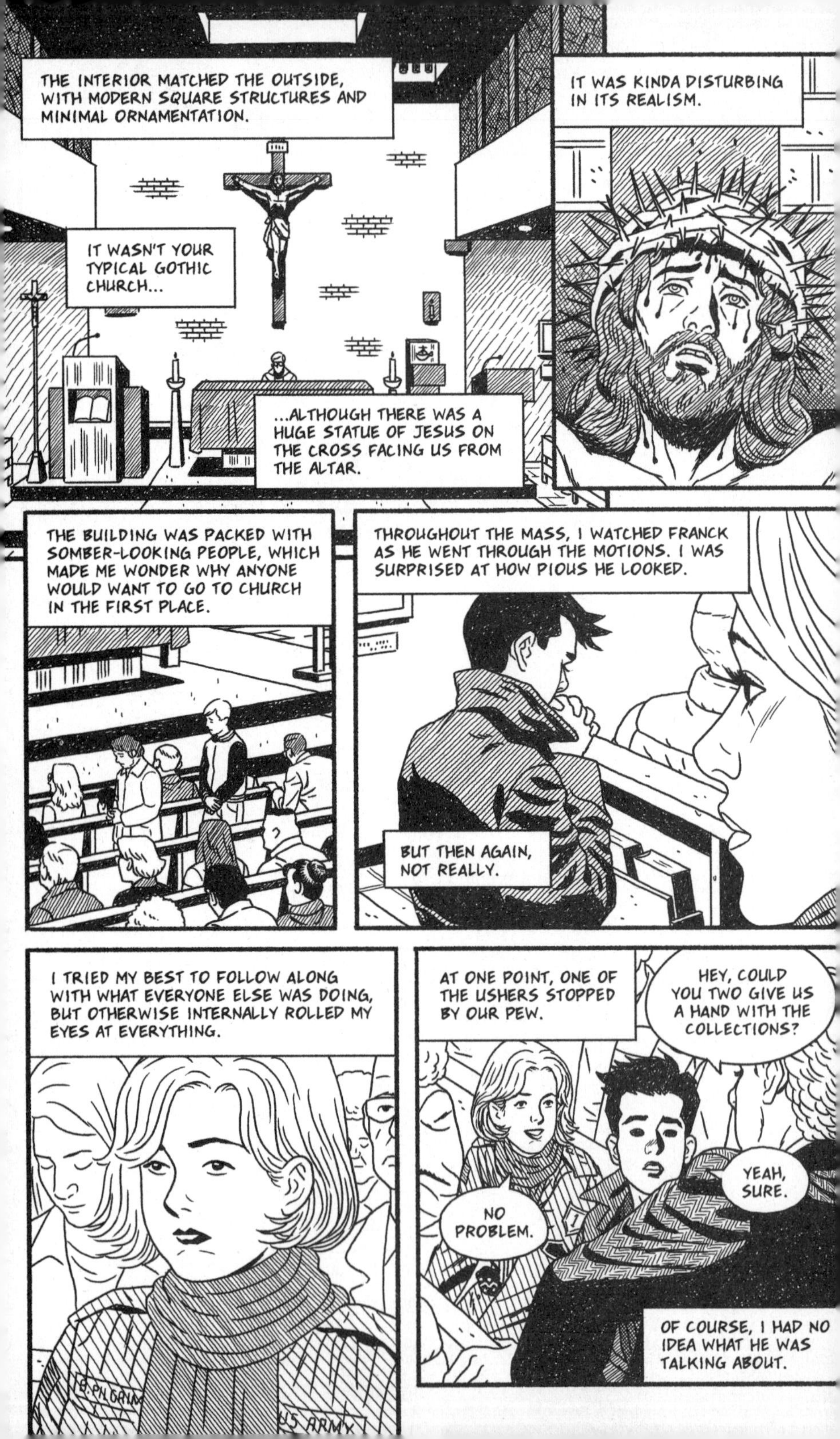
THE INTERIOR MATCHED THE OUTSIDE, WITH MODERN SQUARE STRUCTURES AND MINIMAL ORNAMENTATION.
IT WASN'T YOUR TYPICAL GOTHIC CHURCH...
...ALTHOUGH THERE WAS A HUGE STATUE OF JESUS ON THE CROSS FACING US FROM THE ALTAR.
IT WAS KINDA DISTURBING IN ITS REALISM.
THE BUILDING WAS PACKED WITH SOMBER-LOOKING PEOPLE, WHICH MADE ME WONDER WHY ANYONE WOULD WANT TO GO TO CHURCH IN THE FIRST PLACE.
THROUGHOUT THE MASS, I WATCHED FRANCK AS HE WENT THROUGH THE MOTIONS. I WAS SURPRISED AT HOW PIOUS HE LOOKED.
BUT THEN AGAIN, NOT REALLY.
I TRIED MY BEST TO FOLLOW ALONG WITH WHAT EVERYONE ELSE WAS DOING, BUT OTHERWISE INTERNALLY ROLLED MY EYES AT EVERYTHING.
US ARMY
AT ONE POINT, ONE OF THE USHERS STOPPED BY OUR PEW.
HEY, COULD YOU TWO GIVE US A HAND WITH THE COLLECTIONS?
NO PROBLEM.
YEAH, SURE.
OF COURSE, I HAD NO IDEA WHAT HE WAS TALKING ABOUT.

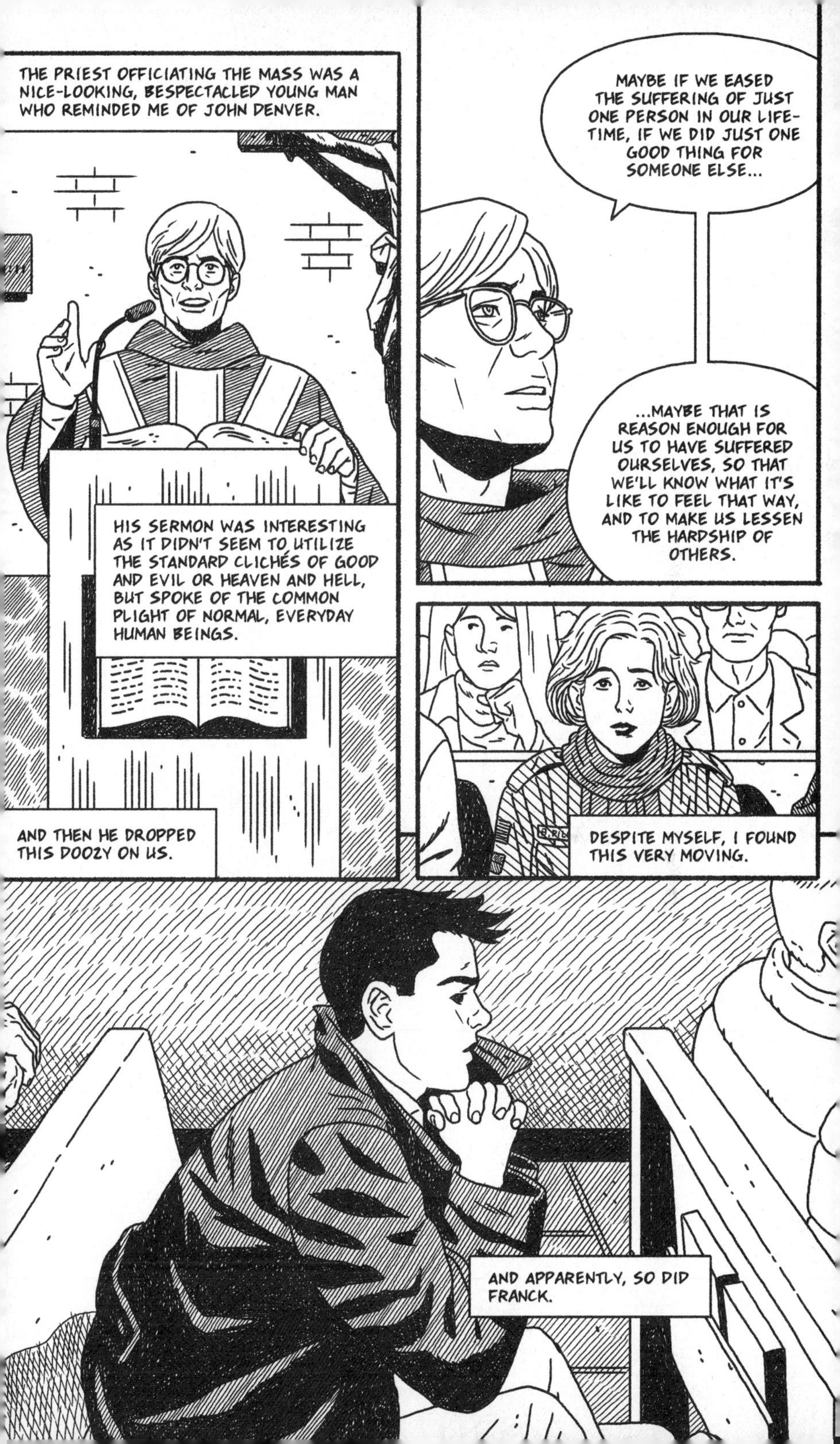
THE PRIEST OFFICIATING THE MASS WAS A NICE-LOOKING, BESPECTACLED YOUNG MAN WHO REMINDED ME OF JOHN DENVER.
HIS SERMON WAS INTERESTING AS IT DIDN'T SEEM TO UTILIZE THE STANDARD CLICHÉS OF GOOD AND EVIL OR HEAVEN AND HELL, BUT SPOKE OF THE COMMON PLIGHT OF NORMAL, EVERYDAY HUMAN BEINGS.
AND THEN HE DROPPED THIS DOOZY ON US.
MAYBE IF WE EASED THE SUFFERING OF JUST ONE PERSON IN OUR LIFE-TIME, IF WE DID JUST ONE GOOD THING FOR SOMEONE ELSE...
...MAYBE THAT IS REASON ENOUGH FOR US TO HAVE SUFFERED OURSELVES, SO THAT WE'LL KNOW WHAT IT'S LIKE TO FEEL THAT WAY, AND TO MAKE US LESSEN THE HARDSHIP OF OTHERS.
DESPITE MYSELF, I FOUND THIS VERY MOVING.
AND APPARENTLY, SO DID FRANCK.

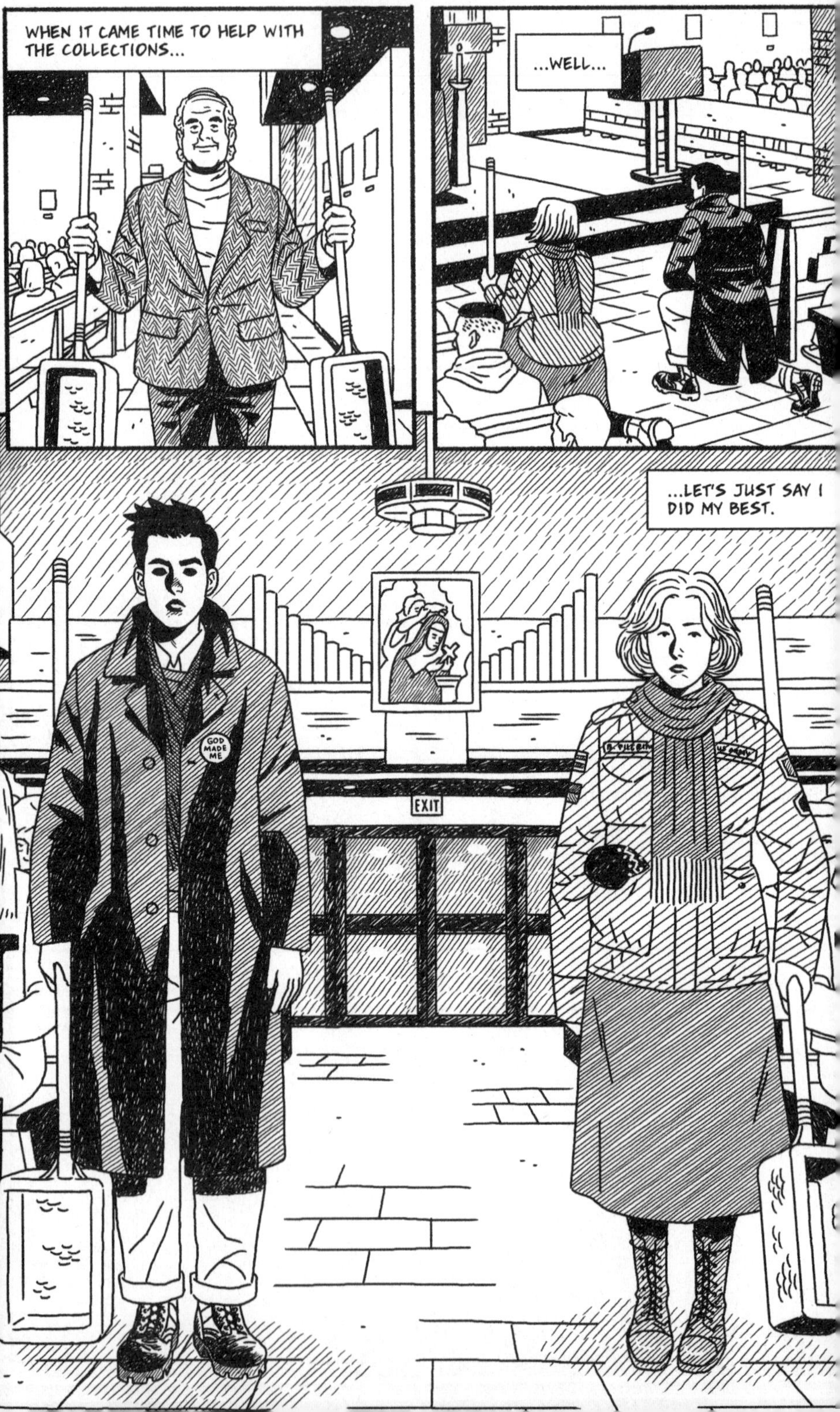
WHEN IT CAME TIME TO HELP WITH THE COLLECTIONS...
...WELL...
...LET'S JUST SAY I DID MY BEST.
GOD MADE ME
EXIT

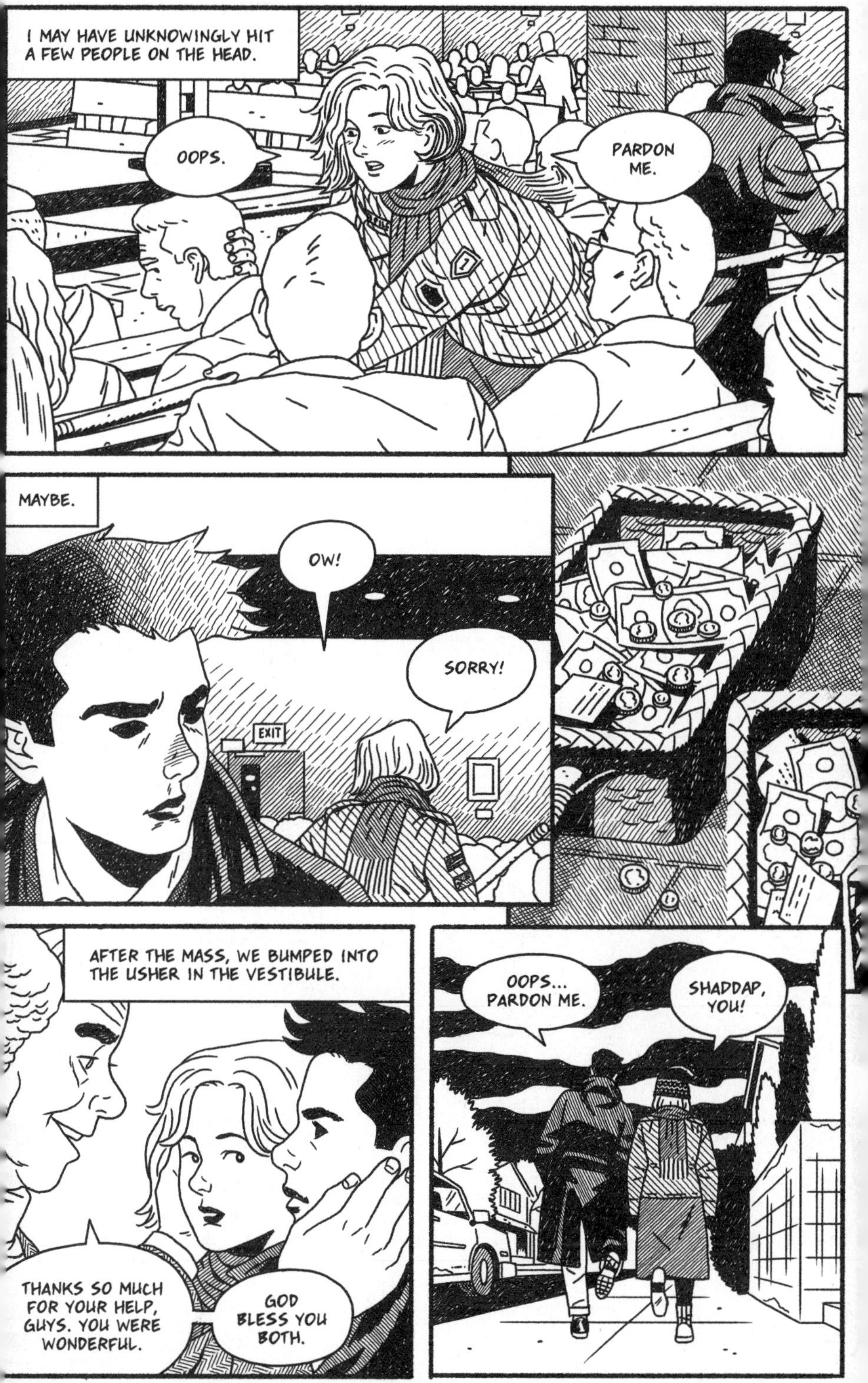
I MAY HAVE UNKNOWINGLY HIT A FEW PEOPLE ON THE HEAD.
OOPS.
PARDON ME.
MAYBE.
OW!
SORRY!
EXIT
AFTER THE MASS, WE BUMPED INTO THE USHER IN THE VESTIBULE.
THANKS SO MUCH FOR YOUR HELP, GUYS. YOU WERE WONDERFUL.
GOD BLESS YOU BOTH.
OOPS... PARDON ME.
SHADDAP, YOU!

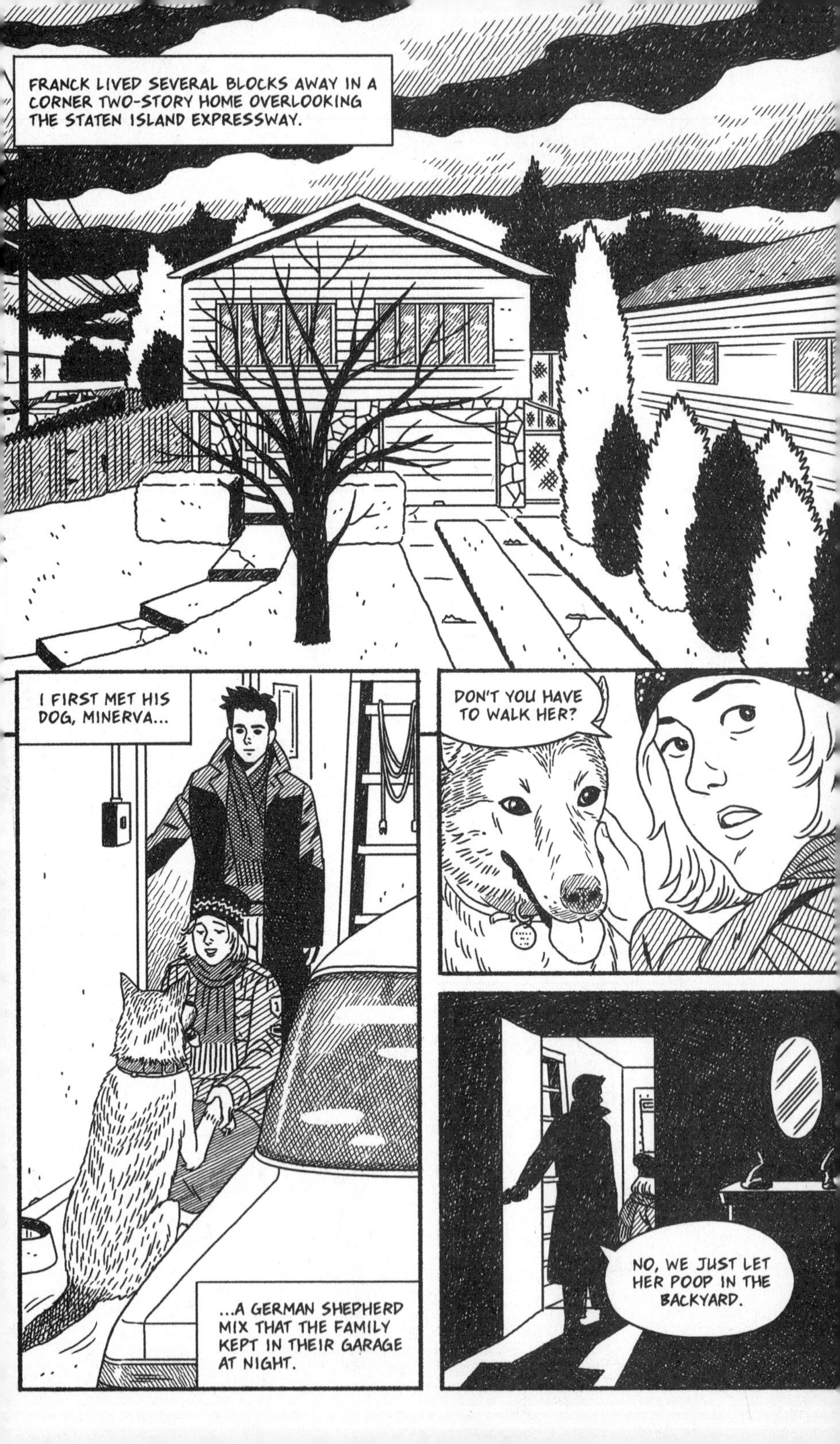
FRANCK LIVED SEVERAL BLOCKS AWAY IN A CORNER TWO-STORY HOME OVERLOOKING THE STATEN ISLAND EXPRESSWAY.
I FIRST MET HIS DOG, MINERVA...
...A GERMAN SHEPHERD MIX THAT THE FAMILY KEPT IN THEIR GARAGE AT NIGHT.
DON'T YOU HAVE TO WALK HER?
NO, WE JUST LET HER POOP IN THE BACKYARD.

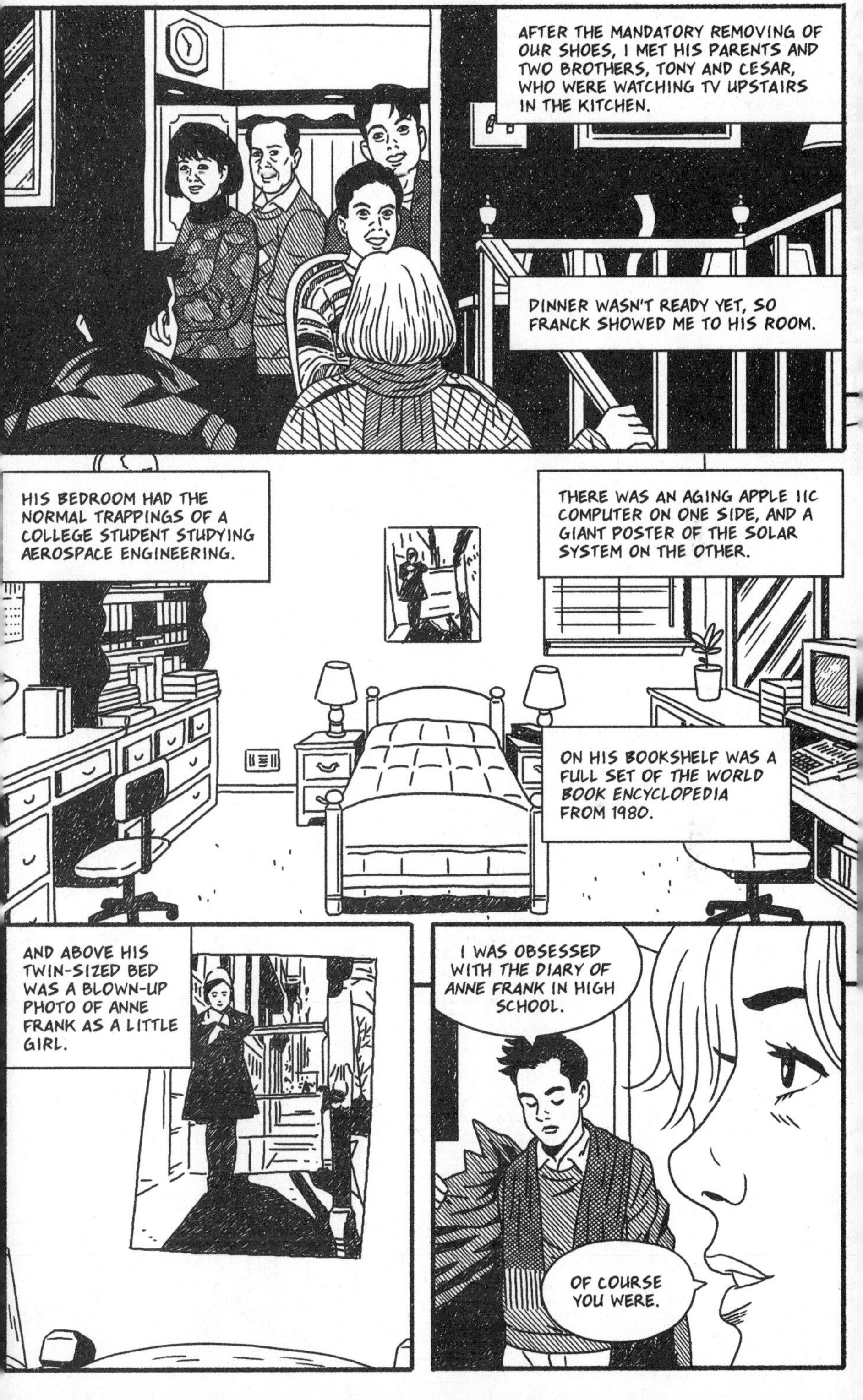
AFTER THE MANDATORY REMOVING OF OUR SHOES, I MET HIS PARENTS AND TWO BROTHERS, TONY AND CESAR, WHO WERE WATCHING TV UPSTAIRS IN THE KITCHEN.
DINNER WASN'T READY YET, SO FRANCK SHOWED ME TO HIS ROOM.
HIS BEDROOM HAD THE NORMAL TRAPPINGS OF A COLLEGE STUDENT STUDYING AEROSPACE ENGINEERING.
THERE WAS AN AGING APPLE IIC COMPUTER ON ONE SIDE, AND A GIANT POSTER OF THE SOLAR SYSTEM ON THE OTHER.
ON HIS BOOKSHELF WAS A FULL SET OF THE WORLD BOOK ENCYCLOPEDIA FROM 1980.
AND ABOVE HIS TWIN-SIZED BED WAS A BLOWN-UP PHOTO OF ANNE FRANK AS A LITTLE GIRL.
I WAS OBSESSED WITH THE DIARY OF ANNE FRANK IN HIGH SCHOOL.
OF COURSE YOU WERE.

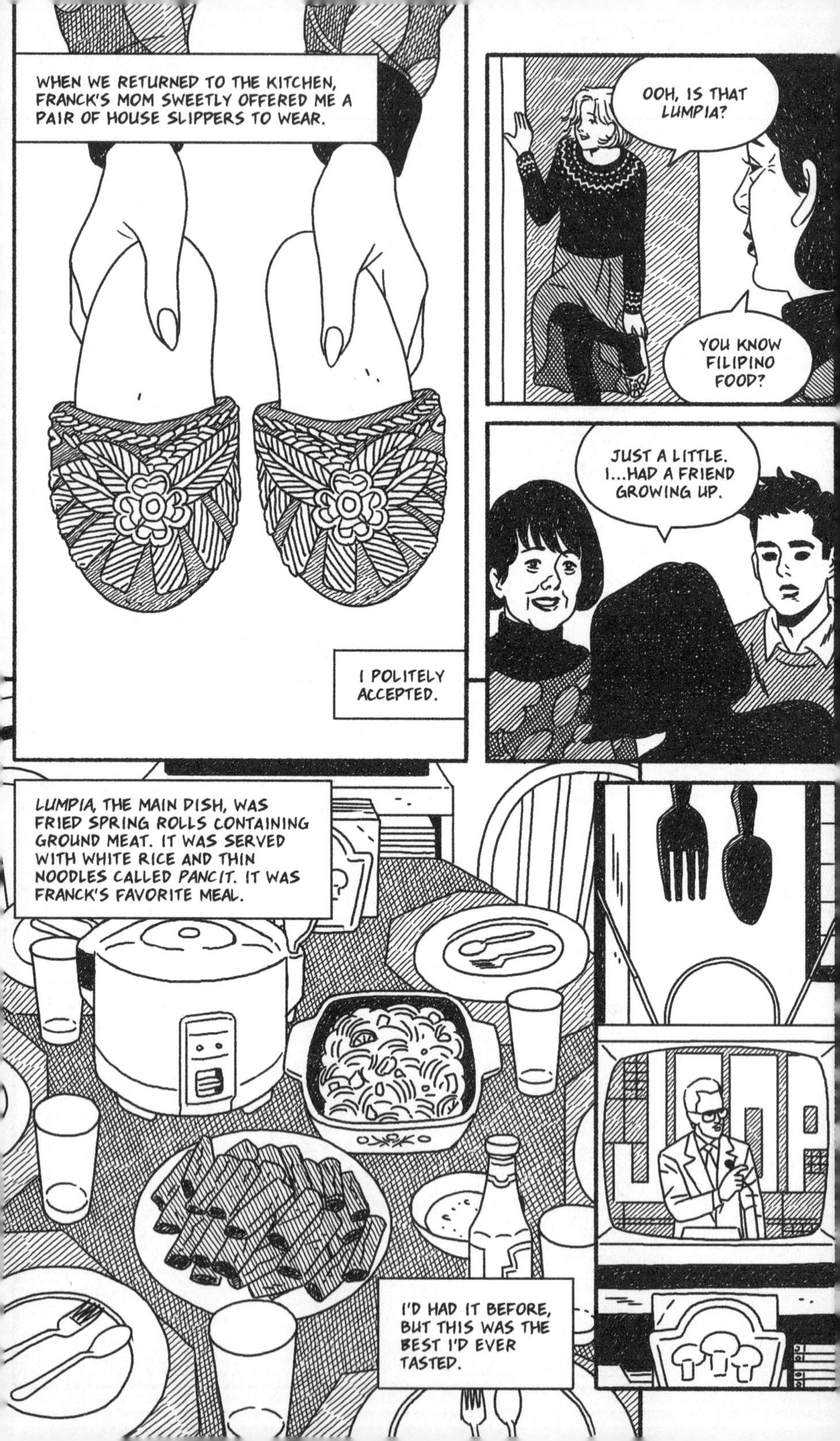
WHEN WE RETURNED TO THE KITCHEN, FRANCK'S MOM SWEETLY OFFERED ME A PAIR OF HOUSE SLIPPERS TO WEAR.
I POLITELY ACCEPTED.
OOH, IS THAT *LUMPIA*?
YOU KNOW FILIPINO FOOD?
JUST A LITTLE. I...HAD A FRIEND GROWING UP.
LUMPIA, THE MAIN DISH, WAS FRIED SPRING ROLLS CONTAINING GROUND MEAT. IT WAS SERVED WITH WHITE RICE AND THIN NOODLES CALLED *PANCIT*. IT WAS FRANCK'S FAVORITE MEAL.
I'D HAD IT BEFORE, BUT THIS WAS THE BEST I'D EVER TASTED.

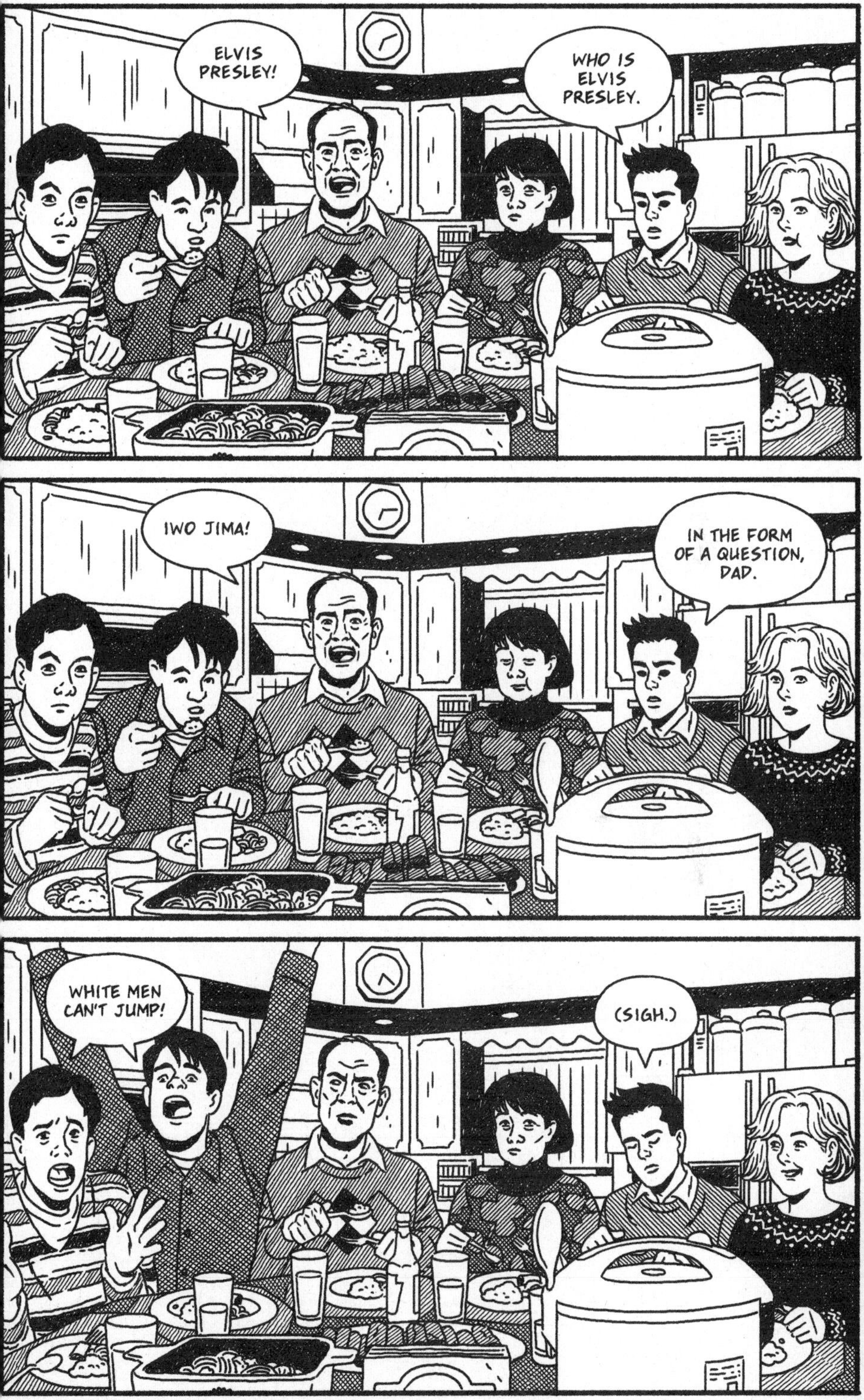
ELVIS PRESLEY!
WHO IS ELVIS PRESLEY.
IWO JIMA!
IN THE FORM OF A QUESTION, DAD.
WHITE MEN CAN'T JUMP!
(SIGH.)

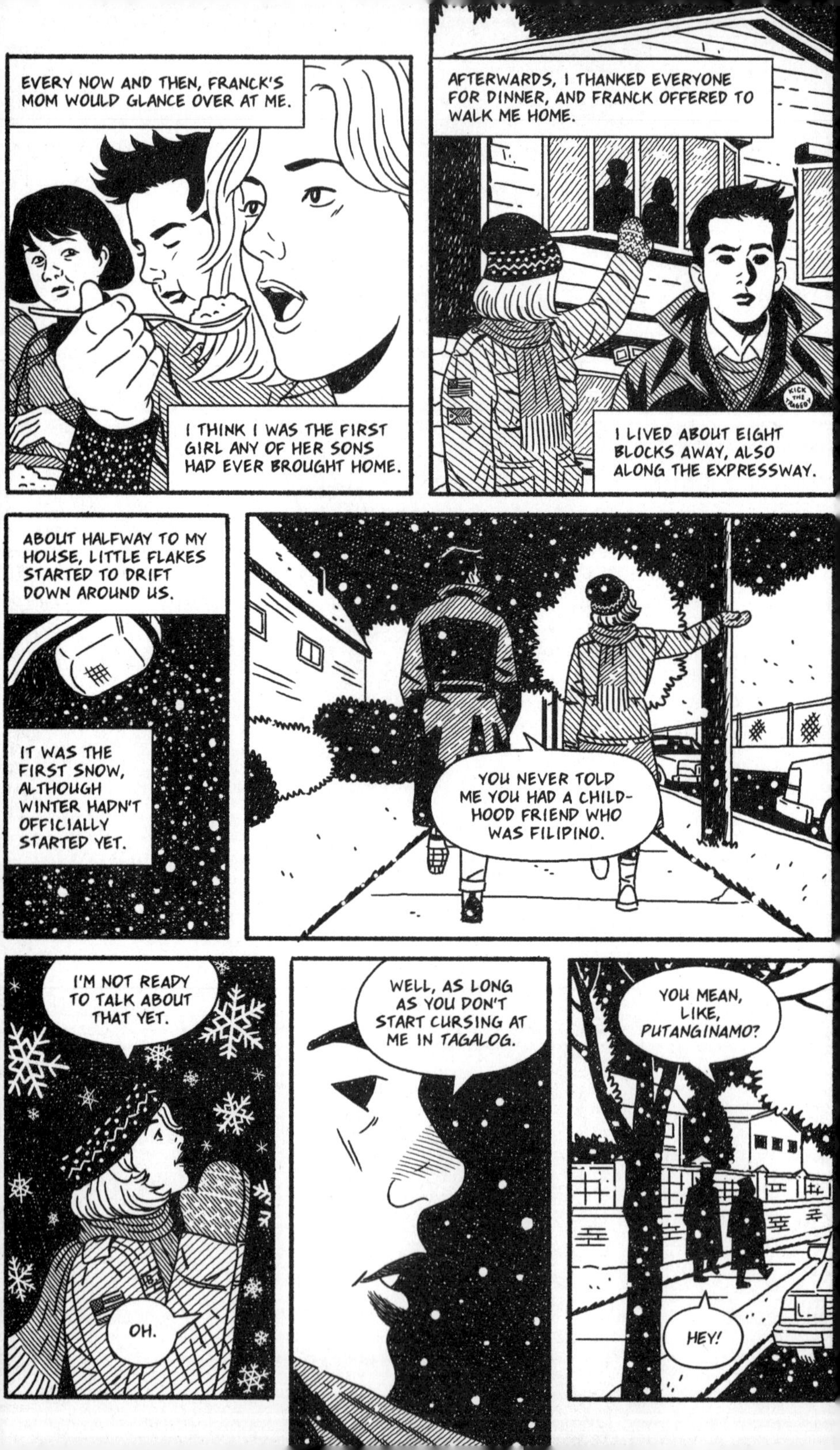
EVERY NOW AND THEN, FRANCK'S MOM WOULD GLANCE OVER AT ME.
I THINK I WAS THE FIRST GIRL ANY OF HER SONS HAD EVER BROUGHT HOME.
AFTERWARDS, I THANKED EVERYONE FOR DINNER, AND FRANCK OFFERED TO WALK ME HOME.
KICK THE TRAGEDY
I LIVED ABOUT EIGHT BLOCKS AWAY, ALSO ALONG THE EXPRESSWAY.
ABOUT HALFWAY TO MY HOUSE, LITTLE FLAKES STARTED TO DRIFT DOWN AROUND US.
IT WAS THE FIRST SNOW, ALTHOUGH WINTER HADN'T OFFICIALLY STARTED YET.
YOU NEVER TOLD ME YOU HAD A CHILDHOOD FRIEND WHO WAS FILIPINO.
I'M NOT READY TO TALK ABOUT THAT YET.
OH.
WELL, AS LONG AS YOU DON'T START CURSING AT ME IN TAGALOG.
YOU MEAN, LIKE, PUTANGINAMO?
HEY!

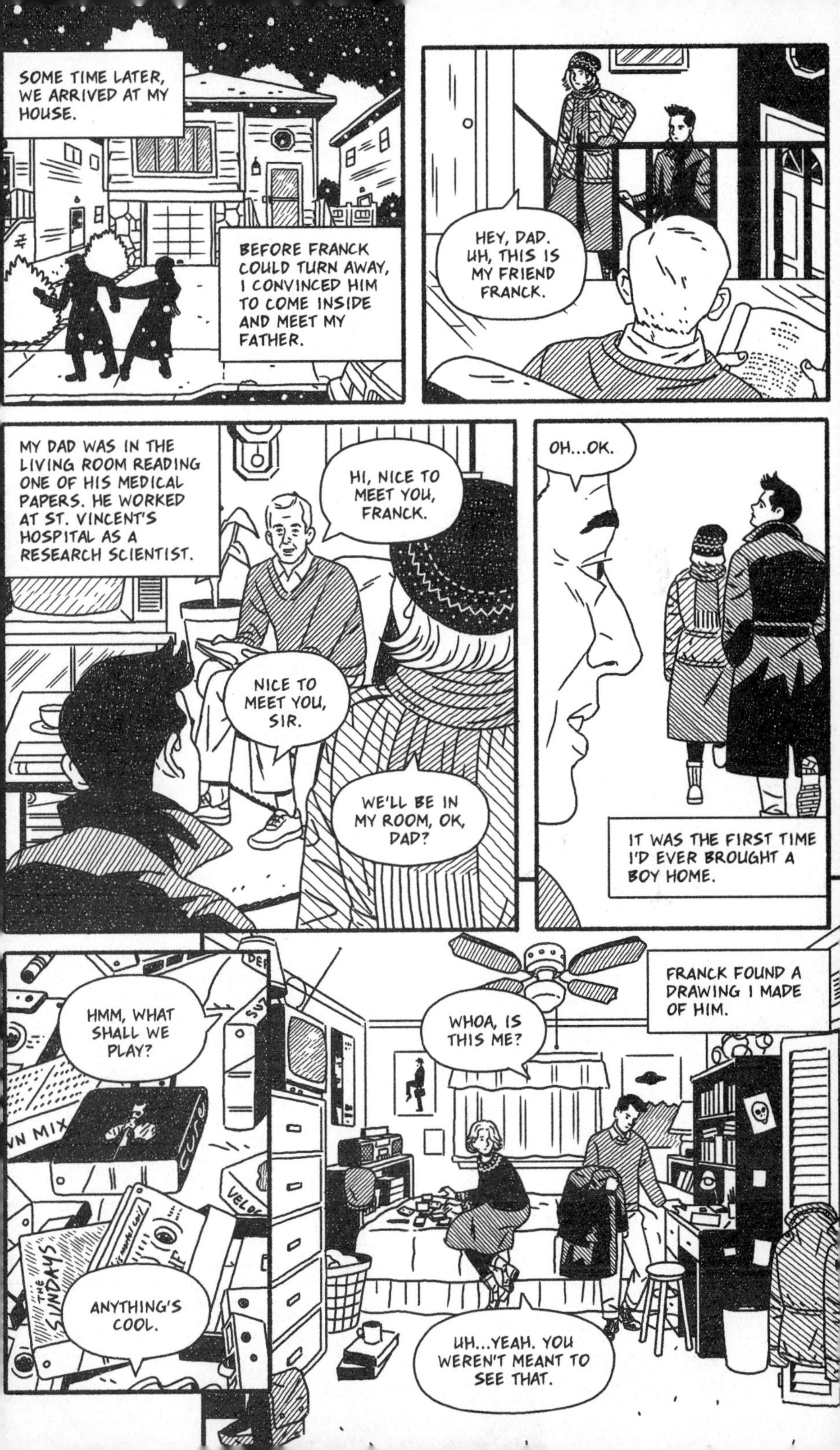
SOME TIME LATER, WE ARRIVED AT MY HOUSE.
BEFORE FRANCK COULD TURN AWAY, I CONVINCED HIM TO COME INSIDE AND MEET MY FATHER.
HEY, DAD. UH, THIS IS MY FRIEND FRANCK.
MY DAD WAS IN THE LIVING ROOM READING ONE OF HIS MEDICAL PAPERS. HE WORKED AT ST. VINCENT'S HOSPITAL AS A RESEARCH SCIENTIST.
HI, NICE TO MEET YOU, FRANCK.
NICE TO MEET YOU, SIR.
WE'LL BE IN MY ROOM, OK, DAD?
OH...OK.
IT WAS THE FIRST TIME I'D EVER BROUGHT A BOY HOME.
HMM, WHAT SHALL WE PLAY?
cure
THE SUNDAYS
ANYTHING'S COOL.
FRANCK FOUND A DRAWING I MADE OF HIM.
WHOA, IS THIS ME?
UH...YEAH. YOU WEREN'T MEANT TO SEE THAT.

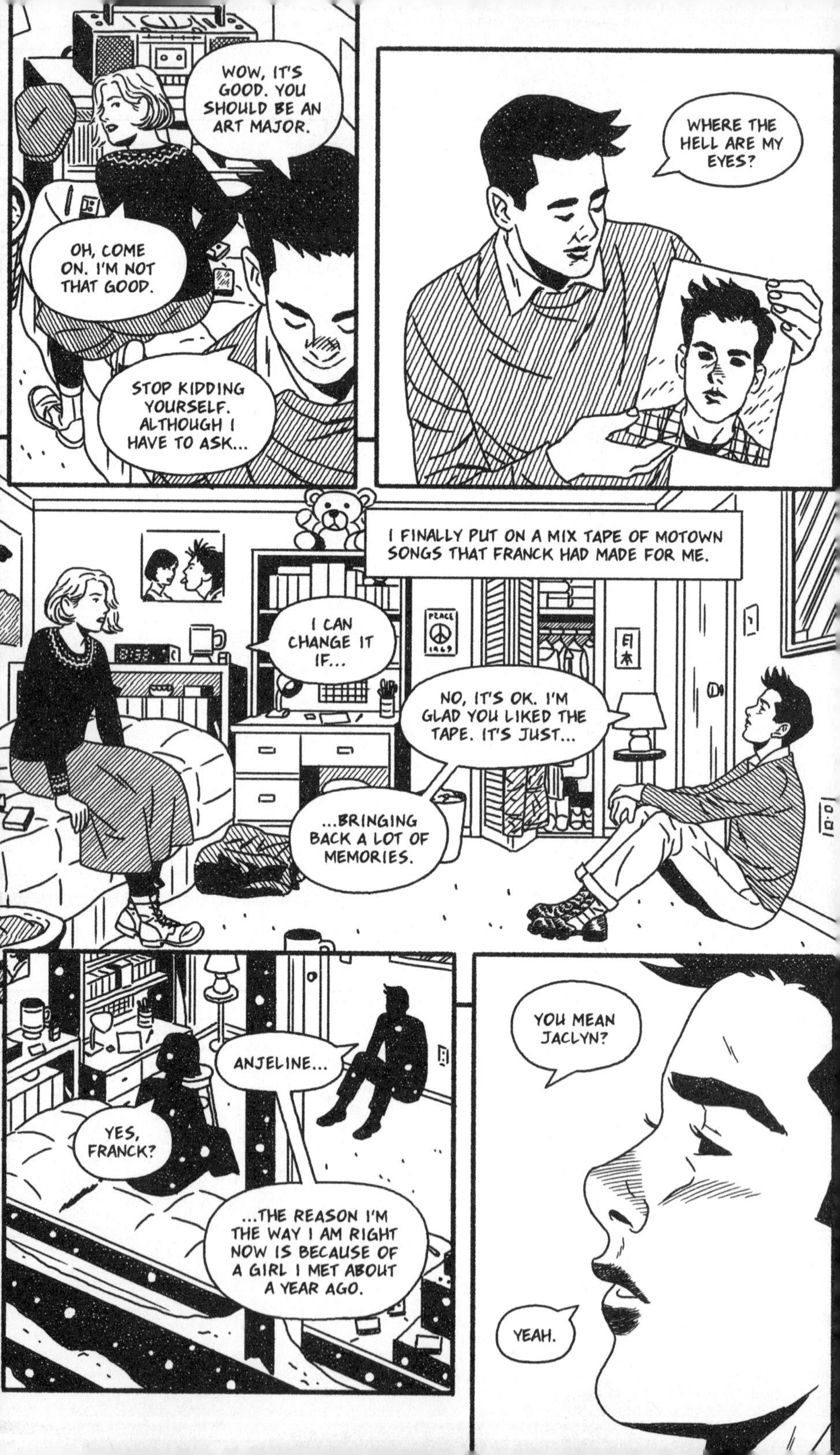
WOW, IT'S GOOD. YOU SHOULD BE AN ART MAJOR.
OH, COME ON. I'M NOT THAT GOOD.
STOP KIDDING YOURSELF. ALTHOUGH I HAVE TO ASK...
WHERE THE HELL ARE MY EYES?
I FINALLY PUT ON A MIX TAPE OF MOTOWN SONGS THAT FRANCK HAD MADE FOR ME.
PEACE 1969
I CAN CHANGE IT IF...
NO, IT'S OK. I'M GLAD YOU LIKED THE TAPE. IT'S JUST...
...BRINGING BACK A LOT OF MEMORIES.
ANJELINE...
YES, FRANCK?
...THE REASON I'M THE WAY I AM RIGHT NOW IS BECAUSE OF A GIRL I MET ABOUT A YEAR AGO.
YOU MEAN JACLYN?
YEAH.

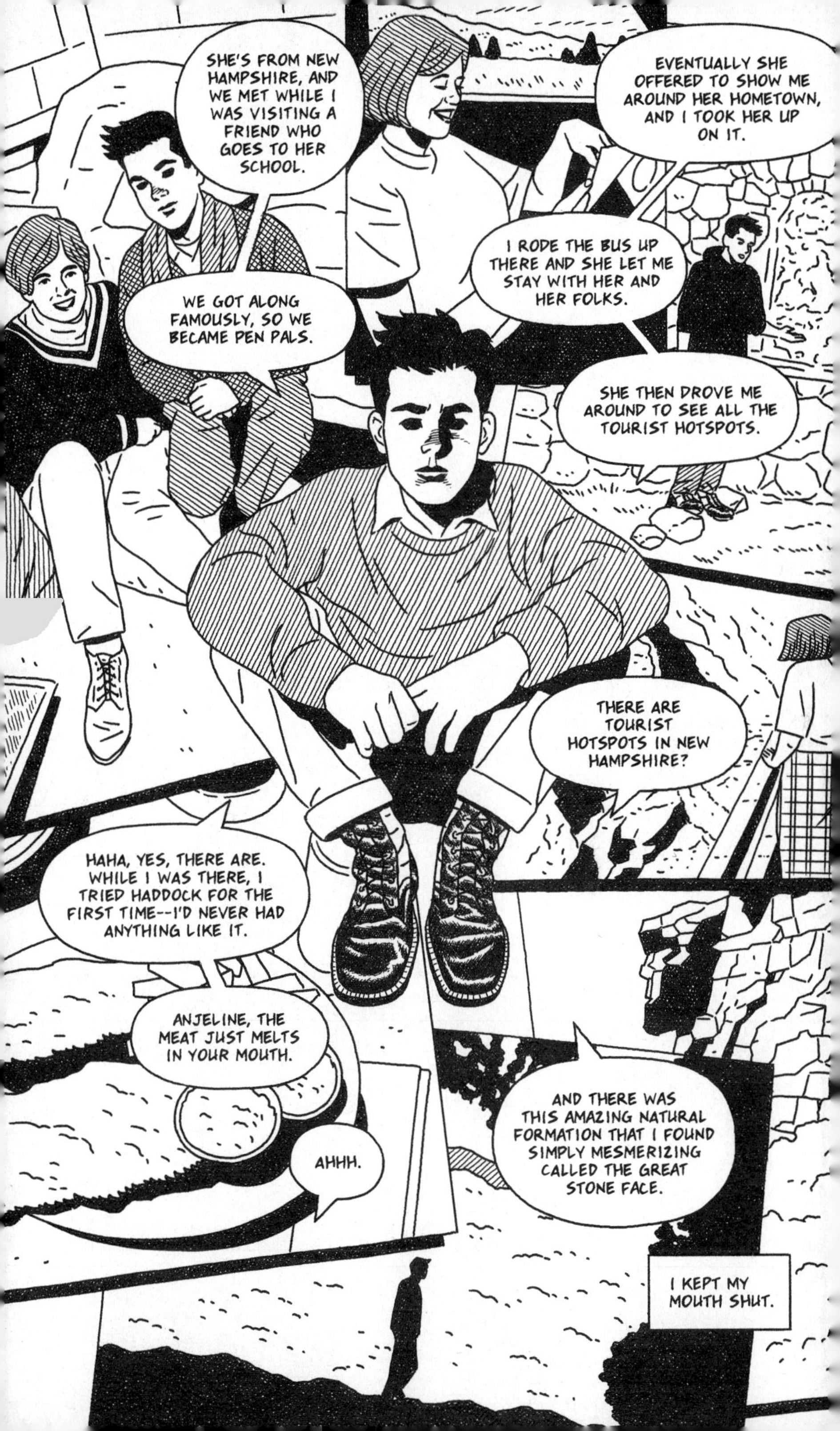
SHE'S FROM NEW HAMPSHIRE, AND WE MET WHILE I WAS VISITING A FRIEND WHO GOES TO HER SCHOOL.
WE GOT ALONG FAMOUSLY, SO WE BECAME PEN PALS.
EVENTUALLY SHE OFFERED TO SHOW ME AROUND HER HOMETOWN, AND I TOOK HER UP ON IT.
I RODE THE BUS UP THERE AND SHE LET ME STAY WITH HER AND HER FOLKS.
SHE THEN DROVE ME AROUND TO SEE ALL THE TOURIST HOTSPOTS.
THERE ARE TOURIST HOTSPOTS IN NEW HAMPSHIRE?
HAHA, YES, THERE ARE. WHILE I WAS THERE, I TRIED HADDOCK FOR THE FIRST TIME--I'D NEVER HAD ANYTHING LIKE IT.
ANJELINE, THE MEAT JUST MELTS IN YOUR MOUTH.
AHHH.
AND THERE WAS THIS AMAZING NATURAL FORMATION THAT I FOUND SIMPLY MESMERIZING CALLED THE GREAT STONE FACE.
I KEPT MY MOUTH SHUT.

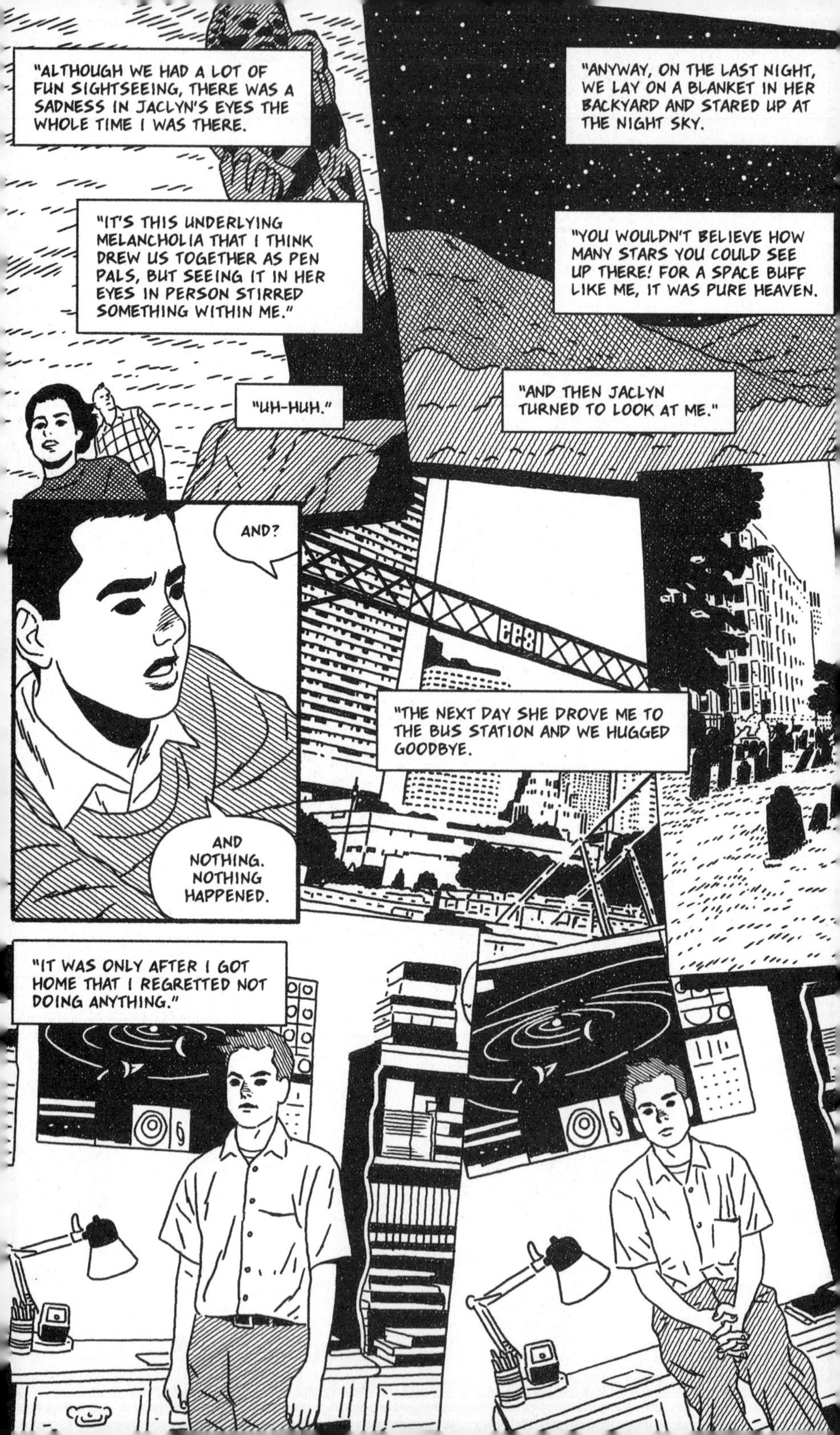
"ALTHOUGH WE HAD A LOT OF FUN SIGHTSEEING, THERE WAS A SADNESS IN JACLYN'S EYES THE WHOLE TIME I WAS THERE.
"IT'S THIS UNDERLYING MELANCHOLIA THAT I THINK DREW US TOGETHER AS PEN PALS, BUT SEEING IT IN HER EYES IN PERSON STIRRED SOMETHING WITHIN ME."
"UH-HUH."
"ANYWAY, ON THE LAST NIGHT, WE LAY ON A BLANKET IN HER BACKYARD AND STARED UP AT THE NIGHT SKY.
"YOU WOULDN'T BELIEVE HOW MANY STARS YOU COULD SEE UP THERE! FOR A SPACE BUFF LIKE ME, IT WAS PURE HEAVEN.
"AND THEN JACLYN TURNED TO LOOK AT ME."
AND?
AND NOTHING. NOTHING HAPPENED.
"THE NEXT DAY SHE DROVE ME TO THE BUS STATION AND WE HUGGED GOODBYE.
"IT WAS ONLY AFTER I GOT HOME THAT I REGRETTED NOT DOING ANYTHING."

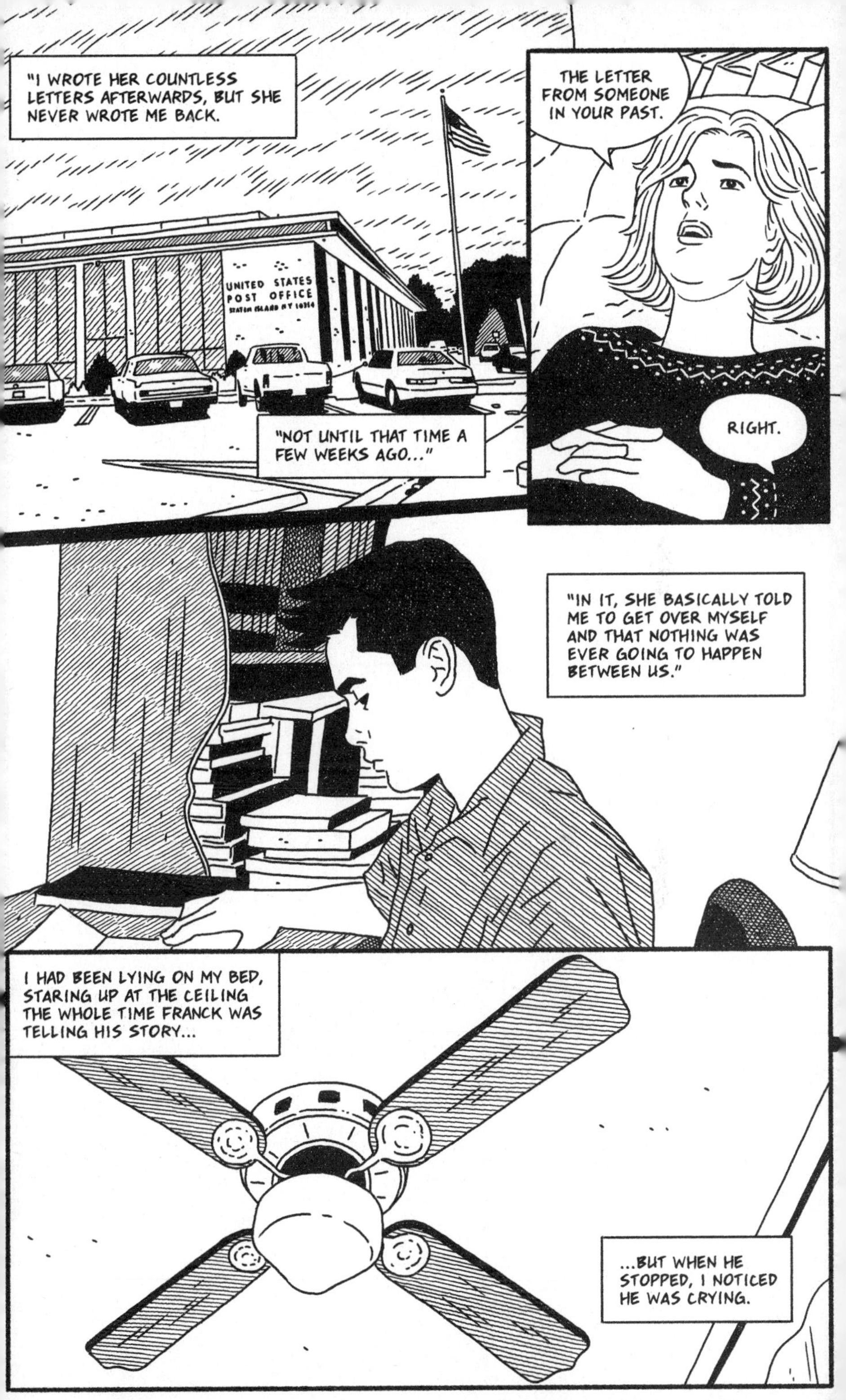
"I WROTE HER COUNTLESS LETTERS AFTERWARDS, BUT SHE NEVER WROTE ME BACK.
UNITED STATES POST OFFICE
"NOT UNTIL THAT TIME A FEW WEEKS AGO..."
THE LETTER FROM SOMEONE IN YOUR PAST.
RIGHT.
"IN IT, SHE BASICALLY TOLD ME TO GET OVER MYSELF AND THAT NOTHING WAS EVER GOING TO HAPPEN BETWEEN US."
I HAD BEEN LYING ON MY BED, STARING UP AT THE CEILING THE WHOLE TIME FRANCK WAS TELLING HIS STORY...
...BUT WHEN HE STOPPED, I NOTICED HE WAS CRYING.

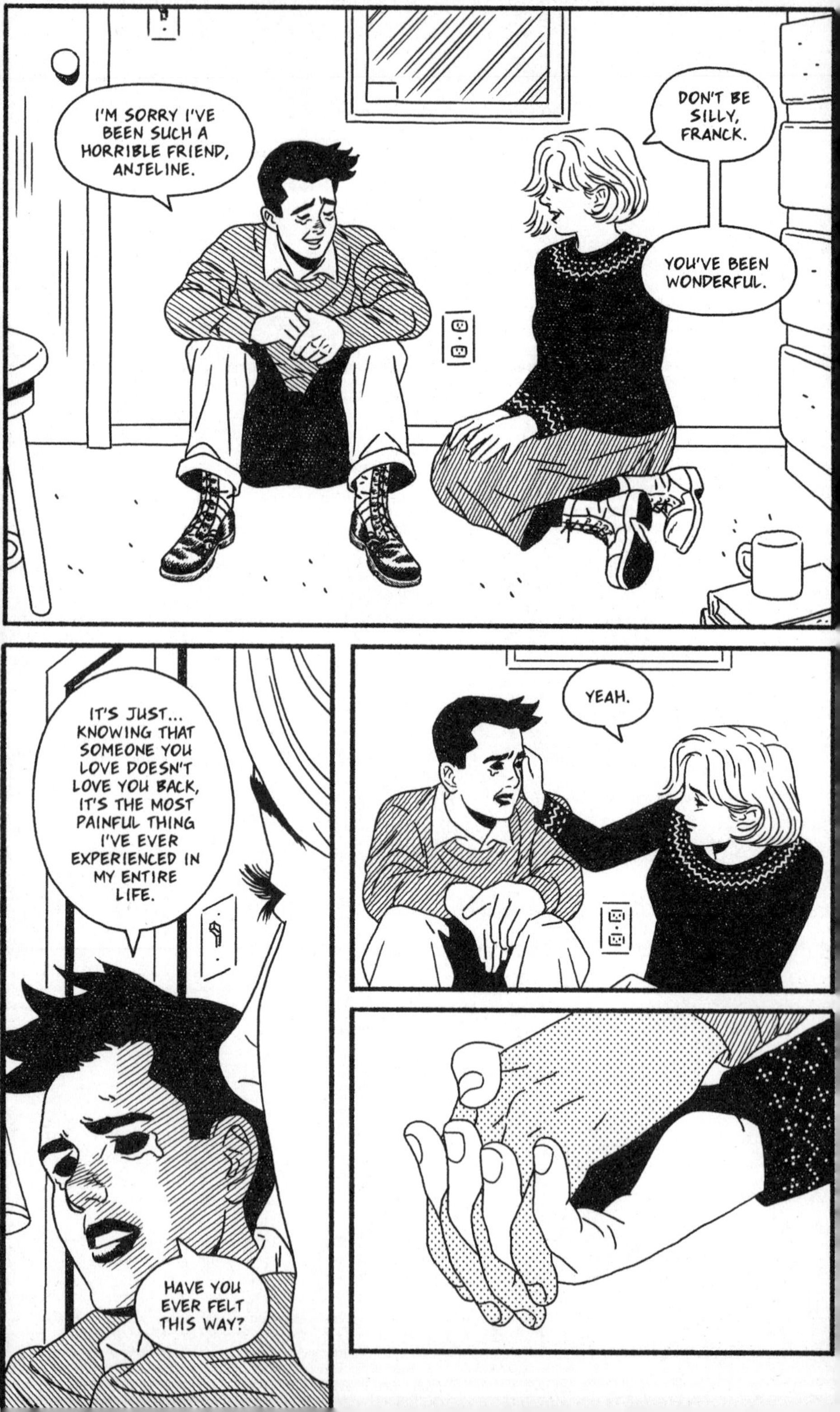
I'M SORRY I'VE BEEN SUCH A HORRIBLE FRIEND, ANJELINE.
DON'T BE SILLY, FRANCK.
YOU'VE BEEN WONDERFUL.
IT'S JUST... KNOWING THAT SOMEONE YOU LOVE DOESN'T LOVE YOU BACK, IT'S THE MOST PAINFUL THING I'VE EVER EXPERIENCED IN MY ENTIRE LIFE.
HAVE YOU EVER FELT THIS WAY?
YEAH.

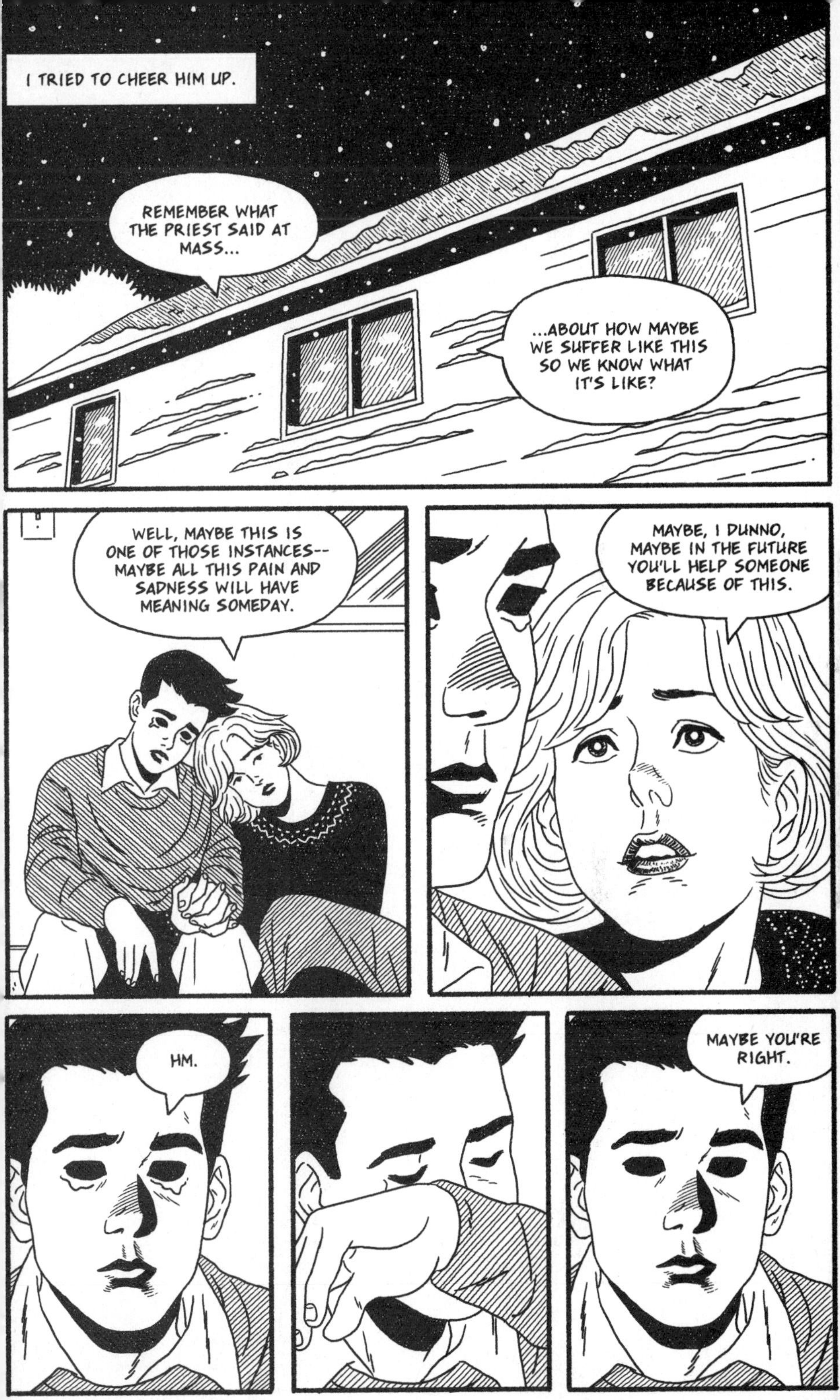
I TRIED TO CHEER HIM UP.
REMEMBER WHAT THE PRIEST SAID AT MASS...
...ABOUT HOW MAYBE WE SUFFER LIKE THIS SO WE KNOW WHAT IT'S LIKE?
WELL, MAYBE THIS IS ONE OF THOSE INSTANCES-- MAYBE ALL THIS PAIN AND SADNESS WILL HAVE MEANING SOMEDAY.
MAYBE, I DUNNO, MAYBE IN THE FUTURE YOU'LL HELP SOMEONE BECAUSE OF THIS.
HM.
MAYBE YOU'RE RIGHT.

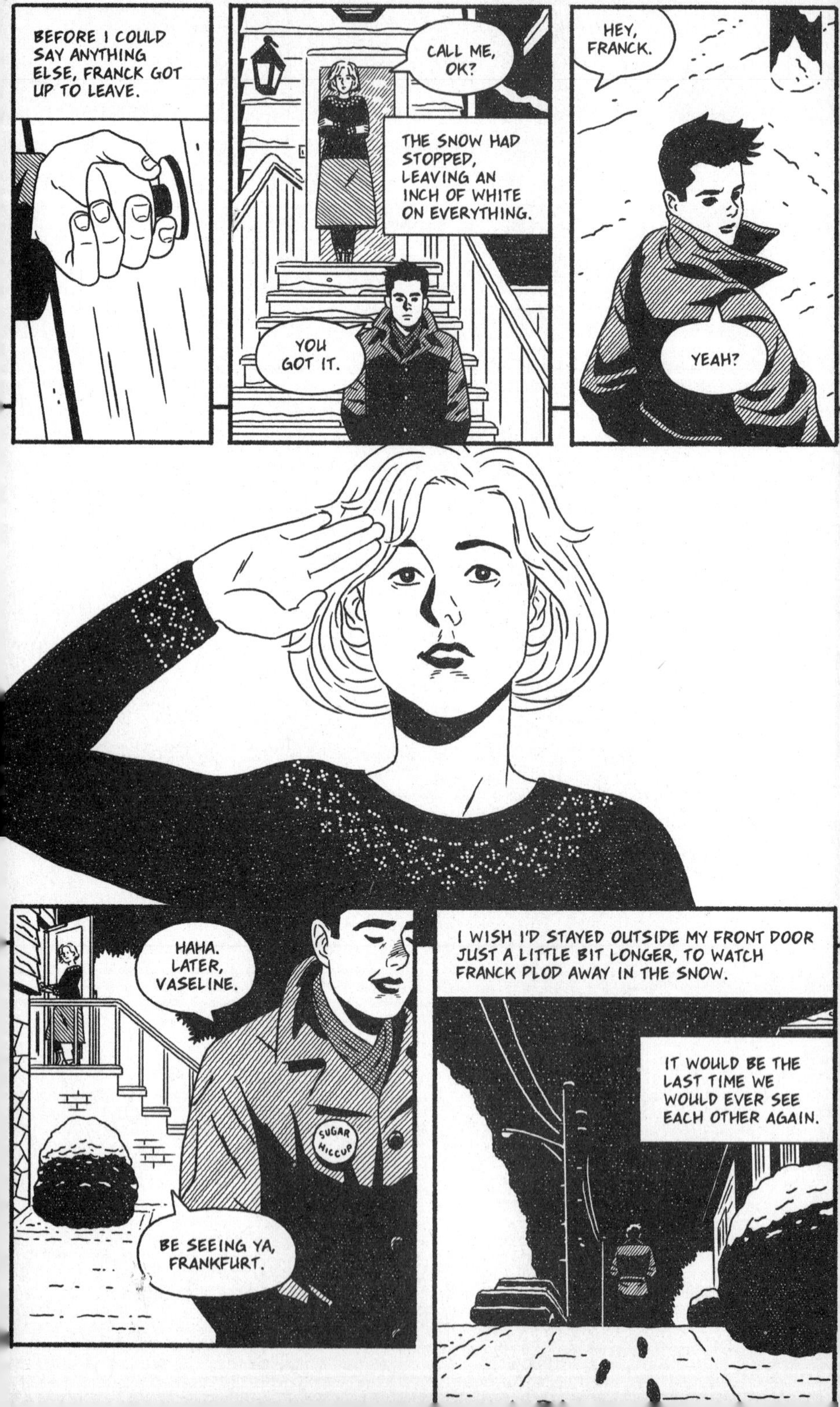
BEFORE I COULD SAY ANYTHING ELSE, FRANCK GOT UP TO LEAVE.
CALL ME, OK?
THE SNOW HAD STOPPED, LEAVING AN INCH OF WHITE ON EVERYTHING.
YOU GOT IT.
HEY, FRANCK.
YEAH?
HAHA. LATER, VASELINE.
SUGAR HICCUP
BE SEEING YA, FRANKFURT.
I WISH I'D STAYED OUTSIDE MY FRONT DOOR JUST A LITTLE BIT LONGER, TO WATCH FRANCK PLOD AWAY IN THE SNOW.
IT WOULD BE THE LAST TIME WE WOULD EVER SEE EACH OTHER AGAIN.

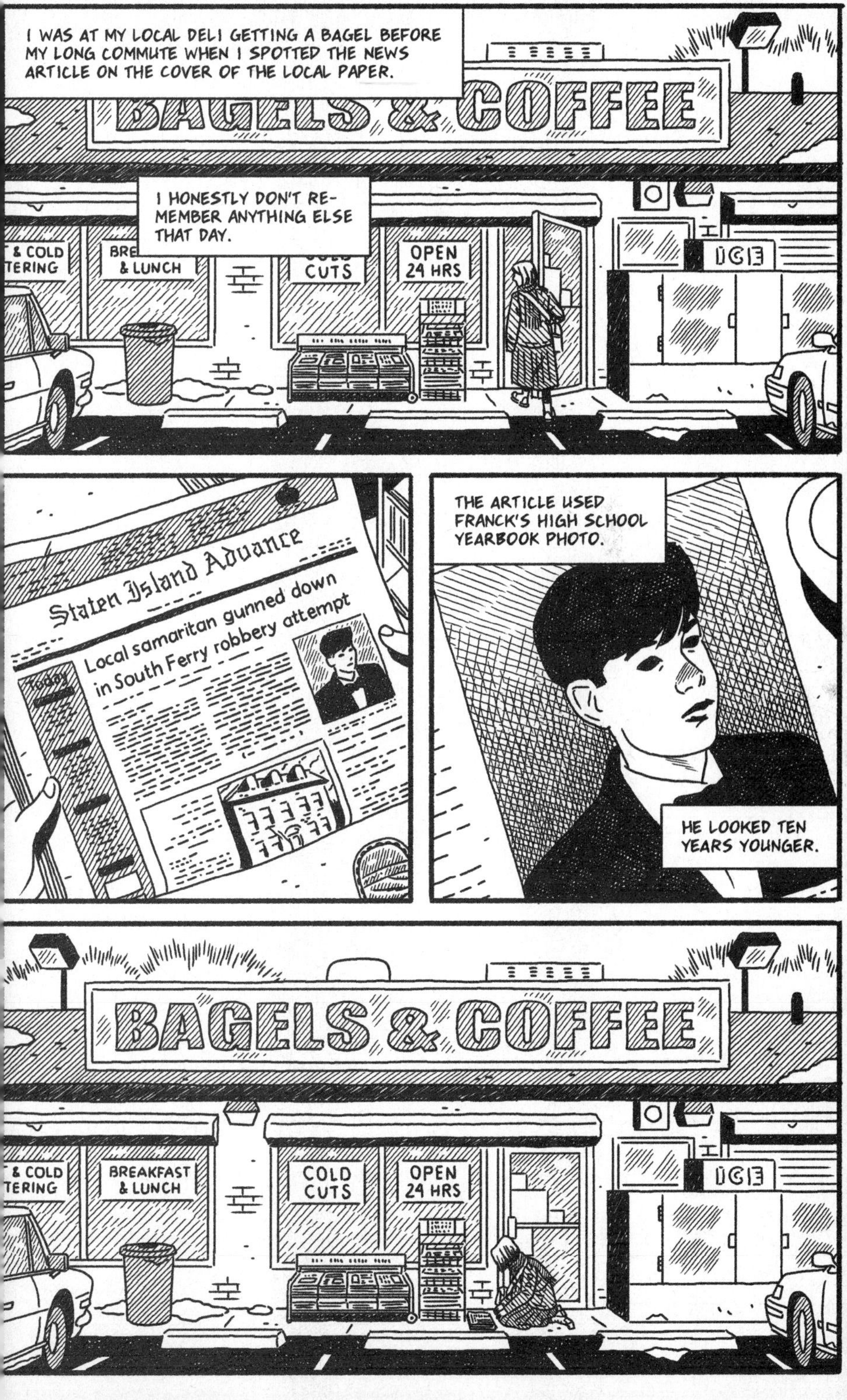
I WAS AT MY LOCAL DELI GETTING A BAGEL BEFORE MY LONG COMMUTE WHEN I SPOTTED THE NEWS ARTICLE ON THE COVER OF THE LOCAL PAPER.
I HONESTLY DON'T RE-MEMBER ANYTHING ELSE THAT DAY.
OPEN 24 HRS
Staten Island Advance
Local samaritan gunned down in South Ferry robbery attempt
THE ARTICLE USED FRANCK'S HIGH SCHOOL YEARBOOK PHOTO.
HE LOOKED TEN YEARS YOUNGER.
BAGELS & COFFEE
BREAKFAST & LUNCH
COLD CUTS
OPEN 24 HRS

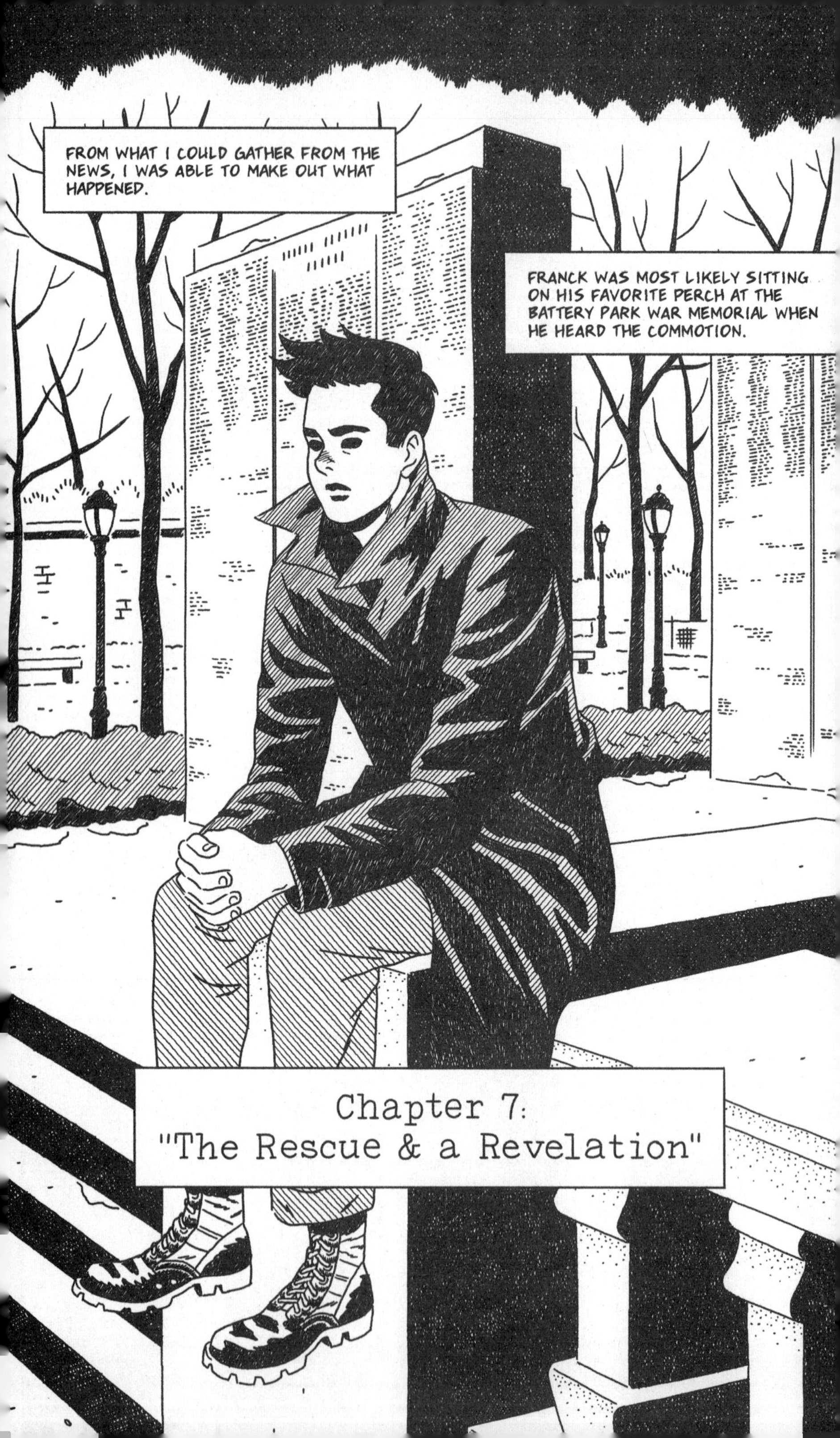
FROM WHAT I COULD GATHER FROM THE NEWS, I WAS ABLE TO MAKE OUT WHAT HAPPENED.
FRANCK WAS MOST LIKELY SITTING ON HIS FAVORITE PERCH AT THE BATTERY PARK WAR MEMORIAL WHEN HE HEARD THE COMMOTION.
Chapter 7:
"The Rescue & a Revelation"

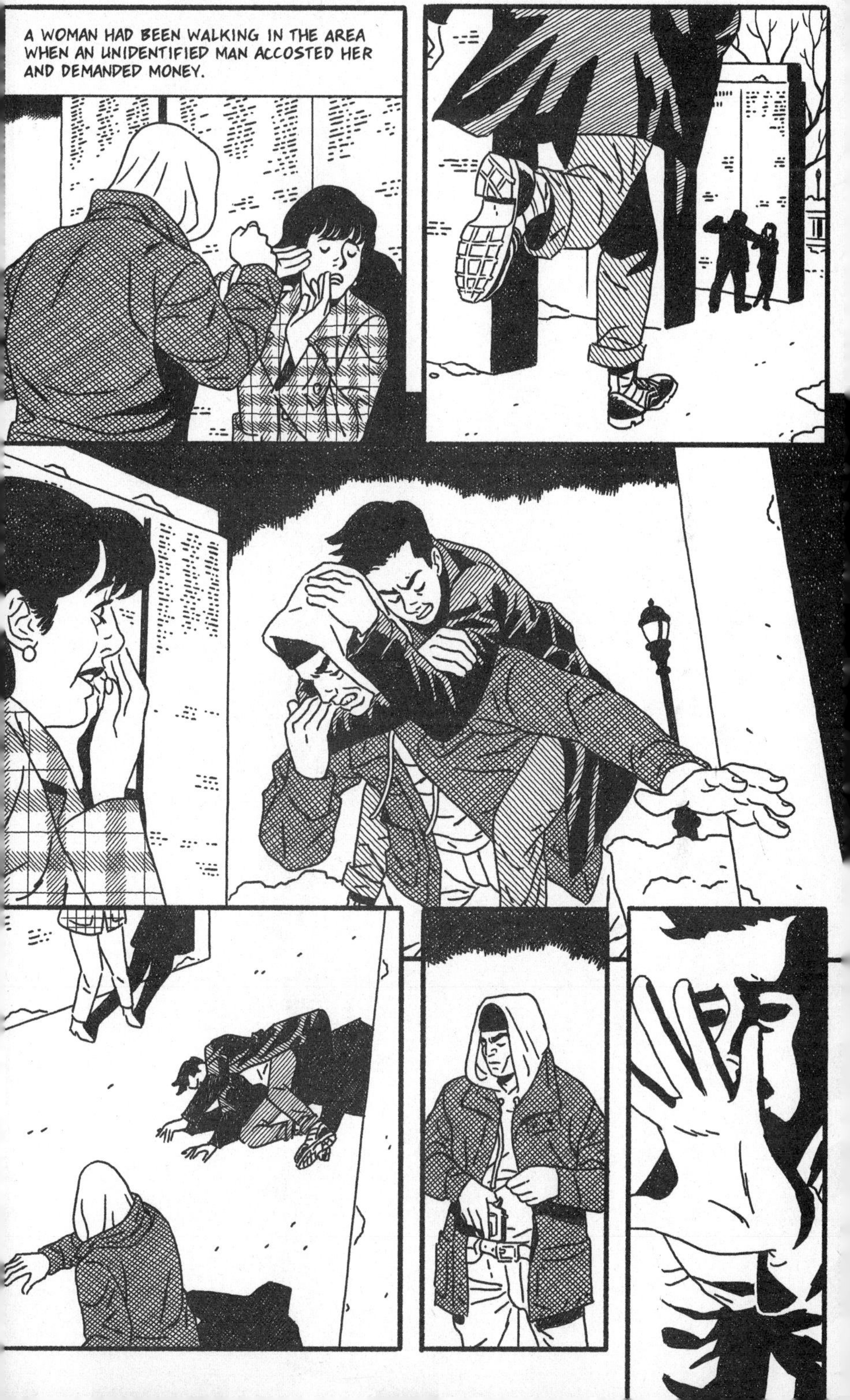
A WOMAN HAD BEEN WALKING IN THE AREA WHEN AN UNIDENTIFIED MAN ACCOSTED HER AND DEMANDED MONEY.

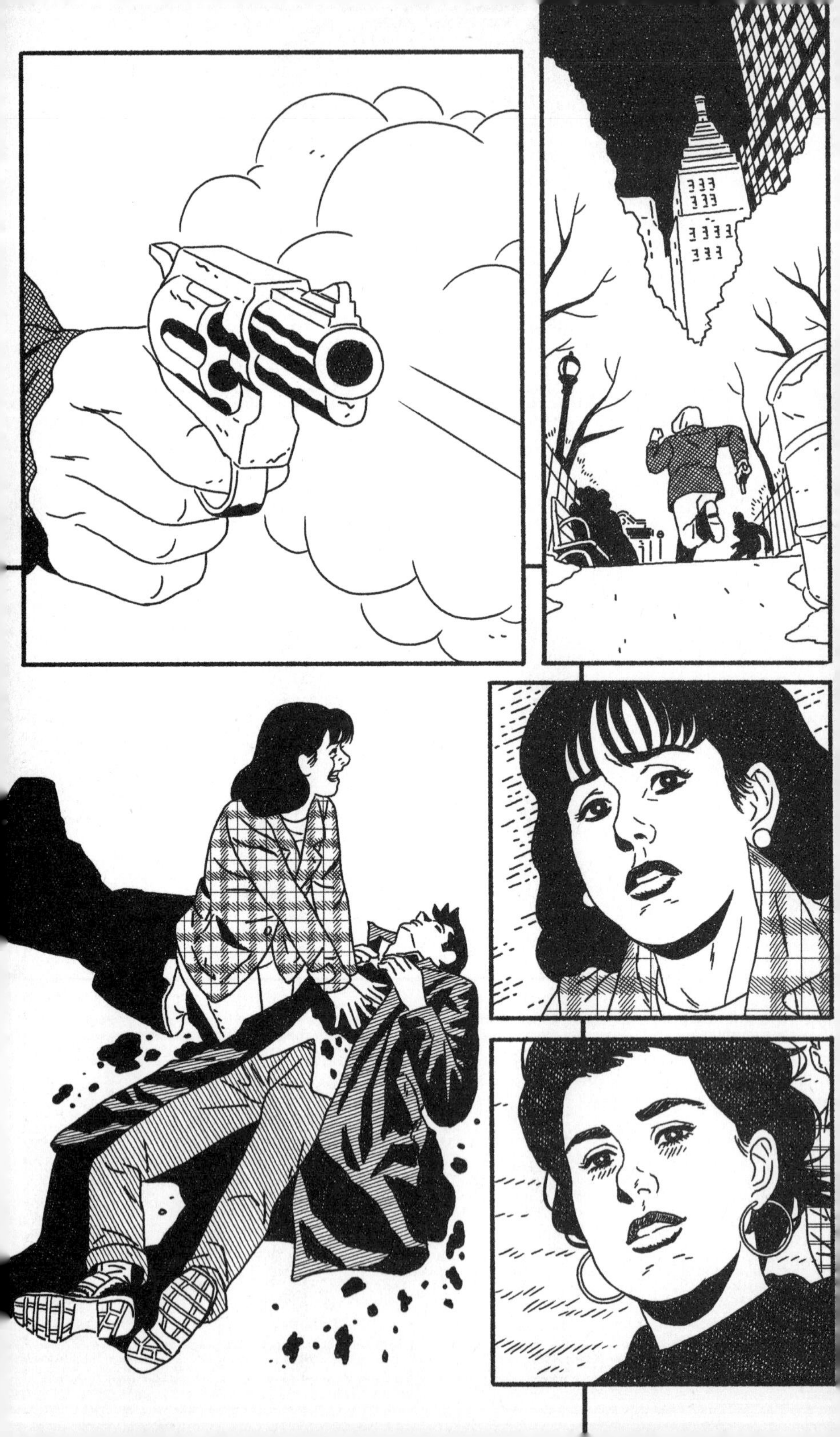

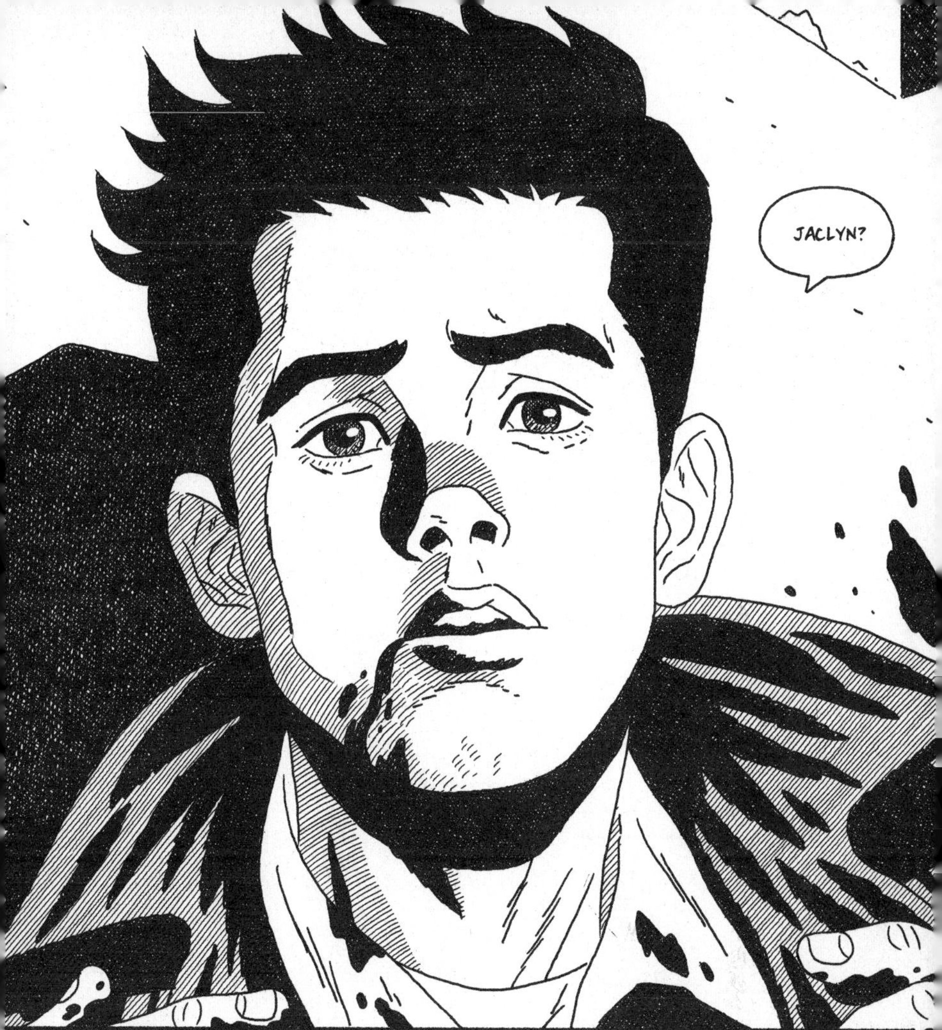
JACLYN?

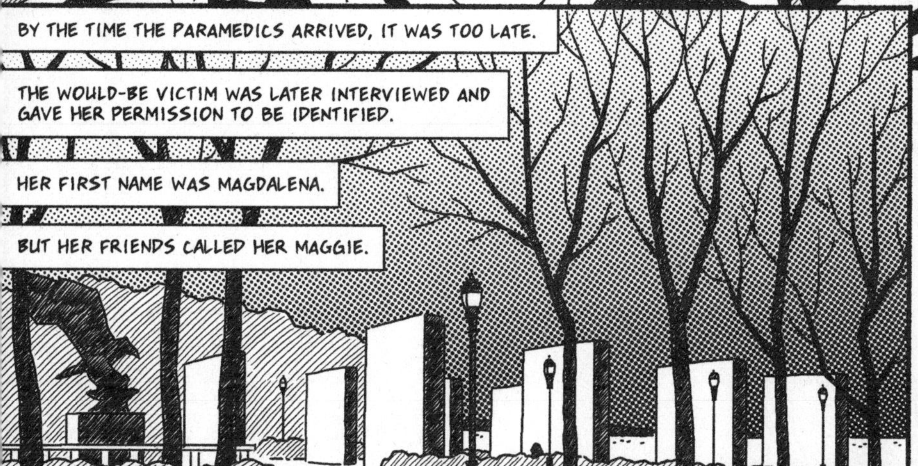
BY THE TIME THE PARAMEDICS ARRIVED, IT WAS TOO LATE.
THE WOULD-BE VICTIM WAS LATER INTERVIEWED AND GAVE HER PERMISSION TO BE IDENTIFIED.
HER FIRST NAME WAS MAGDALENA.
BUT HER FRIENDS CALLED HER MAGGIE.

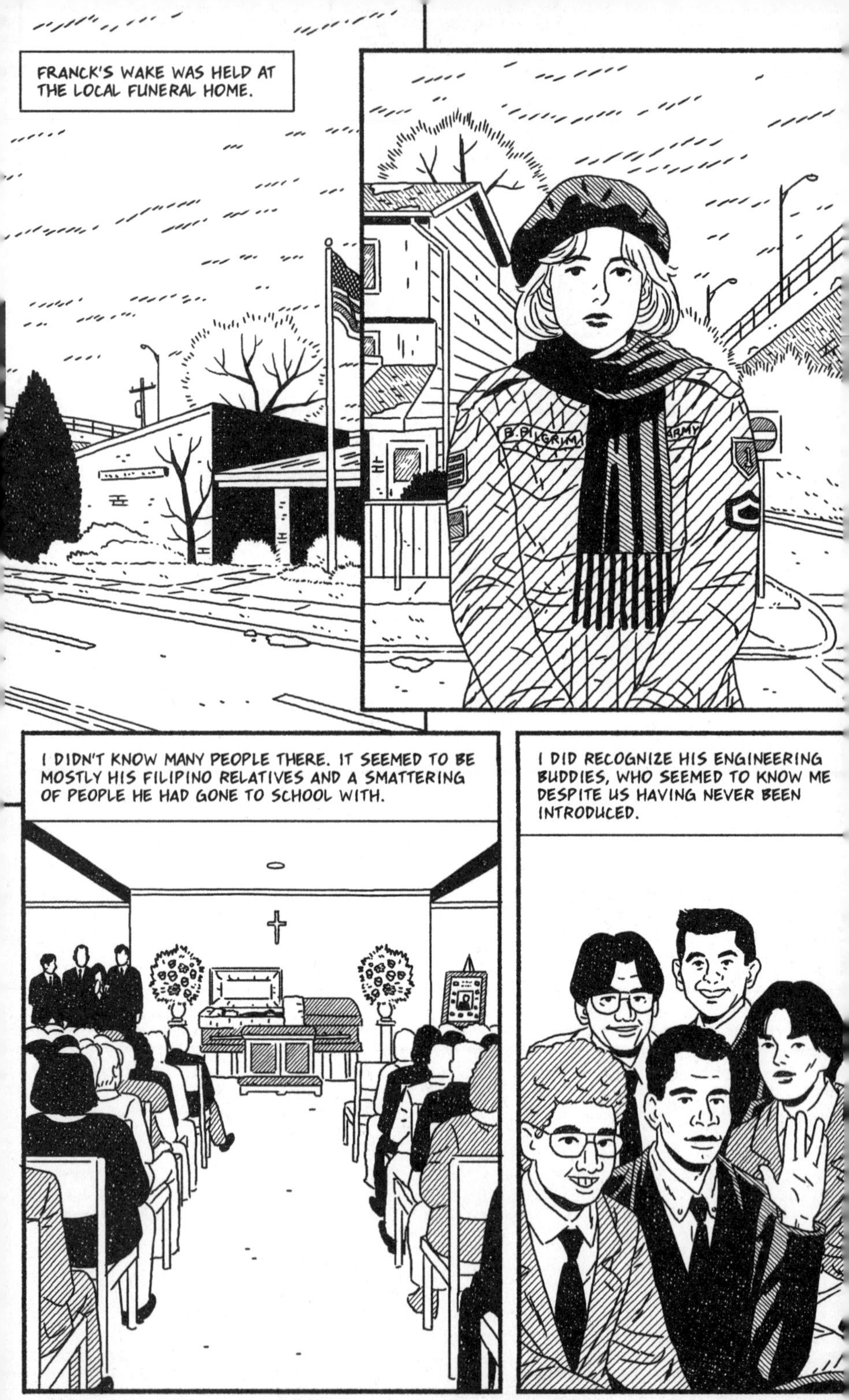
FRANCK'S WAKE WAS HELD AT THE LOCAL FUNERAL HOME.
B. PILGRIM
ARMY
I DIDN'T KNOW MANY PEOPLE THERE. IT SEEMED TO BE MOSTLY HIS FILIPINO RELATIVES AND A SMATTERING OF PEOPLE HE HAD GONE TO SCHOOL WITH.
I DID RECOGNIZE HIS ENGINEERING BUDDIES, WHO SEEMED TO KNOW ME DESPITE US HAVING NEVER BEEN INTRODUCED.

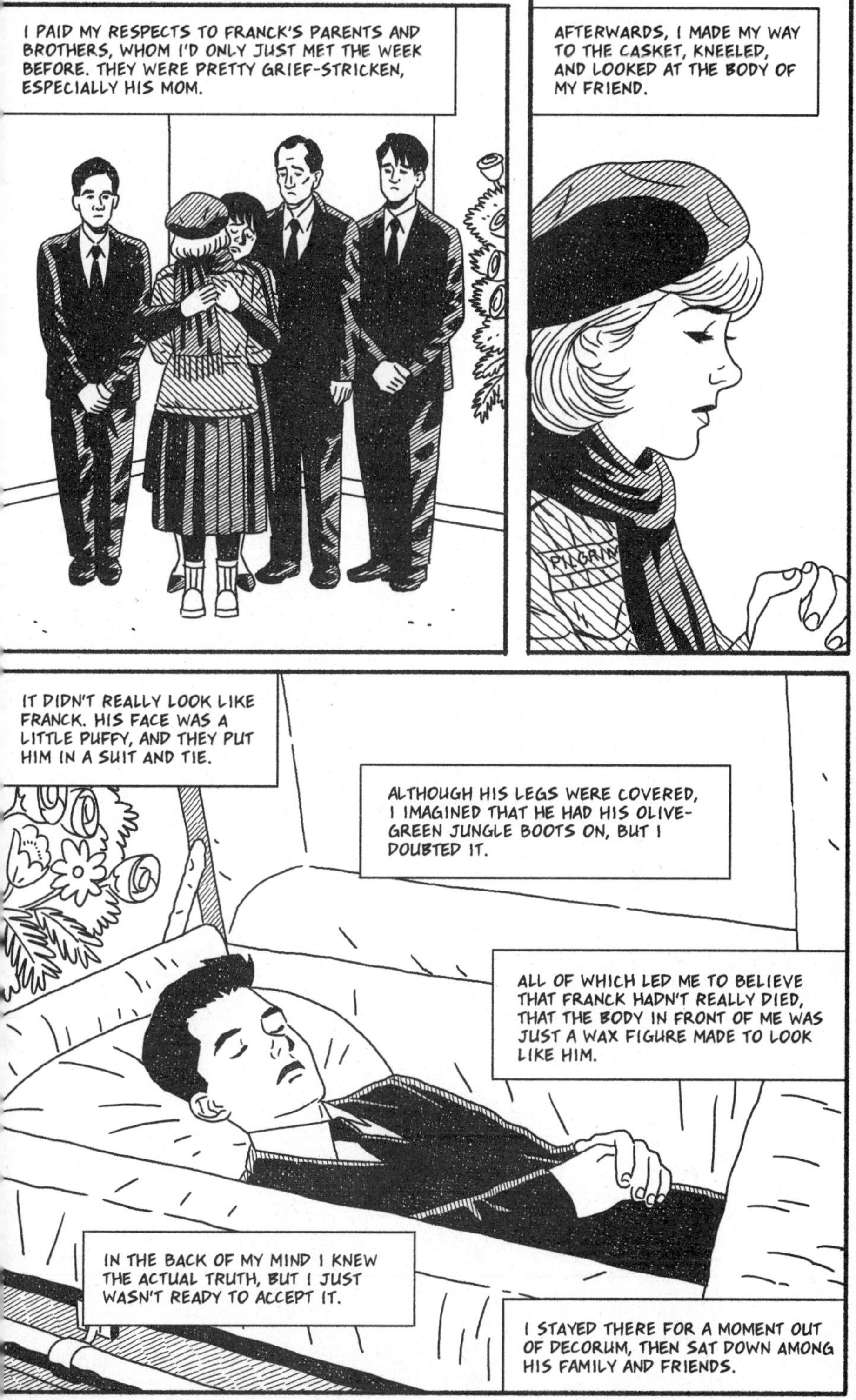
I PAID MY RESPECTS TO FRANCK'S PARENTS AND BROTHERS, WHOM I'D ONLY JUST MET THE WEEK BEFORE. THEY WERE PRETTY GRIEF-STRICKEN, ESPECIALLY HIS MOM.
AFTERWARDS, I MADE MY WAY TO THE CASKET, KNEELED, AND LOOKED AT THE BODY OF MY FRIEND.
PILGRIM
IT DIDN'T REALLY LOOK LIKE FRANCK. HIS FACE WAS A LITTLE PUFFY, AND THEY PUT HIM IN A SUIT AND TIE.
ALTHOUGH HIS LEGS WERE COVERED, I IMAGINED THAT HE HAD HIS OLIVE-GREEN JUNGLE BOOTS ON, BUT I DOUBTED IT.
ALL OF WHICH LED ME TO BELIEVE THAT FRANCK HADN'T REALLY DIED, THAT THE BODY IN FRONT OF ME WAS JUST A WAX FIGURE MADE TO LOOK LIKE HIM.
IN THE BACK OF MY MIND I KNEW THE ACTUAL TRUTH, BUT I JUST WASN'T READY TO ACCEPT IT.
I STAYED THERE FOR A MOMENT OUT OF DECORUM, THEN SAT DOWN AMONG HIS FAMILY AND FRIENDS.

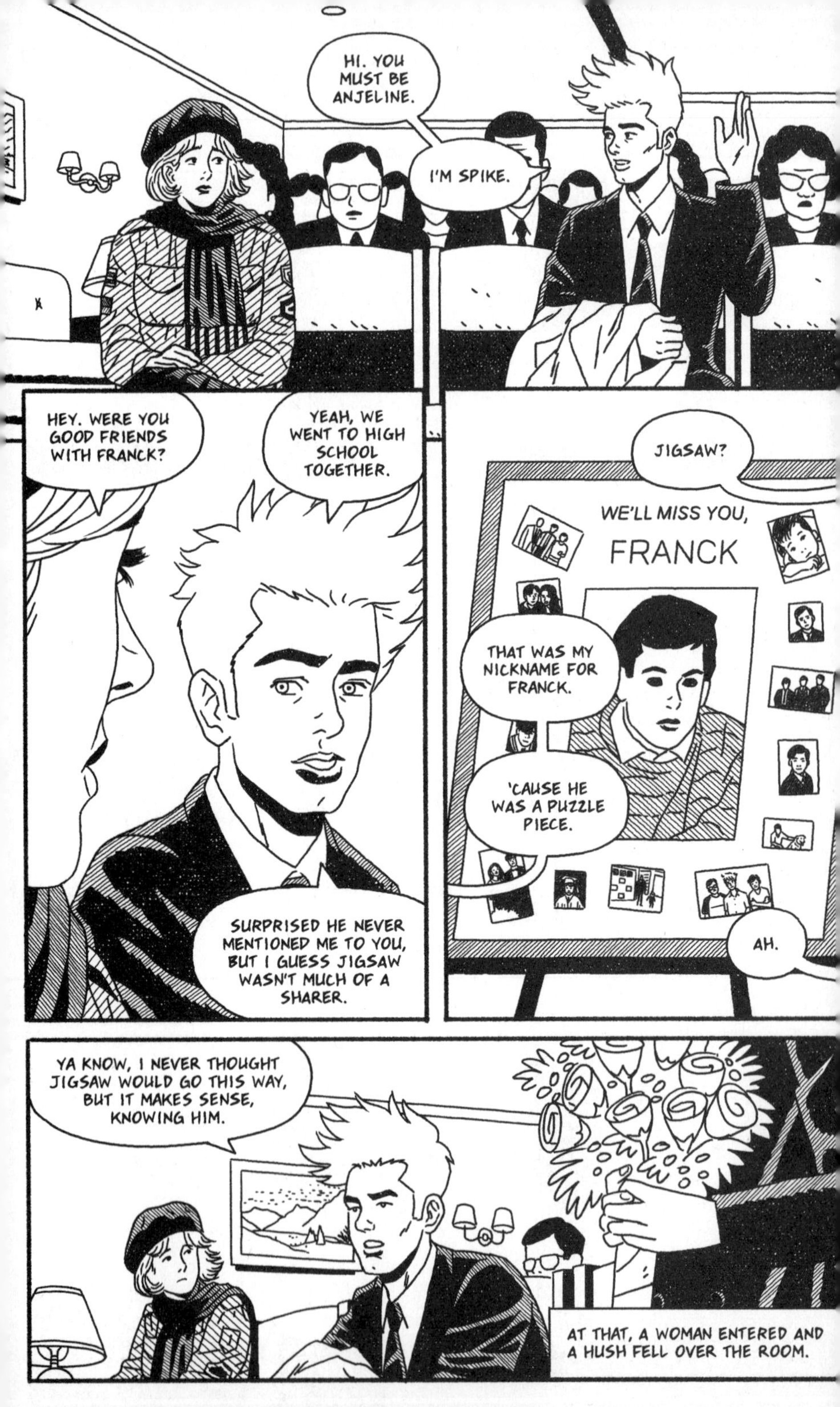
HI. YOU MUST BE ANJELINE.
I'M SPIKE.
HEY. WERE YOU GOOD FRIENDS WITH FRANCK?
YEAH, WE WENT TO HIGH SCHOOL TOGETHER.
SURPRISED HE NEVER MENTIONED ME TO YOU, BUT I GUESS JIGSAW WASN'T MUCH OF A SHARER.
JIGSAW?
WE'LL MISS YOU,
FRANCK
THAT WAS MY NICKNAME FOR FRANCK.
'CAUSE HE WAS A PUZZLE PIECE.
AH.
YA KNOW, I NEVER THOUGHT JIGSAW WOULD GO THIS WAY, BUT IT MAKES SENSE, KNOWING HIM.
AT THAT, A WOMAN ENTERED AND A HUSH FELL OVER THE ROOM.

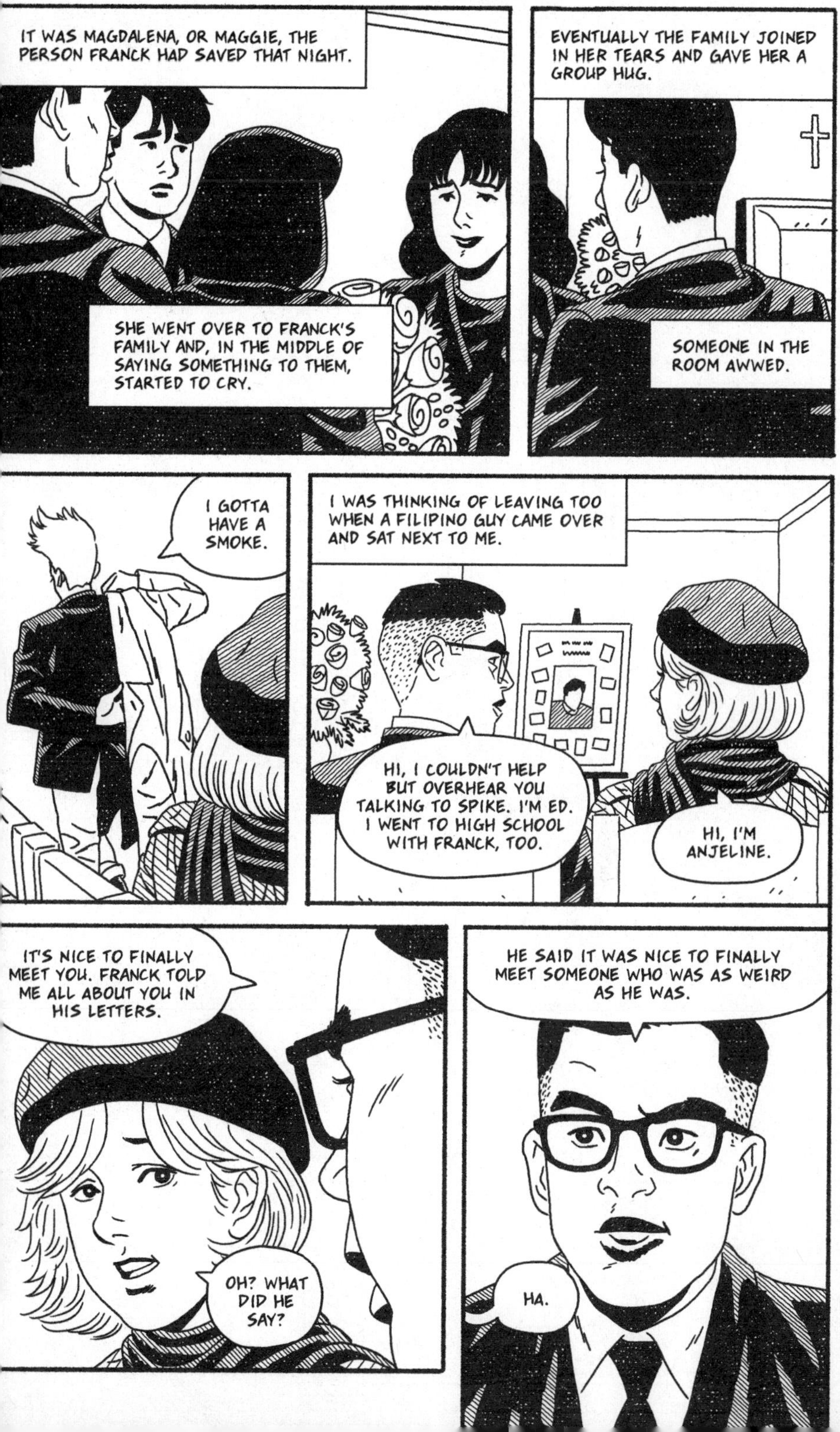
IT WAS MAGDALENA, OR MAGGIE, THE PERSON FRANCK HAD SAVED THAT NIGHT.
SHE WENT OVER TO FRANCK'S FAMILY AND, IN THE MIDDLE OF SAYING SOMETHING TO THEM, STARTED TO CRY.
EVENTUALLY THE FAMILY JOINED IN HER TEARS AND GAVE HER A GROUP HUG.
SOMEONE IN THE ROOM AWWED.
I GOTTA HAVE A SMOKE.
I WAS THINKING OF LEAVING TOO WHEN A FILIPINO GUY CAME OVER AND SAT NEXT TO ME.
HI, I COULDN'T HELP BUT OVERHEAR YOU TALKING TO SPIKE. I'M ED. I WENT TO HIGH SCHOOL WITH FRANCK, TOO.
HI, I'M ANJELINE.
IT'S NICE TO FINALLY MEET YOU. FRANCK TOLD ME ALL ABOUT YOU IN HIS LETTERS.
OH? WHAT DID HE SAY?
HE SAID IT WAS NICE TO FINALLY MEET SOMEONE WHO WAS AS WEIRD AS HE WAS.
HA.

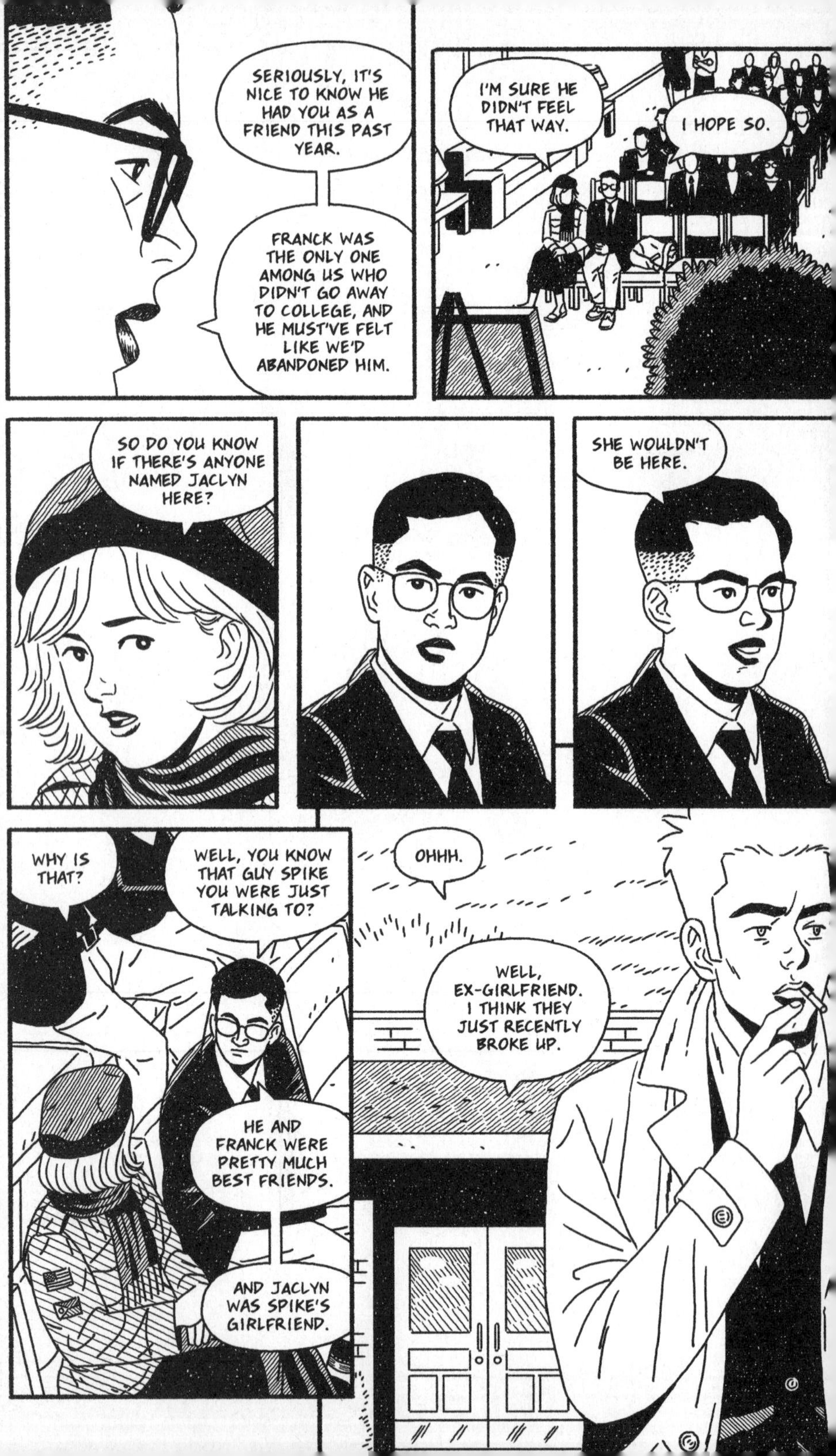
SERIOUSLY, IT'S NICE TO KNOW HE HAD YOU AS A FRIEND THIS PAST YEAR.
FRANCK WAS THE ONLY ONE AMONG US WHO DIDN'T GO AWAY TO COLLEGE, AND HE MUST'VE FELT LIKE WE'D ABANDONED HIM.
I'M SURE HE DIDN'T FEEL THAT WAY.
I HOPE SO.
SO DO YOU KNOW IF THERE'S ANYONE NAMED JACLYN HERE?
SHE WOULDN'T BE HERE.
WHY IS THAT?
WELL, YOU KNOW THAT GUY SPIKE YOU WERE JUST TALKING TO?
HE AND FRANCK WERE PRETTY MUCH BEST FRIENDS.
AND JACLYN WAS SPIKE'S GIRLFRIEND.
OHHH.
WELL, EX-GIRLFRIEND. I THINK THEY JUST RECENTLY BROKE UP.

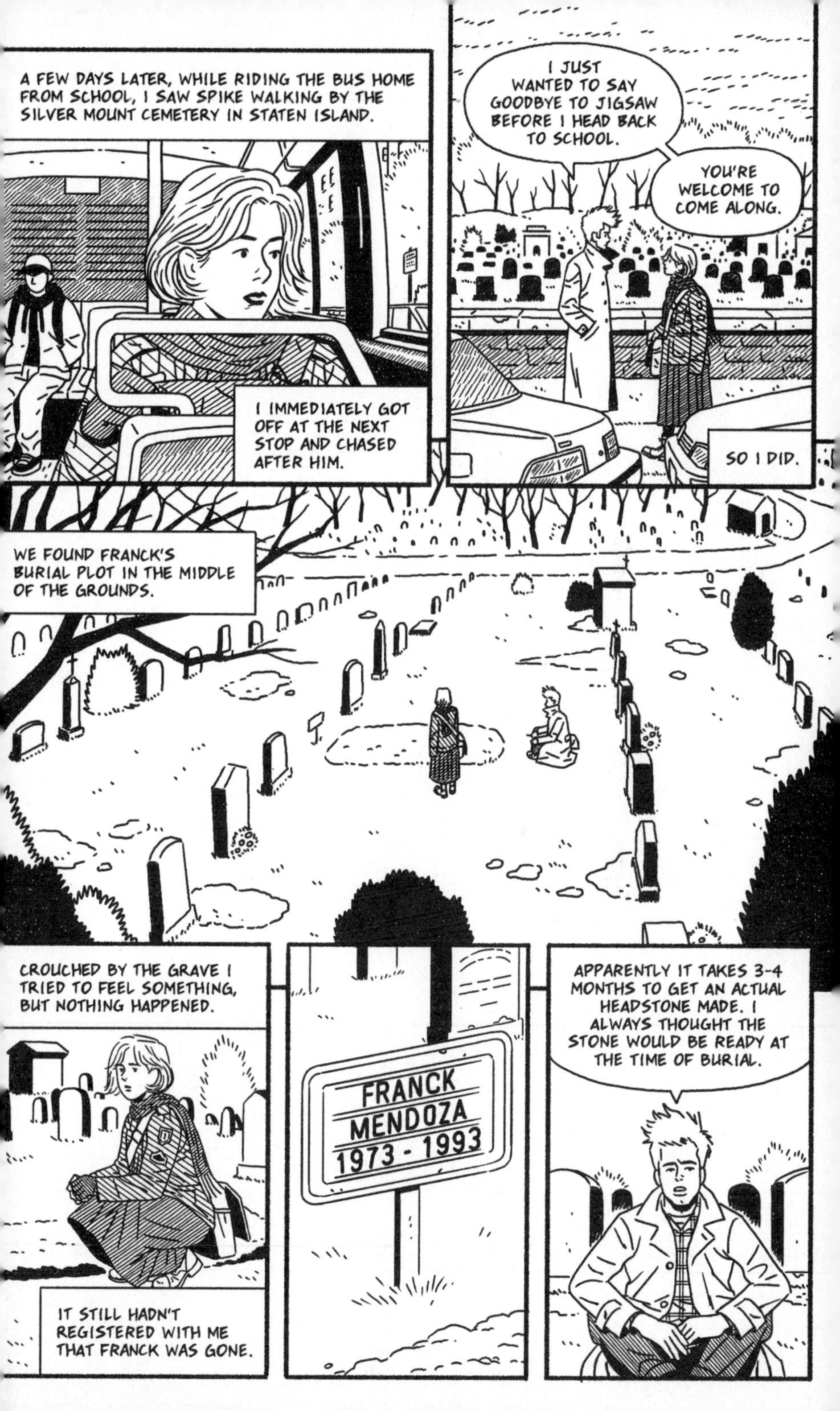
A FEW DAYS LATER, WHILE RIDING THE BUS HOME FROM SCHOOL, I SAW SPIKE WALKING BY THE SILVER MOUNT CEMETERY IN STATEN ISLAND.
I IMMEDIATELY GOT OFF AT THE NEXT STOP AND CHASED AFTER HIM.
I JUST WANTED TO SAY GOODBYE TO JIGSAW BEFORE I HEAD BACK TO SCHOOL.
YOU'RE WELCOME TO COME ALONG.
SO I DID.
WE FOUND FRANCK'S BURIAL PLOT IN THE MIDDLE OF THE GROUNDS.
CROUCHED BY THE GRAVE I TRIED TO FEEL SOMETHING, BUT NOTHING HAPPENED.
IT STILL HADN'T REGISTERED WITH ME THAT FRANCK WAS GONE.
FRANCK MENDOZA 1973 - 1993
APPARENTLY IT TAKES 3-4 MONTHS TO GET AN ACTUAL HEADSTONE MADE. I ALWAYS THOUGHT THE STONE WOULD BE READY AT THE TIME OF BURIAL.

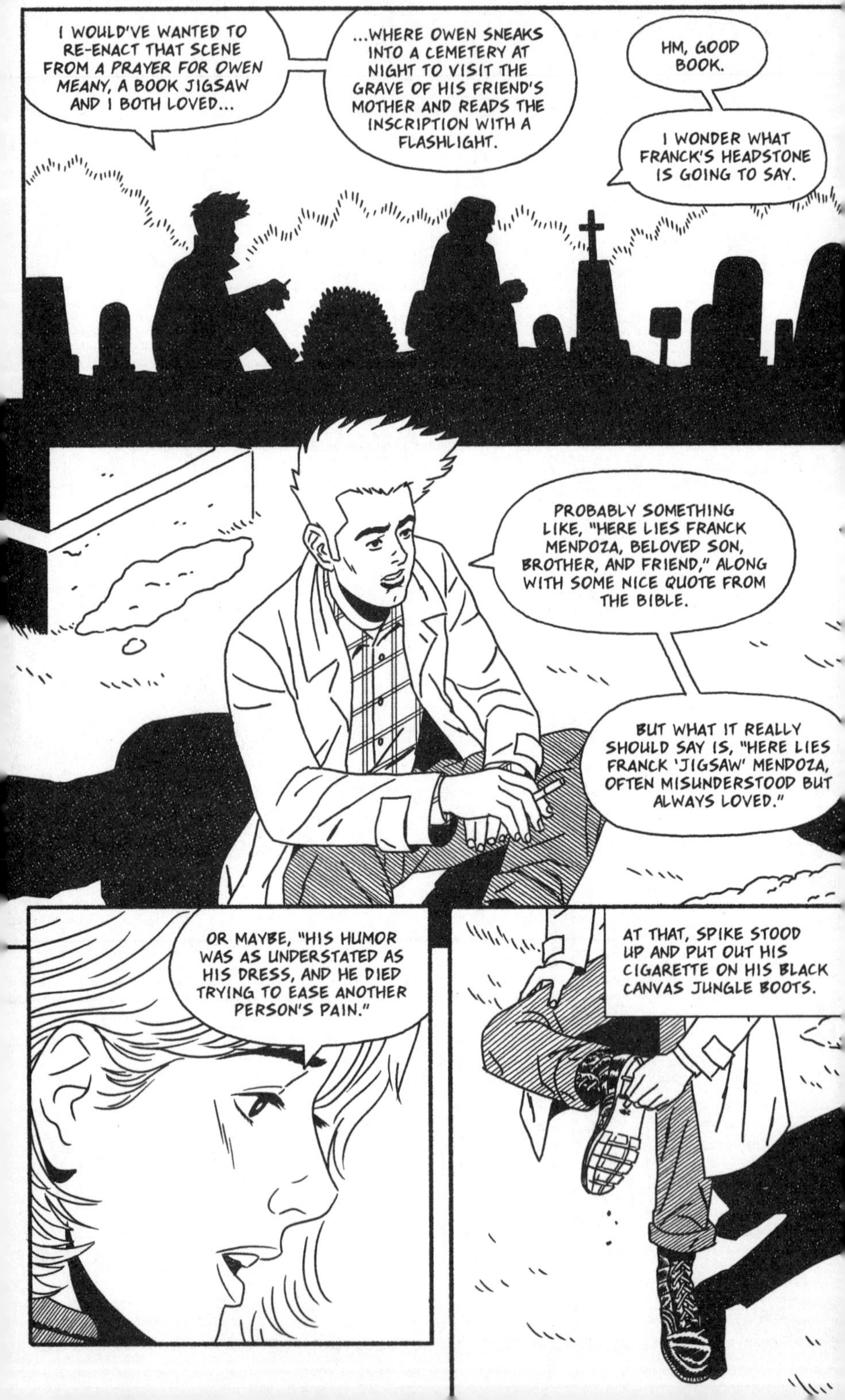
I WOULD'VE WANTED TO RE-ENACT THAT SCENE FROM A *PRAYER FOR OWEN MEANY*, A BOOK JIGSAW AND I BOTH LOVED...
...WHERE OWEN SNEAKS INTO A CEMETERY AT NIGHT TO VISIT THE GRAVE OF HIS FRIEND'S MOTHER AND READS THE INSCRIPTION WITH A FLASHLIGHT.
HM, GOOD BOOK.
I WONDER WHAT FRANCK'S HEADSTONE IS GOING TO SAY.
PROBABLY SOMETHING LIKE, "HERE LIES FRANCK MENDOZA, BELOVED SON, BROTHER, AND FRIEND," ALONG WITH SOME NICE QUOTE FROM THE BIBLE.
BUT WHAT IT REALLY SHOULD SAY IS, "HERE LIES FRANCK 'JIGSAW' MENDOZA, OFTEN MISUNDERSTOOD BUT ALWAYS LOVED."
OR MAYBE, "HIS HUMOR WAS AS UNDERSTATED AS HIS DRESS, AND HE DIED TRYING TO EASE ANOTHER PERSON'S PAIN."
AT THAT, SPIKE STOOD UP AND PUT OUT HIS CIGARETTE ON HIS BLACK CANVAS JUNGLE BOOTS.

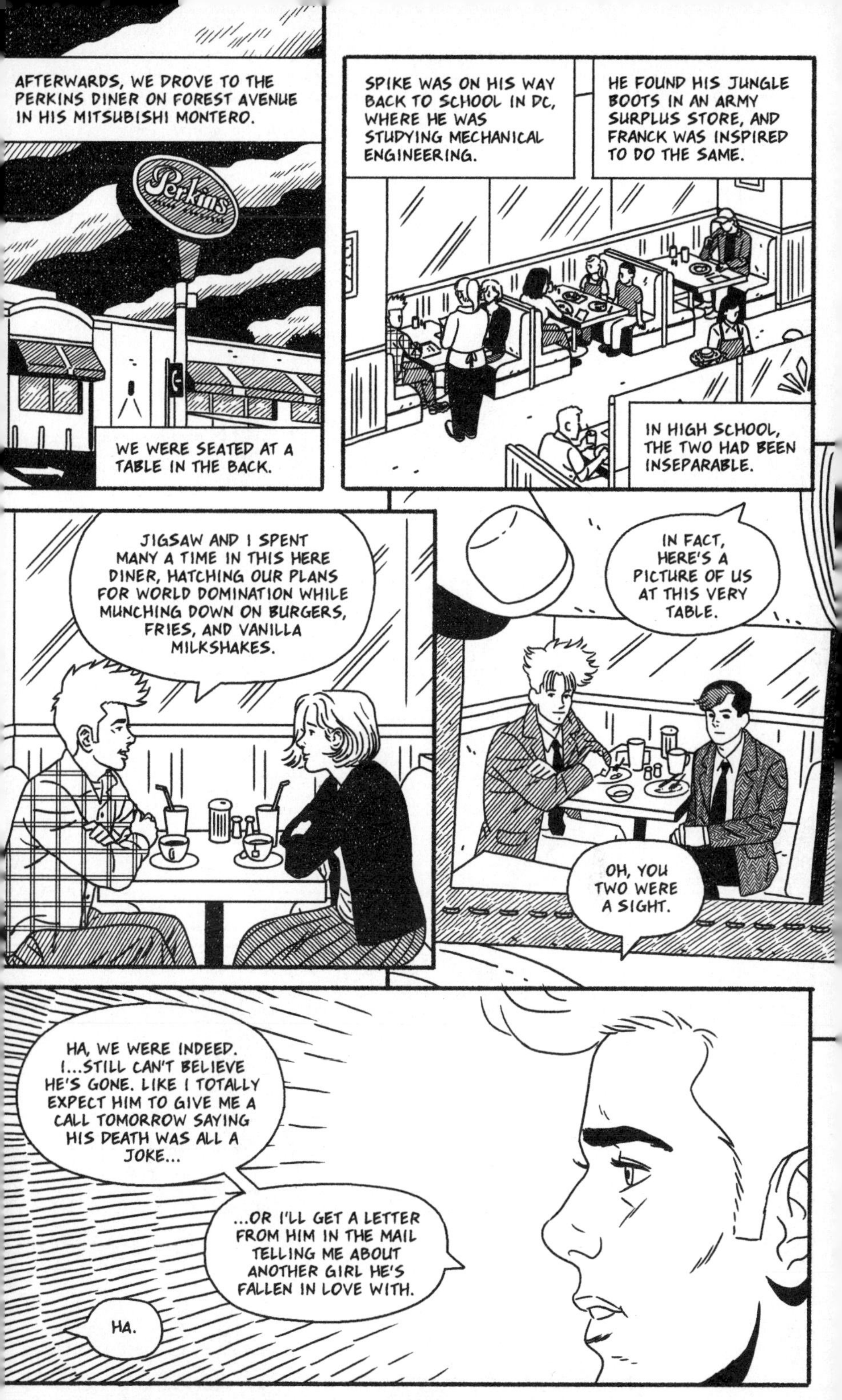
AFTERWARDS, WE DROVE TO THE PERKINS DINER ON FOREST AVENUE IN HIS MITSUBISHI MONTERO.
Perkins
WE WERE SEATED AT A TABLE IN THE BACK.
SPIKE WAS ON HIS WAY BACK TO SCHOOL IN DC, WHERE HE WAS STUDYING MECHANICAL ENGINEERING.
HE FOUND HIS JUNGLE BOOTS IN AN ARMY SURPLUS STORE, AND FRANCK WAS INSPIRED TO DO THE SAME.
IN HIGH SCHOOL, THE TWO HAD BEEN INSEPARABLE.
JIGSAW AND I SPENT MANY A TIME IN THIS HERE DINER, HATCHING OUR PLANS FOR WORLD DOMINATION WHILE MUNCHING DOWN ON BURGERS, FRIES, AND VANILLA MILKSHAKES.
IN FACT, HERE'S A PICTURE OF US AT THIS VERY TABLE.
OH, YOU TWO WERE A SIGHT.
HA, WE WERE INDEED. I...STILL CAN'T BELIEVE HE'S GONE. LIKE I TOTALLY EXPECT HIM TO GIVE ME A CALL TOMORROW SAYING HIS DEATH WAS ALL A JOKE...
...OR I'LL GET A LETTER FROM HIM IN THE MAIL TELLING ME ABOUT ANOTHER GIRL HE'S FALLEN IN LOVE WITH.
HA.

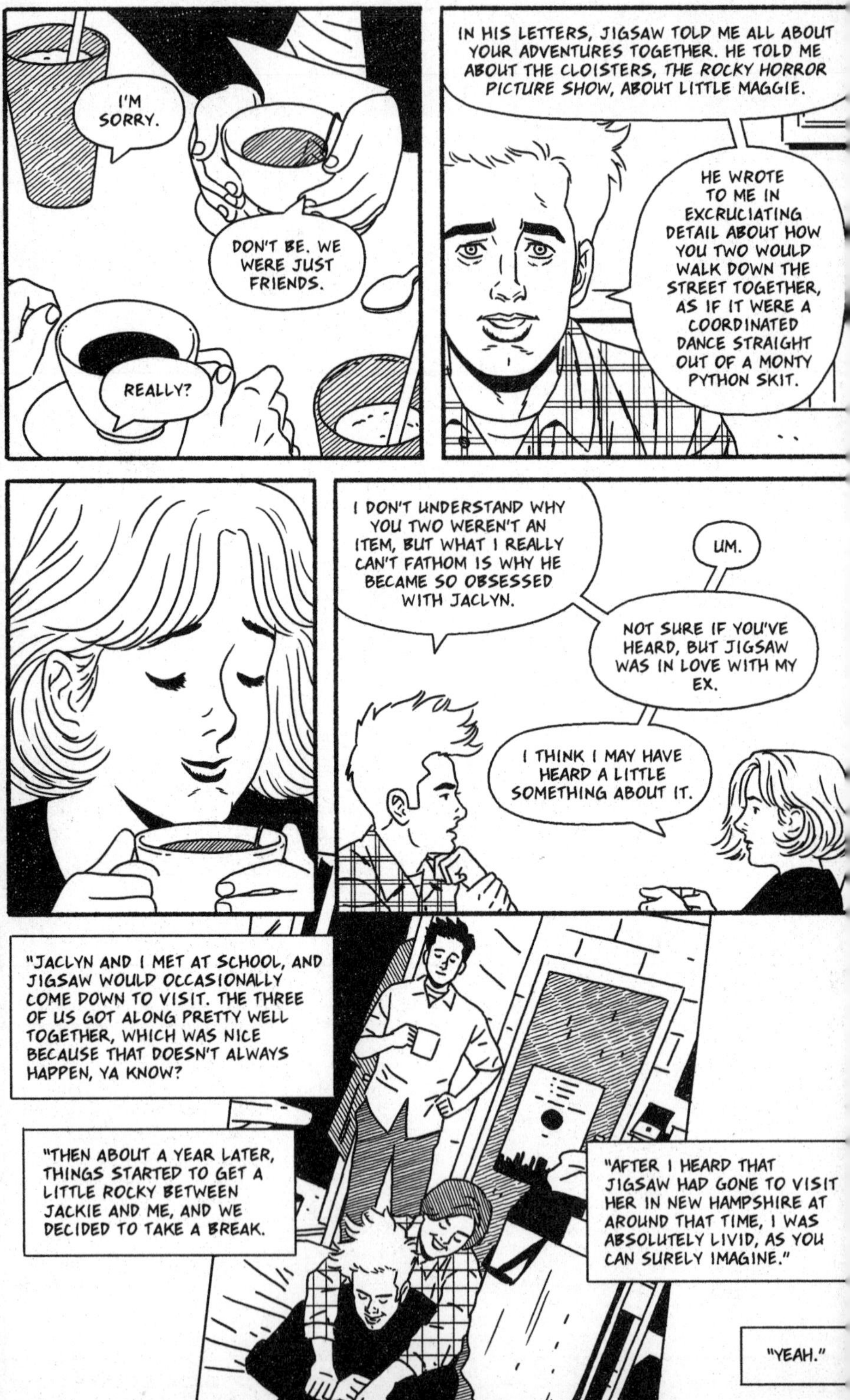
I'M SORRY.
DON'T BE. WE WERE JUST FRIENDS.
REALLY?
IN HIS LETTERS, JIGSAW TOLD ME ALL ABOUT YOUR ADVENTURES TOGETHER. HE TOLD ME ABOUT THE CLOISTERS, THE *ROCKY HORROR PICTURE SHOW*, ABOUT LITTLE MAGGIE.
HE WROTE TO ME IN EXCRUCIATING DETAIL ABOUT HOW YOU TWO WOULD WALK DOWN THE STREET TOGETHER, AS IF IT WERE A COORDINATED DANCE STRAIGHT OUT OF A MONTY PYTHON SKIT.
I DON'T UNDERSTAND WHY YOU TWO WEREN'T AN ITEM, BUT WHAT I REALLY CAN'T FATHOM IS WHY HE BECAME SO OBSESSED WITH JACLYN.
UM.
NOT SURE IF YOU'VE HEARD, BUT JIGSAW WAS IN LOVE WITH MY EX.
I THINK I MAY HAVE HEARD A LITTLE SOMETHING ABOUT IT.
"JACLYN AND I MET AT SCHOOL, AND JIGSAW WOULD OCCASIONALLY COME DOWN TO VISIT. THE THREE OF US GOT ALONG PRETTY WELL TOGETHER, WHICH WAS NICE BECAUSE THAT DOESN'T ALWAYS HAPPEN, YA KNOW?
"THEN ABOUT A YEAR LATER, THINGS STARTED TO GET A LITTLE ROCKY BETWEEN JACKIE AND ME, AND WE DECIDED TO TAKE A BREAK.
"AFTER I HEARD THAT JIGSAW HAD GONE TO VISIT HER IN NEW HAMPSHIRE AT AROUND THAT TIME, I WAS ABSOLUTELY LIVID, AS YOU CAN SURELY IMAGINE."
"YEAH."

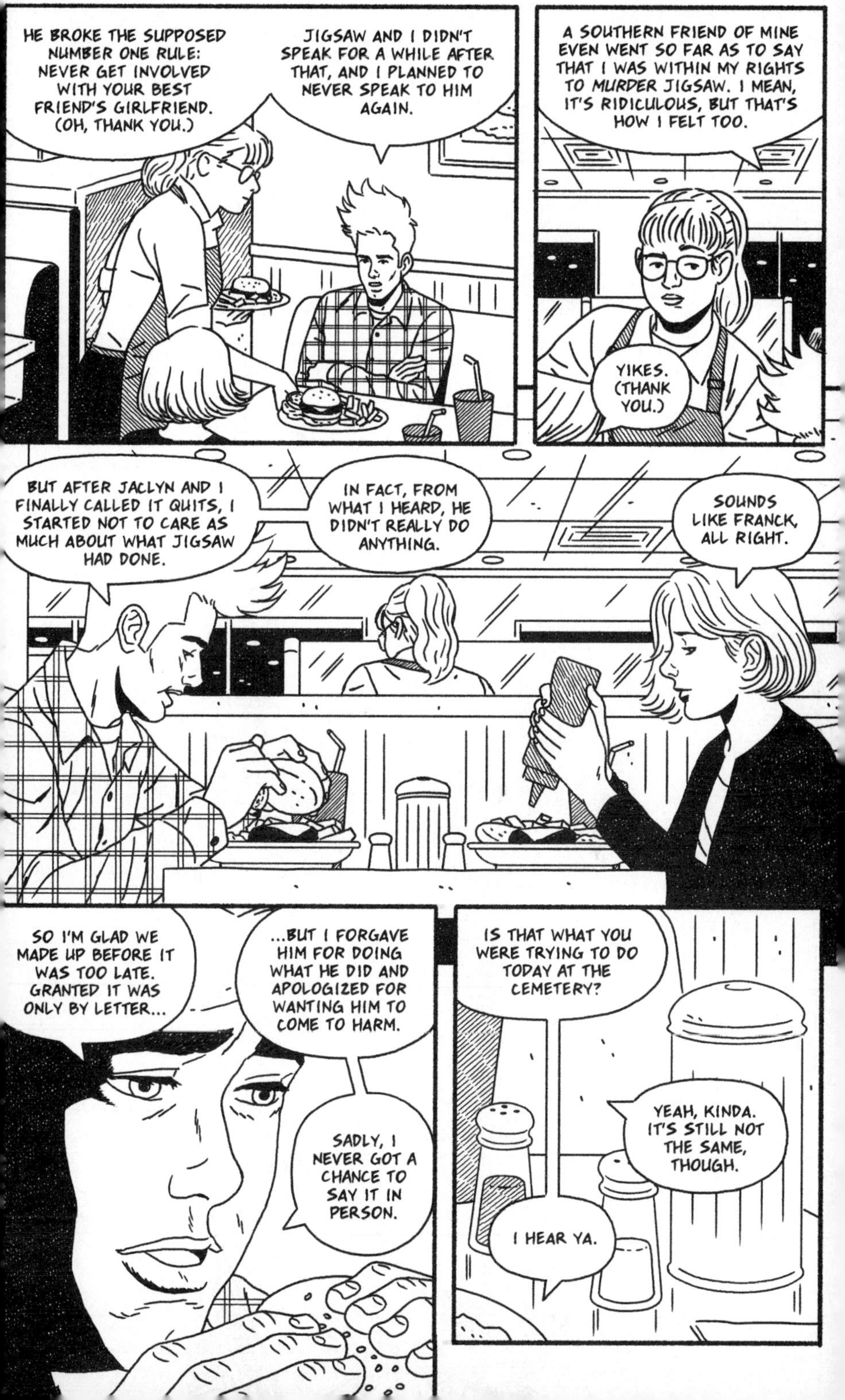
HE BROKE THE SUPPOSED NUMBER ONE RULE: NEVER GET INVOLVED WITH YOUR BEST FRIEND'S GIRLFRIEND. (OH, THANK YOU.)
JIGSAW AND I DIDN'T SPEAK FOR A WHILE AFTER THAT, AND I PLANNED TO NEVER SPEAK TO HIM AGAIN.
A SOUTHERN FRIEND OF MINE EVEN WENT SO FAR AS TO SAY THAT I WAS WITHIN MY RIGHTS TO *MURDER* JIGSAW. I MEAN, IT'S RIDICULOUS, BUT THAT'S HOW I FELT TOO.
YIKES. (THANK YOU.)
BUT AFTER JACLYN AND I FINALLY CALLED IT QUITS, I STARTED NOT TO CARE AS MUCH ABOUT WHAT JIGSAW HAD DONE.
IN FACT, FROM WHAT I HEARD, HE DIDN'T REALLY DO ANYTHING.
SOUNDS LIKE FRANCK, ALL RIGHT.
SO I'M GLAD WE MADE UP BEFORE IT WAS TOO LATE. GRANTED IT WAS ONLY BY LETTER...
...BUT I FORGAVE HIM FOR DOING WHAT HE DID AND APOLOGIZED FOR WANTING HIM TO COME TO HARM.
SADLY, I NEVER GOT A CHANCE TO SAY IT IN PERSON.
IS THAT WHAT YOU WERE TRYING TO DO TODAY AT THE CEMETERY?
YEAH, KINDA. IT'S STILL NOT THE SAME, THOUGH.
I HEAR YA.

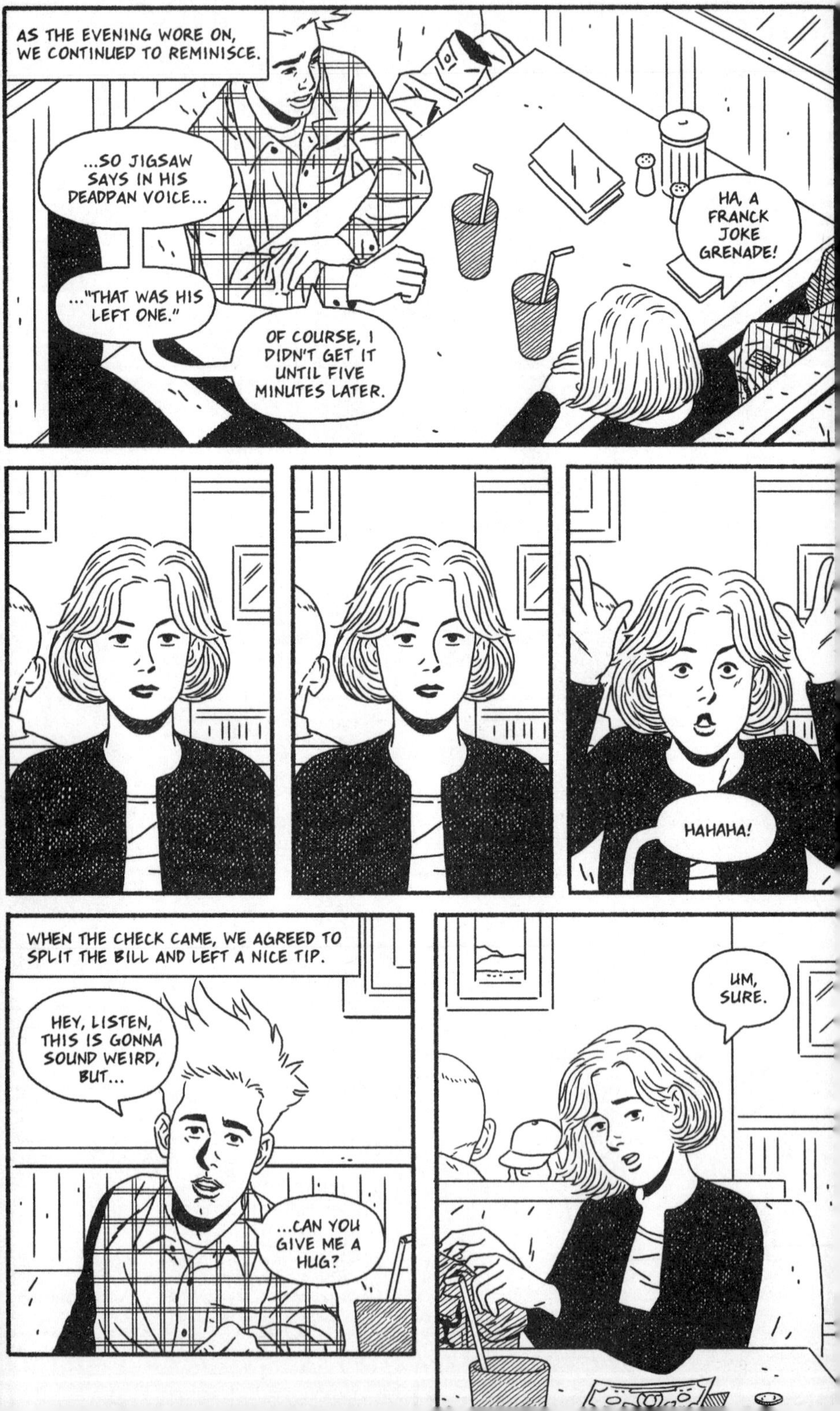
AS THE EVENING WORE ON, WE CONTINUED TO REMINISCE.
...SO JIGSAW SAYS IN HIS DEADPAN VOICE...
..."THAT WAS HIS LEFT ONE."
OF COURSE, I DIDN'T GET IT UNTIL FIVE MINUTES LATER.
HA, A FRANCK JOKE GRENADE!
HAHAHA!
WHEN THE CHECK CAME, WE AGREED TO SPLIT THE BILL AND LEFT A NICE TIP.
HEY, LISTEN, THIS IS GONNA SOUND WEIRD, BUT...
...CAN YOU GIVE ME A HUG?
UM, SURE.

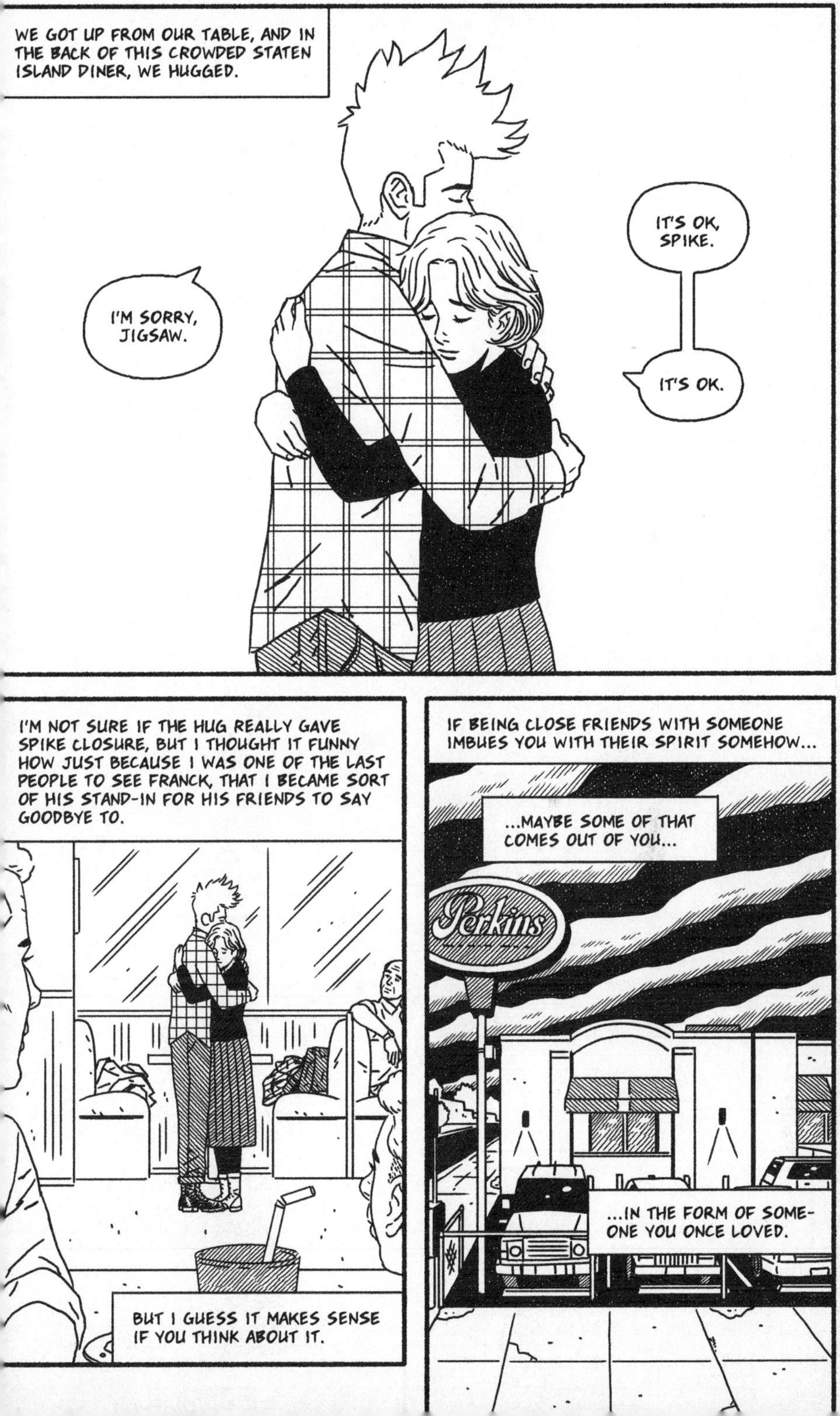
WE GOT UP FROM OUR TABLE, AND IN THE BACK OF THIS CROWDED STATEN ISLAND DINER, WE HUGGED.
I'M SORRY, JIGSAW.
IT'S OK, SPIKE.
IT'S OK.
I'M NOT SURE IF THE HUG REALLY GAVE SPIKE CLOSURE, BUT I THOUGHT IT FUNNY HOW JUST BECAUSE I WAS ONE OF THE LAST PEOPLE TO SEE FRANCK, THAT I BECAME SORT OF HIS STAND-IN FOR HIS FRIENDS TO SAY GOODBYE TO.
BUT I GUESS IT MAKES SENSE IF YOU THINK ABOUT IT.
IF BEING CLOSE FRIENDS WITH SOMEONE IMBUES YOU WITH THEIR SPIRIT SOMEHOW...
...MAYBE SOME OF THAT COMES OUT OF YOU...
Perkins
...IN THE FORM OF SOME-ONE YOU ONCE LOVED.

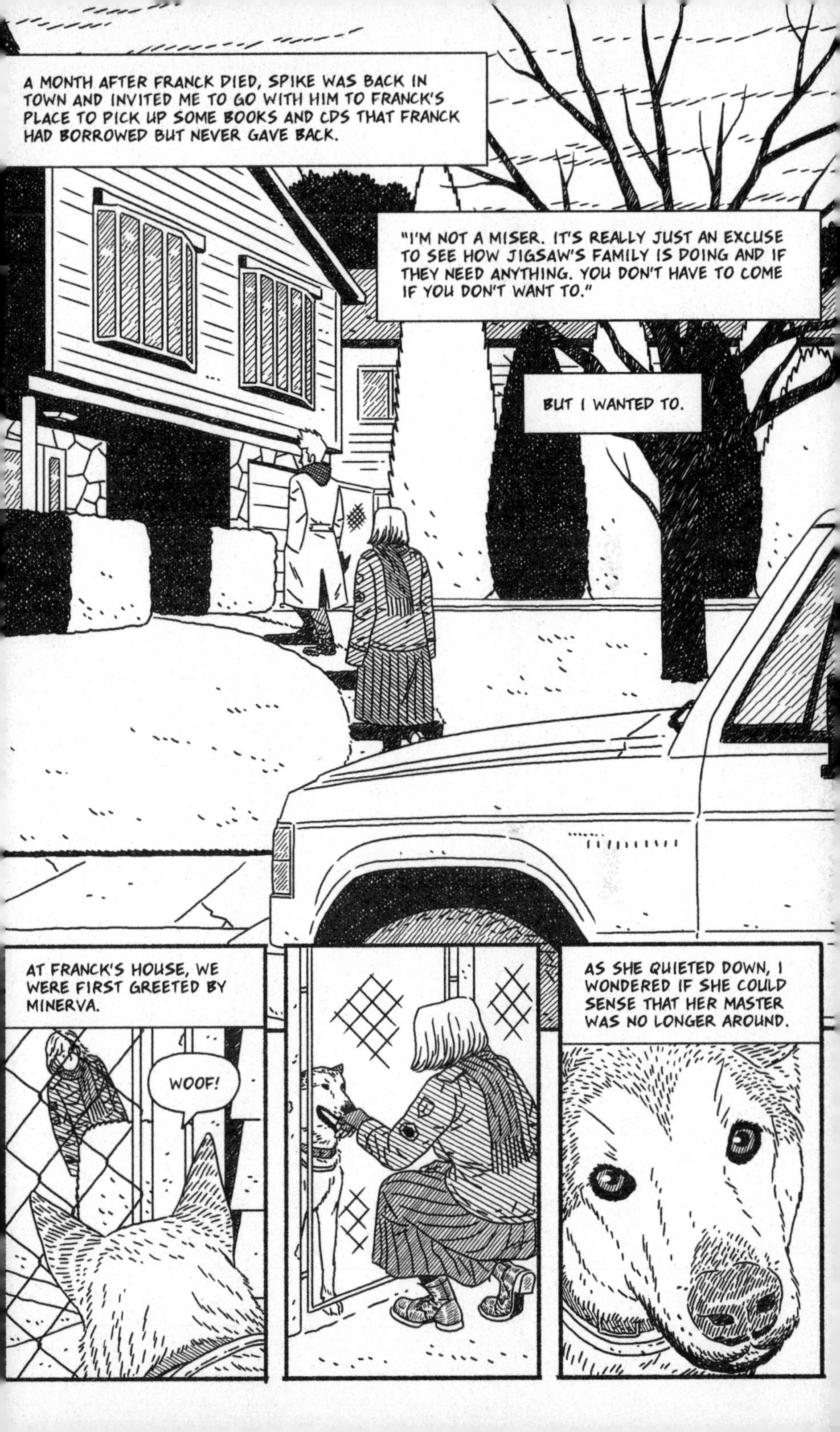
A MONTH AFTER FRANCK DIED, SPIKE WAS BACK IN TOWN AND INVITED ME TO GO WITH HIM TO FRANCK'S PLACE TO PICK UP SOME BOOKS AND CDS THAT FRANCK HAD BORROWED BUT NEVER GAVE BACK.
"I'M NOT A MISER. IT'S REALLY JUST AN EXCUSE TO SEE HOW JIGSAW'S FAMILY IS DOING AND IF THEY NEED ANYTHING. YOU DON'T HAVE TO COME IF YOU DON'T WANT TO."
BUT I WANTED TO.
AT FRANCK'S HOUSE, WE WERE FIRST GREETED BY MINERVA.
WOOF!
AS SHE QUIETED DOWN, I WONDERED IF SHE COULD SENSE THAT HER MASTER WAS NO LONGER AROUND.

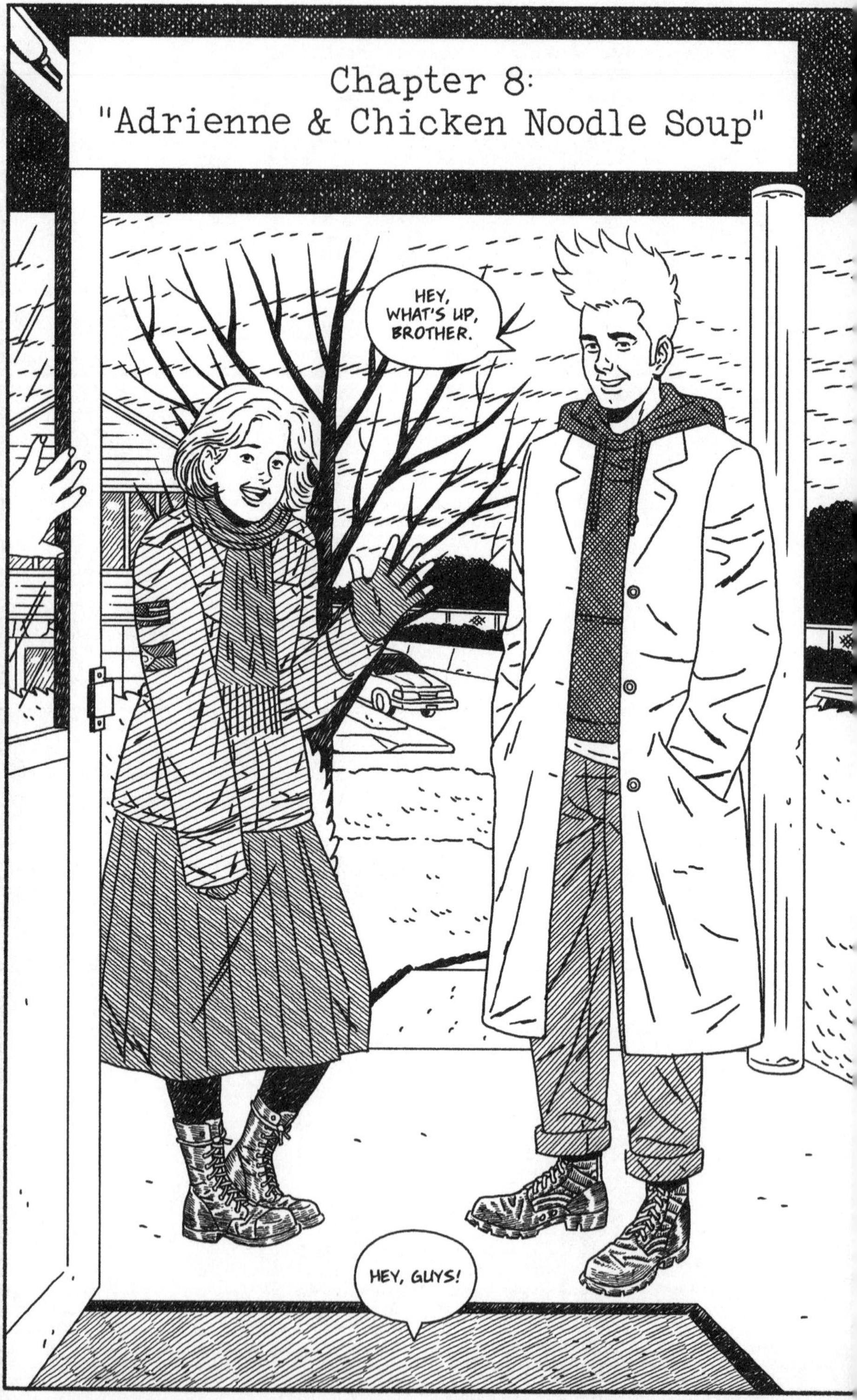
Chapter 8:
"Adrienne & Chicken Noodle Soup"
HEY, WHAT'S UP, BROTHER.
HEY, GUYS!

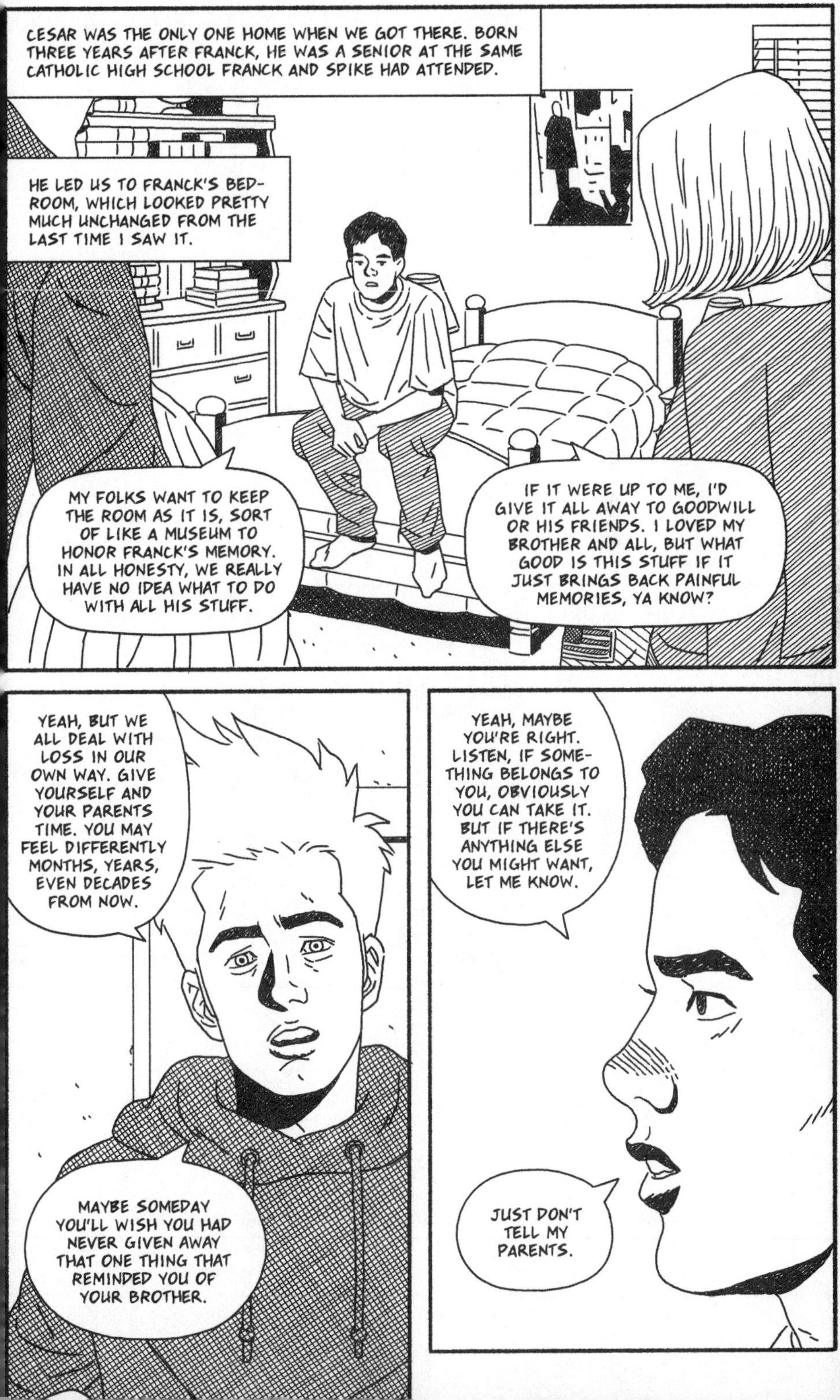
CESAR WAS THE ONLY ONE HOME WHEN WE GOT THERE. BORN THREE YEARS AFTER FRANCK, HE WAS A SENIOR AT THE SAME CATHOLIC HIGH SCHOOL FRANCK AND SPIKE HAD ATTENDED.
HE LED US TO FRANCK'S BEDROOM, WHICH LOOKED PRETTY MUCH UNCHANGED FROM THE LAST TIME I SAW IT.
MY FOLKS WANT TO KEEP THE ROOM AS IT IS, SORT OF LIKE A MUSEUM TO HONOR FRANCK'S MEMORY. IN ALL HONESTY, WE REALLY HAVE NO IDEA WHAT TO DO WITH ALL HIS STUFF.
IF IT WERE UP TO ME, I'D GIVE IT ALL AWAY TO GOODWILL OR HIS FRIENDS. I LOVED MY BROTHER AND ALL, BUT WHAT GOOD IS THIS STUFF IF IT JUST BRINGS BACK PAINFUL MEMORIES, YA KNOW?
YEAH, BUT WE ALL DEAL WITH LOSS IN OUR OWN WAY. GIVE YOURSELF AND YOUR PARENTS TIME. YOU MAY FEEL DIFFERENTLY MONTHS, YEARS, EVEN DECADES FROM NOW.
MAYBE SOMEDAY YOU'LL WISH YOU HAD NEVER GIVEN AWAY THAT ONE THING THAT REMINDED YOU OF YOUR BROTHER.
YEAH, MAYBE YOU'RE RIGHT. LISTEN, IF SOMETHING BELONGS TO YOU, OBVIOUSLY YOU CAN TAKE IT. BUT IF THERE'S ANYTHING ELSE YOU MIGHT WANT, LET ME KNOW.
JUST DON'T TELL MY PARENTS.

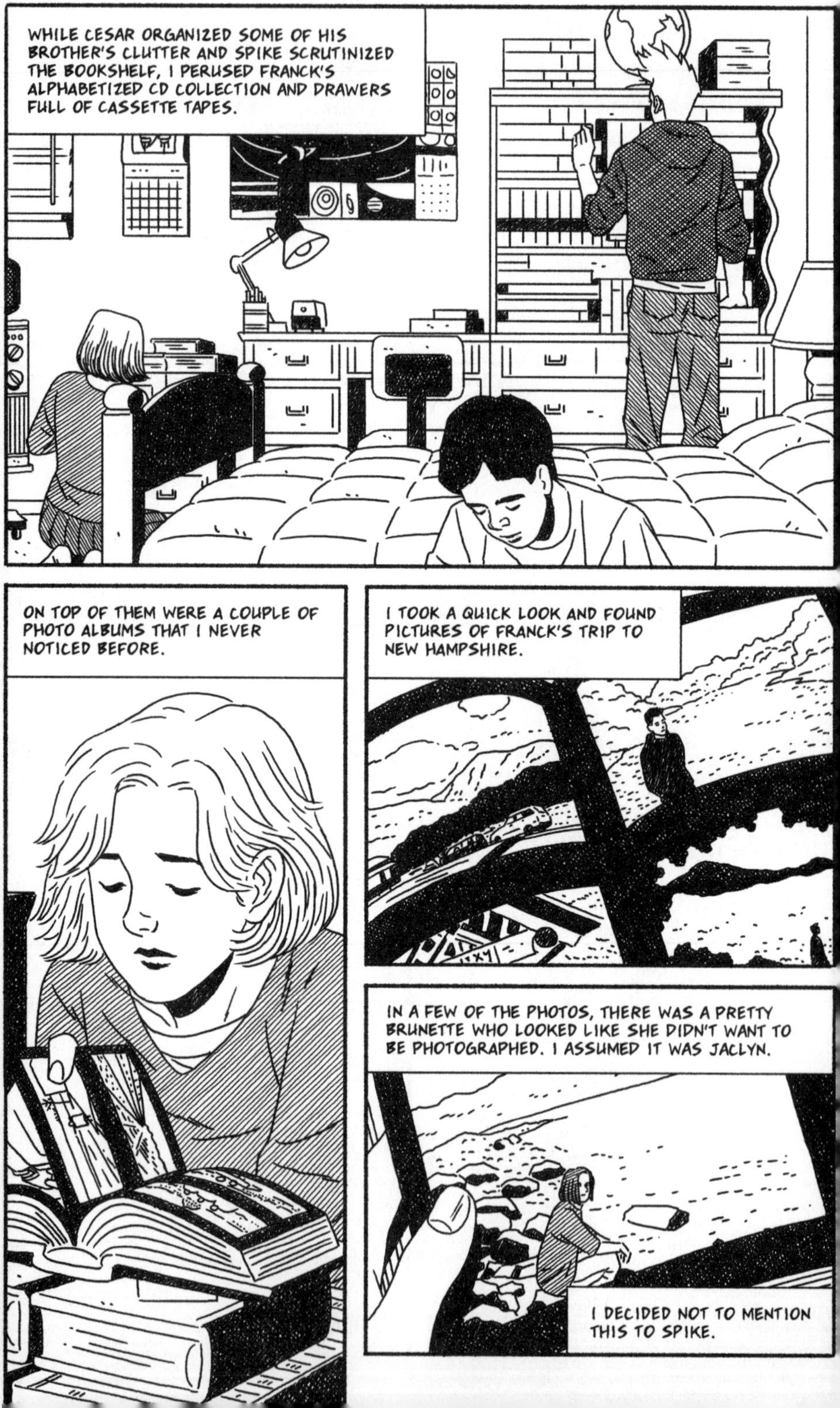
WHILE CESAR ORGANIZED SOME OF HIS BROTHER'S CLUTTER AND SPIKE SCRUTINIZED THE BOOKSHELF, I PERUSED FRANCK'S ALPHABETIZED CD COLLECTION AND DRAWERS FULL OF CASSETTE TAPES.
ON TOP OF THEM WERE A COUPLE OF PHOTO ALBUMS THAT I NEVER NOTICED BEFORE.
I TOOK A QUICK LOOK AND FOUND PICTURES OF FRANCK'S TRIP TO NEW HAMPSHIRE.
IN A FEW OF THE PHOTOS, THERE WAS A PRETTY BRUNETTE WHO LOOKED LIKE SHE DIDN'T WANT TO BE PHOTOGRAPHED. I ASSUMED IT WAS JACLYN.
I DECIDED NOT TO MENTION THIS TO SPIKE.

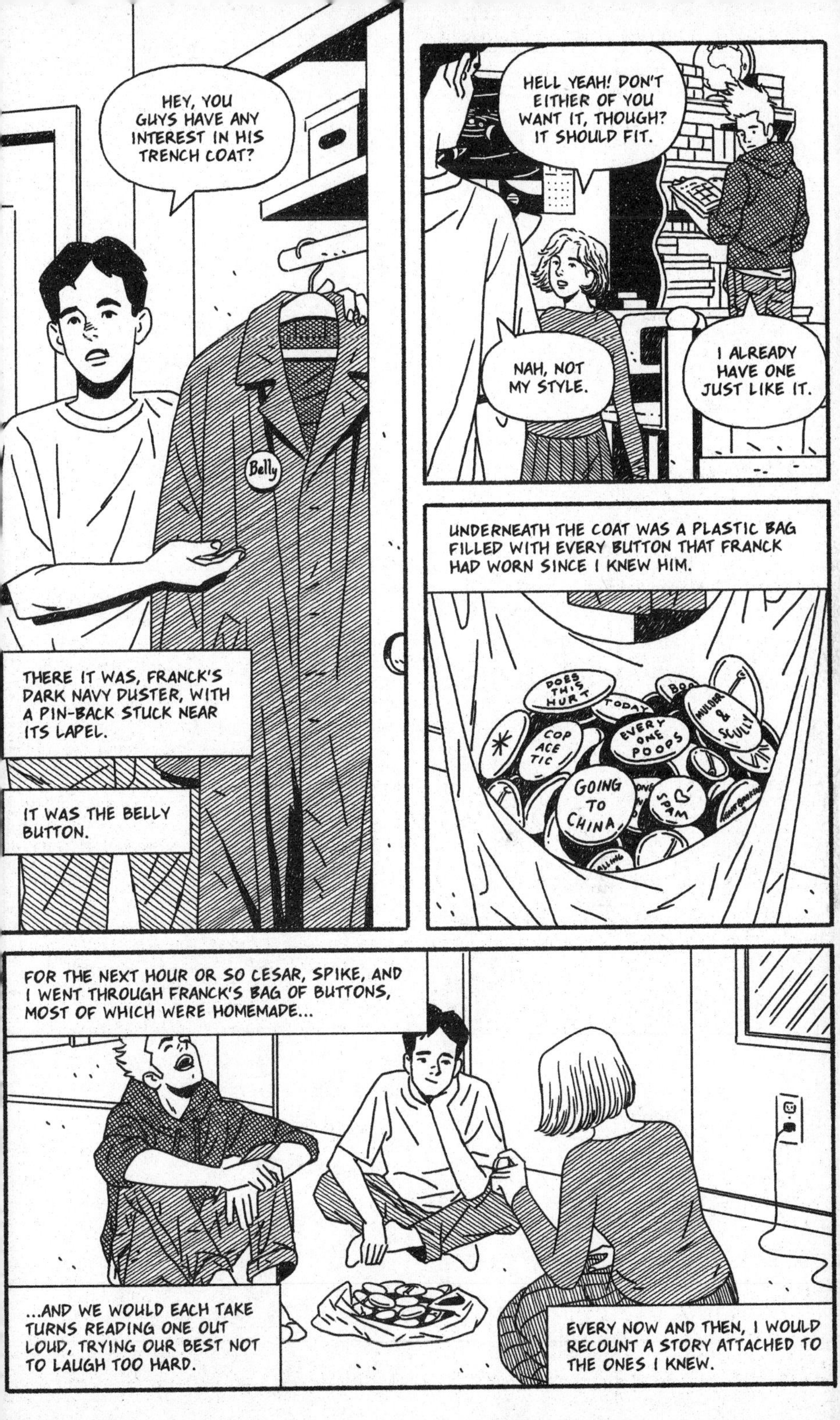
HEY, YOU GUYS HAVE ANY INTEREST IN HIS TRENCH COAT?
Belly
THERE IT WAS, FRANCK'S DARK NAVY DUSTER, WITH A PIN-BACK STUCK NEAR ITS LAPEL.
IT WAS THE BELLY BUTTON.
HELL YEAH! DON'T EITHER OF YOU WANT IT, THOUGH? IT SHOULD FIT.
NAH, NOT MY STYLE.
I ALREADY HAVE ONE JUST LIKE IT.
UNDERNEATH THE COAT WAS A PLASTIC BAG FILLED WITH EVERY BUTTON THAT FRANCK HAD WORN SINCE I KNEW HIM.
DOES THIS HURT
MULDER & SCULLY
COP ACE TIC
EVERY ONE POOPS
GOING TO CHINA
SPAM
FOR THE NEXT HOUR OR SO CESAR, SPIKE, AND I WENT THROUGH FRANCK'S BAG OF BUTTONS, MOST OF WHICH WERE HOMEMADE...
...AND WE WOULD EACH TAKE TURNS READING ONE OUT LOUD, TRYING OUR BEST NOT TO LAUGH TOO HARD.
EVERY NOW AND THEN, I WOULD RECOUNT A STORY ATTACHED TO THE ONES I KNEW.

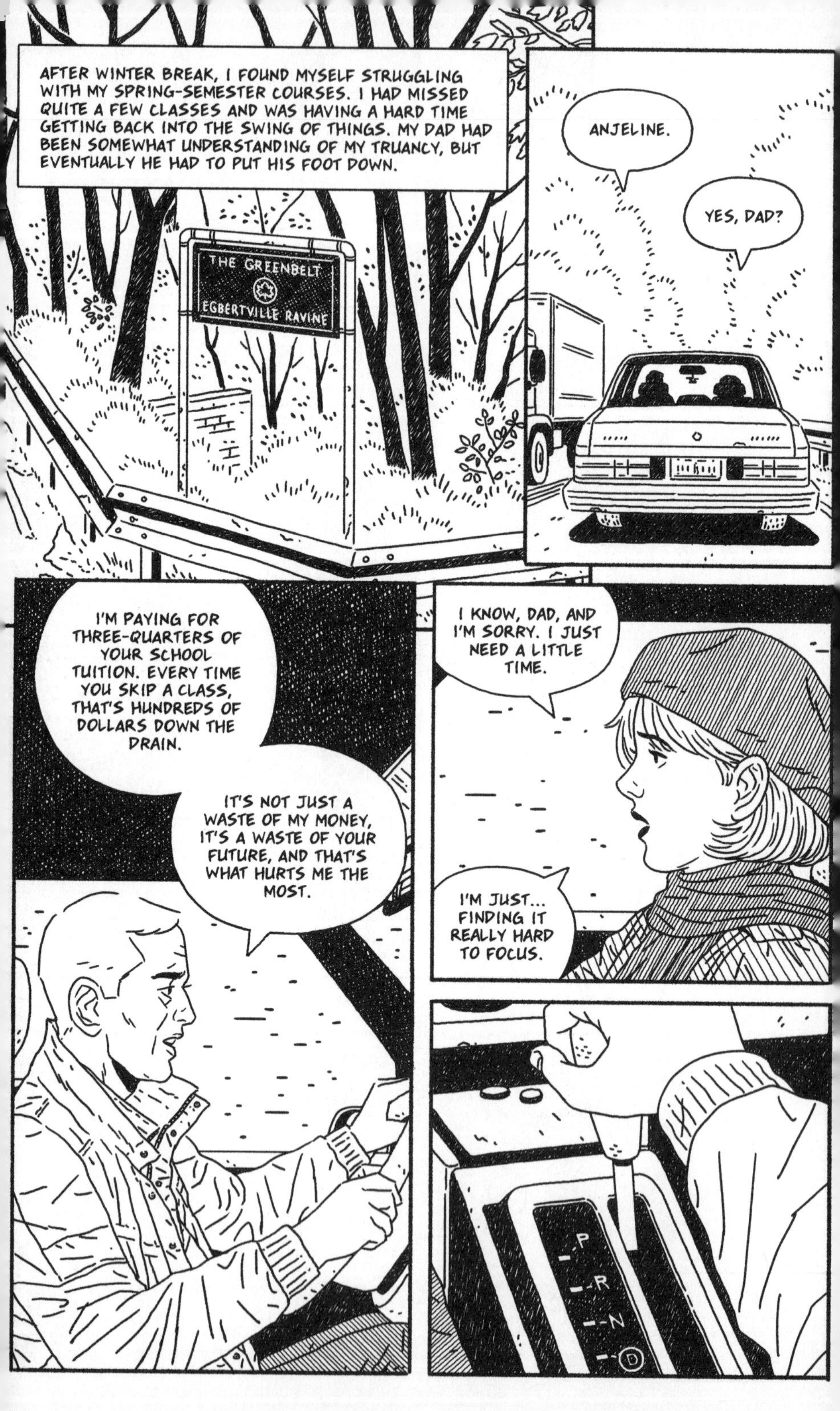
AFTER WINTER BREAK, I FOUND MYSELF STRUGGLING WITH MY SPRING-SEMESTER COURSES. I HAD MISSED QUITE A FEW CLASSES AND WAS HAVING A HARD TIME GETTING BACK INTO THE SWING OF THINGS. MY DAD HAD BEEN SOMEWHAT UNDERSTANDING OF MY TRUANCY, BUT EVENTUALLY HE HAD TO PUT HIS FOOT DOWN.
THE GREENBELT
EGBERTVILLE RAVINE
ANJELINE.
YES, DAD?
I'M PAYING FOR THREE-QUARTERS OF YOUR SCHOOL TUITION. EVERY TIME YOU SKIP A CLASS, THAT'S HUNDREDS OF DOLLARS DOWN THE DRAIN.
IT'S NOT JUST A WASTE OF MY MONEY, IT'S A WASTE OF YOUR FUTURE, AND THAT'S WHAT HURTS ME THE MOST.
I KNOW, DAD, AND I'M SORRY. I JUST NEED A LITTLE TIME.
I'M JUST... FINDING IT REALLY HARD TO FOCUS.
P
R
N
D

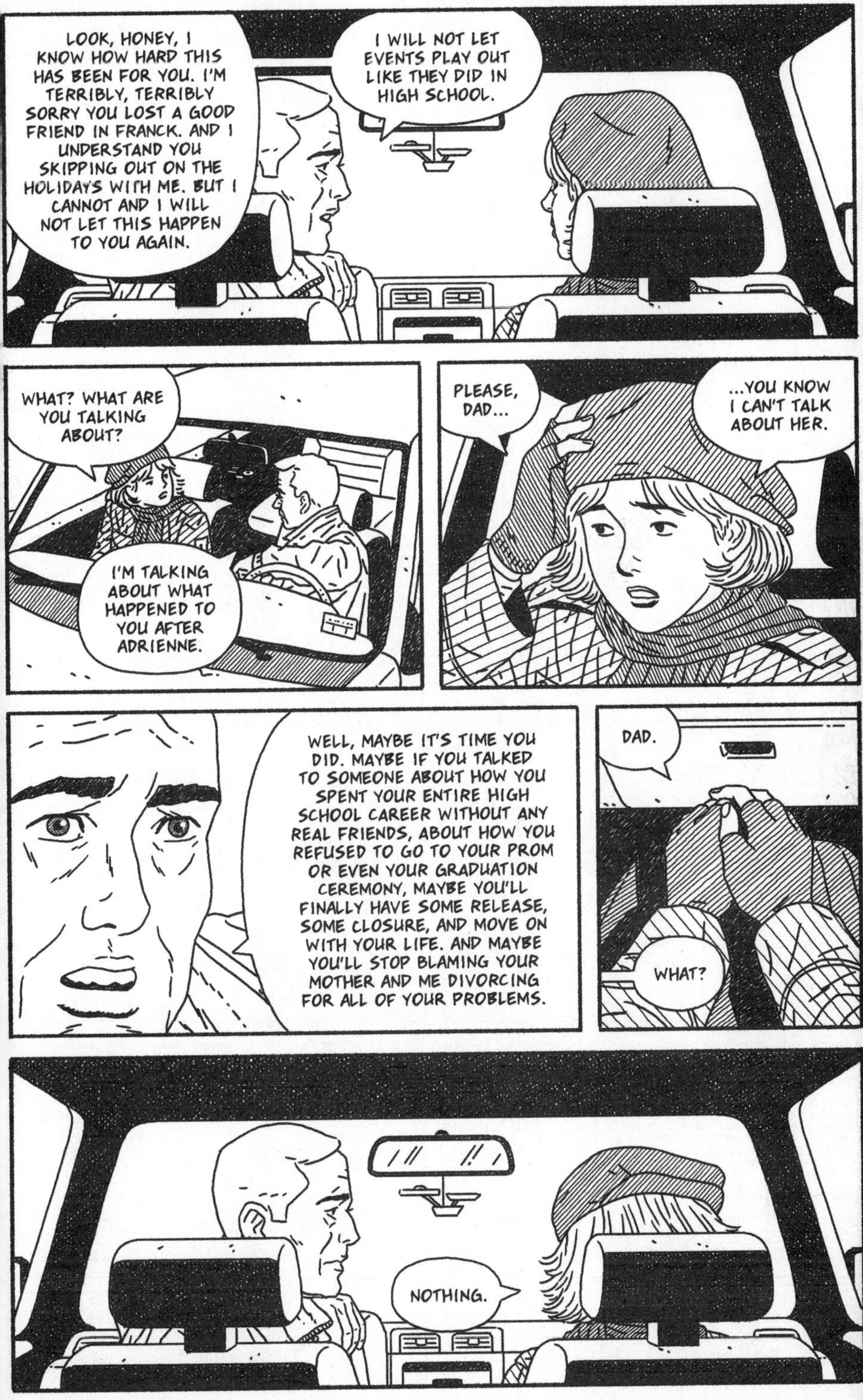
LOOK, HONEY, I KNOW HOW HARD THIS HAS BEEN FOR YOU. I'M TERRIBLY, TERRIBLY SORRY YOU LOST A GOOD FRIEND IN FRANCK. AND I UNDERSTAND YOU SKIPPING OUT ON THE HOLIDAYS WITH ME. BUT I CANNOT AND I WILL NOT LET THIS HAPPEN TO YOU AGAIN.
I WILL NOT LET EVENTS PLAY OUT LIKE THEY DID IN HIGH SCHOOL.
WHAT? WHAT ARE YOU TALKING ABOUT?
I'M TALKING ABOUT WHAT HAPPENED TO YOU AFTER ADRIENNE.
PLEASE, DAD...
...YOU KNOW I CAN'T TALK ABOUT HER.
WELL, MAYBE IT'S TIME YOU DID. MAYBE IF YOU TALKED TO SOMEONE ABOUT HOW YOU SPENT YOUR ENTIRE HIGH SCHOOL CAREER WITHOUT ANY REAL FRIENDS, ABOUT HOW YOU REFUSED TO GO TO YOUR PROM OR EVEN YOUR GRADUATION CEREMONY, MAYBE YOU'LL FINALLY HAVE SOME RELEASE, SOME CLOSURE, AND MOVE ON WITH YOUR LIFE. AND MAYBE YOU'LL STOP BLAMING YOUR MOTHER AND ME DIVORCING FOR ALL OF YOUR PROBLEMS.
DAD.
WHAT?
NOTHING.

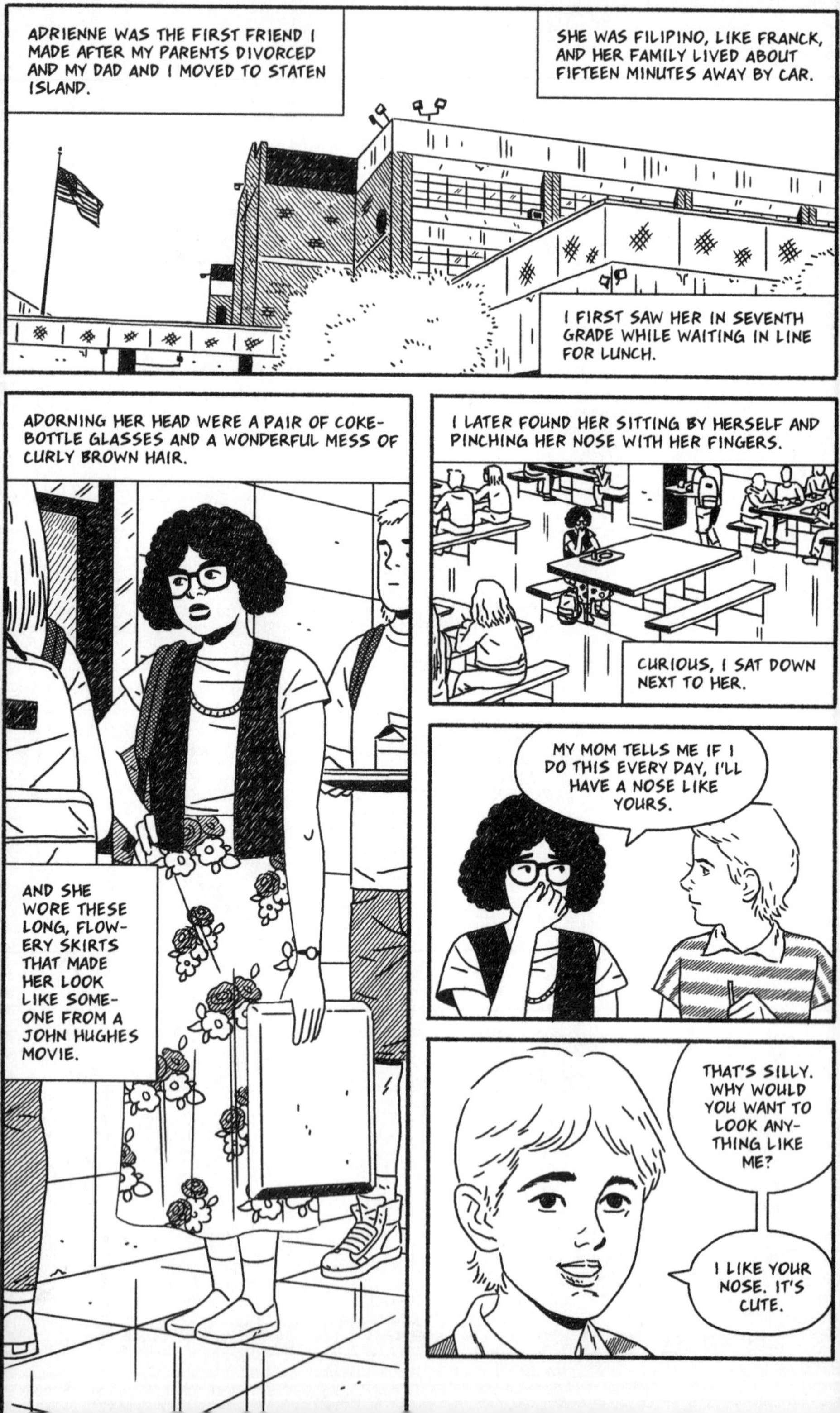
ADRIENNE WAS THE FIRST FRIEND I MADE AFTER MY PARENTS DIVORCED AND MY DAD AND I MOVED TO STATEN ISLAND.
SHE WAS FILIPINO, LIKE FRANCK, AND HER FAMILY LIVED ABOUT FIFTEEN MINUTES AWAY BY CAR.
I FIRST SAW HER IN SEVENTH GRADE WHILE WAITING IN LINE FOR LUNCH.
ADORNING HER HEAD WERE A PAIR OF COKE-BOTTLE GLASSES AND A WONDERFUL MESS OF CURLY BROWN HAIR.
AND SHE WORE THESE LONG, FLOWERY SKIRTS THAT MADE HER LOOK LIKE SOMEONE FROM A JOHN HUGHES MOVIE.
I LATER FOUND HER SITTING BY HERSELF AND PINCHING HER NOSE WITH HER FINGERS.
CURIOUS, I SAT DOWN NEXT TO HER.
MY MOM TELLS ME IF I DO THIS EVERY DAY, I'LL HAVE A NOSE LIKE YOURS.
THAT'S SILLY. WHY WOULD YOU WANT TO LOOK ANYTHING LIKE ME?
I LIKE YOUR NOSE. IT'S CUTE.

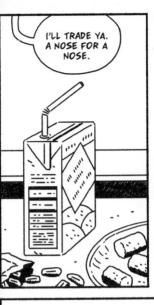

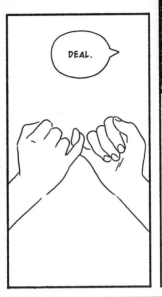

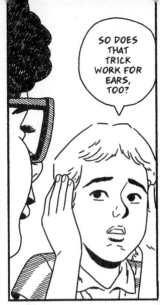

I'LL TRADE YA. A NOSE FOR A NOSE.
DEAL.
SO DOES THAT TRICK WORK FOR EARS, TOO?
AFTER REMINISCING ABOUT ADRIENNE, I DUG UP SOME OLD PHOTOS OF THE TWO OF US.
DIARY

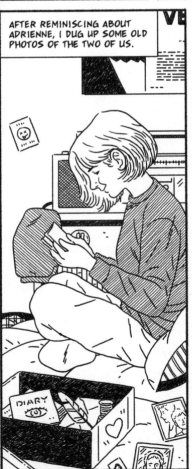

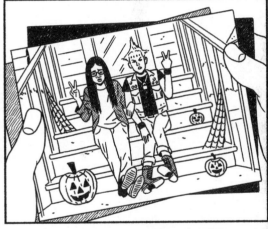

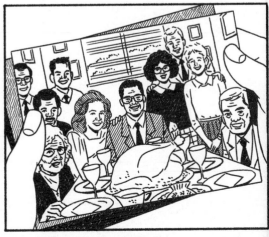

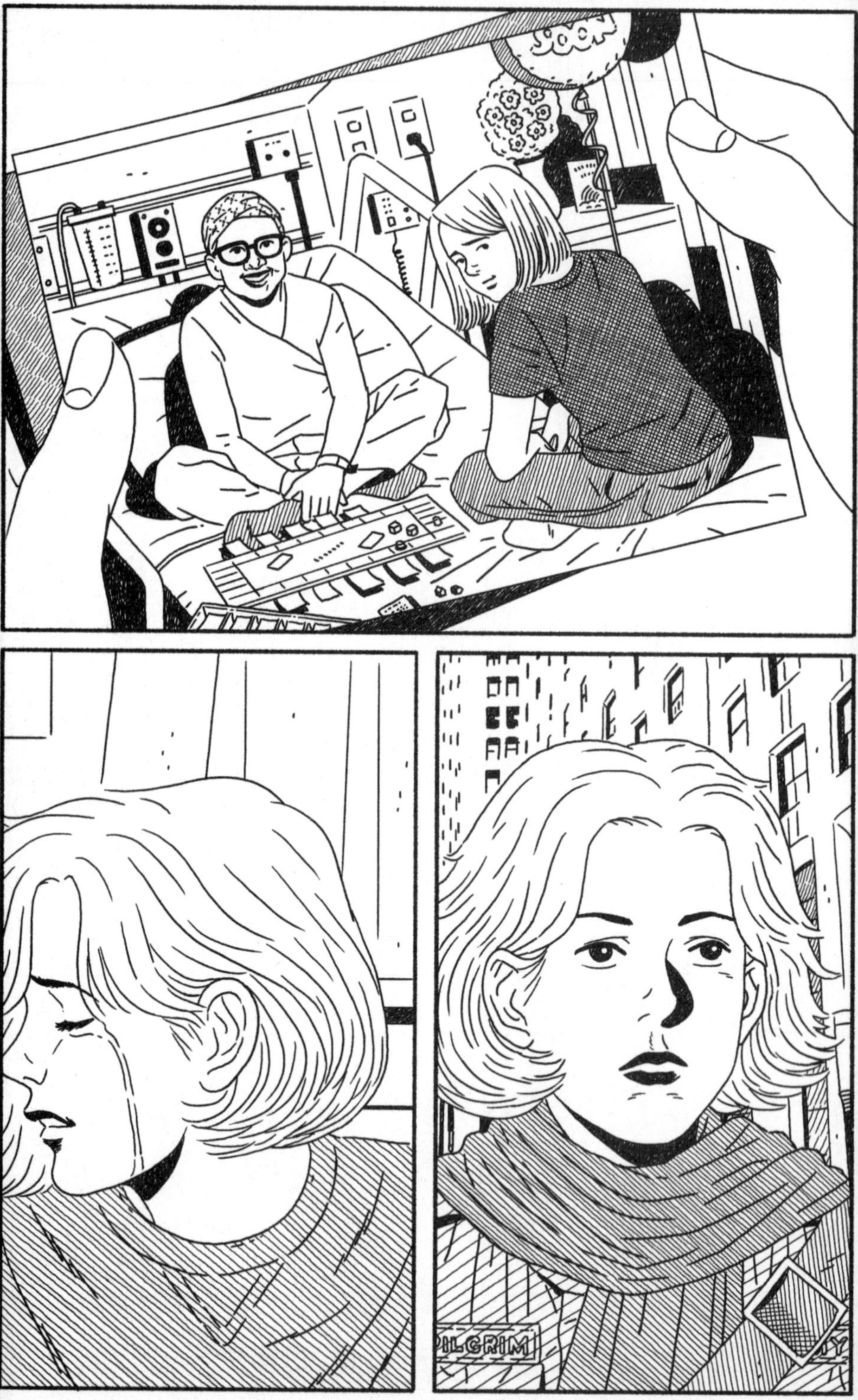
PILGRIM

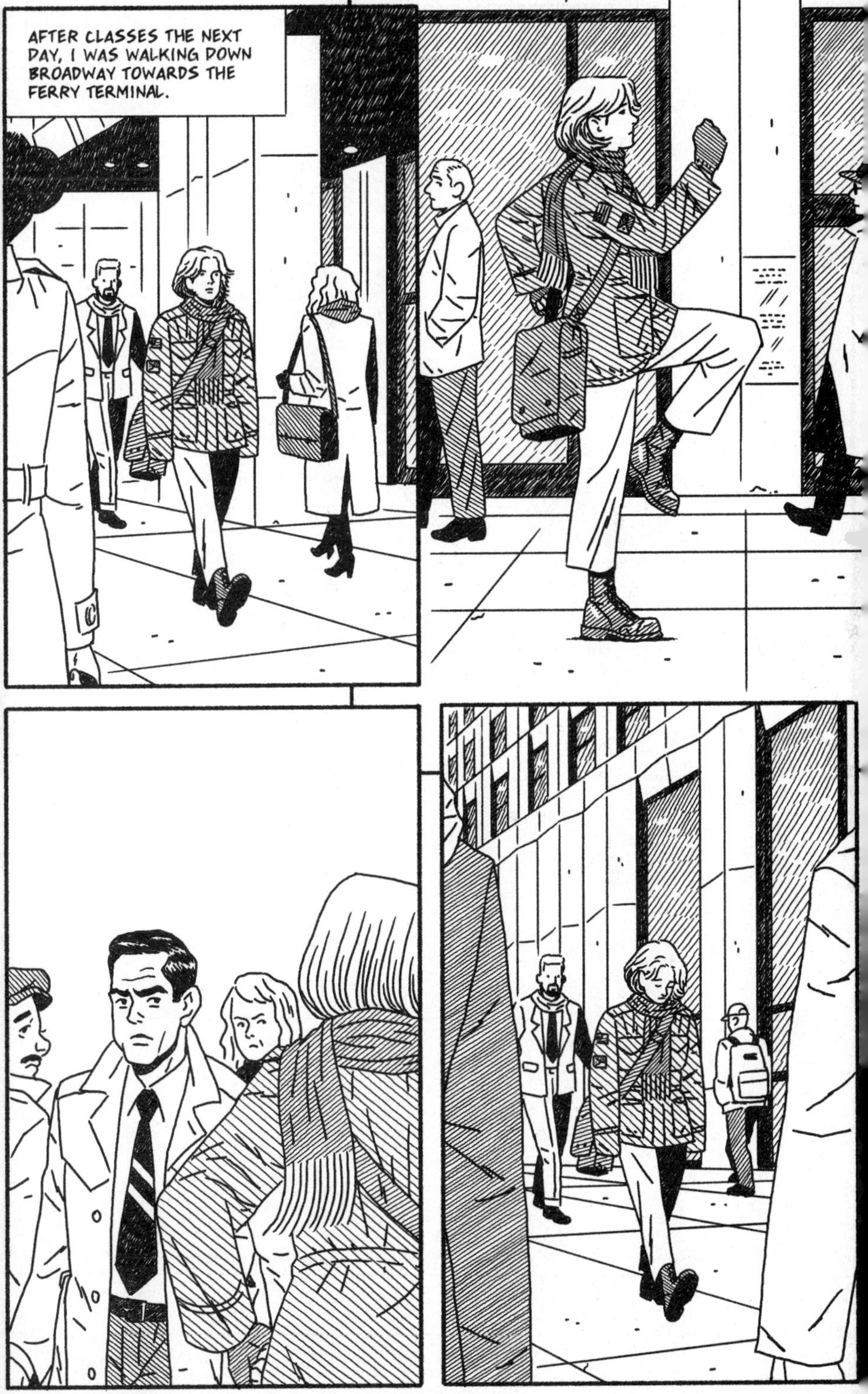
AFTER CLASSES THE NEXT DAY, I WAS WALKING DOWN BROADWAY TOWARDS THE FERRY TERMINAL.

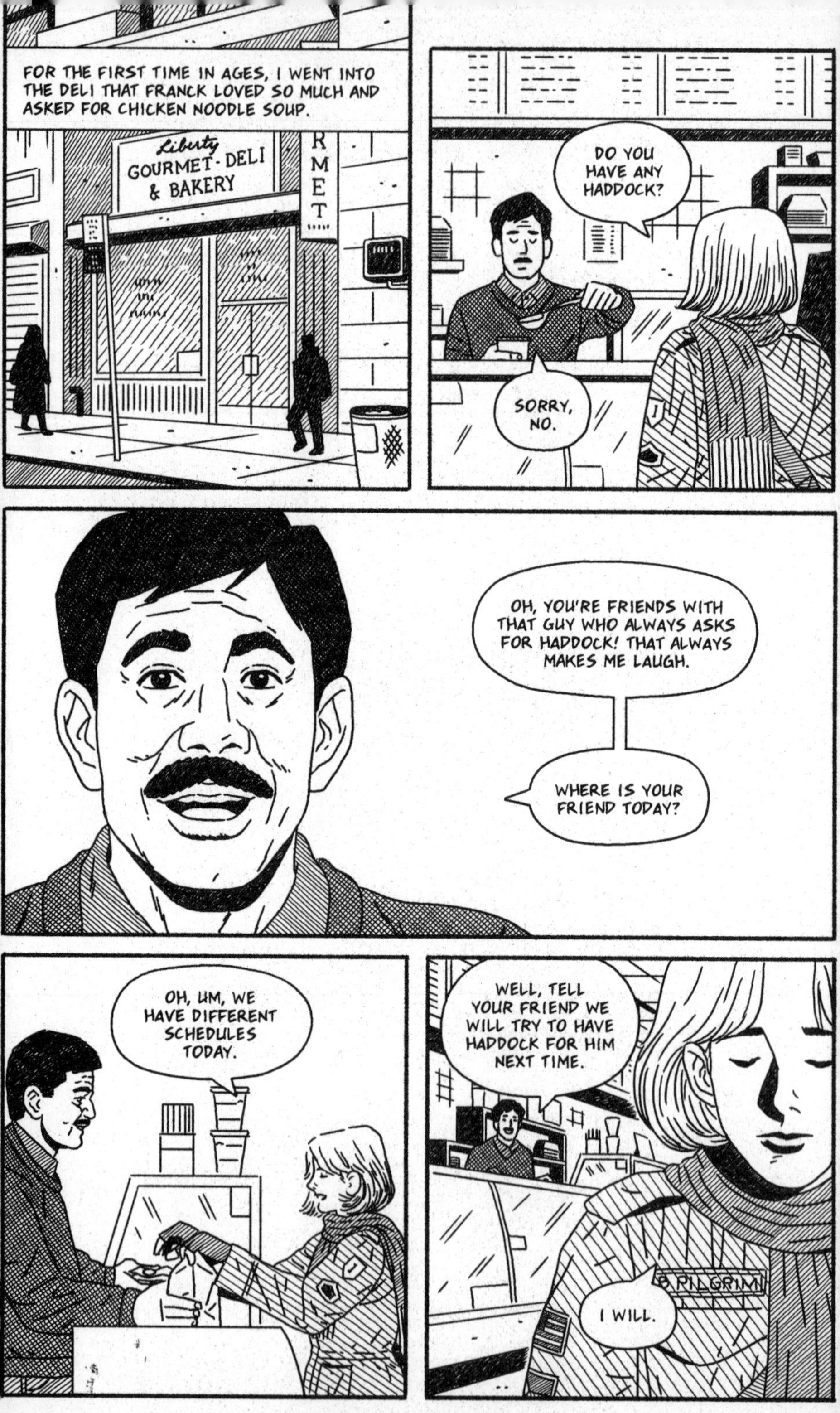
FOR THE FIRST TIME IN AGES, I WENT INTO THE DELI THAT FRANCK LOVED SO MUCH AND ASKED FOR CHICKEN NOODLE SOUP.
Liberty GOURMET - DELI & BAKERY
RMET
DO YOU HAVE ANY HADDOCK?
SORRY, NO.
OH, YOU'RE FRIENDS WITH THAT GUY WHO ALWAYS ASKS FOR HADDOCK! THAT ALWAYS MAKES ME LAUGH.
WHERE IS YOUR FRIEND TODAY?
OH, UM, WE HAVE DIFFERENT SCHEDULES TODAY.
WELL, TELL YOUR FRIEND WE WILL TRY TO HAVE HADDOCK FOR HIM NEXT TIME.
B. PILGRIM
I WILL.

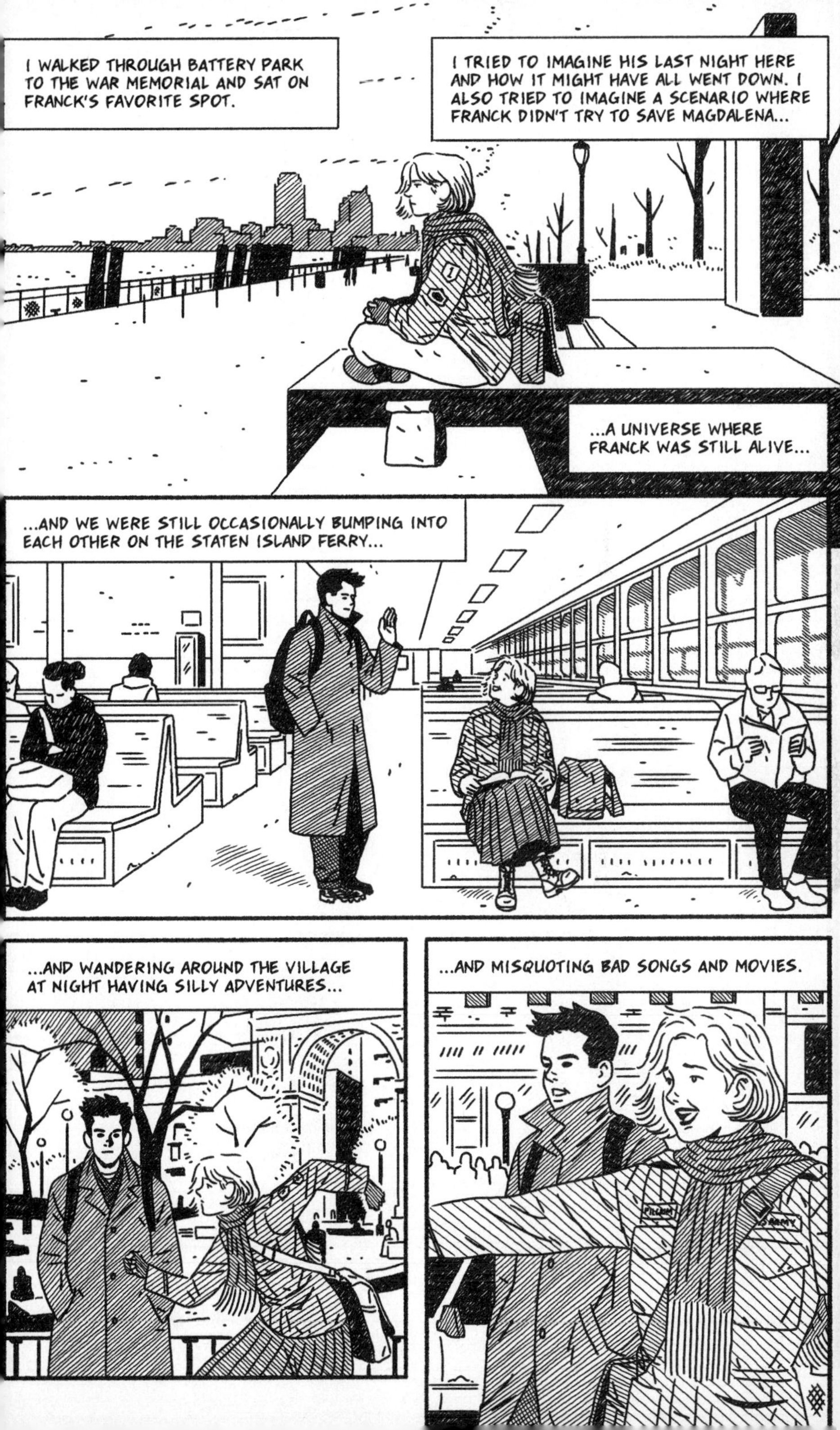
I WALKED THROUGH BATTERY PARK TO THE WAR MEMORIAL AND SAT ON FRANCK'S FAVORITE SPOT.
I TRIED TO IMAGINE HIS LAST NIGHT HERE AND HOW IT MIGHT HAVE ALL WENT DOWN. I ALSO TRIED TO IMAGINE A SCENARIO WHERE FRANCK DIDN'T TRY TO SAVE MAGDALENA...
...A UNIVERSE WHERE FRANCK WAS STILL ALIVE...
...AND WE WERE STILL OCCASIONALLY BUMPING INTO EACH OTHER ON THE STATEN ISLAND FERRY...
...AND WANDERING AROUND THE VILLAGE AT NIGHT HAVING SILLY ADVENTURES...
...AND MISQUOTING BAD SONGS AND MOVIES.

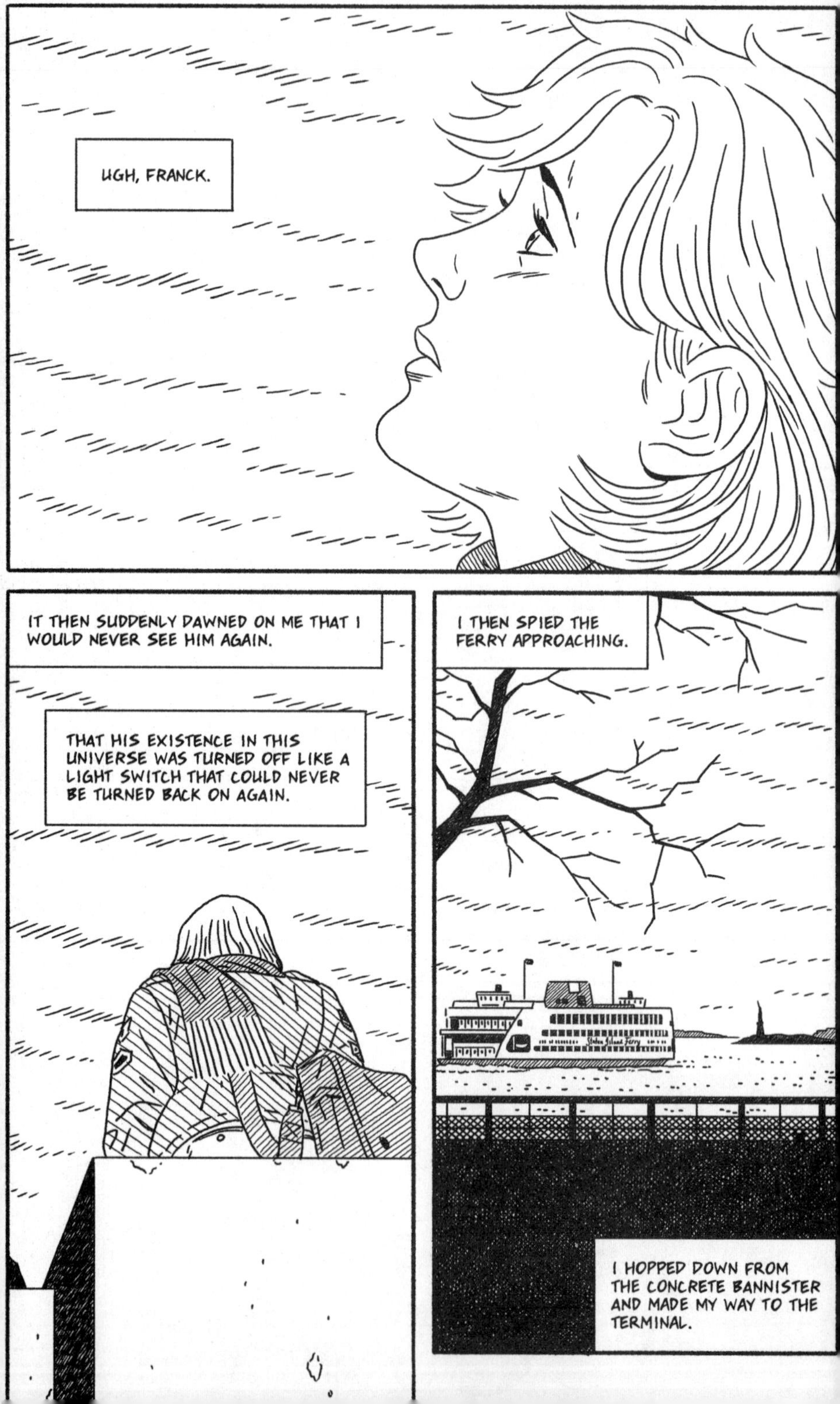
UGH, FRANCK.
IT THEN SUDDENLY DAWNED ON ME THAT I WOULD NEVER SEE HIM AGAIN.
THAT HIS EXISTENCE IN THIS UNIVERSE WAS TURNED OFF LIKE A LIGHT SWITCH THAT COULD NEVER BE TURNED BACK ON AGAIN.
I THEN SPIED THE FERRY APPROACHING.
I HOPPED DOWN FROM THE CONCRETE BANNISTER AND MADE MY WAY TO THE TERMINAL.

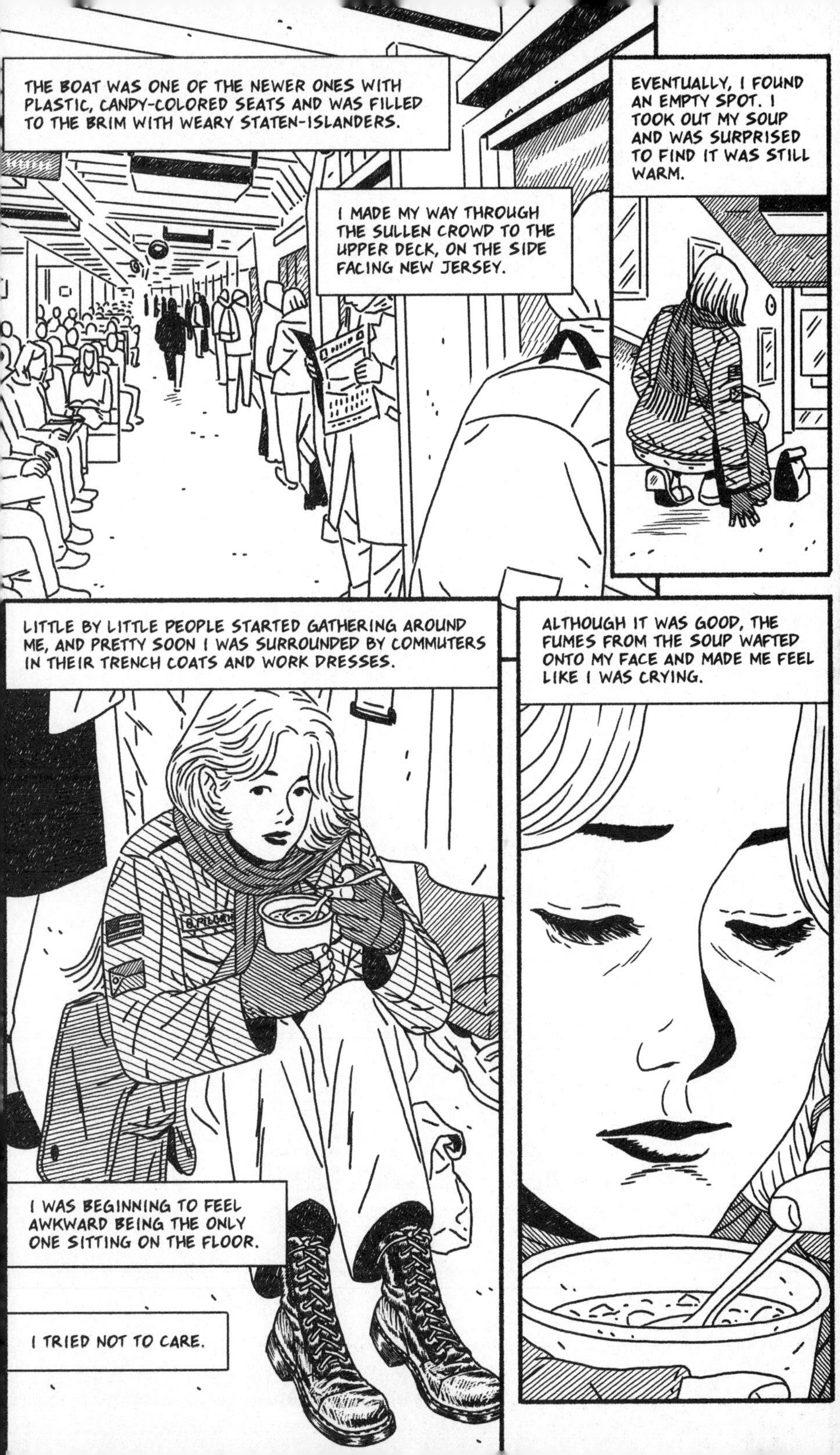
THE BOAT WAS ONE OF THE NEWER ONES WITH PLASTIC, CANDY-COLORED SEATS AND WAS FILLED TO THE BRIM WITH WEARY STATEN-ISLANDERS.
I MADE MY WAY THROUGH THE SULLEN CROWD TO THE UPPER DECK, ON THE SIDE FACING NEW JERSEY.
EVENTUALLY, I FOUND AN EMPTY SPOT. I TOOK OUT MY SOUP AND WAS SURPRISED TO FIND IT WAS STILL WARM.
LITTLE BY LITTLE PEOPLE STARTED GATHERING AROUND ME, AND PRETTY SOON I WAS SURROUNDED BY COMMUTERS IN THEIR TRENCH COATS AND WORK DRESSES.
I WAS BEGINNING TO FEEL AWKWARD BEING THE ONLY ONE SITTING ON THE FLOOR.
I TRIED NOT TO CARE.
ALTHOUGH IT WAS GOOD, THE FUMES FROM THE SOUP WAFTED ONTO MY FACE AND MADE ME FEEL LIKE I WAS CRYING.

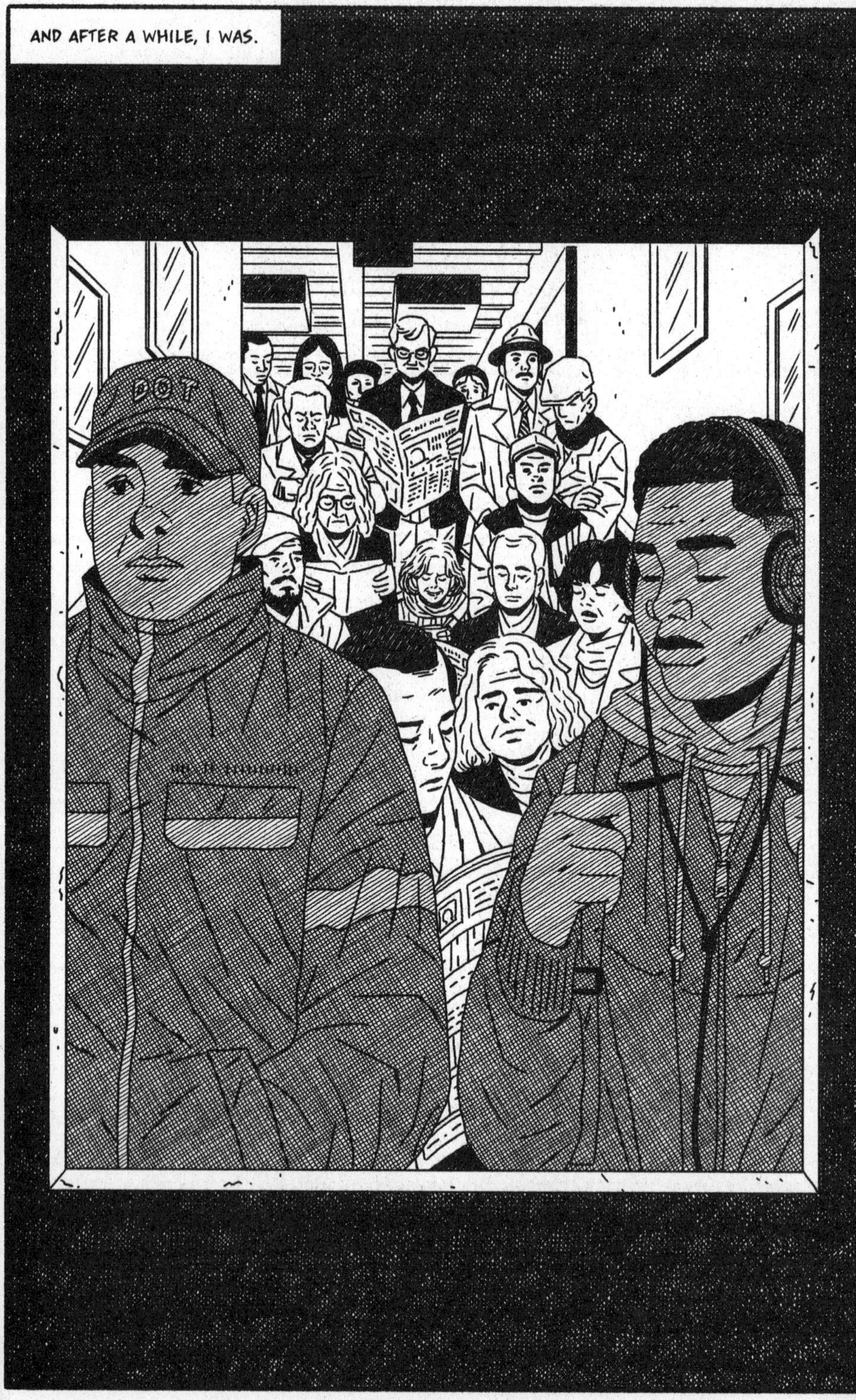
AND AFTER A WHILE, I WAS.
DOT

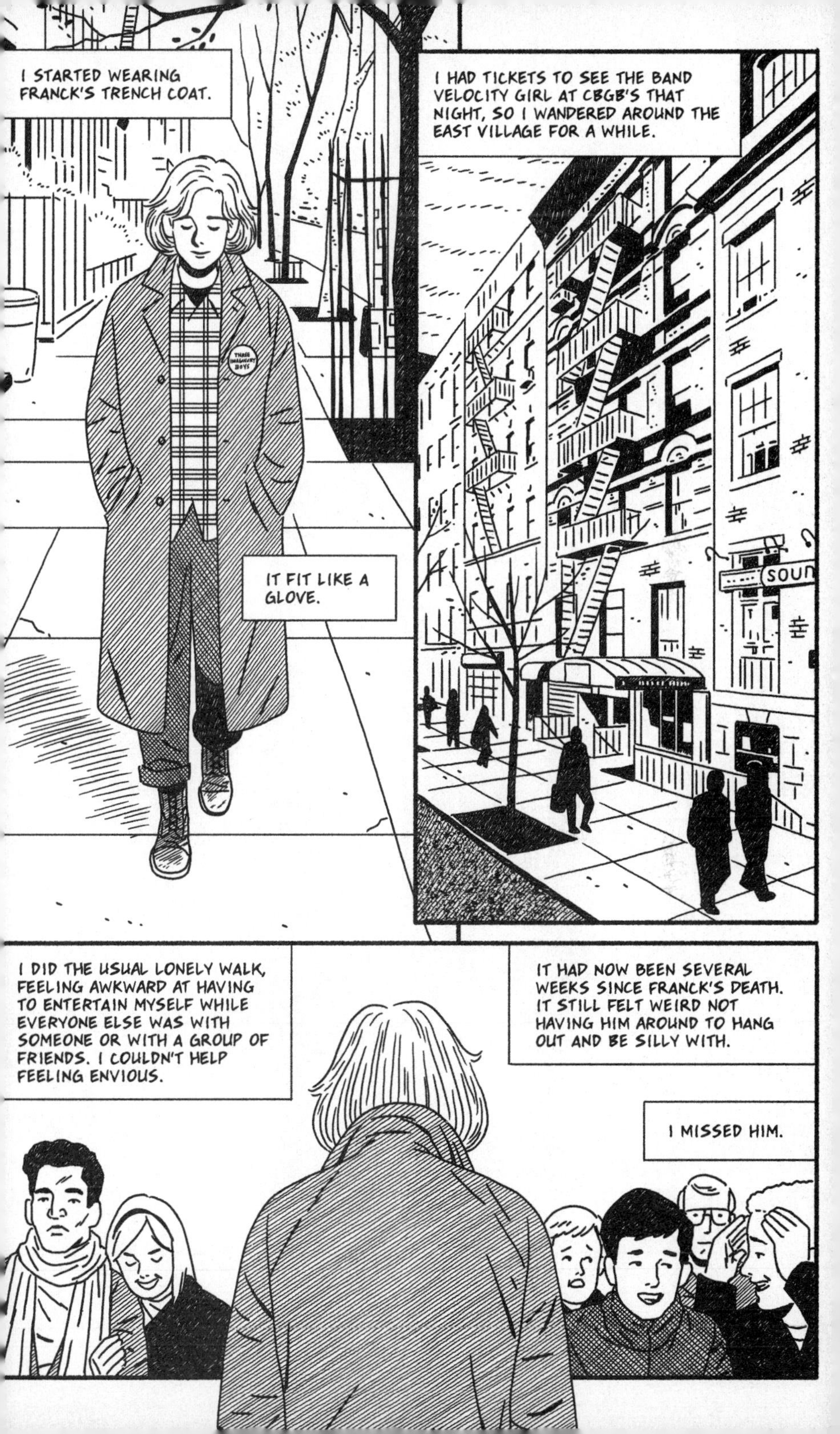

I STARTED WEARING FRANCK'S TRENCH COAT.
THREE IMAGINARY BOYS
IT FIT LIKE A GLOVE.
I HAD TICKETS TO SEE THE BAND VELOCITY GIRL AT CBGB'S THAT NIGHT, SO I WANDERED AROUND THE EAST VILLAGE FOR A WHILE.
SOUN
I DID THE USUAL LONELY WALK, FEELING AWKWARD AT HAVING TO ENTERTAIN MYSELF WHILE EVERYONE ELSE WAS WITH SOMEONE OR WITH A GROUP OF FRIENDS. I COULDN'T HELP FEELING ENVIOUS.
IT HAD NOW BEEN SEVERAL WEEKS SINCE FRANCK'S DEATH. IT STILL FELT WEIRD NOT HAVING HIM AROUND TO HANG OUT AND BE SILLY WITH.
I MISSED HIM.

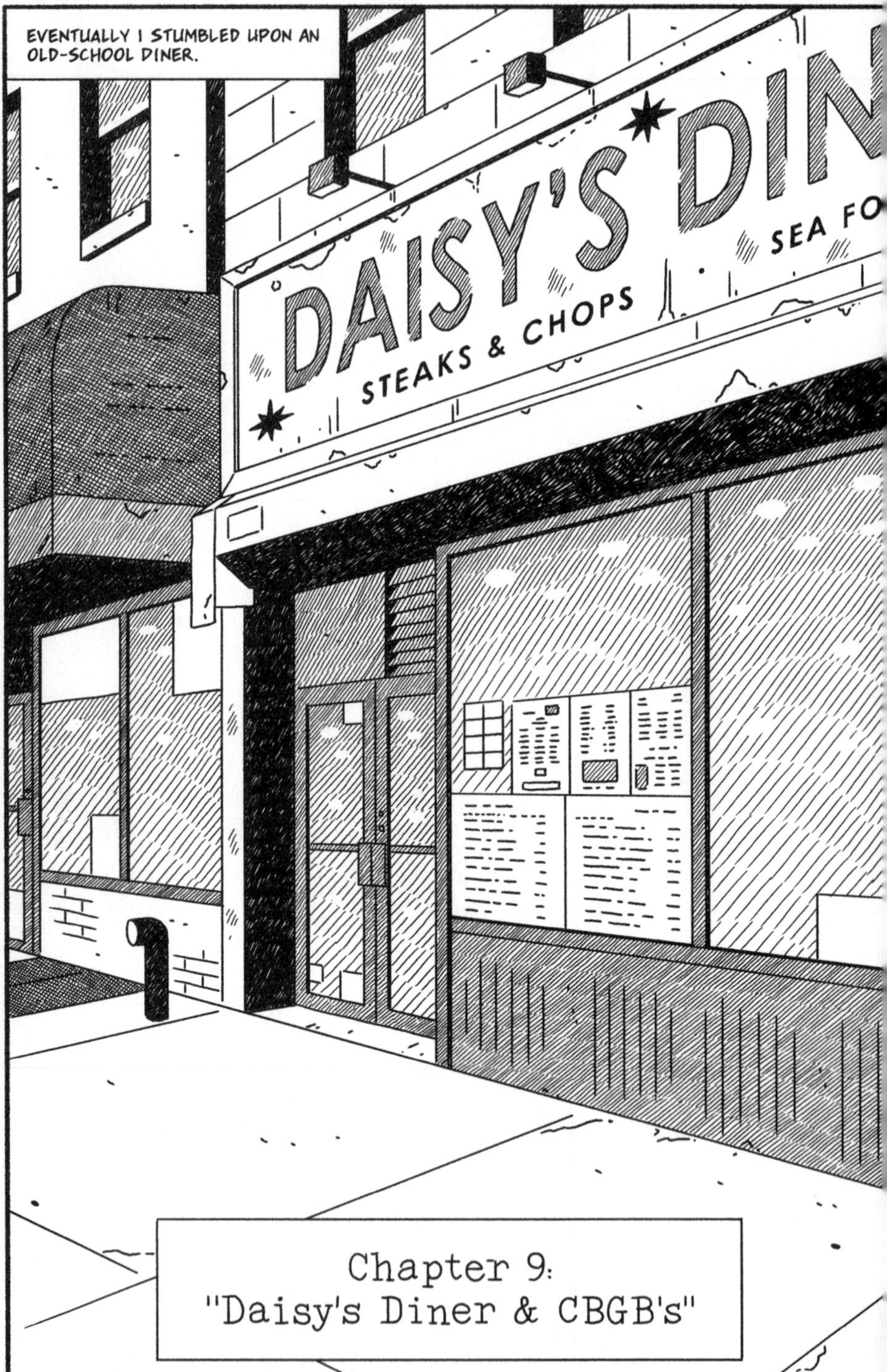
EVENTUALLY I STUMBLED UPON AN OLD-SCHOOL DINER.
DAISY'S DIN
STEAKS & CHOPS
SEA FO

Chapter 9: "Daisy's Diner & CBGB's"

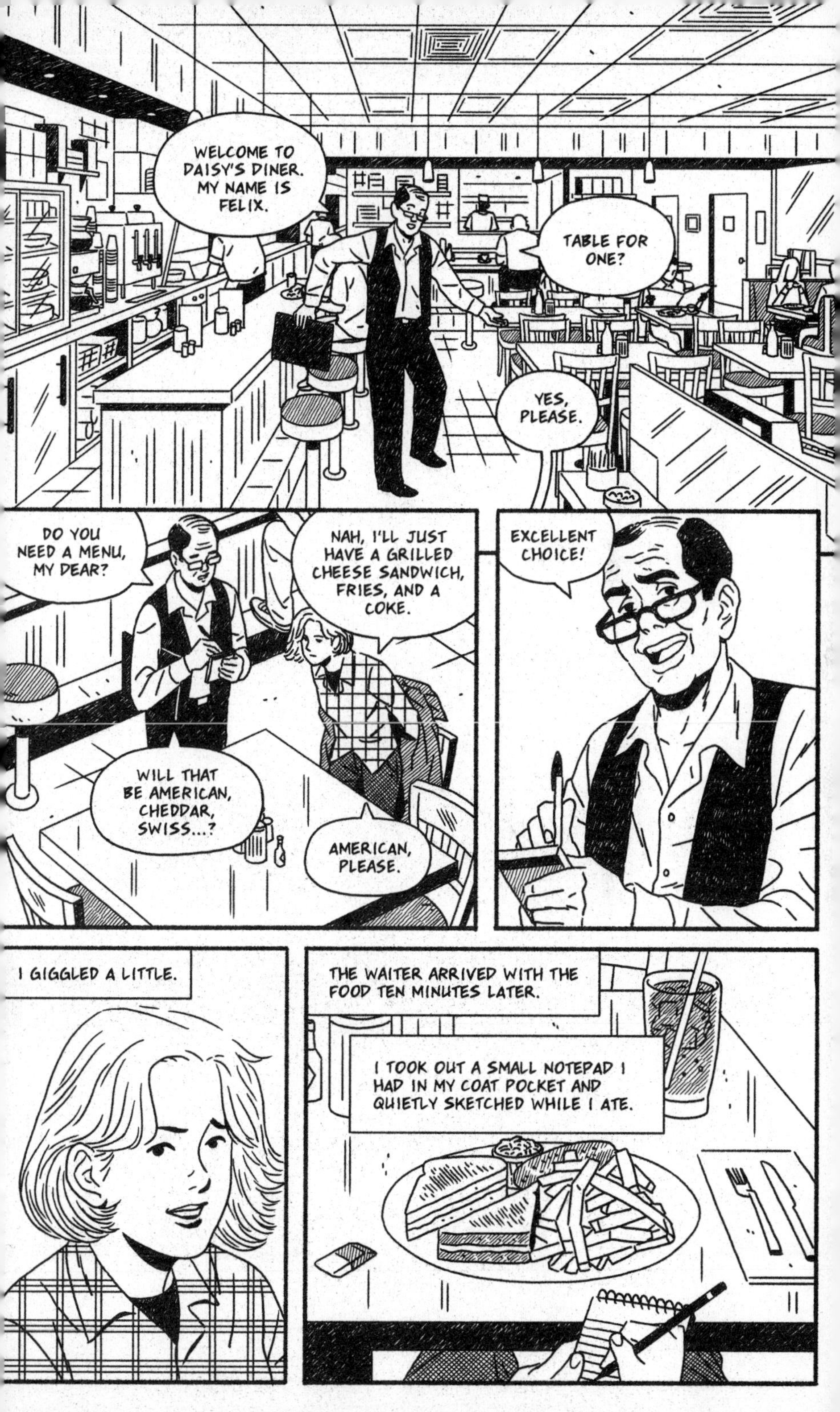
WELCOME TO DAISY'S DINER. MY NAME IS FELIX.
TABLE FOR ONE?
YES, PLEASE.
DO YOU NEED A MENU, MY DEAR?
NAH, I'LL JUST HAVE A GRILLED CHEESE SANDWICH, FRIES, AND A COKE.
WILL THAT BE AMERICAN, CHEDDAR, SWISS...?
AMERICAN, PLEASE.
EXCELLENT CHOICE!
I GIGGLED A LITTLE.
THE WAITER ARRIVED WITH THE FOOD TEN MINUTES LATER.
I TOOK OUT A SMALL NOTEPAD I HAD IN MY COAT POCKET AND QUIETLY SKETCHED WHILE I ATE.

WAS IT GOOD?

IT WAS DELICIOUS.

IT REALLY WAS.

OH, THAT MAKES ME SO HAPPY!

HAHA, I'M GLAD.

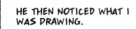

HE THEN NOTICED WHAT I WAS DRAWING.

WOW, THAT'S QUITE GOOD. YOU'RE VERY TALENTED!

OH, THANKS, THEY'RE JUST DOODLES.

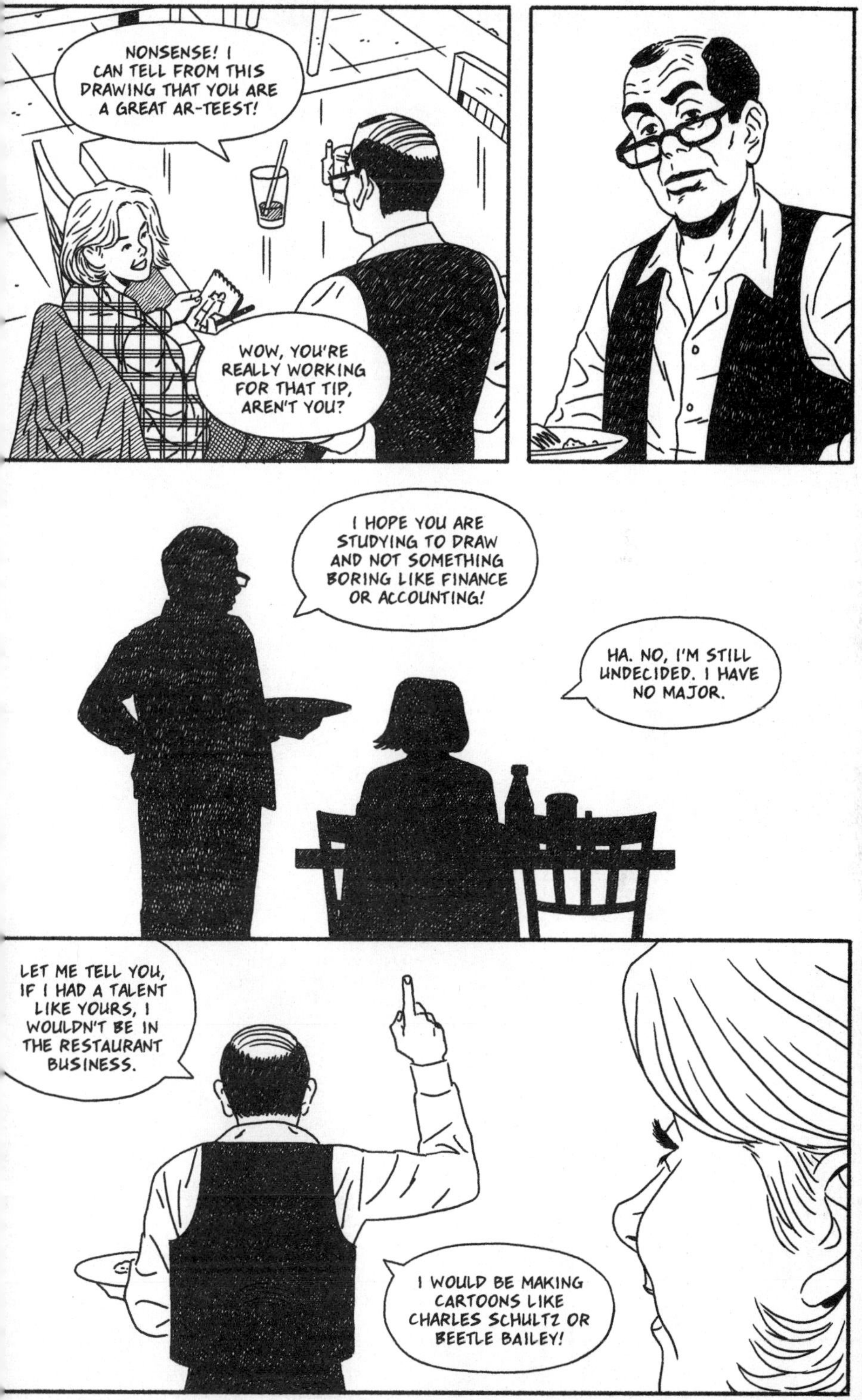
NONSENSE! I CAN TELL FROM THIS DRAWING THAT YOU ARE A GREAT AR-TEEST!
WOW, YOU'RE REALLY WORKING FOR THAT TIP, AREN'T YOU?
I HOPE YOU ARE STUDYING TO DRAW AND NOT SOMETHING BORING LIKE FINANCE OR ACCOUNTING!
HA. NO, I'M STILL UNDECIDED. I HAVE NO MAJOR.
LET ME TELL YOU, IF I HAD A TALENT LIKE YOURS, I WOULDN'T BE IN THE RESTAURANT BUSINESS.
I WOULD BE MAKING CARTOONS LIKE CHARLES SCHULTZ OR BEETLE BAILEY!

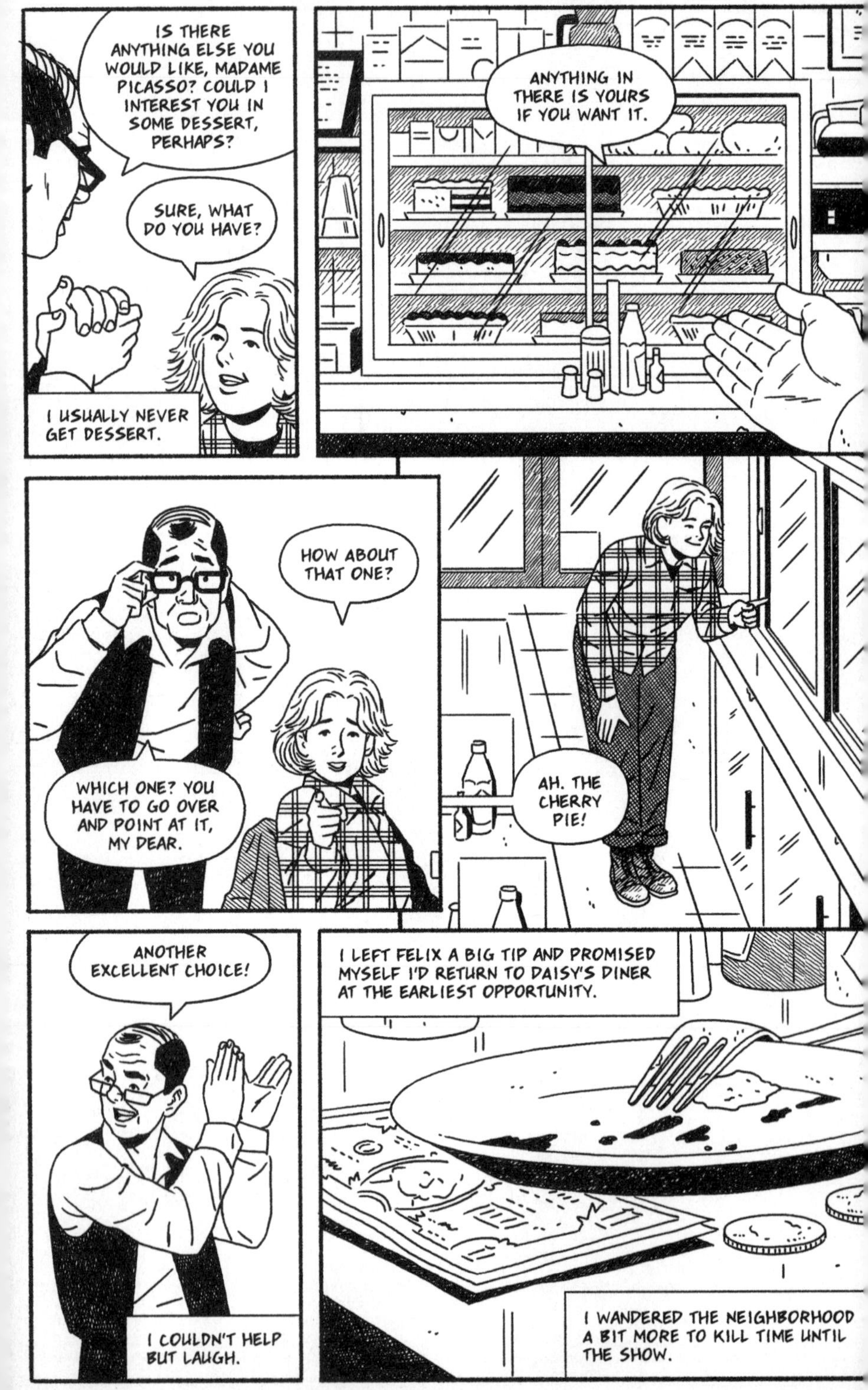
IS THERE ANYTHING ELSE YOU WOULD LIKE, MADAME PICASSO? COULD I INTEREST YOU IN SOME DESSERT, PERHAPS?
SURE, WHAT DO YOU HAVE?
I USUALLY NEVER GET DESSERT.
ANYTHING IN THERE IS YOURS IF YOU WANT IT.
HOW ABOUT THAT ONE?
WHICH ONE? YOU HAVE TO GO OVER AND POINT AT IT, MY DEAR.
AH. THE CHERRY PIE!
ANOTHER EXCELLENT CHOICE!
I COULDN'T HELP BUT LAUGH.
I LEFT FELIX A BIG TIP AND PROMISED MYSELF I'D RETURN TO DAISY'S DINER AT THE EARLIEST OPPORTUNITY.
I WANDERED THE NEIGHBORHOOD A BIT MORE TO KILL TIME UNTIL THE SHOW.

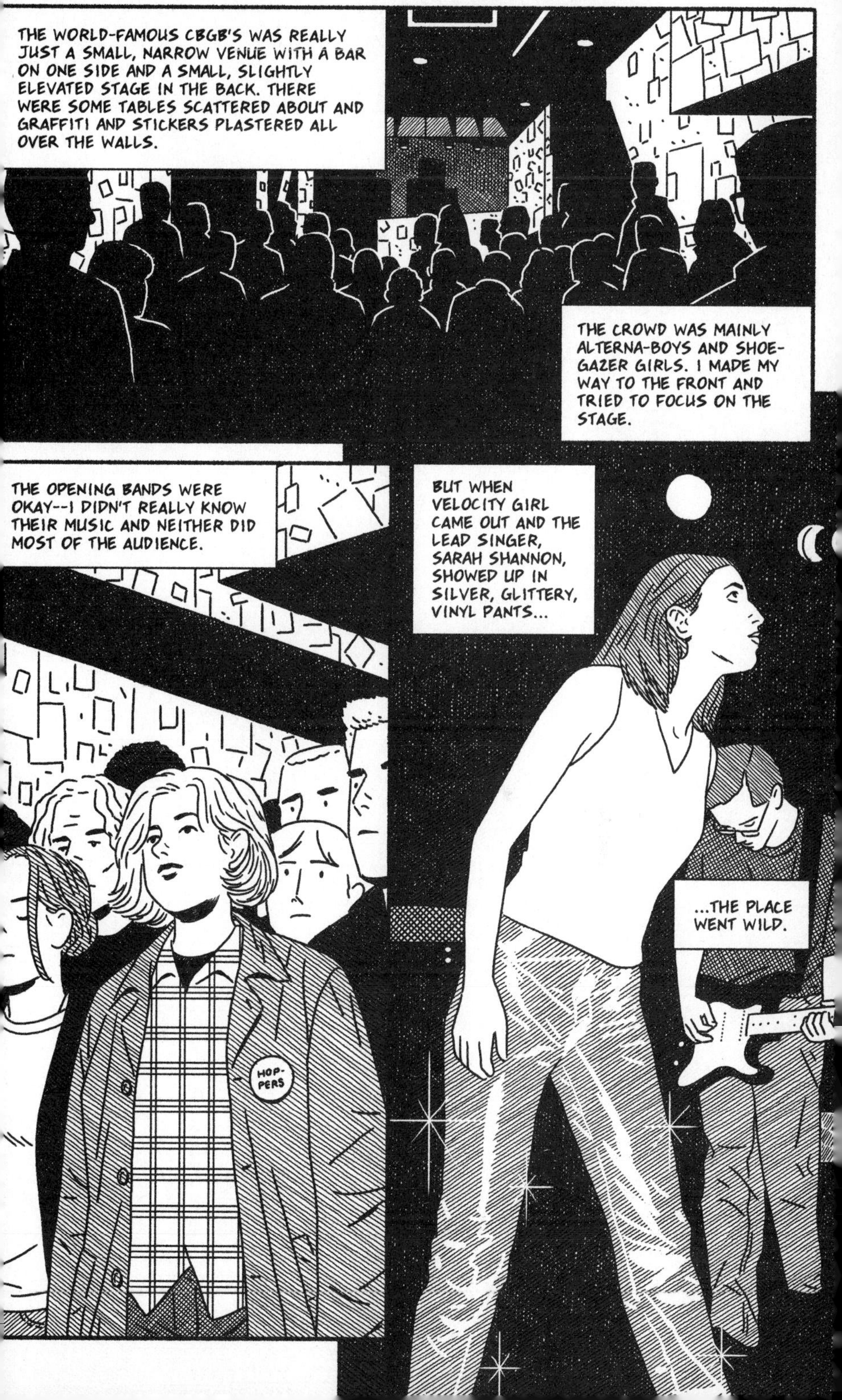
THE WORLD-FAMOUS CBGB'S WAS REALLY JUST A SMALL, NARROW VENUE WITH A BAR ON ONE SIDE AND A SMALL, SLIGHTLY ELEVATED STAGE IN THE BACK. THERE WERE SOME TABLES SCATTERED ABOUT AND GRAFFITI AND STICKERS PLASTERED ALL OVER THE WALLS.
THE CROWD WAS MAINLY ALTERNA-BOYS AND SHOE-GAZER GIRLS. I MADE MY WAY TO THE FRONT AND TRIED TO FOCUS ON THE STAGE.
THE OPENING BANDS WERE OKAY--I DIDN'T REALLY KNOW THEIR MUSIC AND NEITHER DID MOST OF THE AUDIENCE.
HOP-PERS
BUT WHEN VELOCITY GIRL CAME OUT AND THE LEAD SINGER, SARAH SHANNON, SHOWED UP IN SILVER, GLITTERY, VINYL PANTS...
...THE PLACE WENT WILD.

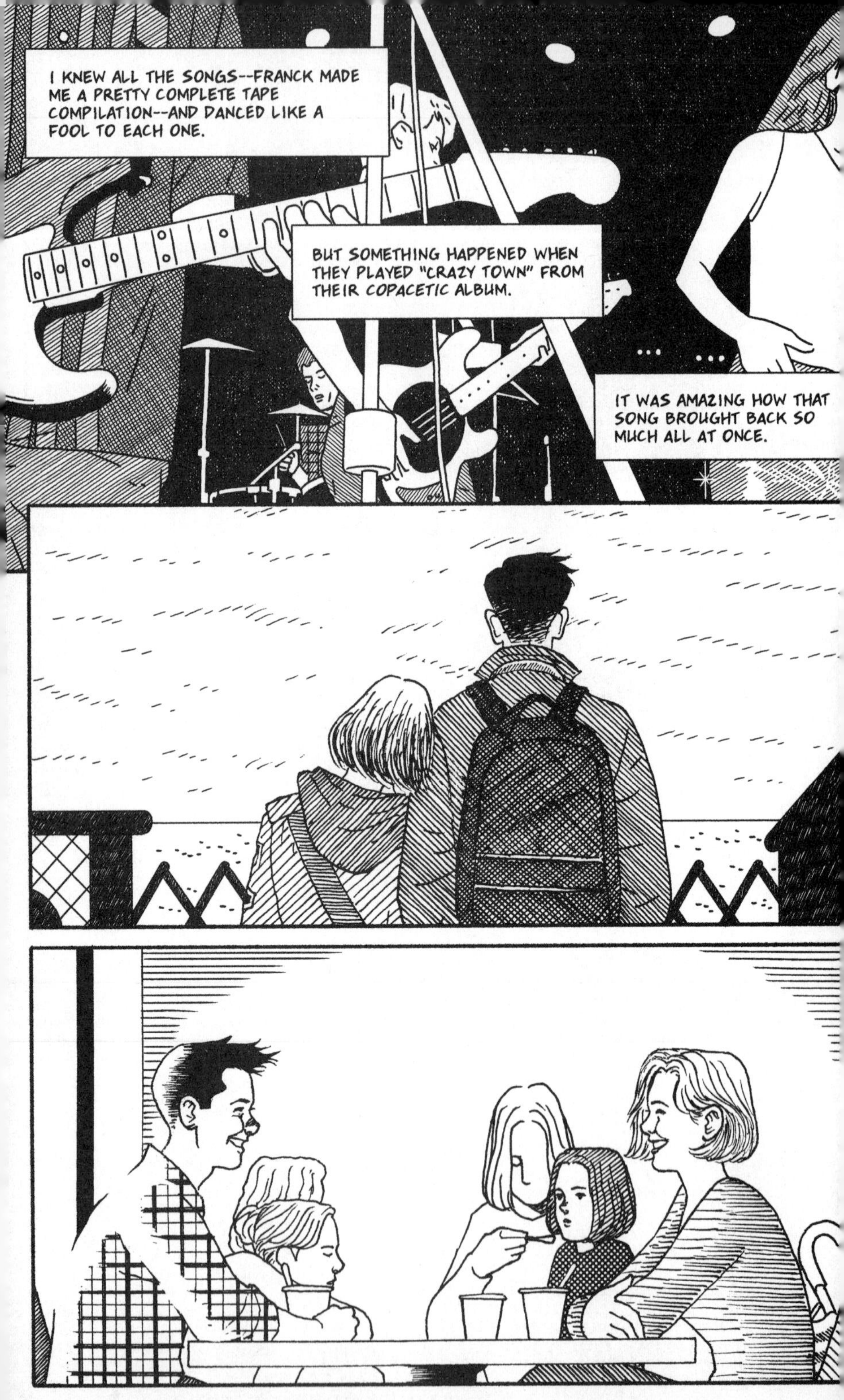
I KNEW ALL THE SONGS--FRANCK MADE ME A PRETTY COMPLETE TAPE COMPILATION--AND DANCED LIKE A FOOL TO EACH ONE.
BUT SOMETHING HAPPENED WHEN THEY PLAYED "CRAZY TOWN" FROM THEIR COPACETIC ALBUM.
IT WAS AMAZING HOW THAT SONG BROUGHT BACK SO MUCH ALL AT ONCE.

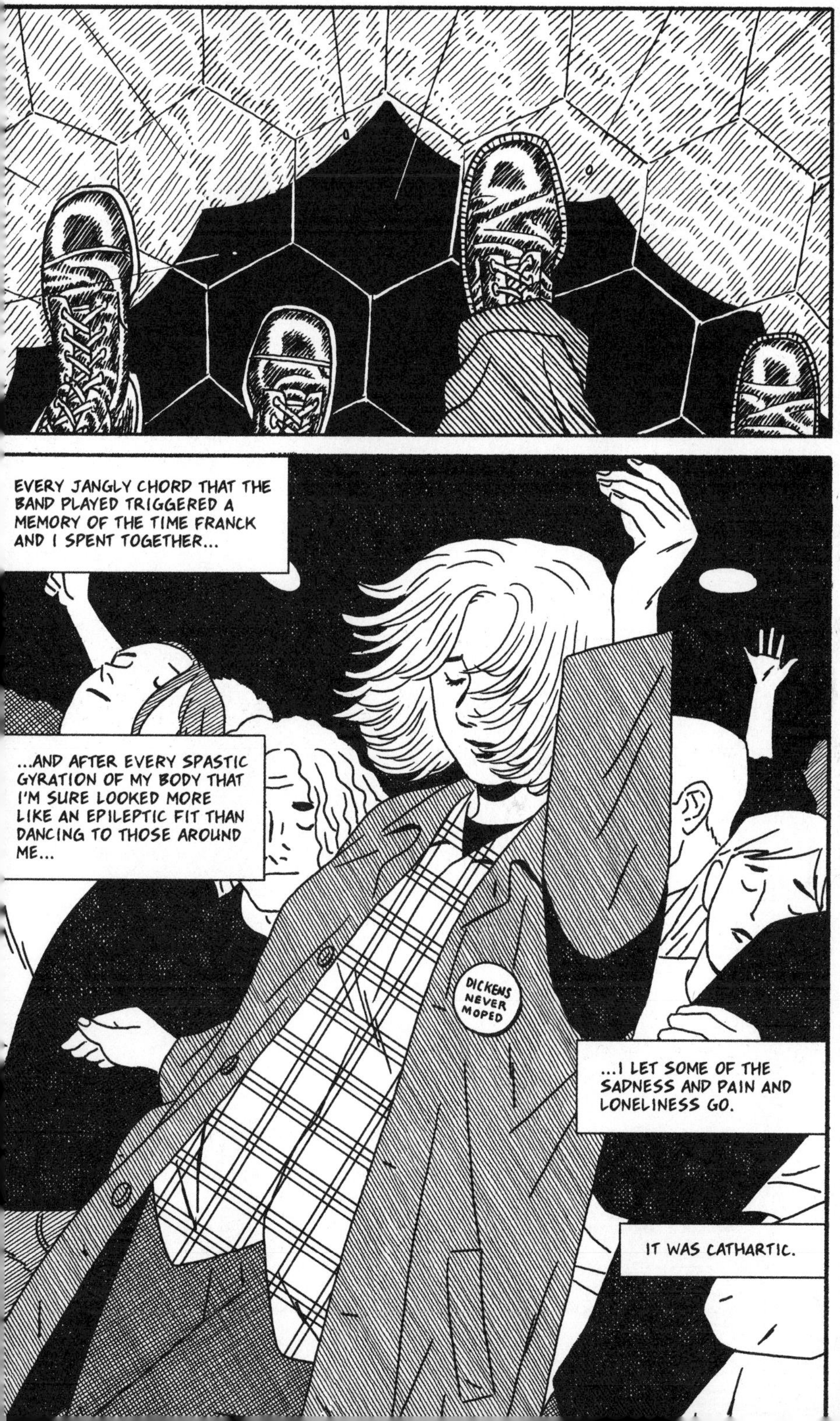
EVERY JANGLY CHORD THAT THE BAND PLAYED TRIGGERED A MEMORY OF THE TIME FRANCK AND I SPENT TOGETHER...
...AND AFTER EVERY SPASTIC GYRATION OF MY BODY THAT I'M SURE LOOKED MORE LIKE AN EPILEPTIC FIT THAN DANCING TO THOSE AROUND ME...
DICKENS NEVER MOPED
...I LET SOME OF THE SADNESS AND PAIN AND LONELINESS GO.
IT WAS CATHARTIC.

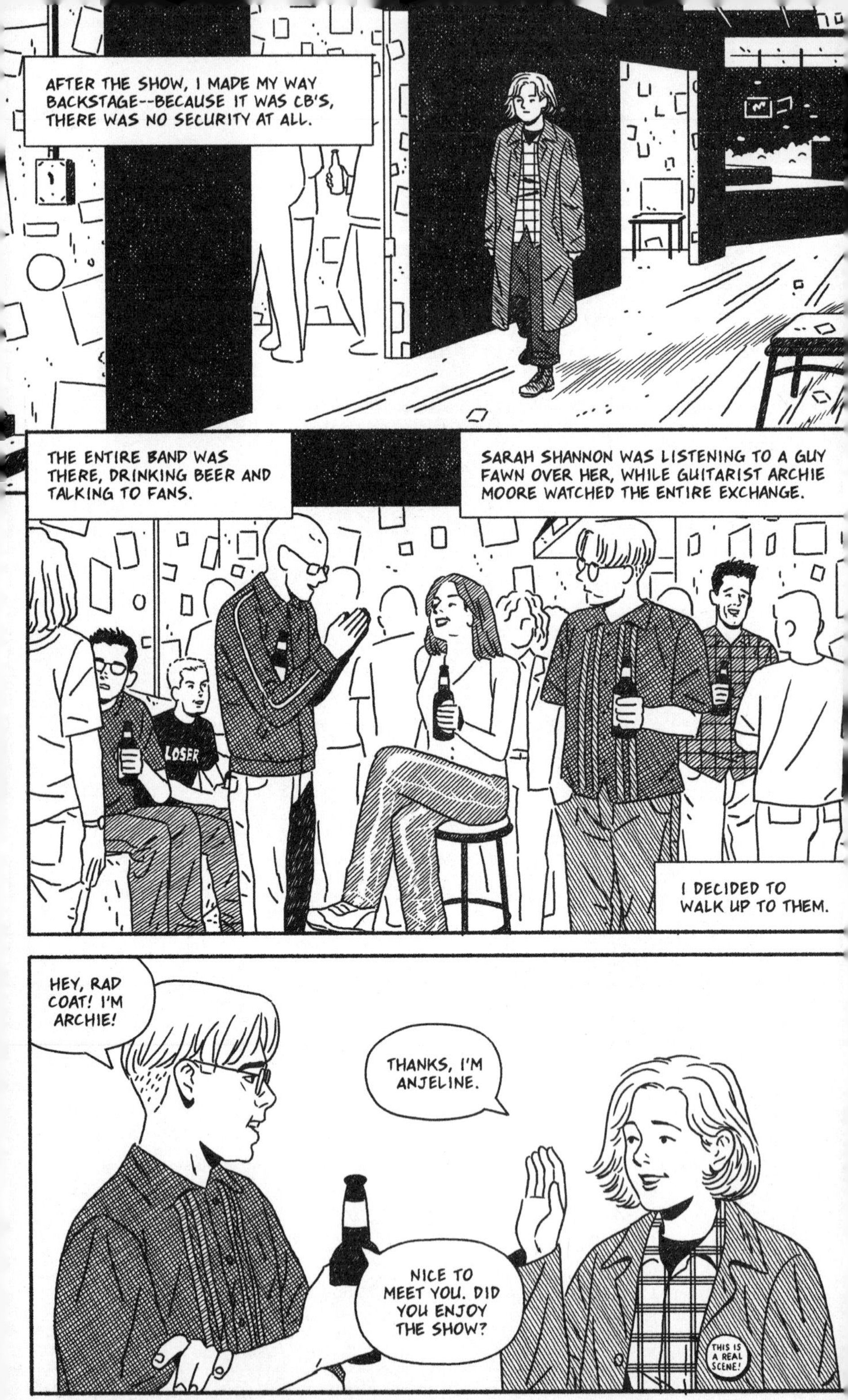

AFTER THE SHOW, I MADE MY WAY BACKSTAGE--BECAUSE IT WAS CB'S, THERE WAS NO SECURITY AT ALL.
THE ENTIRE BAND WAS THERE, DRINKING BEER AND TALKING TO FANS.
SARAH SHANNON WAS LISTENING TO A GUY FAWN OVER HER, WHILE GUITARIST ARCHIE MOORE WATCHED THE ENTIRE EXCHANGE.
LOSER
I DECIDED TO WALK UP TO THEM.
HEY, RAD COAT! I'M ARCHIE!
THANKS, I'M ANJELINE.
NICE TO MEET YOU. DID YOU ENJOY THE SHOW?
THIS IS A REAL SCENE!

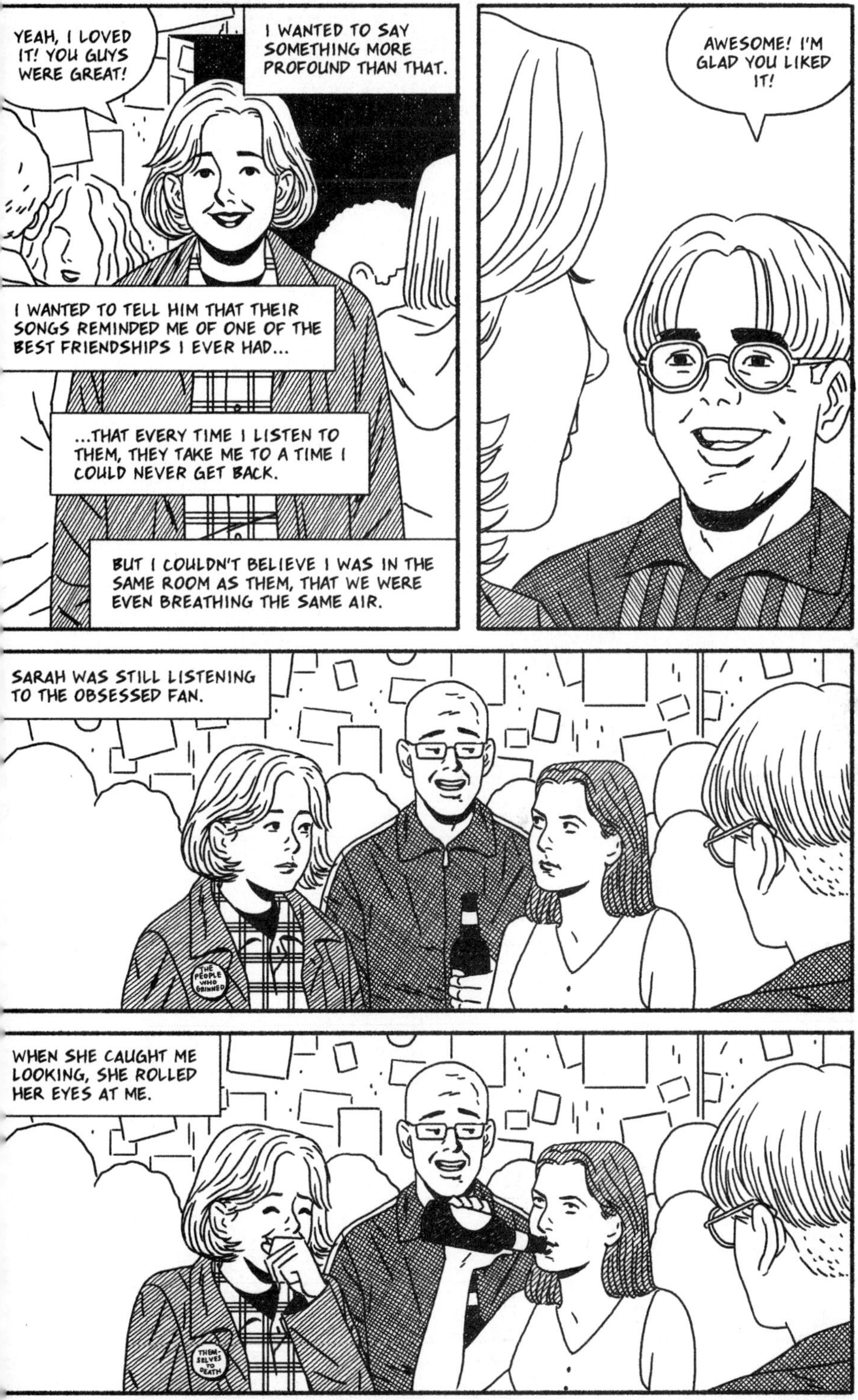
YEAH, I LOVED IT! YOU GUYS WERE GREAT!
I WANTED TO SAY SOMETHING MORE PROFOUND THAN THAT.
I WANTED TO TELL HIM THAT THEIR SONGS REMINDED ME OF ONE OF THE BEST FRIENDSHIPS I EVER HAD...
...THAT EVERY TIME I LISTEN TO THEM, THEY TAKE ME TO A TIME I COULD NEVER GET BACK.
BUT I COULDN'T BELIEVE I WAS IN THE SAME ROOM AS THEM, THAT WE WERE EVEN BREATHING THE SAME AIR.
AWESOME! I'M GLAD YOU LIKED IT!
SARAH WAS STILL LISTENING TO THE OBSESSED FAN.
THE PEOPLE WHO GRINNED
WHEN SHE CAUGHT ME LOOKING, SHE ROLLED HER EYES AT ME.
THEMSELVES TO DEATH

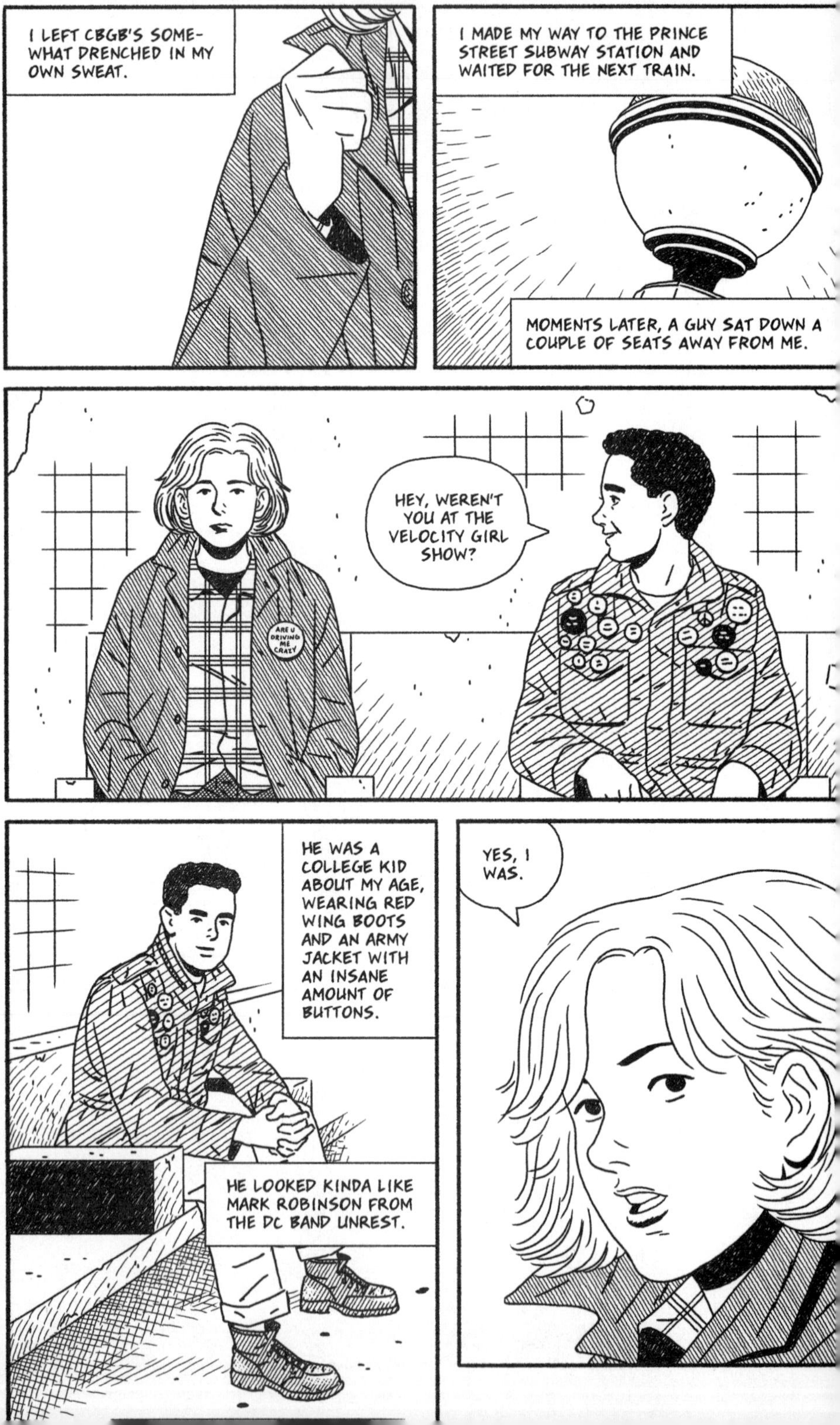
I LEFT CBGB'S SOME-WHAT DRENCHED IN MY OWN SWEAT.
I MADE MY WAY TO THE PRINCE STREET SUBWAY STATION AND WAITED FOR THE NEXT TRAIN.
MOMENTS LATER, A GUY SAT DOWN A COUPLE OF SEATS AWAY FROM ME.
HEY, WEREN'T YOU AT THE VELOCITY GIRL SHOW?
ARE U DRIVING ME CRAZY
HE WAS A COLLEGE KID ABOUT MY AGE, WEARING RED WING BOOTS AND AN ARMY JACKET WITH AN INSANE AMOUNT OF BUTTONS.
HE LOOKED KINDA LIKE MARK ROBINSON FROM THE DC BAND UNREST.
YES, I WAS.

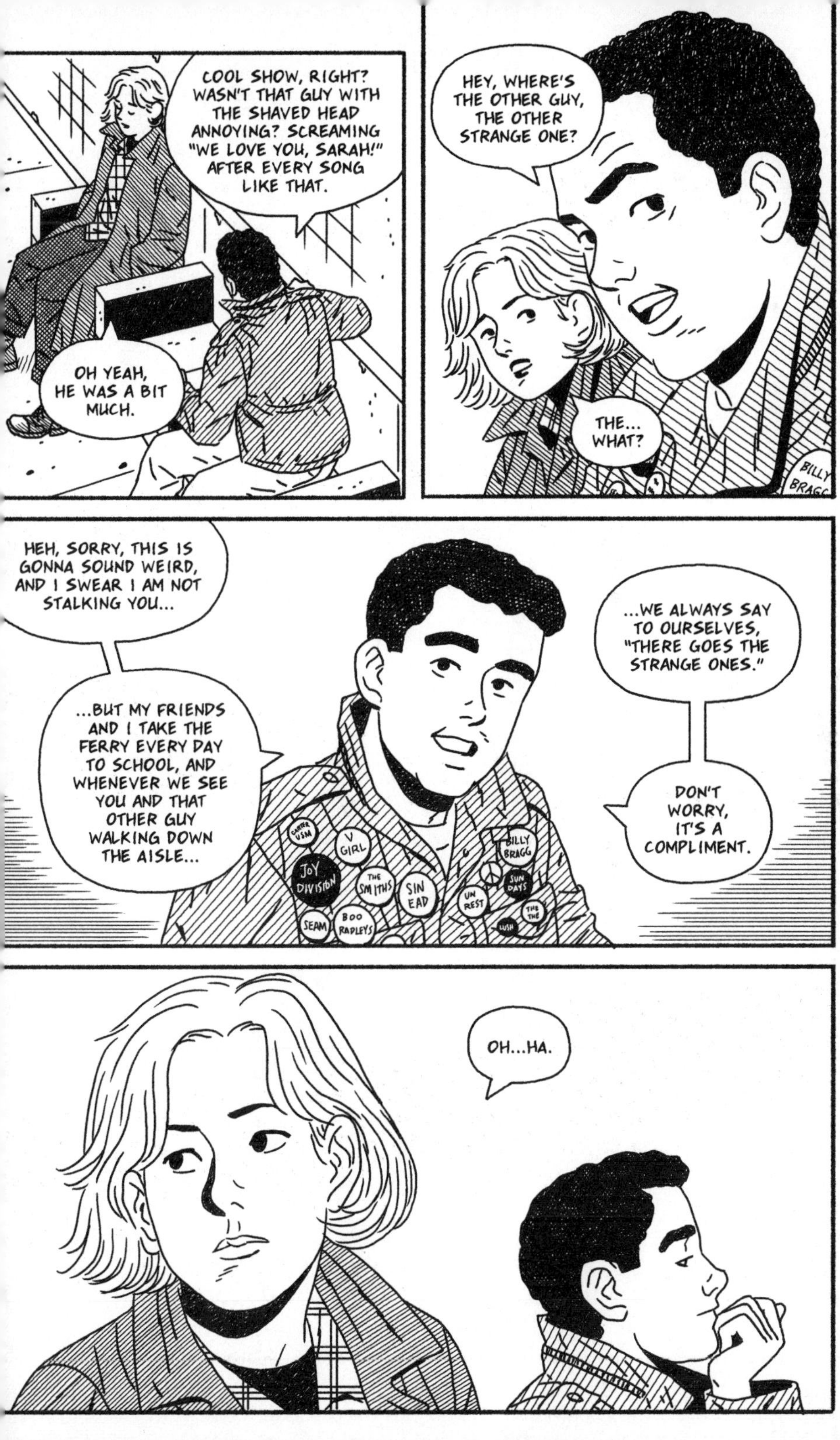
COOL SHOW, RIGHT? WASN'T THAT GUY WITH THE SHAVED HEAD ANNOYING? SCREAMING "WE LOVE YOU, SARAH!" AFTER EVERY SONG LIKE THAT.
OH YEAH, HE WAS A BIT MUCH.
HEY, WHERE'S THE OTHER GUY, THE OTHER STRANGE ONE?
THE... WHAT?
BILLY BRAGG
HEH, SORRY, THIS IS GONNA SOUND WEIRD, AND I SWEAR I AM NOT STALKING YOU...
...BUT MY FRIENDS AND I TAKE THE FERRY EVERY DAY TO SCHOOL, AND WHENEVER WE SEE YOU AND THAT OTHER GUY WALKING DOWN THE AISLE...
...WE ALWAYS SAY TO OURSELVES, "THERE GOES THE STRANGE ONES."
DON'T WORRY, IT'S A COMPLIMENT.
CARTER USM
V GIRL
JOY DIVISION
THE SMITHS
SIN EAD
BILLY BRAGG
SUN DAYS
UN REST
THE THE
LUSH
SEAM
BOO RADLEYS
OH...HA.

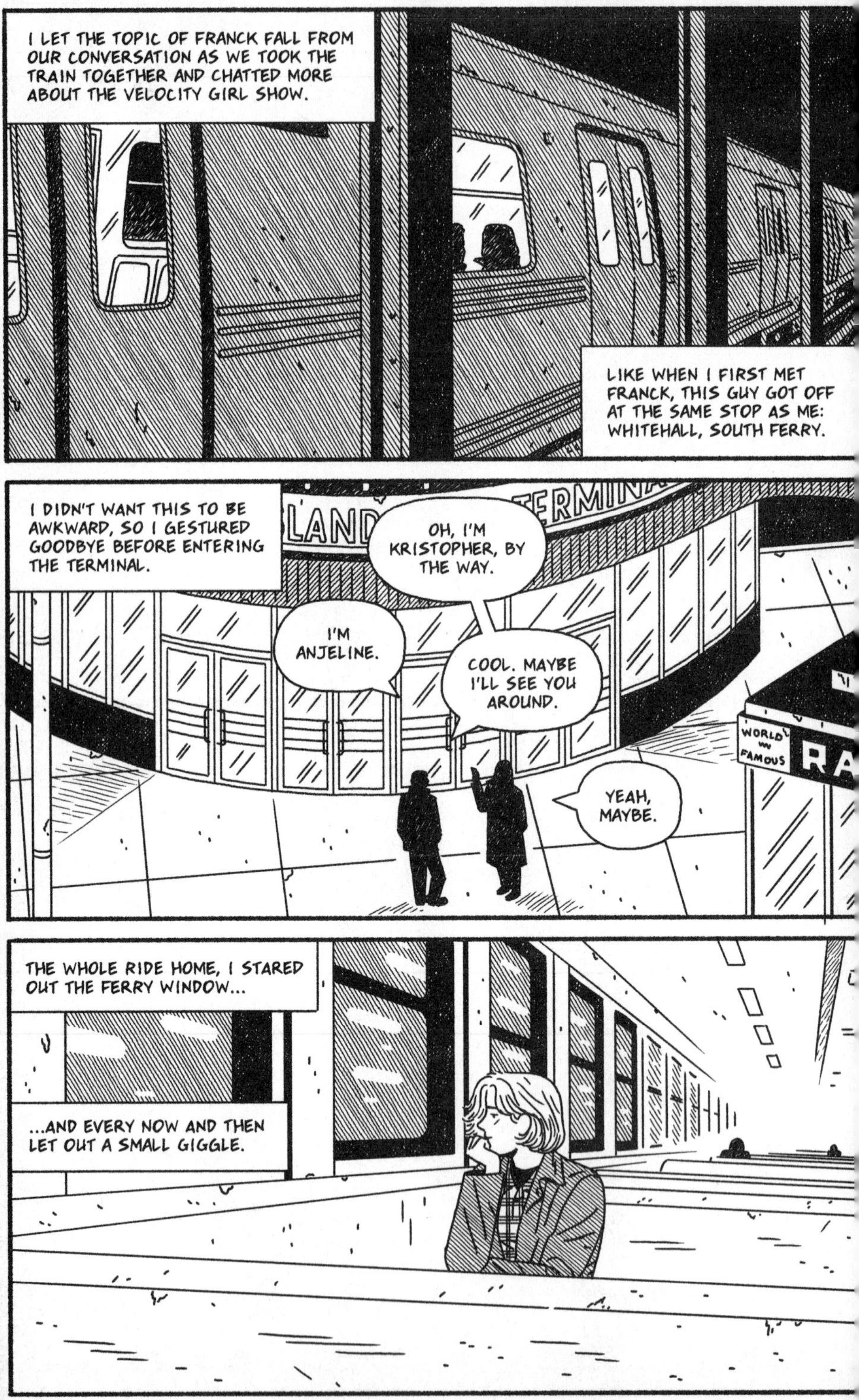
I LET THE TOPIC OF FRANCK FALL FROM OUR CONVERSATION AS WE TOOK THE TRAIN TOGETHER AND CHATTED MORE ABOUT THE VELOCITY GIRL SHOW.
LIKE WHEN I FIRST MET FRANCK, THIS GUY GOT OFF AT THE SAME STOP AS ME: WHITEHALL, SOUTH FERRY.
I DIDN'T WANT THIS TO BE AWKWARD, SO I GESTURED GOODBYE BEFORE ENTERING THE TERMINAL.
OH, I'M KRISTOPHER, BY THE WAY.
I'M ANJELINE.
COOL. MAYBE I'LL SEE YOU AROUND.
YEAH, MAYBE.
WORLD FAMOUS
THE WHOLE RIDE HOME, I STARED OUT THE FERRY WINDOW...
...AND EVERY NOW AND THEN LET OUT A SMALL GIGGLE.

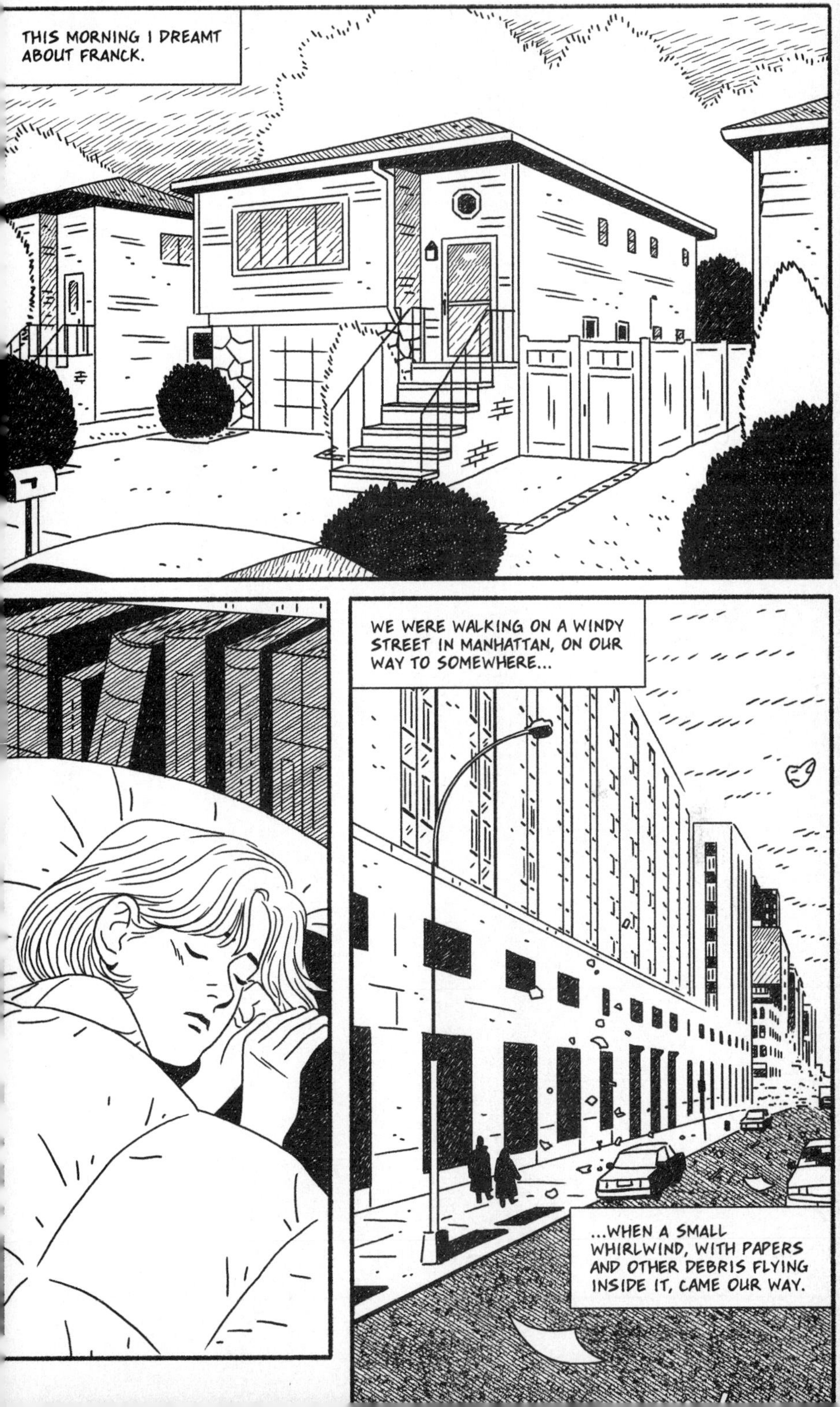
THIS MORNING I DREAMT ABOUT FRANCK.
WE WERE WALKING ON A WINDY STREET IN MANHATTAN, ON OUR WAY TO SOMEWHERE...
...WHEN A SMALL WHIRLWIND, WITH PAPERS AND OTHER DEBRIS FLYING INSIDE IT, CAME OUR WAY.

Chapter 10: "The Dream & Kristopher"

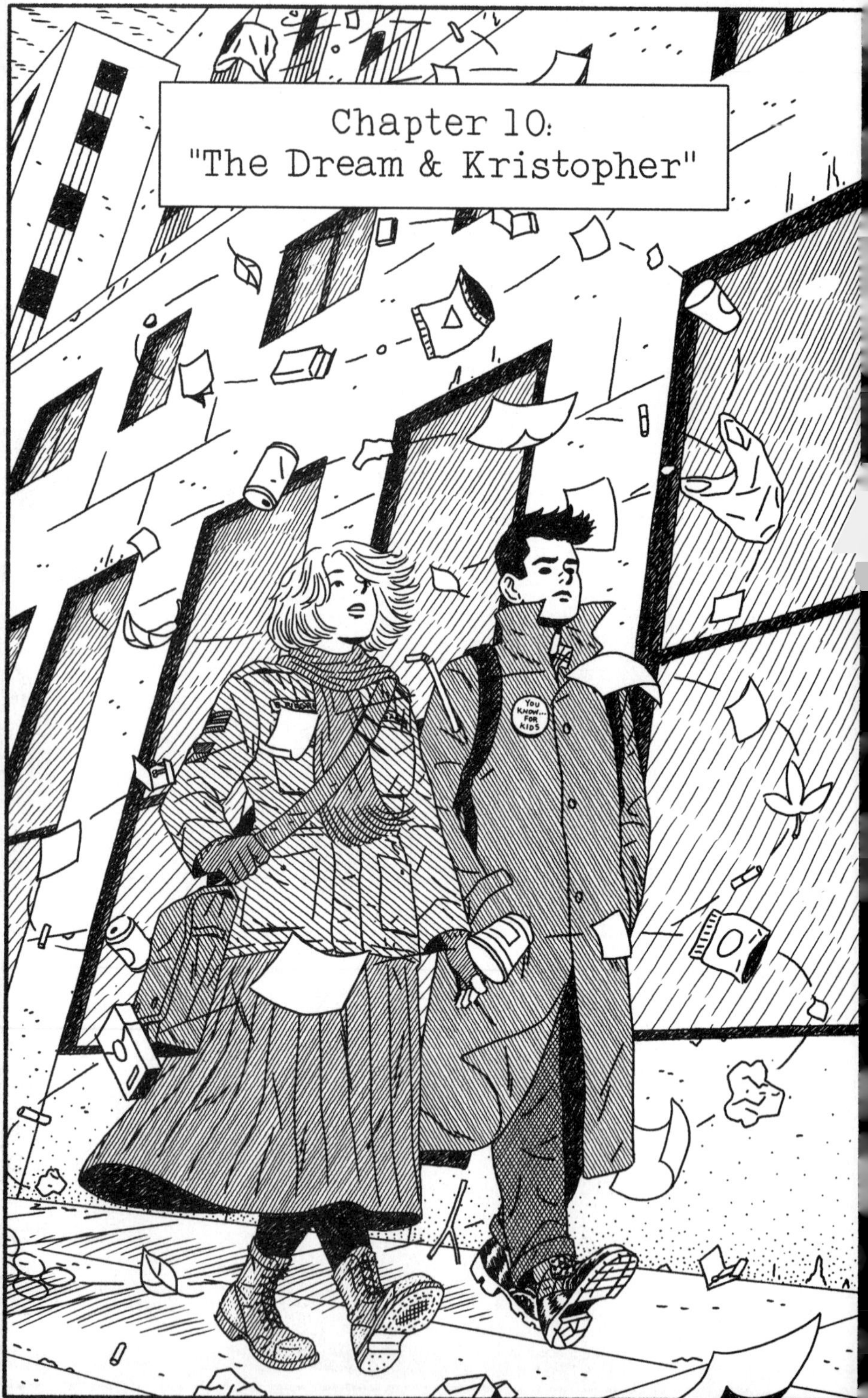
YOU KNOW... FOR KIDS

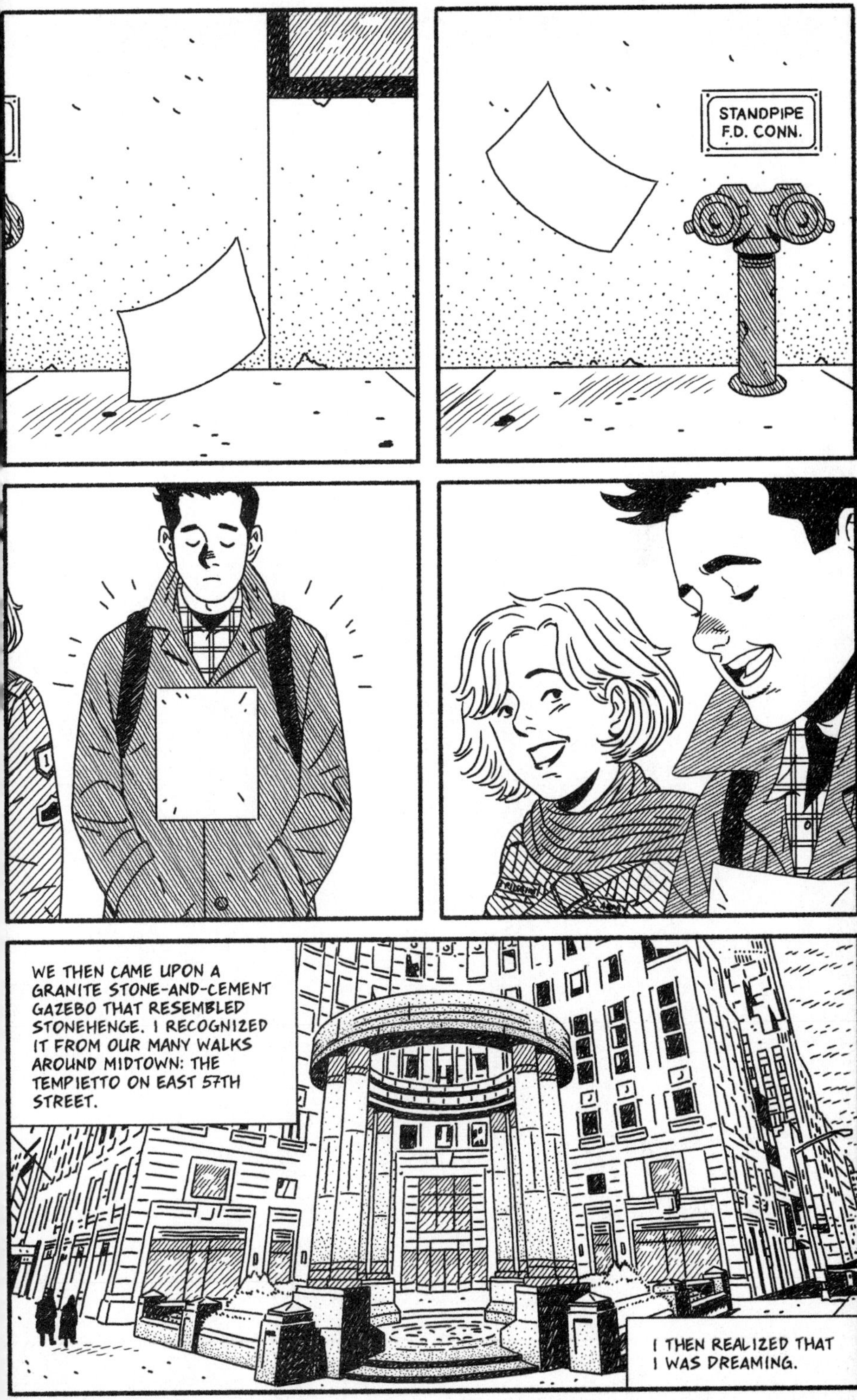
STANDPIPE
F.D. CONN.
WE THEN CAME UPON A GRANITE STONE-AND-CEMENT GAZEBO THAT RESEMBLED STONEHENGE. I RECOGNIZED IT FROM OUR MANY WALKS AROUND MIDTOWN: THE TEMPIETTO ON EAST 57TH STREET.
I THEN REALIZED THAT I WAS DREAMING.

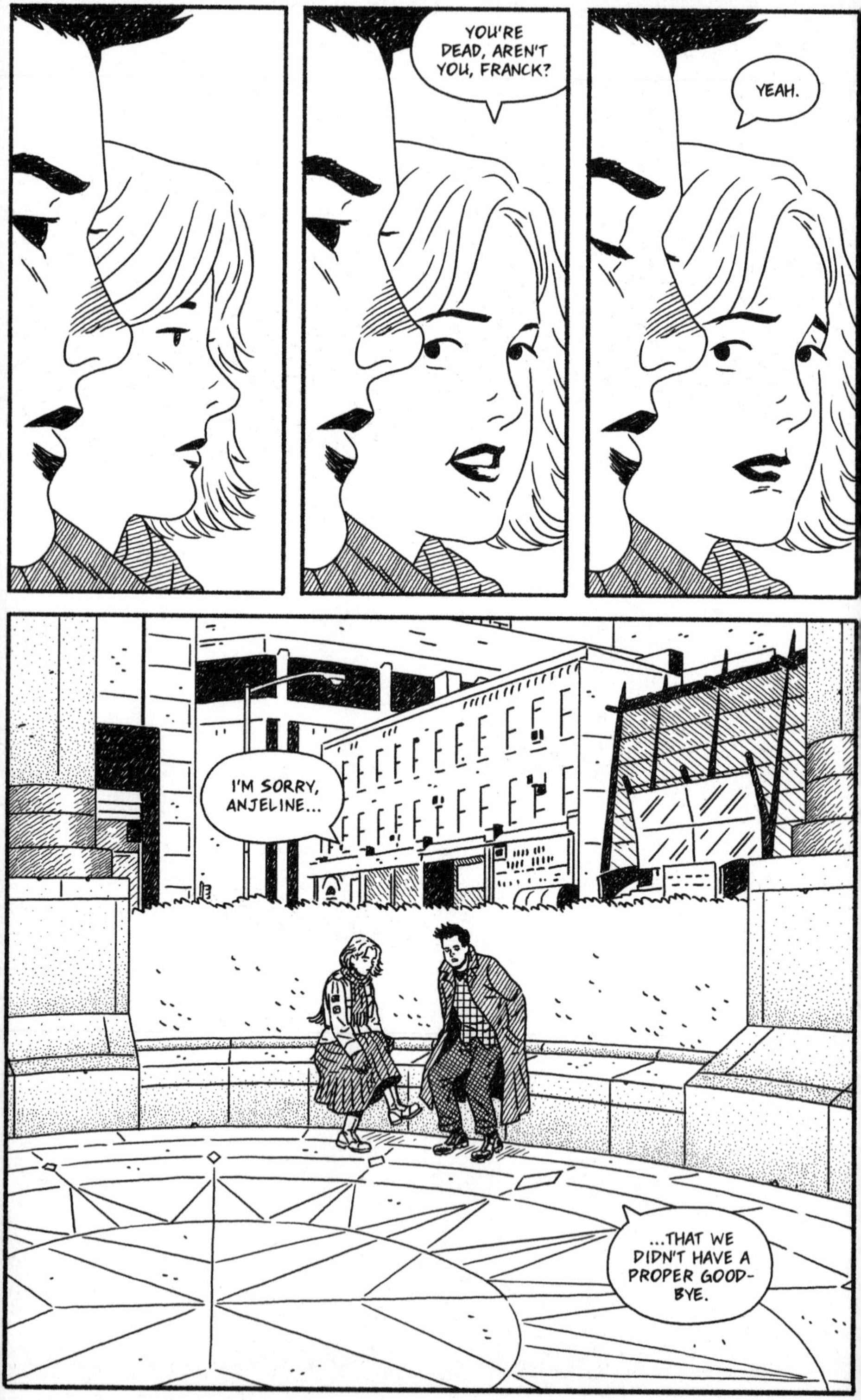
YOU'RE DEAD, AREN'T YOU, FRANCK?
YEAH.
I'M SORRY, ANJELINE...
...THAT WE DIDN'T HAVE A PROPER GOOD-BYE.

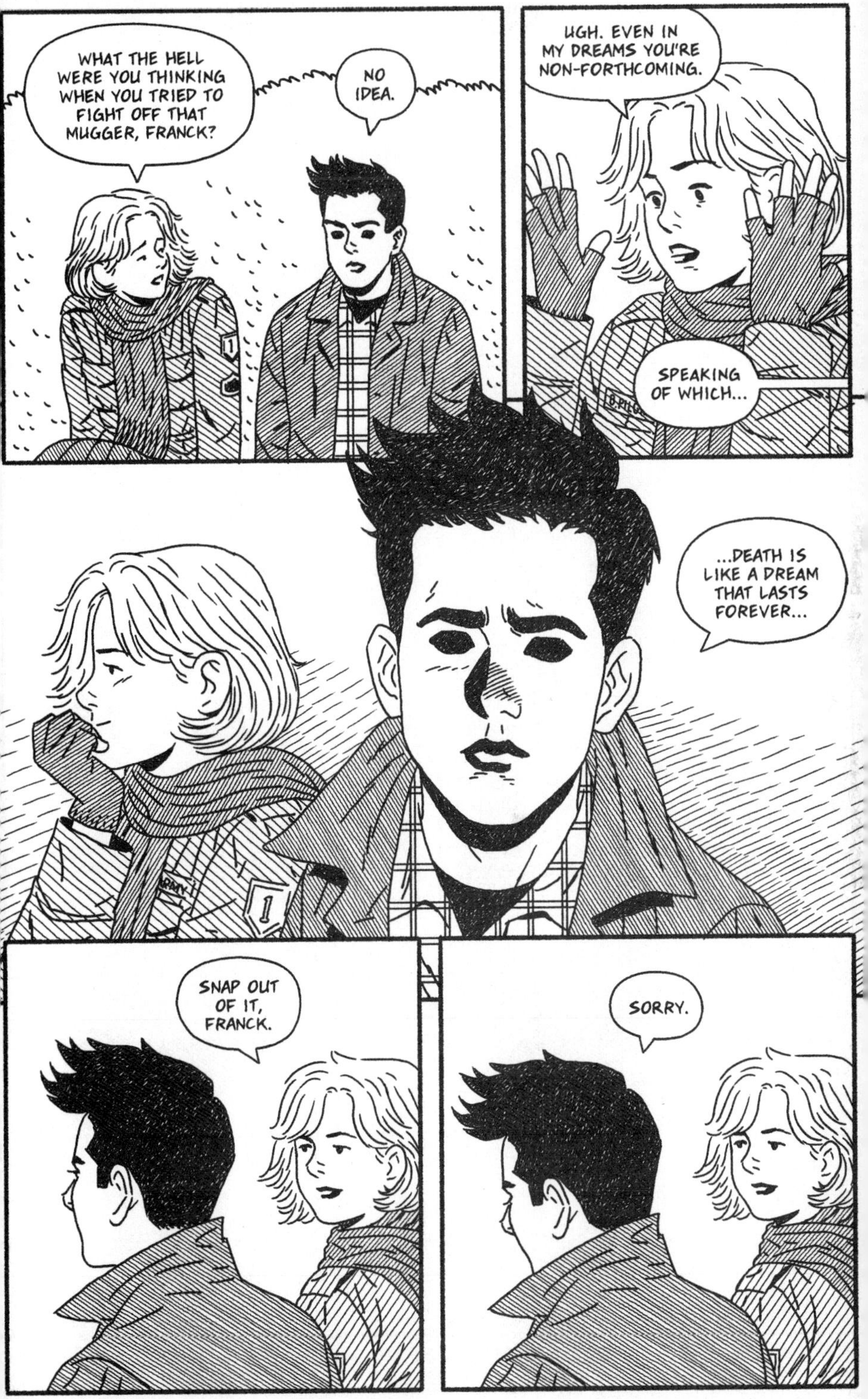
WHAT THE HELL WERE YOU THINKING WHEN YOU TRIED TO FIGHT OFF THAT MUGGER, FRANCK?
NO IDEA.
UGH. EVEN IN MY DREAMS YOU'RE NON-FORTHCOMING.
SPEAKING OF WHICH...
...DEATH IS LIKE A DREAM THAT LASTS FOREVER...
SNAP OUT OF IT, FRANCK.
SORRY.

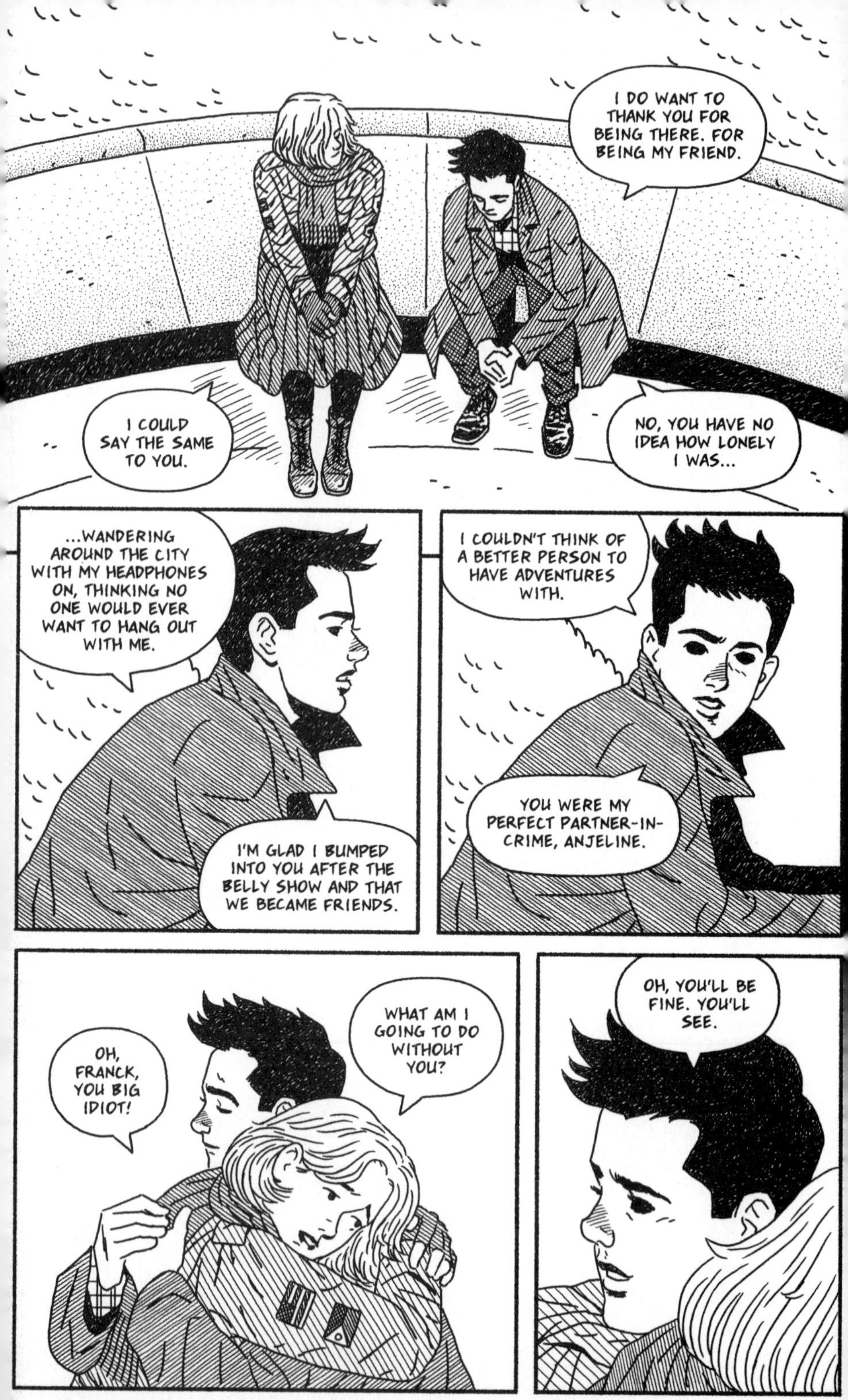
I DO WANT TO THANK YOU FOR BEING THERE. FOR BEING MY FRIEND.
I COULD SAY THE SAME TO YOU.
NO, YOU HAVE NO IDEA HOW LONELY I WAS...
...WANDERING AROUND THE CITY WITH MY HEADPHONES ON, THINKING NO ONE WOULD EVER WANT TO HANG OUT WITH ME.
I'M GLAD I BUMPED INTO YOU AFTER THE BELLY SHOW AND THAT WE BECAME FRIENDS.
I COULDN'T THINK OF A BETTER PERSON TO HAVE ADVENTURES WITH.
YOU WERE MY PERFECT PARTNER-IN-CRIME, ANJELINE.
WHAT AM I GOING TO DO WITHOUT YOU?
OH, FRANCK, YOU BIG IDIOT!
OH, YOU'LL BE FINE. YOU'LL SEE.

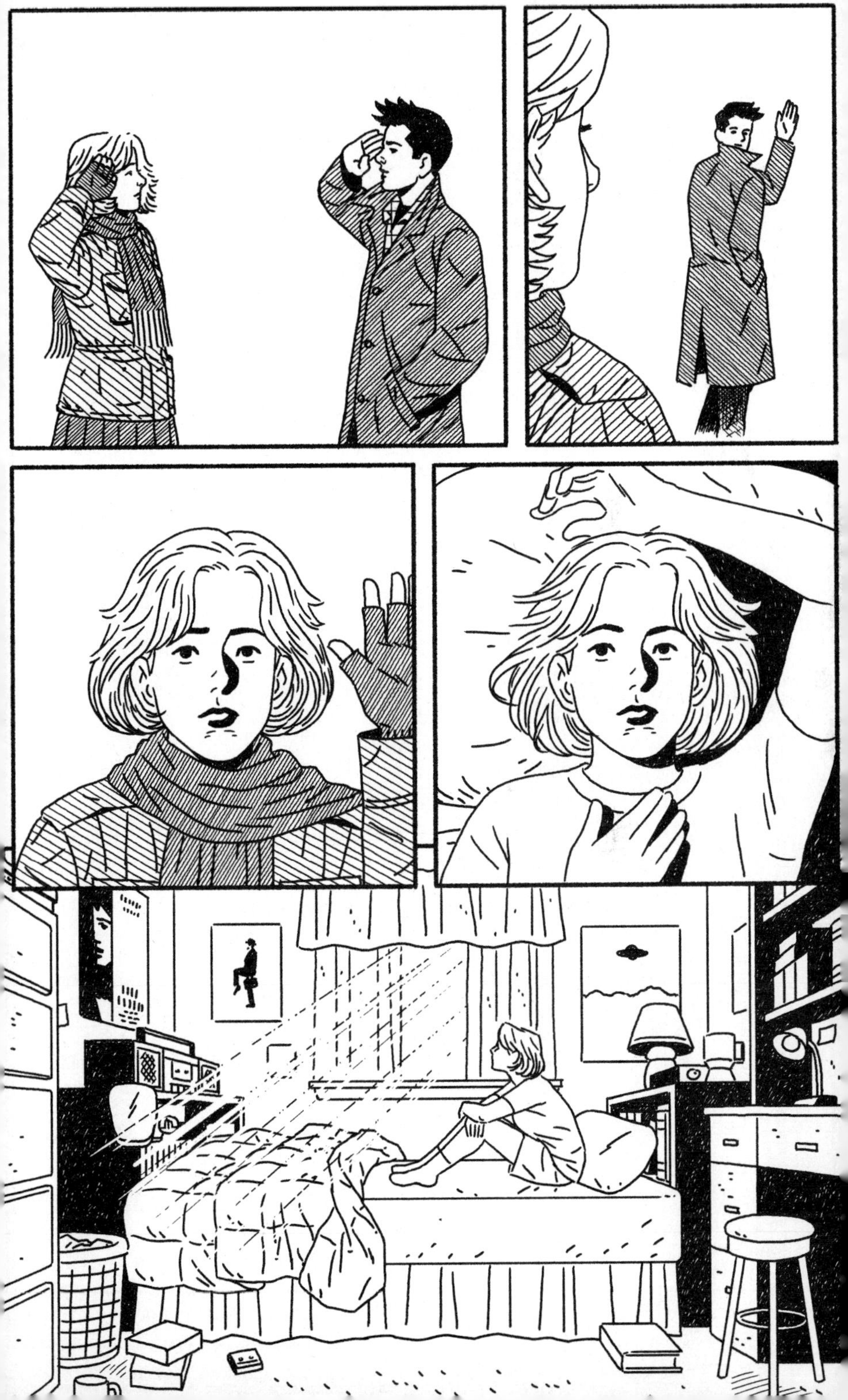

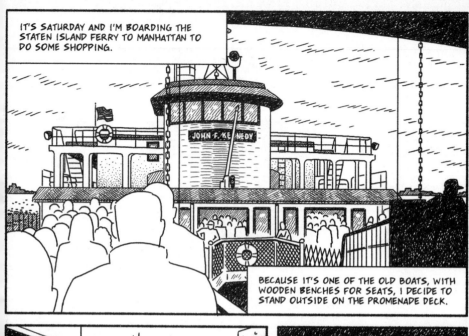

IT'S SATURDAY AND I'M BOARDING THE STATEN ISLAND FERRY TO MANHATTAN TO DO SOME SHOPPING.

BECAUSE IT'S ONE OF THE OLD BOATS, WITH WOODEN BENCHES FOR SEATS, I DECIDE TO STAND OUTSIDE ON THE PROMENADE DECK.

ALTHOUGH IT'S OFFICIALLY SPRING, THERE'S A COLD BREEZE IN THE AIR, AND I AM THE ONLY ONE OUT HERE.

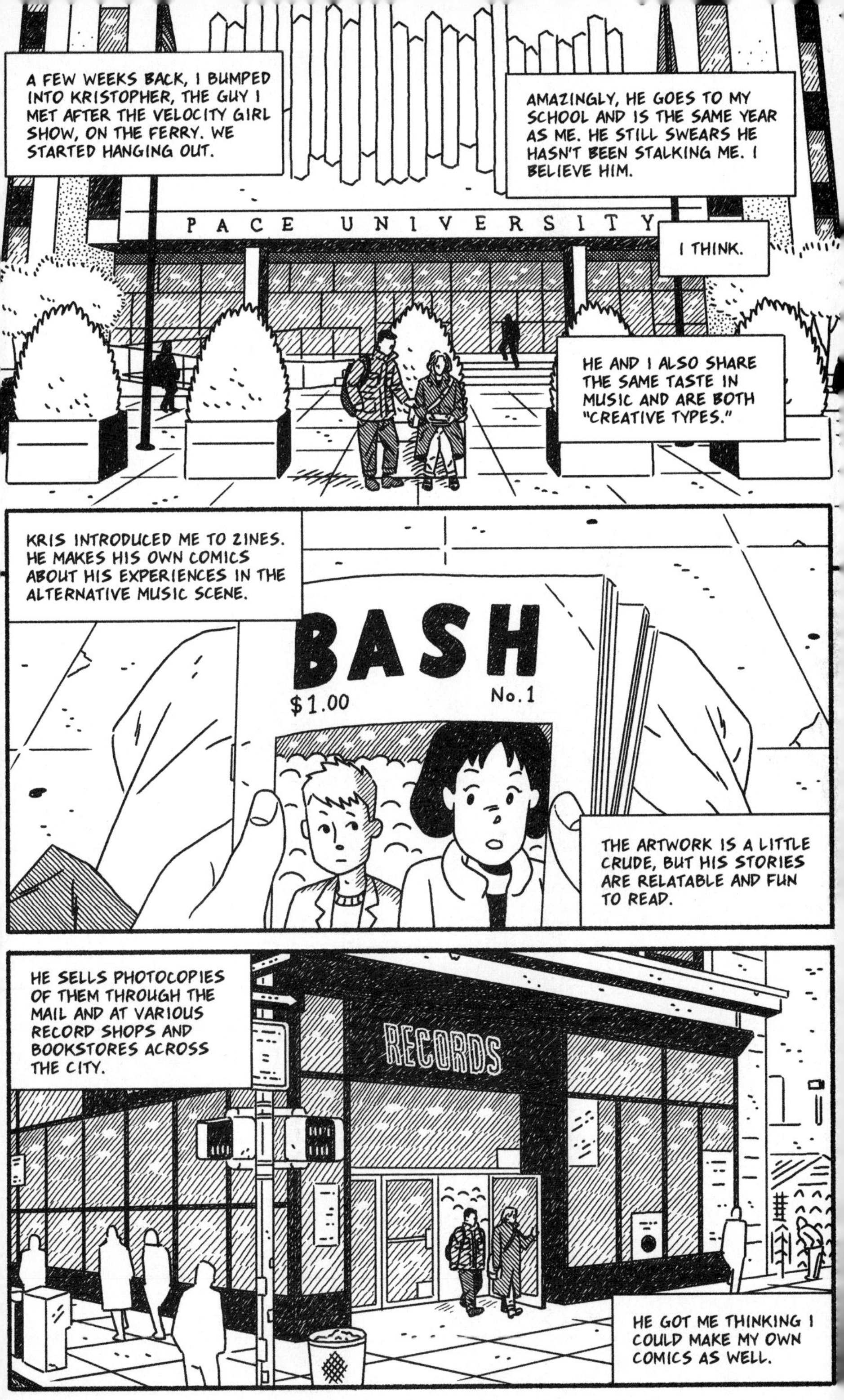
A FEW WEEKS BACK, I BUMPED INTO KRISTOPHER, THE GUY I MET AFTER THE VELOCITY GIRL SHOW, ON THE FERRY. WE STARTED HANGING OUT.
AMAZINGLY, HE GOES TO MY SCHOOL AND IS THE SAME YEAR AS ME. HE STILL SWEARS HE HASN'T BEEN STALKING ME. I BELIEVE HIM.
PACE UNIVERSITY
I THINK.
HE AND I ALSO SHARE THE SAME TASTE IN MUSIC AND ARE BOTH "CREATIVE TYPES."
KRIS INTRODUCED ME TO ZINES. HE MAKES HIS OWN COMICS ABOUT HIS EXPERIENCES IN THE ALTERNATIVE MUSIC SCENE.
BASH
$1.00
No. 1
THE ARTWORK IS A LITTLE CRUDE, BUT HIS STORIES ARE RELATABLE AND FUN TO READ.
HE SELLS PHOTOCOPIES OF THEM THROUGH THE MAIL AND AT VARIOUS RECORD SHOPS AND BOOKSTORES ACROSS THE CITY.
RECORDS
HE GOT ME THINKING I COULD MAKE MY OWN COMICS AS WELL.

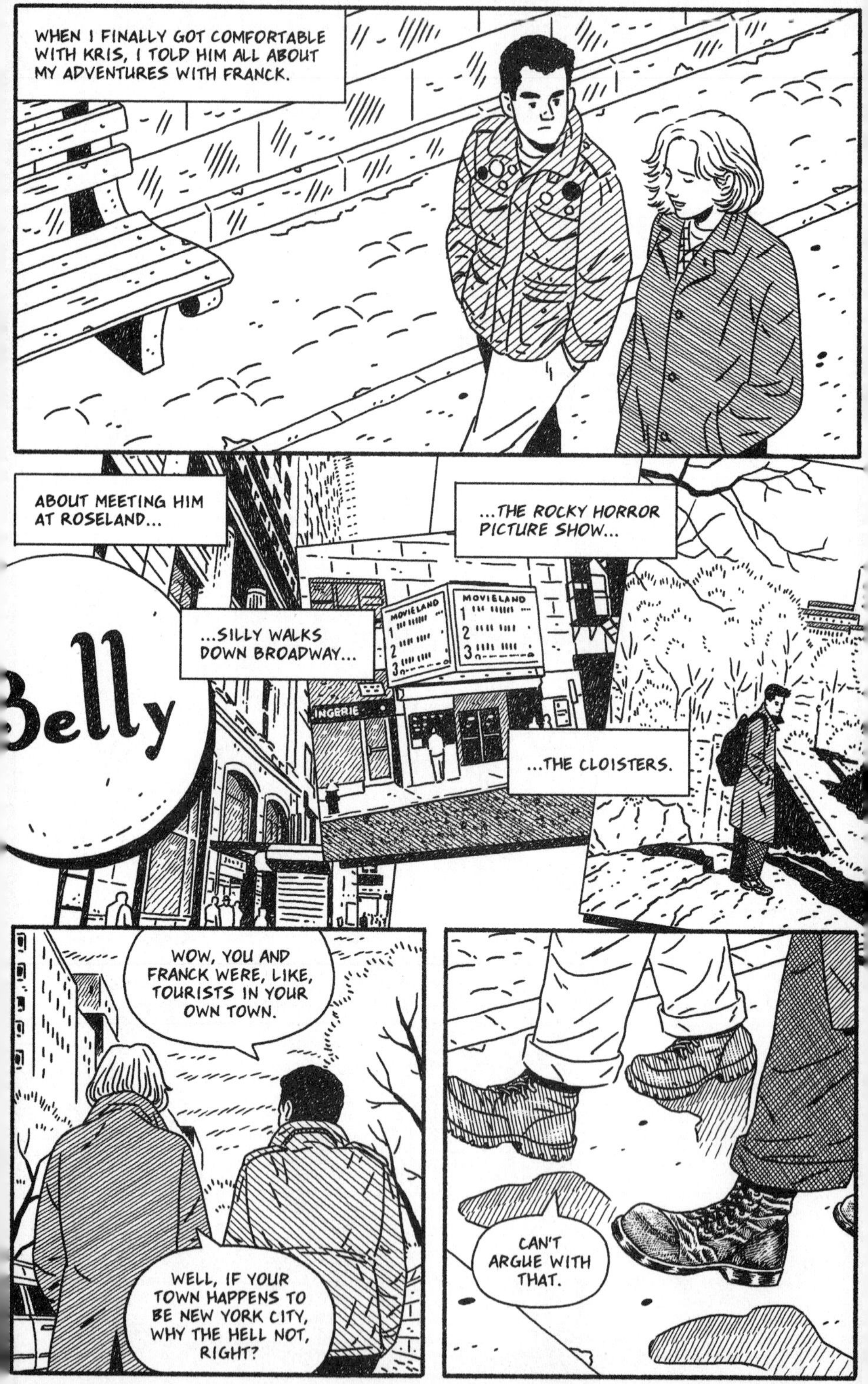
WHEN I FINALLY GOT COMFORTABLE WITH KRIS, I TOLD HIM ALL ABOUT MY ADVENTURES WITH FRANCK.
ABOUT MEETING HIM AT ROSELAND...
Belly
...SILLY WALKS DOWN BROADWAY...
MOVIELAND
LINGERIE
...THE ROCKY HORROR PICTURE SHOW...
...THE CLOISTERS.
WOW, YOU AND FRANCK WERE, LIKE, TOURISTS IN YOUR OWN TOWN.
WELL, IF YOUR TOWN HAPPENS TO BE NEW YORK CITY, WHY THE HELL NOT, RIGHT?
CAN'T ARGUE WITH THAT.

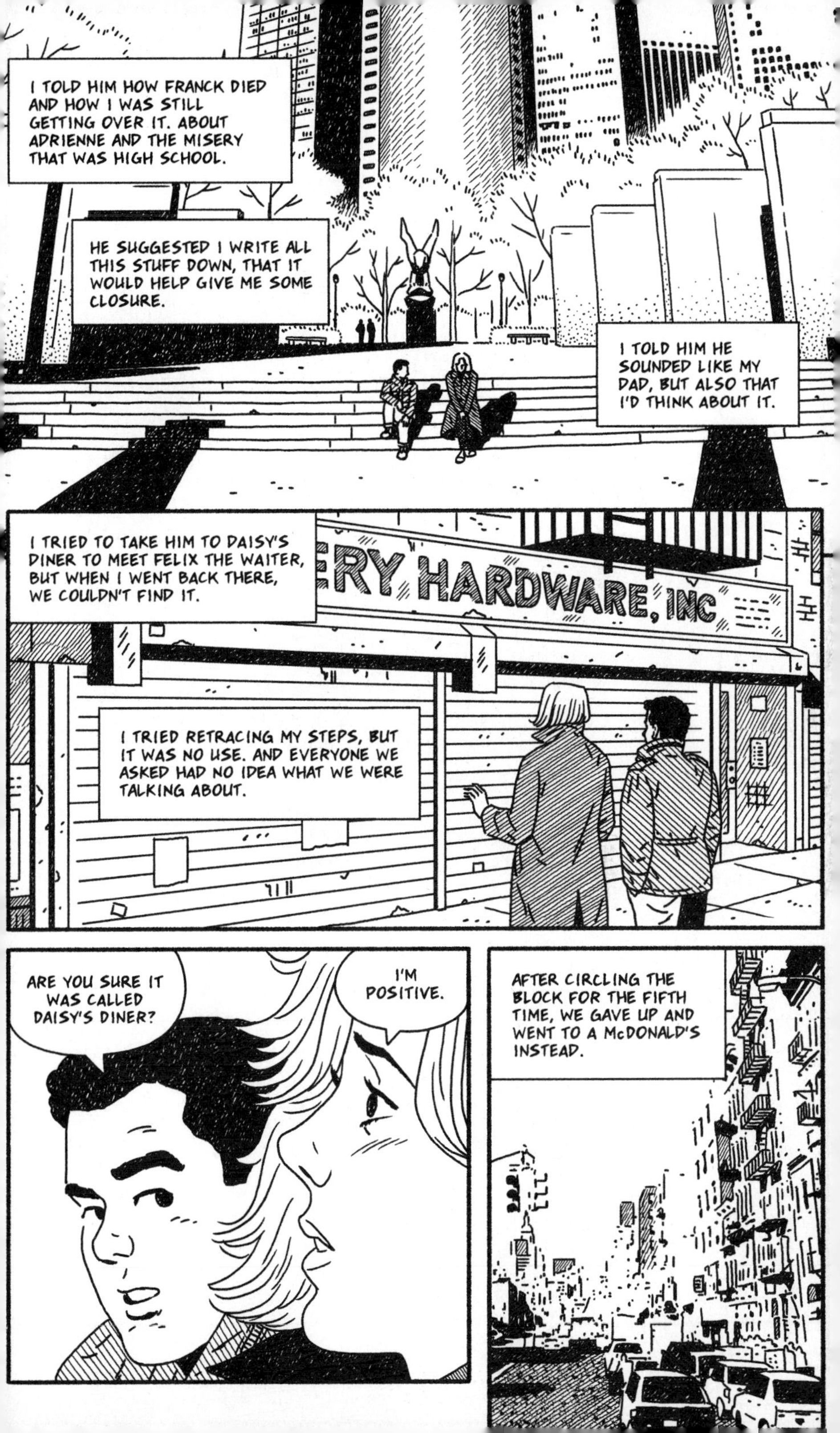
I TOLD HIM HOW FRANCK DIED AND HOW I WAS STILL GETTING OVER IT. ABOUT ADRIENNE AND THE MISERY THAT WAS HIGH SCHOOL.
HE SUGGESTED I WRITE ALL THIS STUFF DOWN, THAT IT WOULD HELP GIVE ME SOME CLOSURE.
I TOLD HIM HE SOUNDED LIKE MY DAD, BUT ALSO THAT I'D THINK ABOUT IT.
I TRIED TO TAKE HIM TO DAISY'S DINER TO MEET FELIX THE WAITER, BUT WHEN I WENT BACK THERE, WE COULDN'T FIND IT.
ERY HARDWARE, INC
I TRIED RETRACING MY STEPS, BUT IT WAS NO USE. AND EVERYONE WE ASKED HAD NO IDEA WHAT WE WERE TALKING ABOUT.
ARE YOU SURE IT WAS CALLED DAISY'S DINER?
I'M POSITIVE.
AFTER CIRCLING THE BLOCK FOR THE FIFTH TIME, WE GAVE UP AND WENT TO A McDONALD'S INSTEAD.

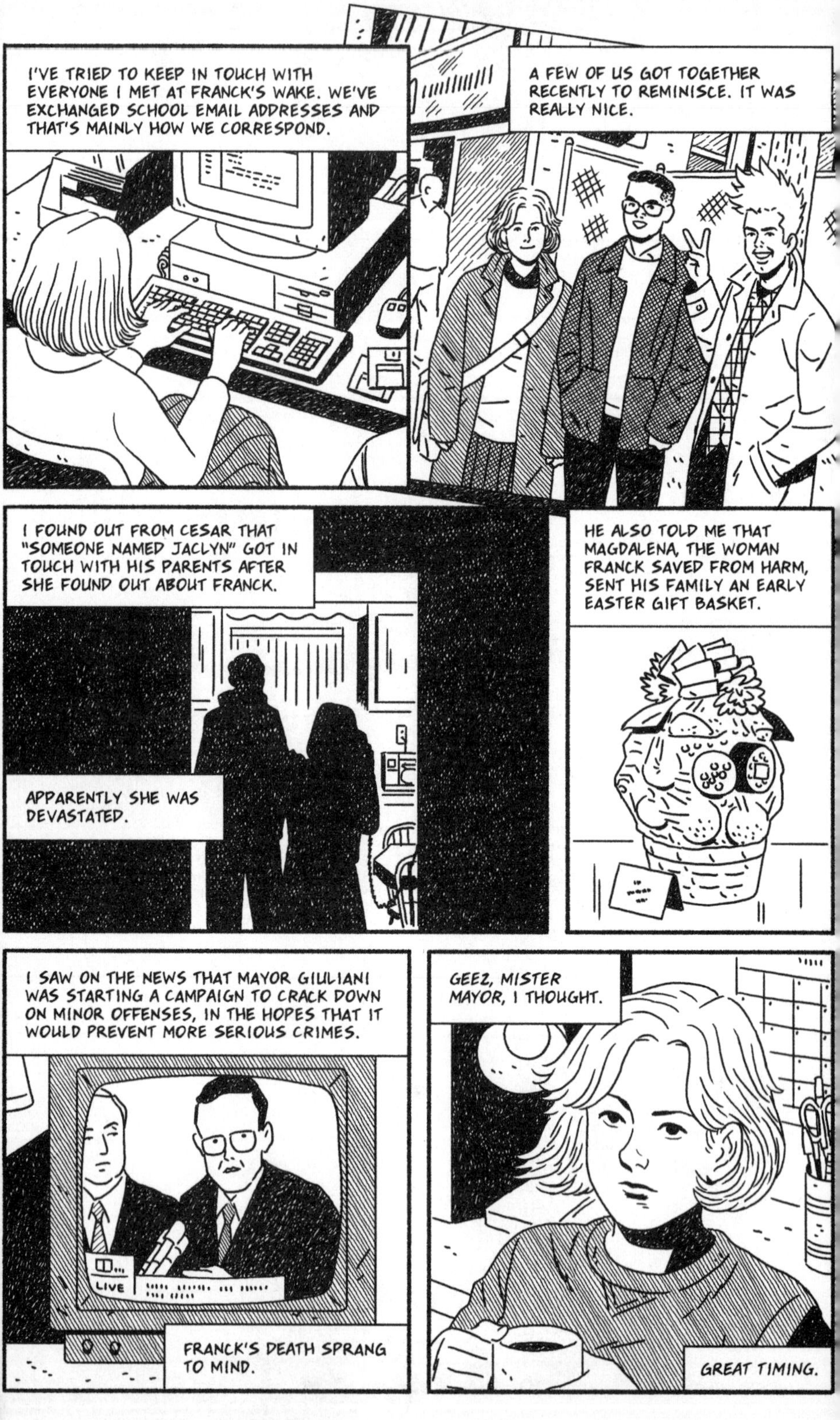
I'VE TRIED TO KEEP IN TOUCH WITH EVERYONE I MET AT FRANCK'S WAKE. WE'VE EXCHANGED SCHOOL EMAIL ADDRESSES AND THAT'S MAINLY HOW WE CORRESPOND.
A FEW OF US GOT TOGETHER RECENTLY TO REMINISCE. IT WAS REALLY NICE.
I FOUND OUT FROM CESAR THAT "SOMEONE NAMED JACLYN" GOT IN TOUCH WITH HIS PARENTS AFTER SHE FOUND OUT ABOUT FRANCK.
APPARENTLY SHE WAS DEVASTATED.
HE ALSO TOLD ME THAT MAGDALENA, THE WOMAN FRANCK SAVED FROM HARM, SENT HIS FAMILY AN EARLY EASTER GIFT BASKET.
I SAW ON THE NEWS THAT MAYOR GIULIANI WAS STARTING A CAMPAIGN TO CRACK DOWN ON MINOR OFFENSES, IN THE HOPES THAT IT WOULD PREVENT MORE SERIOUS CRIMES.
LIVE
FRANCK'S DEATH SPRANG TO MIND.
GEEZ, MISTER MAYOR, I THOUGHT.
GREAT TIMING.

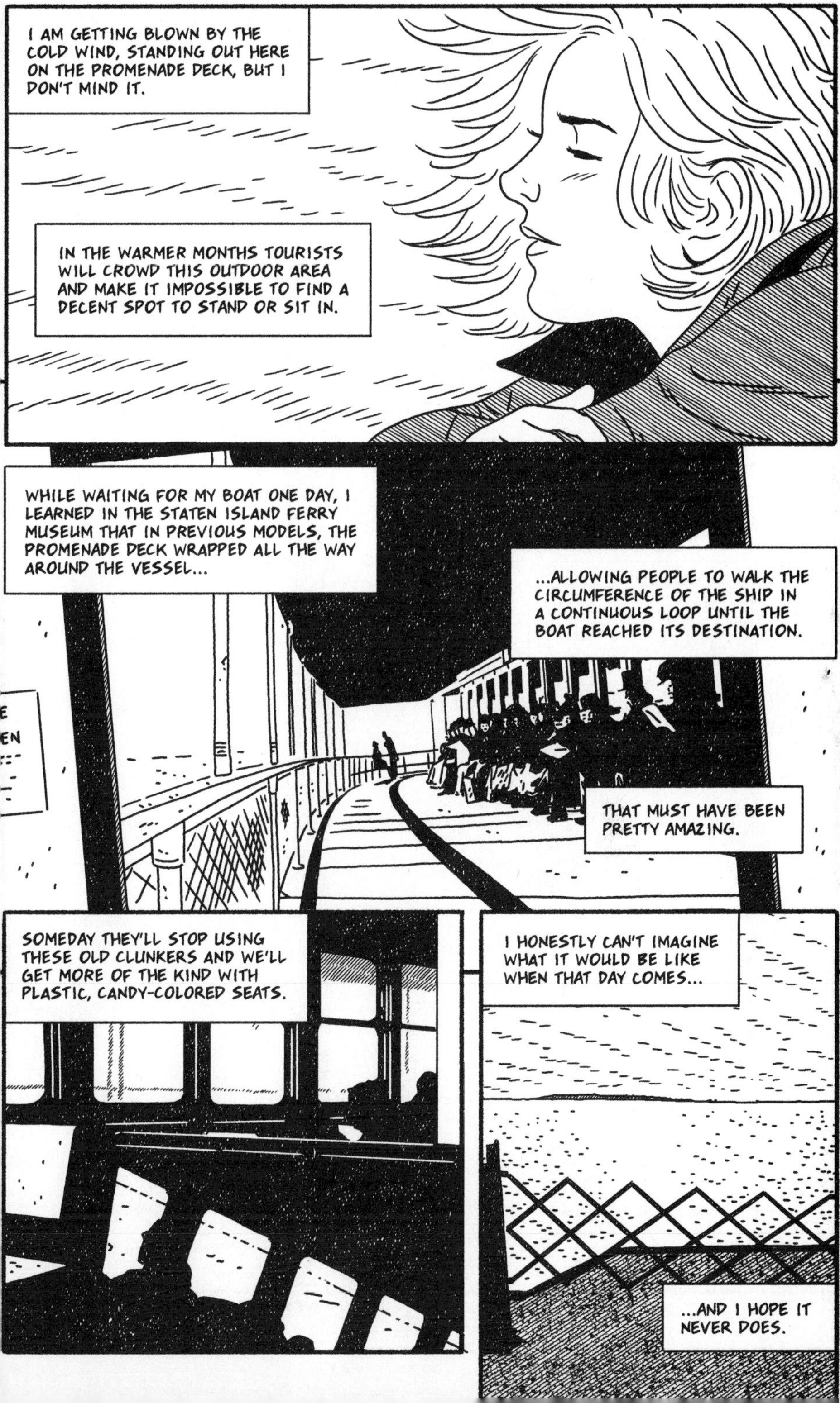
I AM GETTING BLOWN BY THE COLD WIND, STANDING OUT HERE ON THE PROMENADE DECK, BUT I DON'T MIND IT.
IN THE WARMER MONTHS TOURISTS WILL CROWD THIS OUTDOOR AREA AND MAKE IT IMPOSSIBLE TO FIND A DECENT SPOT TO STAND OR SIT IN.
WHILE WAITING FOR MY BOAT ONE DAY, I LEARNED IN THE STATEN ISLAND FERRY MUSEUM THAT IN PREVIOUS MODELS, THE PROMENADE DECK WRAPPED ALL THE WAY AROUND THE VESSEL...
...ALLOWING PEOPLE TO WALK THE CIRCUMFERENCE OF THE SHIP IN A CONTINUOUS LOOP UNTIL THE BOAT REACHED ITS DESTINATION.
THAT MUST HAVE BEEN PRETTY AMAZING.
SOMEDAY THEY'LL STOP USING THESE OLD CLUNKERS AND WE'LL GET MORE OF THE KIND WITH PLASTIC, CANDY-COLORED SEATS.
I HONESTLY CAN'T IMAGINE WHAT IT WOULD BE LIKE WHEN THAT DAY COMES...
...AND I HOPE IT NEVER DOES.

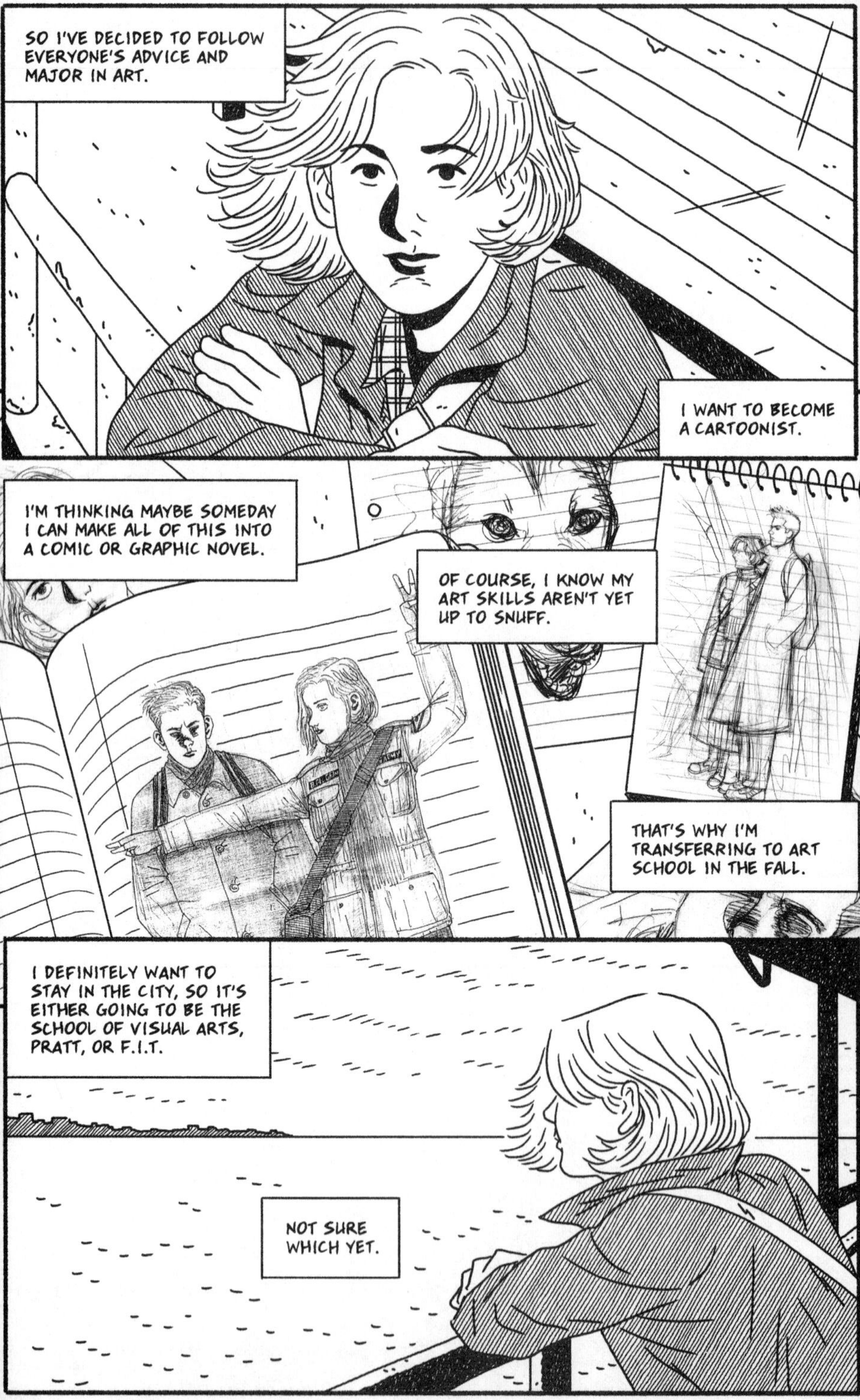
SO I'VE DECIDED TO FOLLOW EVERYONE'S ADVICE AND MAJOR IN ART.
I WANT TO BECOME A CARTOONIST.
I'M THINKING MAYBE SOMEDAY I CAN MAKE ALL OF THIS INTO A COMIC OR GRAPHIC NOVEL.
OF COURSE, I KNOW MY ART SKILLS AREN'T YET UP TO SNUFF.
THAT'S WHY I'M TRANSFERRING TO ART SCHOOL IN THE FALL.
I DEFINITELY WANT TO STAY IN THE CITY, SO IT'S EITHER GOING TO BE THE SCHOOL OF VISUAL ARTS, PRATT, OR F.I.T.
NOT SURE WHICH YET.

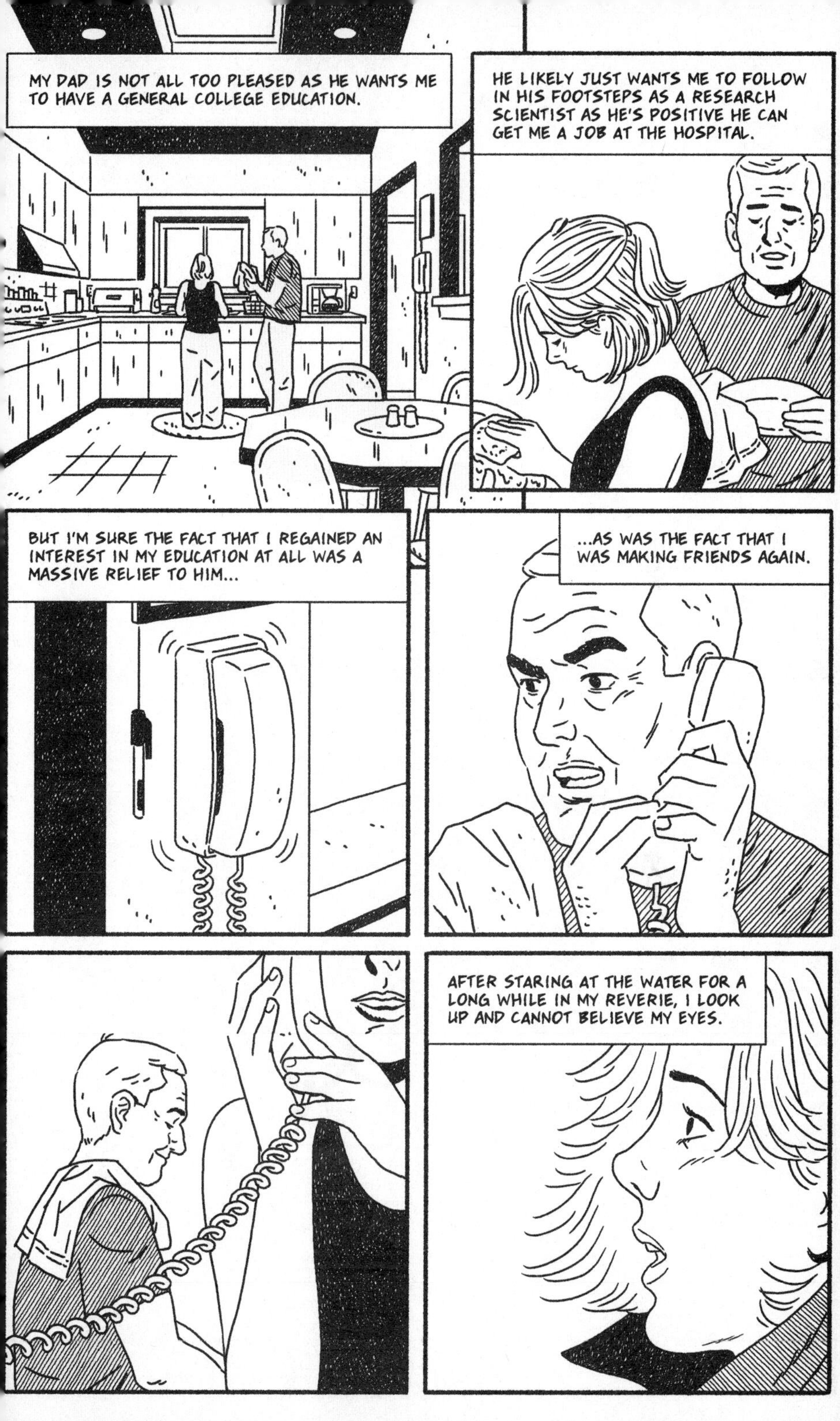
MY DAD IS NOT ALL TOO PLEASED AS HE WANTS ME TO HAVE A GENERAL COLLEGE EDUCATION.
HE LIKELY JUST WANTS ME TO FOLLOW IN HIS FOOTSTEPS AS A RESEARCH SCIENTIST AS HE'S POSITIVE HE CAN GET ME A JOB AT THE HOSPITAL.
BUT I'M SURE THE FACT THAT I REGAINED AN INTEREST IN MY EDUCATION AT ALL WAS A MASSIVE RELIEF TO HIM...
...AS WAS THE FACT THAT I WAS MAKING FRIENDS AGAIN.
AFTER STARING AT THE WATER FOR A LONG WHILE IN MY REVERIE, I LOOK UP AND CANNOT BELIEVE MY EYES.

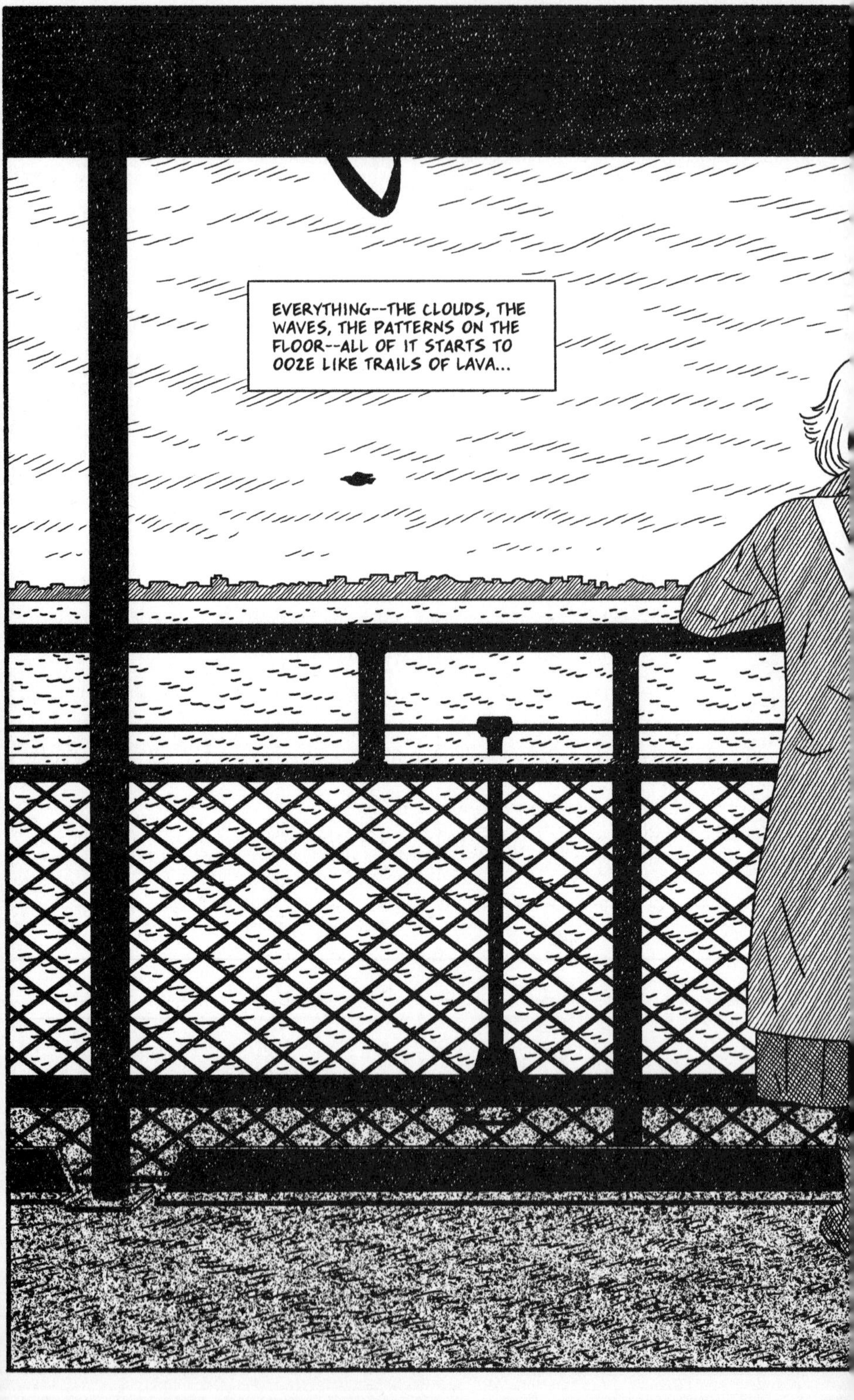
EVERYTHING--THE CLOUDS, THE WAVES, THE PATTERNS ON THE FLOOR--ALL OF IT STARTS TO OOZE LIKE TRAILS OF LAVA...

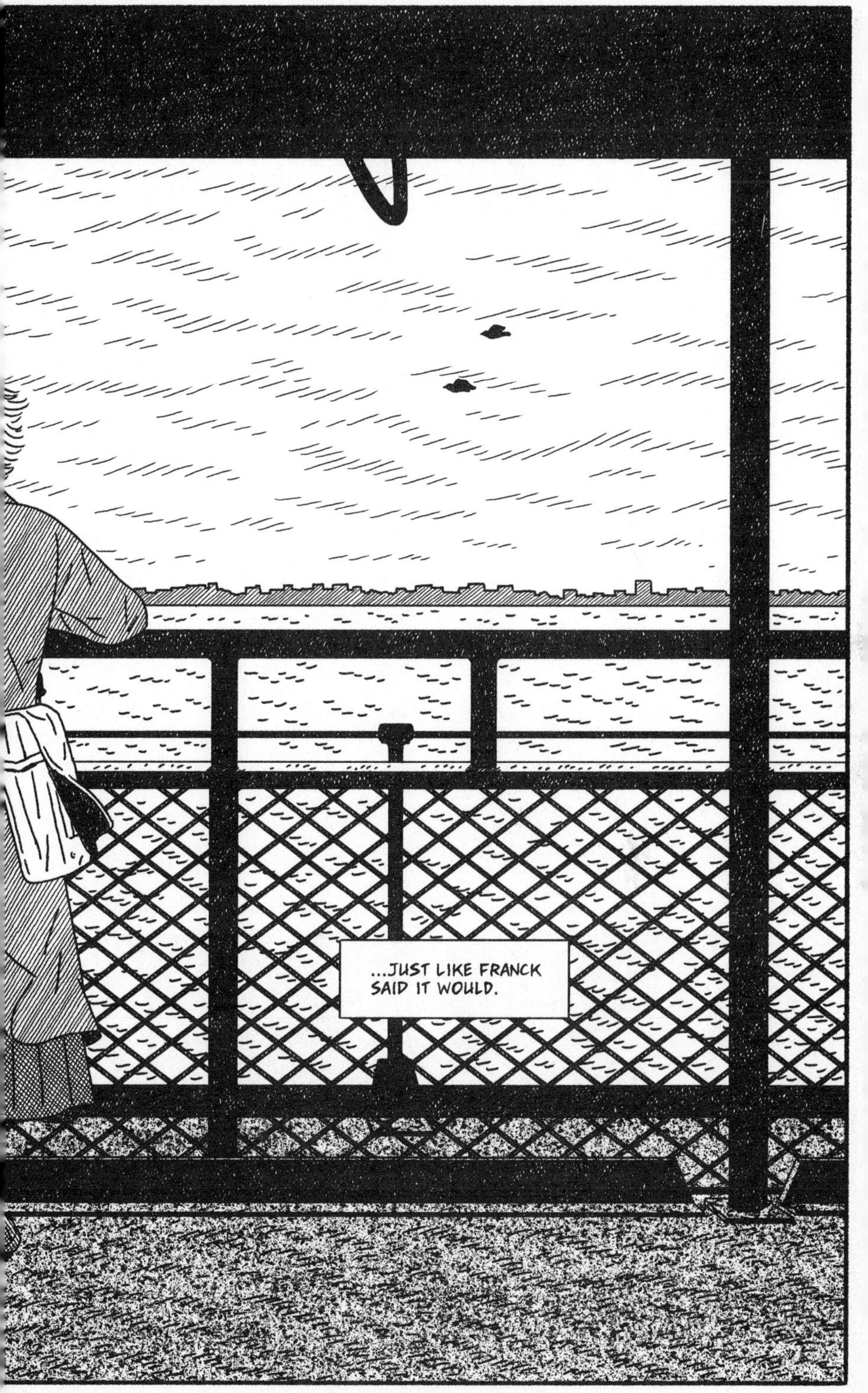
...JUST LIKE FRANCK
SAID IT WOULD.

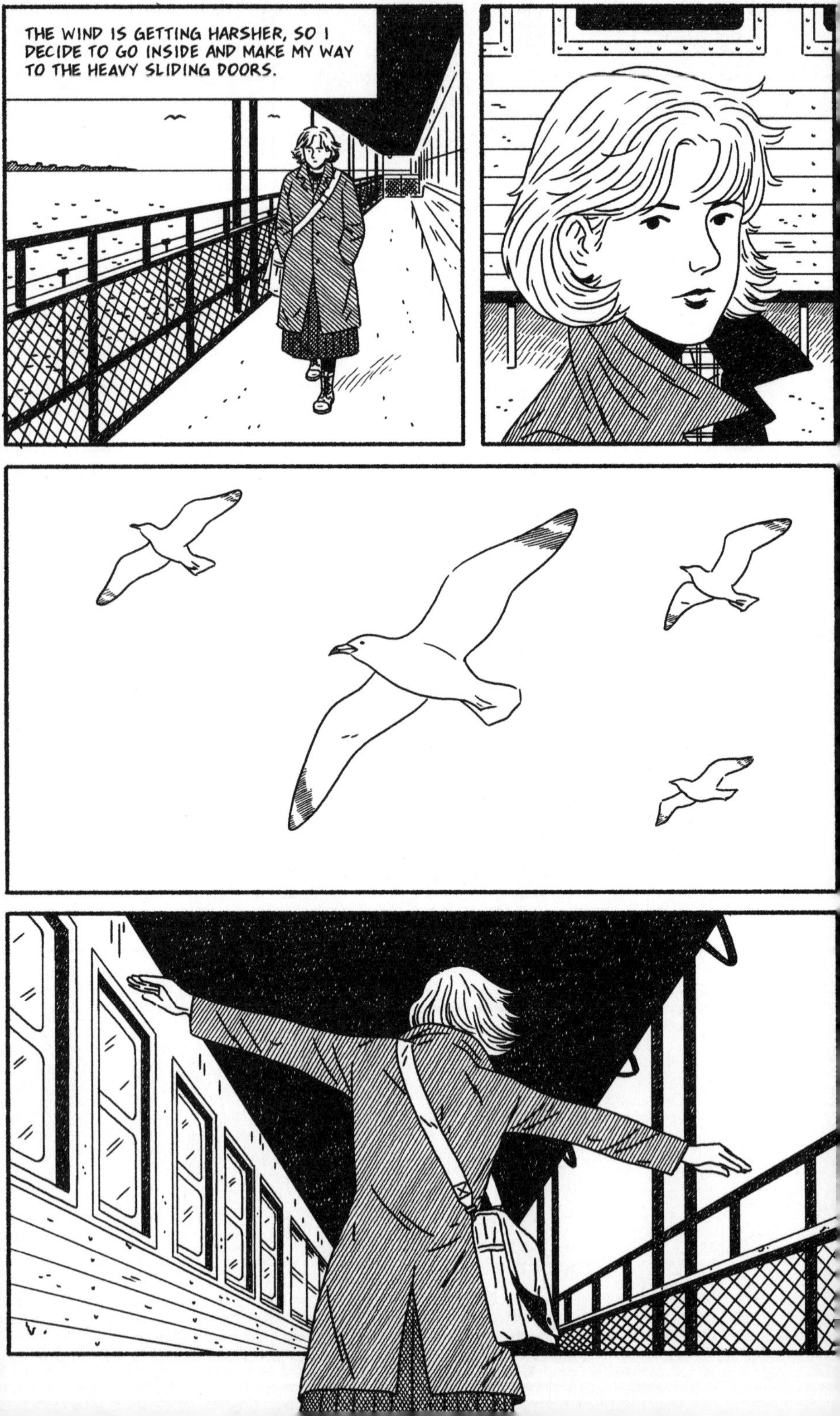
THE WIND IS GETTING HARSHER, SO I DECIDE TO GO INSIDE AND MAKE MY WAY TO THE HEAVY SLIDING DOORS.

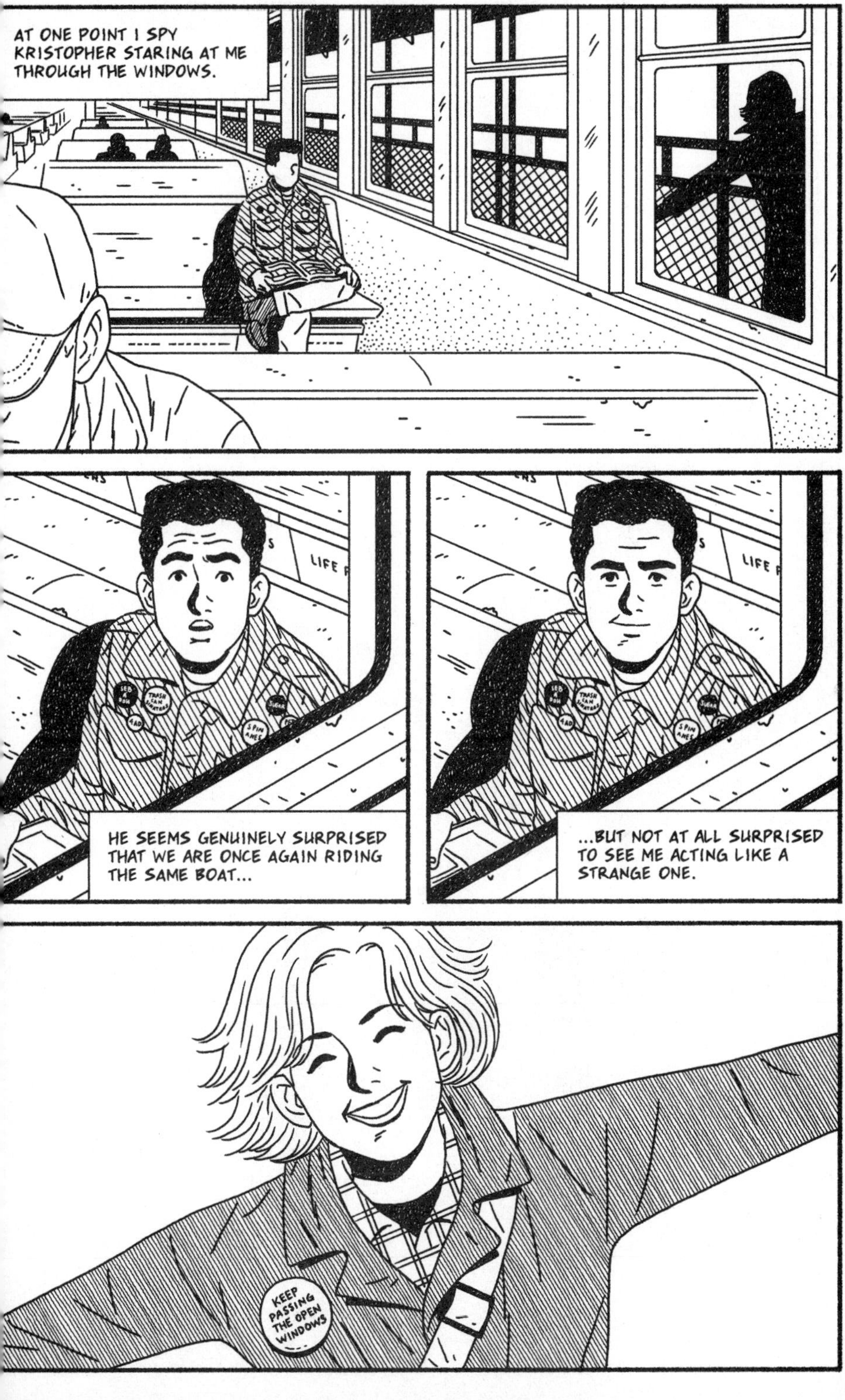
AT ONE POINT I SPY KRISTOPHER STARING AT ME THROUGH THE WINDOWS.
LIFE
HE SEEMS GENUINELY SURPRISED THAT WE ARE ONCE AGAIN RIDING THE SAME BOAT...
LIFE
...BUT NOT AT ALL SURPRISED TO SEE ME ACTING LIKE A STRANGE ONE.
KEEP PASSING THE OPEN WINDOWS

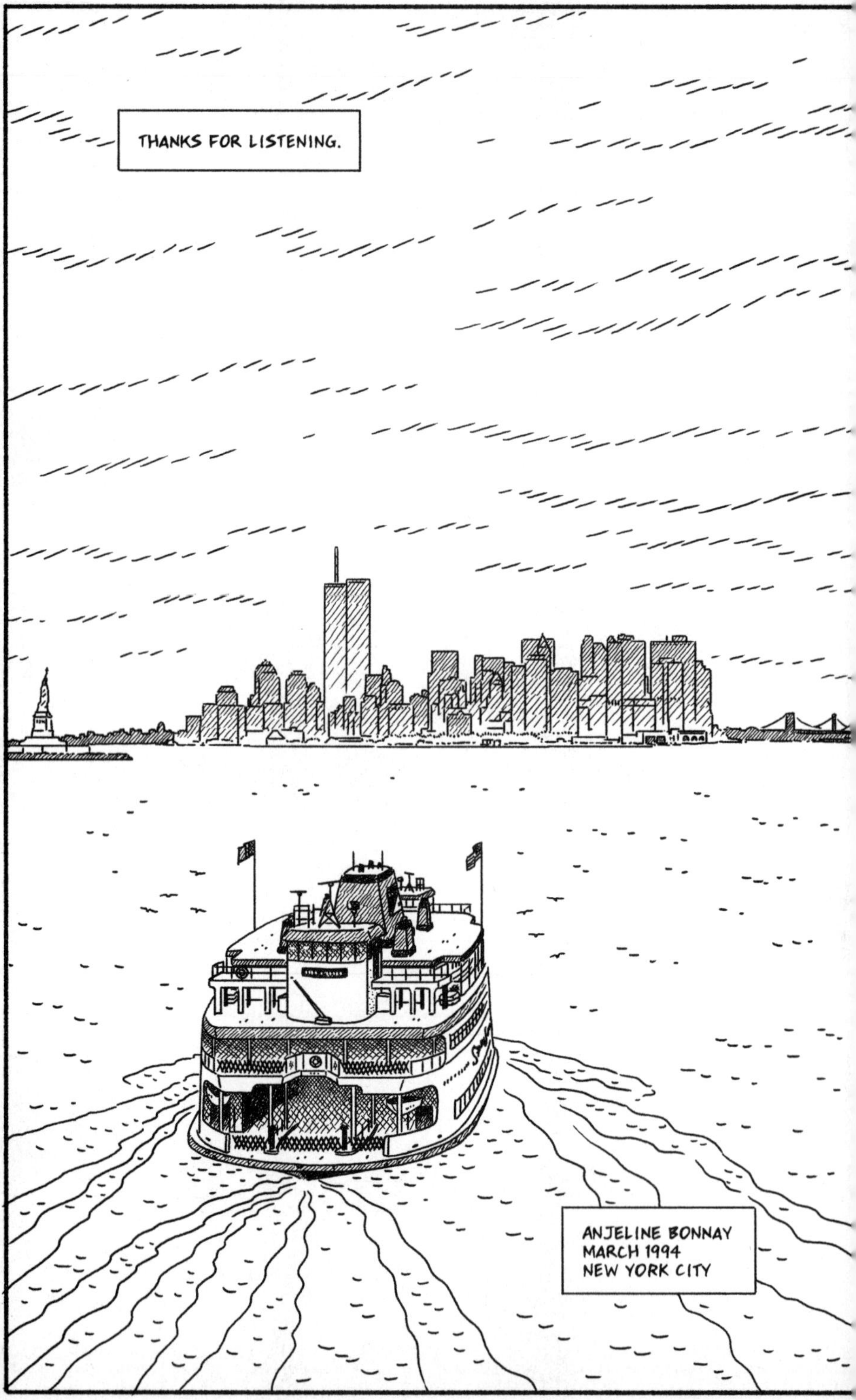
THANKS FOR LISTENING.
ANJELINE BONNAY
MARCH 1994
NEW YORK CITY